INSTIGATOR

STRIKE FORCE (BOOK THREE)

FIONA QUINN

INSTIGATOR

Strike Force

BOOK THREE

FIONA QUINN

THE WORLD OF INIQUUS

Ubicumque, Quoties. Quidquid

Iniquus - /i'ni/kwus/ our strength is unequalled, our tactics unfair – we stretch the law to its breaking point. We do whatever is necessary to bring the enemy down.

THE LYNX SERIES

Weakest Lynx

Missing Lynx

Chain Lynx

Cuff Lynx

Gulf Lynx

Hyper Lynx

MARRIAGE LYNX

STRIKE FORCE

In Too DEEP

JACK Be Quick

InstiGATOR

UNCOMMON ENEMIES

Wasp

Relic

Deadlock

Thorn

FBI JOINT TASK FORCE

Open Secret

Cold Red

Even Odds

KATE HAMILTON MYSTERIES

Mine

Yours

Ours

CERBERUS TACTICAL K9 TEAM ALPHA

Survival Instinct

Protective Instinct

Defender's Instinct

DELTA FORCE ECHO

Danger Signs

Danger Zone

Danger Close

This list was created in 2021. For an up-to-date list, please visit FionaQuinnBooks.com

If you prefer to read the Iniquus World in chronological order you will find a full list at the end

of this book.

There's an unequal amount of good and bad in most things. The 'trick' is to figure out the ratio and act accordingly.

— TH3 J3ST3R

This book is dedicated to all those who see the bigger picture and yet do not despair. Instead, they find a way to do their part— big or small—to bring safety and peace to our world. Thank you.

1

CHRISTEN

Tuesday, Forward Operating Base, Mosul Iraq

"SCRAMBLE. SCRAMBLE. SCRAMBLE."

The PA system's bright, tinny voice yanked Lieutenant Christen Davidson from her curled-up sleep. She found herself standing on the unfinished planks next to her bunk before her eyelids could even pry open. As her feet hit the floor, she criss-crossed her arms and jerked her t-shirt up over her head. Her flight uniform lay draped over the headboard in such a way that there would be no fumbling as adrenaline, Christen's drug of choice, shot excitement through her system.

She scratched her fingers through her short pixie-cut hair, the most she would do to make herself presentable. Vanity was a time suck. Christen's time was spent piling special forces operators into the back of her heli and flying them into the fray. They depended on her. Missions and lives were at stake – *they* were her priority.

Perched on the edge of her cot behind the makeshift privacy curtain formed from a queen-sized striped sheet, Christen pulled on her clothes, yanked the laces of her flight boots, and quickly looped a bow. With a shove of the door, she shot herself into the daylight. The sun glared in her eyes as she ran full-tilt toward the command tent to get her orders.

Christen wasn't normally awake this time of day and didn't normally fly in sunlight. She was a member of the Night Stalkers, the Army's 160th. She was one of the only female pilots in what had been, up until very recently, the only special forces unit that allowed women to apply. She'd earned her place. Anything the male pilots could do, she could do too—maybe better, maybe not. Everyone had their strengths *and* their weaknesses.

Christen's strength was flying low altitude flights in the black of night, hugging the terrain, glossing over its surface, scaring the hell out of the people below her while hiding her customers from any enemy eyes that might be scanning the midnight sky. She'd trained long and hard, year after year. She'd logged hundreds of hours — every hour she could possibly fly, any *thing* she could find to fly.

These last five years, she had flown in every kind of weather, terrain, and impossible-to-survive scenario her commanders at the 160th SOAR(A) at Fort Campbell could contrive. Before this last deployment, she'd received her change of status. She was fully mission qualified. She could go on any assignment required of her – bar none. But daylight? —Christen looked up at the sun as she reached to pull the command tent door open— that's not what Night Stalkers did.

This was odd.

Something was off.

Christen stopped short when she saw her commander barreling toward her.

"Let's move it, Lieutenant." The colonel growled as he strode through the door she held wide. He thrust a clipboard of papers at her, then pointed toward the Little Bird helicopter across the field getting fueled. The tanker truck was positioned far enough away that if an enemy combatant wanted to set it on fire, it wouldn't explode the whole Forward Operating Base, situated just this side of enemy-held territory.

A line of Delta operators formed to her left, with their long hair and bushy beards. The "quiet professionals"—latent death and destruction. Each one laden with weapons, fully geared up in their battle rattle. Christen wondered when they'd flown in. They weren't on base when she'd gone to sleep. The Deltas stepped, one at a time, onto a bathroom scale, and one of their group noted each man's weight on their clipboard. Weight mattered to the speed and the dexterity of a helicopter's maneuvers. If they were being that precise, this wasn't a taxi ride.

Christen looked down at her flight plan and blinked. What the... "What?" She held a hand up to shield her eyes and read her orders again. She flipped to the waypoints marked on her map, and the GPS coordinates she knew were already loaded into her flight computer system. *Wow.*

"I'm not sending you out on a Sunday picnic." Colonel Martin stabbed a finger into her shoulder. "You're our precision flier. Guts forged out of steel, I told 'em. And now, you're going to make sure I don't regret putting my reputation behind you."

It was uncharacteristic of the colonel to point to any one pilot — to lift them up or set them apart in any manner from the rest of the Night Stalkers. Christen didn't like it. She was a team player, period. She didn't seek out and didn't want flattery or recognition. She just wanted to do her job.

And with or without any added pressure, this was going to be one hell of a trick-shot. Christen's gaze scanned down the fuel calculations. With her tank filled to spill--depending on the weight of the Deltas and the opposing wind speeds--she had a little over a two hundred sixty-mile range. With the calculated hover time... Yeah, this was shaving it close. She turned the page to find the weather read-out, then glanced up again at the bright sunshine, not a cloud in the sky. Of course, here in the desert, that could change in the blink of an eye – no matter what the weather report said. Haboobs came when they wanted to. These violent winds carrying blinding dirt and debris could choke an engine and put a bird nose down in the sand quicker than quick. Sunlight, though, totally sucked. She wished they'd let her do this at night when she was in her comfort zone.

Like a vampire, Christen thrived after the sun went down. The 160th Night Stalkers loved the pitch-black of moonless nights. With their FLIR—forward-looking infrared systems—and their night vision goggles along with some rad computer systems, she could sweep over the terrain, almost undetectable, to deliver her customers to the required spot, arriving on time and on target in plus or minus thirty seconds. It was the precision that her customers demanded. The Night Stalkers were the air support for the United States Special Operations units.

The 160th had flown the Osama bin Laden mission, which had been planned and trained for to the Nth degree. Even with the technical problems, that mission could only be seen as a success of vital importance. The 160th had also been the team that zoomed their way into the Hindu Kush Region of Afghanistan when the call was made for an immediate extraction after a SEAL team came under heavy fire during Operation Red Wings. The Night Stalkers in their CH-47 Chinook helicopters took off without a gunship escort, hoping against hope to extract the team in time. The Taliban shot down one of the Night Stalker's helicopters with a rocket-propelled grenade, killing the eight

Navy SEALs and eight special operations aviators on board. The second helicopter was forced to leave the scene. It was a soul-crushing horror of a day. It was the day Christen swore she'd become a Night Stalker, dedicating her work to the memory of those fallen warriors.

Christen chewed on her upper lip, reading over her orders to fly straight into the center of a populated city. She visualized the scene in her mind. This kind of challenge was exactly what she'd signed up for. She reached around and hooked a hand behind the back of her neck as she processed the schematics. The road width with the apron of sidewalks and parking lanes on either side was marked on the satellite photo as thirty-one feet five inches. Her rotor diameter was twenty-seven feet, four inches.

Could she trust these calculations?

Whew! This was going to be one hell of a hairy mission. She'd never trained for this. Never imagined it. Wasn't completely convinced it was possible. But damned, she was glad *she* was given the opportunity to try.

Typically, they'd sit down and plot this out meticulously. They'd practice, practice, practice until go-time, working to find any holes and plug them. But this time, she didn't get to sit down in the wooden chairs and participate in the mission planning. They were spooling up with the pressure of some undefined time constraint. Papers slapped into her hands. There must be an imminent threat—a small window of opportunity.

Christen turned as her stick buddy, Nick Campbell, moved up beside her and read their paperwork over her shoulder. A low whistle blew between his teeth. "How many customers are we taking in our bird?"

"We have four. The Deltas are checking their weight now to make sure we're well below the max takeoff load. The Black

Hawk will have the rest of the customers and the heavier firepower."

"I guess we're glad they've got our backs." His gaze scanned over to the Black Hawk. "I hope they have all the firepower they can cram on there. I have a feeling we're going to need it." He tucked his helmet under his arm and grinned. "It's a good day to die." He raised a hand toward their clients and went to do his pre-flight checks.

2

CHRISTEN

Tuesday, Forward Operating Base, Mosul Iraq

THEY WERE STRAPPED IN, waiting for the colonel to say the mission was a go. Christen hadn't revved her motors yet.

She was clinging to every drop of her precious fuel.

Their four Delta customers patted themselves over, a final gear check. Nerves were sparking. Everyone chomped at the bit anticipating their green light.

"I can't help but think this is gonna get him killed," Nick said.

"Not our call." Christen was of like mind. She couldn't figure out what the hell command was thinking. An American, John Grey, had been captured. Yes, he should be rescued. Yes, she was willing to die trying. But this? Surely, the colonel had weighed the importance of this man against the lives of everyone on her bird and possibly everyone on the Black Hawk, too, not to mention the civilians who would be in their general vicinity. This had disaster written all over it. But Christen turned a blind eye to the writing on the wall. Honestly, it didn't matter. Her creed dictated that she took the missions no one else would try. And she lived her creed. Happily.

Listening to the Deltas talking in their low tones, Christen got the impression John Grey was a CIA operations officer in deep shit with some very big secrets that Uncle Sam would prefer not be wrestled out of him through torture sessions. Everyone had their breaking point.

Everyone.

Still, this move didn't make a heck of a lot of sense.

With a thumbs up and a salute, they were in play.

"Here we go." Christen snapped her helmet into place, revved the motors, and maneuvered the helicopter into the air, heading for the hills and toward their target.

Soon, they soared over the flat roofs of the city. The trip was just long enough that it could encourage complacence. Christen knew better; even a moment's inattention could turn them into a fireball. Every cell in her body was on high alert.

The prison lay just ahead. Nick leaned out the open door as Christen lowered her bird toward the street. He gestured information to her. When she reached eight feet of elevation, she flew them down the road like she would drive to church. She scared the bejeezus out of the lone donkey galloping and bucking below her. All the humans had fled inside.

The helicopter wash kicked up a debris storm that filled the air between the buildings, dancing particles off the hard surfaces, boxing in the air. With nowhere to expand and the downward thrust of the rotating blades roiling and churning up a dust cloud, visibility dropped to almost nothing. Everyone knew they were there. There was no stealth involved, which meant they'd soon have company.

The Black Hawk was above them and to the rear. She knew the Delta operators back there would be dangling from the runners, their rifles aimed and ready, sucking up a lungful of crap.

Christen didn't need a clear line of sight as she negotiated the tight space; she flew night missions, after all. But her sensors weren't happy that the blades were so close to the walls on her left and right. She wasn't thrilled about it either. Micromovements. Firm hands. Laser focus. Christen brought the heli flush to the northwest wall.

Nick counted the windows as she edged their bird forward. "Seven, eight. Steady. Steady. Eleven!"

Christen breathed in a stabilizing breath as she held her stick firmly and, with a practiced hand, maneuvered to lift them straight up.

"Second floor. Third floor. Fourth. Five. Here. Here. Here," he called into the comms.

They hovered until they saw a head behind the bars, peeking out. An American face pressed forward, his hands splayed wide against the window glass. Nick looked down at the photo then back at the man. "We've got him!"

Christen didn't turn her head to look, though she desperately wanted to. Her focus was steady on her instruments. Christen felt rather than saw Nick give Grey a wave before she edged forward a few feet, waiting for a tap on her shoulder, telling her she was lined up. She let air blow in a stream through her pursed lips. Flaring her nostrils and sucking in more oxygen, she worked to calm her adrenal glands. She'd trained for this level of stress. There was no room for error. Inches, not feet, were in play. Her hazard alarms were doing their job warning her. She was well aware that she had only the smallest amount of wiggle room before her blade caught on the side of the buildings. She just needed to keep a cool head. And keep her hands *steady*.

Nick reached over and pressed the button on their stopwatch. Now their precise mission window was in play.

They were all in danger, but none so much as the Delta operator who pushed a ladder between the window sill and the open door, forming a bridge between the building and the helicopter. He was tethered in, so if she took off, he'd take off, too, dangling below her runners. Christen could hear the screech of metal against metal as their helicopter shifted about, rubbing against the ladder. Nothing she could do about it. There was no such thing as holding this beast perfectly still. Front and back, possible up and down micro-sways might be okay. But the prison window sill they'd latched their ladder to couldn't be more than three or four inches wide. She hoped the Deltas were sitting on the back end of their rigged-up bridge because the side to side shift would surely be wider than the width of a hand. Not her problem, Christen reminded herself. They handled their end of the mission, and she handled hers. Straight. Even. Steady. That was the mantra she chanted.

Over the comms, she could hear the customers talking. With a Delta brother on either side holding his ankles, they handed out the tools. This operator, it seemed, was suited up in welder's gear.

"I need the plasma torch," the guy on the ladder called.

No one had run that idea by Christen. Her eyes stretched wide as she thought about sparks and bright-hot metal shards flying so close to her fuel tanks. Well, today might very well be a good day to die.

As that thought bubbled to the surface of her consciousness, a spark landed on her thigh, which was only somewhat protected by her flame-retardant jumpsuit. She had to work at not jerking her leg, not taking her hand off her control stick. Nick flicked the metal off before it seared her skin too badly. Christen made a mental note to thank him later.

Eyes forward. Breath paced. Focus sharp.

Hands sweaty, sure. But steady nonetheless. This is why Night Stalkers trained for every possible scenario under every possible condition. Ready for anything. This one was new, though. Christen never trained for a jailbreak in the middle of a city street in the full glare of the midday sun. Fun times.

Time did the adrenaline dance, making everything seem to take much longer than it actually did. According to the stopwatch mounted on her console, it had been twenty seconds. Was that possible?

Suddenly, pings sounded below them. Even with the engine noise bouncing and echoing off the buildings, Christen could make out that specific sound of metal on metal in a staccato beat of bullets flying from a finger exercising the trigger of a semi-automatic weapon. After every so many rounds, there was a short break. The shooter probably changing magazines.

"He's out our left side aiming for the fuel tanks," Nick's voice was as calm as a summer day fishing. More guns were added to the fight on the street, trying to take her bird down. Or maybe just trying to get the Delta off his ladder bridge. Surely, the guards in the prison were racing toward Grey's cell. Would the Delta's chase through the window after him if Grey was suddenly yanked from the room?

Thirty seconds.

One of the Deltas lay on his stomach out the left door, shooting his rifles downward with his own strafe of firepower to force the shooters behind cover. One of the militants' bullets must have found her fuel tank. She watched her fuel gauge needle slide toward E. Much longer, and she'd get fuel-critical for making their return flight.

Thirty-five seconds.

Of course, that would mean nothing if the idiot below them detonated her fuel tank with a grenade or other incendiary device. That was actually a problem she didn't need to deal with. Either it wouldn't detonate, or she'd be in a million pieces so fast that she would be alive one second and mist the next. *Focus.*

There was a clang, then a second clang to her right. Christen assumed that noise was the jail bars being tossed into the cell and hitting the cement floor.

A third clang.

Forty-two seconds in.

She wondered if the shooter might get up under them and shoot Grey as he was being pulled to freedom. The wash, though, was strong, the debris thick. That might be enough to keep the guy safe.

The Deltas were shouting. "Pull him through! Grab him! Get him on!"

Christen battled curiosity. She forced herself to keep her head straight, even, and forward-facing.

Fifty-four seconds.

A massive clang was followed by a tap on her helmet.

Fingers in her right periphery signaled her forward.

She'd be happy to comply. She waited a nanosecond for Nick to turn, count heads and confirm.

The Night Stalker creed said that she would not/could not leave a comrade to the enemy.

Up, up, up she climbed, banking hard right.

Sixty-seconds, the time allotted to get her customers out of the street. Damned, those Deltas were good!

Eleven-twenty-two hours.

The militants had manned their heavy guns, and Christen thought it was insane that opposition forces were shooting at her in the middle of the city. She moved to get between the enemy and the sun, so she would be lost in the glare. There was no cheering. No congratulations. Even if Grey couldn't hear her over the comms, telling the Black Hawk she was in dire straits, the Deltas could. Things were about to get hairier.

She zipped her bird into the hills, then brought the heli down to ten feet and slowed her motors, trying to conserve energy. She glided over the terrain, undulating the bird up and down, following the curves of Mother Earth. Her objective was to get as far as she could from the militants.

Just then, her fellow Night Stalker, Shawn Promin, better known as Prominator, called out. "Mayday. Mayday. Mayday. We're hit. They got our tail rotor. We're going down."

She hadn't seen the RPG in the air. Hadn't heard the explosion. She could hear the whistle of the Black Hawk as it spun in place. Christen wrenched her bird in a tight circle, bringing herself around. The Deltas' guns blasted from the Little Bird's open doors. The operators pulled out their own launcher, and the air brightened with a flash of light as they hit some explosive target in the distance.

Christen found a patch of what looked like even ground for her to set down.

A hand slapped her shoulder. "No, ma'am, we have to get the precious cargo back to base." The Delta called into the comms gesturing forward. "We have to deliver Grey."

"You don't understand," Christen replied. "We're out of fuel." She tapped the gauge. "We were never going to make it back. That Black Hawk was our ticket home."

3

GATOR

Tuesday, The Dodoma Rock Hotel, Dodoma Tanzania

INIQUUS' Strike Force crowded into a tiny room in their Tanzanian hotel. Shoulder to shoulder, knee to back, sitting on the bed, squatting on the floor, leaning into the walls, they crammed themselves together. Just a can of sardines focused hard on the computer screen, waiting for their commander, General Elliot, to give them the sitrep on their teammate Randy.

Randy had been hot-footed out of the country by a corporate executive who'd been pulled by an Iniquus team from some hole, in some part of a flea-bitten, backwater, life-threatening hell last year. At the time, he'd said, "Anything you need. No. Seriously. *Anything* you need, ever, you call me." That call went out. They needed his corporate jet stat for a direct flight to D.C. And his was the closest one they could lay hands on. The guy happily obliged.

Randy had barely survived the attack on Ngorongoro Imperial Hotel. Life could sure change in the blink of an eye. Just three days ago, he'd nigh on bled out. That picture bloomed in Gator's imagination: Randy lying in the parking lot, black of night, blood spurting. It only took about a minute after you sever an artery. It was a quick way to go. It was the goal of the knife tactics Gator had trained on as a Marine Raider to take down the enemy.

Randy wasn't stabbed, though. He'd taken a ricochet that sliced his femoral artery when the terrorists corralled their hostages into the hotel's parking lot at Ngorongoro Crater. He was bleeding out fast when his sister Meg tied the shredded ends of his artery into knots, and Randy's partner Honey cinched down with a tourniquet. The two of them stuffed Randy under a boulder, hoping he would be left for dead as the two of them, along with the other captives, were shucked into the trucks and taken into the conservation area where they were hidden in the wilds.

Gator slowly twisted the cap off his water bottle, his back pressed against the cream-colored wall.

Funny how you leave a hot zone for a little R&R, and the fight just seems to follow along behind you like stink on a pig.

He tipped the bottle back and took a swig. Seemed that lately, there was nowhere he could go and feel peaceful. He'd been feeling an undercurrent of anticipation. Something looming. Something damned turbulent.

Home, maybe.

Home might give him some peace--out on the bayou where his mama would throw fresh-caught shrimp in the pot to boil up with some corn on the cob and sausages. Crickets would set the tempo for his uncles Jean-Claude and Sebastian, as they picked up their instruments and joined in. Maybe a pretty girl in a pair of cut-offs would be settin' on his knee, laughing and squirming when he tickled her ribs.

He took another drink and wiped the drops from his mouth with the back of his hand.

It had been a long time since he'd been home and gone to bed with the frogs grumping in the background.

Home…He had this odd sense of emptiness. Maybe it was a sentimental hole that needed filling. Maybe he needed some time floatin' on the sun-warmed water and thinking about nothing. Certainly not thinking about this.

Randy's near-miss had sucker-punched Gator. Winded him in a way he wasn't used to. Gator, by nature, let his yesterdays roll off his back like water off a duck's feathers. But this time? It stuck.

Clung.

All Honey and Randy wanted to do was go hang out with Randy's sister Meg in Tanzania. Go on a safari with her scientist buddies. Stare at the wildebeests, maybe spot a lion. And boom! They're right there in the thick of another disaster.

Disasters were Iniquus's bread and butter. Well, *averting* disaster was. And Gator loved his job as an Iniquus operator. It was some kinda fun; he wasn't going to lie about it. Gator reveled in the physical and mental challenges, the do-or-die nature of their business. It was Russian roulette. Winning meant not only getting to live to see another day, but also the honor of serving the United States.

But this last hell-storm with Randy?

Sucker punch.

And crazily enough, the thing that gave Randy a fighting chance at survival, as far as Gator could tell, was the kid sitting in front of Meg on the other side of the bed. From what they'd been told, that eight-year-old thin-as-a-stick boy had been the life preserver that let Randy live to see another day.

Couldn't have been just any eight-year-old kid.

It had to be the right one.

That one.

Gator'd seen kids walking down the street in the middle of the war zone, stepping over land mines. Kids playing soccer that lacked the wherewithal—the survival instinct—to run when the shooting started. He had seen his share of little kids who stood in the middle of a field where all hell was breaking loose. He'd felt compelled to run into the shitstorm and grab 'em up. Hide them behind his armored vehicle to protect them. Give them some water and some candy — a smile. It was the best he could do to lend them comfort while his unit was under attack.

He'd also seen his share of kids wander by where his team had hunkered down. The kid would whistle a song as they strolled on by, but as soon as they were a bit down the road, they'd go running and screaming to the adults, pointing out the Marine's hiding spot. Those kids didn't get it - if they'd hushed their mouths, let the team lie low, and sneak away in the dark, lives would have been saved. Including their own. Eight-year-old kids were predictable in their unpredictability.

Gator looked at the stringy kid sitting on the floor, amazed.

It boggled his mind.

If it hadn't been for Ahbou getting him help, Randy would be dead.

Yeah, that there thought was a hard one to process.

Gator took another swig of water. He rattled the last two drops around in the bottom of the plastic bottle.

The image of a little girl played across Gator's thoughts. She was out with her father herding goats, dressed in clothes way too big for her slight frame, a red bandana around the tangled curls of her black hair. She was watching the sky, thinking she saw a second sun or maybe a fire against the blue expanse. It was replaced with a black spot that seemed to spin and fall. Another black spot was falling much slower. These things meant nothing to her, and she wanted to understand. But the spots were gone now, and she wasn't sure how to ask her father about them. She didn't have the right words to explain what she'd seen. The bells tied around the necks of the herd clanged around her, and she was distracted from the strange sight by a scraggly goat that nibbled at the roses that encircled the bottom of her dress. Gator had the urge to put his finger to his lips to signal her to keep quiet about what she'd seen.

That image came and went. Surely a memory from long ago, some time he'd been in the hills of Iraq. That's the impression he had—Hills of Iraq.

Impression was a better word than memory. It felt more like he was watching something in real-time over computer imagery. It was an odd sensation. Like he was a voyeur.

Gator shifted around uncomfortably.

It was hell waiting for the general to give them some news.

General Elliot liked everything run like clockwork. If he said eleven-thirty hours, then you'd better be at attention at eleven-thirty hours on the dot. The fact that he was late brought up the stress in the room. The heat level was rising with their concern. Gator could see sweat shadows on the guys' t-shirts. Blaze leaned over and turned the fan up another notch. The ancient air conditioner didn't have the muscle to keep up with all the bodies they'd squished in here.

Over next to Blaze, Meg sat cross-legged between Honey's feet. She wrapped her arms around her knees, making herself as small as possible in the overcrowded room. Honey rested his hands on her shoulders. Meg still looked like she was in shock.

That might take a while to shake off. Randy being okay would probably help that along.

Meg turned her head and tipped her chin down to kiss Honey's hand, then rested her cheek there.

It was tender.

Ahbou leaned back and said something to Meg. And Meg, in turn, sought out Gator's attention, miming a bottle of water.

With a nod, Gator moved to the closet where they'd put a cooler. He grabbed two handfuls of bottles and passed them around. He flipped one through the air, and Ahbou snatched it up.

"Thank you, Mr. Alligator, sir." Ahbou liked to layer on the names like butter and jam on a breakfast biscuit.

Gator gave him a grin and a wink.

Hell of a kid.

Meg said she was going to adopt him since he'd lost the last of his biological family in the terror attack at the hotel. Looked to Gator like Honey was hitching his wagon up for that ride too.

They made a nice family.

There it was again—that brush of ennui.

And Gator made the mistake of searching for some kind of understanding in that sensation. What he got was a flash of the red bandana on the girl, a wave of foreboding, of imminent danger. Gator wished he'd had a little more time seeing what had been in the sky. It was important. But the goats? They gave him nothing.

Nothing but the whisper of … something.

It kept flitting like a firefly into Gator's consciousness. Lighting here, flying off, lighting there. Never illuminating long enough for him to figure out what was going on.

It *felt* important.

Gator thought about Lynx, his Strike Force teammate who

was back at Headquarters in Washington D.C. Lynx would call this "psychic static." *I need to talk to her.* Lynx might be able to help him figure out what this buzz was all about.

Whatever was going on, he didn't like it none. Gator arched his shoulders and pressed against the wall, rubbing back and forth as if he could scrape the feeling off. It was darned uncomfortable.

Yeah, a chat with Lynx would help. She was a lot more practiced with her psychic abilities than he was. Gator's skills were still kind of new to him. He was still somewhere climbing the learning curve, figuring out how to master this stuff. When he said that out loud to Lynx, she'd laughed. "Yeah, let me know when you get that mastered." She wasn't being flip or nothin'. She just meant that it was always bigger than she was.

Always stronger.

She said it was learning how to live without feeling a sense of control—submission to the higher plane.

Gator wasn't big on submission.

What he was feeling was like a mosquito that buzzed in his ear then disappeared when he went to swat it.

On missions, Lynx would pick up information from the ether. "Ugh," she'd say. "It's just out of reach. I keep grabbing at it, and it's gone." This must be what she was describing.

I'll call Lynx when we get done in here.

As soon as the thought formed, his phone buzzed in his jeans' pocket. It was Lynx. He knew it for certain.

4

GENERAL ELLIOT MOVED into view on the computer screen and everyone in the Tanzanian hotel room stilled. Elliot was as tough and worn as shoe leather. He'd seen his fair share of disaster and atrocity and done his damnedest to give as good as his men got. More. If the enemy shot a bullet, he'd throw a grenade. "This isn't t-ball, boys!" he'd yell. "This is the big leagues. Bat'er out of the ballpark."

The general settled into the executive's chair. His tie was loose at the neck, the top button of his heavily-starched shirt undone, the sleeves rolled up to his elbows. "I'm not going to sugar-coat it. It's going to be one hell of a fight," he said. "I'm sorry to be late, but I had a call with the hospital." The general didn't wait for the men to acknowledge the apology. "Randy's plane landed at zero four ten Zulu time. He's at Suburban

Hospital now, in guarded condition. I'm told that the Tanzanian doctors did an adequate job getting him stabilized and packaged up. But I'm not trusting Randy's leg to Dr. Who's-available. As soon as we got Striker's first report, we flew in Dr. Silverman and his team from London. He's cutting edge on limb-saving techniques." His eyes glared from behind the permanent squint he'd developed in Nam. "No pun intended."

Gator was pretty sure no one in the room heard that last sentence as funny.

Only their commander, Striker Rheas, had been allowed to see Randy before he got loaded onto the corporate jet that Elliot had wrangled. Striker had said nothin' about Randy's chances of survival, but he had that grim set to his jaw that didn't bode too well. Randy being at Suburban Hospital, meant he was in good hands, though.

It lifted some of the weight off Gator's chest.

"They're prepping the O.R.," the general said. "I'll let you know as soon as we have anything new."

There was a stir in the room as the men digested the information. Gator watched Honey rub Meg's trembling shoulders.

It was Meg who had invited Honey and Randy to join her in Tanzania, where they got caught up in a terrorists' attack. She must feel responsible on some level.

"Ahbou, young man, we are indebted to you." The general's voice softened as he spoke to the boy.

While Gator and his fellow Strike Force team were still in the air, hard-charging onto the scene, Ahbou had snuck out of his hiding place in a tree and gotten Randy to the hospital, driving a hotel delivery van standing up so he could see out the front window and reach the pedals at the same time.

One hell of a feat.

Even though the kid had lost the last of his family in the

hotel's explosion, he was still able to think and act. Gator had been on the battlefield and seen full-grown men turn chicken-shit in the face of much less.

Gator felt the magnetic pull of the new family in front of him — Honey, Meg, and Ahbou.

He flexed his muscles to stop the weird vibration moving through his system.

Are they in danger? He asked himself.

No. That didn't feel right.

Gator thought back to the little girl with the goats. Yes, somewhere out there in the desert hills was where the danger lay. He felt he should warn someone; they needed to get out of that area. Bad things were headed their way. But Gator had no clue who this kid was. He couldn't remember meeting her. He rubbed his hand over his face, hoping to rid himself of the sensation. But it didn't help any.

Gator wanted more than anything to get the information about Randy's condition and then get into the hall to call Lynx.

As he thought that, his cell phone gave a quick buzz as a text dropped into his inbox. Gator pulled the phone from his pocket and held it by his side.

Ahbou grinned at the general. "Thank you, Mr. General Elliot, sir."

"There are few men with the moxy to contrive that rescue." The general said. "I have my eye on you. You just might be an Iniquus warrior in the making."

Ahbou covered his smile with his hand and blinked his big eyes at General Elliot.

"Meg?" the general said.

"Yes." Meg stopped to clear her throat. "Yes, sir," she tried again.

"I've made some phone calls. We're going to get the diplomatic channels lit up and find a way to get you and Ahbou state-side to be with Randy. Sit tight."

"Yes, sir. Thank you, sir." Meg said quietly.

"Team, I'm sure your prayers and good thoughts would be appreciated right about now." The general chewed on his cheek and stared straight ahead of him with that mile-long gaze of his as if he could see right into the future. "We're projecting good outcomes, but we're here for Randy no matter what. Iniquus is family. Period." He punctuated that sentence with a nod of his head.

The men of Strike Force returned the general's nod. Silent agreement. Not all for one and one for all, but the same heartbeat. The same blood.

"Jack McCullen has not yet been cleared for fieldwork by his doctors. He continues to work out of Headquarters. And now, Randy will be out for a while," Elliot was saying. "Striker, your team is short-manned and over-due for some R&R. I'm sorry to say this, but I need two volunteers for a short assignment which begins right there in Tanzania. Tomorrow."

Every hand in the room shot up.

The general scrunched his lips together, trying to hide the smile that wanted to paint across his face. Another nod, this time of approval. "Put your hands down and listen up. First, this assignment needs operators with surfing skills. Second, Strike Force has been overseas for months. If you're in a long-term relationship, when I ask again, keep your hand down. You need to take care of those who love you by spending quality time with them."

Surfing? The thick fog that had swirled around Gator suddenly lifted. He felt the tug of excitement. Lighter. Eager. The first relief he'd felt since he'd stepped into the room. No doubt, this assignment was where he needed to be.

"I'm not saying this is going to be a vacation assignment, we all know how that worked out for Honey and Randy, but I am going to say that I've been assigned to worse places than you're going to go. I need two of you. Okay, now do I have any volunteers?"

As Gator raised his hand to take the job, his phone vibrated a third time. He turned his head toward the buzz of another phone, that one belonged to Blaze, the only other Strike Force operator with his hand in the air.

"Blaze," the general said. "You have a fiancée. I said no one with a long-term relationship."

"Sir, Faith is a long-time girlfriend. We're not engaged. While it would be great to see her, she's out of town for the next ten days, so if the assignment's a short one, I'm good to go."

"Ten days will more than do it. Alright, I need to speak with Gator and Blaze. Striker stay put. Axel, Deep, and Honey, go get your gear in order. You'll be headed to the airport for a flight at thirteen-fifteen hours, local time. Dismissed."

"Sir," they said, coming to their feet. There was a shuffle, and the room emptied out.

"Meg," General Elliot said. "If you don't mind, I need to speak to my men."

"Oh!" Meg exclaimed. "Of course." She scrambled to her feet and touched Ahbou on his shoulder, and they scurried out the door. Yeah, the general could have that effect on folks.

Gator swiped his cell phone screen to take a quick peek at the text messages.

Lynx: **Do you need me?**

Lynx: **You're making me twitchy.**

Gator grinned, looked like Lynx's antennae was dialed to "high" and tuned to his station.

The last message, the one that came in as his hand went up:
This is the house that Jack built.

Son of a gun.

5

CHRISTEN

Tuesday, The hills of somewhere

THE DELTA OPERATORS were calling the shots. Christen outranked them, but she placed lives over ego. She was the expert in the air, but on the ground, her training was thinner.

She could run and evade with the best of them. Her handgun shots were dead-on at ten yards. She could do some damage with a rifle. But for the Delta operators, this was their world, like the night sky was hers. She'd cut them loose as she set the runners on the ground. "Gentlemen, Nick of Time and I are at your disposal."

Before she could pull her helmet from her head and unstrap her safety harness, her customers had leaped into action. Two had raced toward the downed Black Hawk, one had taken off to do recon of the area. One had grabbed a fistful of Grey's shirt collar and maneuvered him toward the cover of the tree line and a massive boulder. Grey had been suited up with a flak jacket and a helmet. He was only wearing one shoe.

Christen checked over her helicopter. When the rotors came to a stop, she'd whip out her new space-age camouflage fabric and throw it over their bird. By staking out the corners, they'd have a place to camp until the Calvary—or in this case, the PJs —could get to them. PJs were the pararescuemen whose task it was to recover personnel and treat their medical needs in combat environments. Christen hated that their recovery mission would be putting the PJs in harm's way. But she was grateful to know they were coming... eventually.

Christen leaned over a rock outcropping and peered down the hill, trying to interpret the movement around the Black Hawk. There was no yelling, no hustle. That could go either way. Things had either gone very well or incredibly badly. Anything in between and there would be a lot more activity and noise.

From this distance, the men looked the same, so Christen couldn't tell if the heads she saw belonged to the Little Bird's customers or they were survivors from the Black Hawk crash. They hadn't called her to help, so she was hopeful Prominator had found a way to the ground with minimal pain. She pulled her binoculars from the Little Bird. From what she could discern through their lenses, Christen was guessing the impact had gone better than expected.

She turned the lenses to scan around her, looking for any signs of danger. From where she stood, there wasn't much to see. It all seemed empty and barren. Hills. Dirt. Rocks. Oak trees grew in sparse clumps like the first hair plugs on a bald man's head. But she knew they weren't alone. Someone knew to shoot at them. Someone knew that there had been a hit and a crash. Someone was out there. How *many* someones? A lone guy who was now trying to pass the information on? That might buy them enough time to get the rescue crew in. A band of militants? That would make their situation a lot less tenable.

Below her, Christen--with the help of her binoculars--could now count more heads and see the activity. It seemed to be centered around equipment and not wounded warriors. The operators on the Black Hawk had pulled out their camouflage material and were spreading it over the wreckage.

Poof, the behemoth disappeared like magic. It was the same space-aged material she carried on the Little Bird. Designed by DARPA—Defense Advanced Research Projects Agency—the fabric was offered to the Night Stalkers to test in real-world situations. According to the government scientists, the material bent the light waves around the object rendering everything under the fabric invisible, like Harry Potter's cloak.

The 160th had given it a try at their base. It was a pretty remarkable development, as long as it was in the good guy's hands alone. It would suck for the enemy to have this to use against them. That was the danger of research and development. New discoveries didn't stay secret for long. Soon the enemy shared the technology, and counter-technology would need to be developed. The same as it had been from club, to spear, to gun, to atomic bomb. It was always a race to get the newest, most effective means of dominance.

Power was a mind-warping drug, mostly measured in wealth and clout. People, once they had a shot of it flow through their veins, craved more and more at any cost. Christen knew that from her own family of addicts.

Christen thought herself lucky that she found her highs in a different way--this way-- hopefully edging the world toward a safer, more peaceful existence.

Sensing movement behind her, Christen turned. Nick was unfolding and laying out their own invisibility cloak. The rotors had stopped. Christen pulled the Delta's ladder from behind her seat and used it to climb to the top of the helicopter. She crawled to the center of the fuselage and reached down for the corner that Nick stretched toward her. She and Nick had trained side by side for years on end. They didn't need a lot of words between them. They each knew how the other would think and act. They functioned together like a fine-tuned machine as they prepped their hide.

From the top of the helicopter, Christen did another scan of the horizon. She could see puffs of brown clouds scattered along the horizon. It could be militants on the move; it could be a flock of animals. She thought back to the movie *13 Hours*. The private security contractors working for GRS were watching video feed of sheep outside the walls of the CIA complex in Benghazi the night that they fought to protect American CIA and State lives. The Security team couldn't tell what they were seeing. Either men were crawling under the sheep, or the sheep were humping. "At 2:30 at night?" one of them asked. "I don't know anything about sheep." Christen looked at the cloud of dirt. She had no idea what she was seeing. Good. Bad. Or indifferent.

Whatever it was, she hoped it stayed in the far distance. They hadn't heard anything about a rescue ETA to their location. Base was probably in the development stages where they planned and debated strategies. She'd requested bladders of fuel for her bird and left Prominator to figure out what should be done about his copter. Until she spoke with him, she wouldn't know if a quick parts change would do the trick or if they'd need to explode the helicopter to keep it from enemy hands.

Christen imagined herself sitting in the strategy room, drawing up the plans. What would make the difference in their decision making? It very well could be the area was too hot after she'd flown down Main Street, thumbing her nose at both the locals and insurgents alike. It might well be that rescue would need to wait until the cover of darkness before they sent anyone. Christen thought command's decision making would have a lot to do with the seriousness of any injuries sustained on the Black Hawk. And whether command needed Grey back alive or if they just needed him out of enemy hands.

"Hey," Nick called. "That's a weird look on your face. What are you thinking about?"

"Sheep humping," Christen said, as the left-hand side of her mouth twitched into a wry smile.

Nick chuckled. "I should have guessed."

"You?" Christen held the light-weight camouflage fabric high over her head so Nick could work it along the rotor blade.

"I heard an interview on the BBC this morning. Sent a chill down my spine, and I haven't been able to warm up since."

"I'm listening." Christen crawled past the rotor and pulled on the fabric to get it centered.

"It was about this SAS guy who killed an ISIS fighter by drowning the tango in a puddle."

"Where exactly do you find a puddle in the desert?"

"Smartass."

"I'm serious." She held on to the fabric while Nick moved to stake out the near corners.

"The British operators were down in a river bed when they figured out they'd been surrounded by ISIS fighters. They check their supplies only to discover they're down to ten bullets between them and about fifty combatants skirting their location. The militants held the high ground."

"If they'd been captured..." She sat down with her legs stretched out in front of her. She swept her binocular across the horizon with closer scrutiny.

"Wouldn't that be a propaganda nightmare? ISIS parading

the British Special Air Service operators through the streets, beating them in the public square, torturing them for their intel, then beheading them on videos." Nick stopped talking while he forced a stake into the ground. He sauntered to the other corner pulling the edge taut. "The SAS decided that was their Alamo."

Christen bent her leg and wrapped her hands around her shin, ducking her head to use her knee to shield her eyes from the sun. "They know about the Alamo?"

"My words, not theirs. They decided they were going to die fighting, take out as many of the tangos as they could on their way out of this world."

"Where'd this go down?"

"They were gathering intelligence in northern Iraq past Mosul. So not too far away from here." Nick walked to the other side of the helicopter, and Christen worked the fabric under her and pushed it over the edge.

"The fight starts," Nick said. "The Brits shoot at the tangoes until their ammo is dry."

"Which was pretty fast with only ten bullets."

Nick grunted while he pushed the third stake in place, then looked up at her from where he squatted. "Then they were down to caveman tactics. They beat the tangoes with their rifle barrels. Stabbed them. Hand-to-hand shit. The one SAS shoves the tango's head into the puddle and drowns him, grabs a rock and pummels another one in the head."

"Wow." Christen blinked. "Wow. That's… wow."

"You feelin' my chill now?"

"You could say that. Did the SAS lose any of their operators?"

"Nope. A couple of them got shot. But they battled on. They counted thirty-two ISIS tangos down when the rest of the militants bugged out. Epic shit. They fought it out for four hours straight."

Christen's gaze held on the Delta operator, who had corralled Grey into the woods. He was standing on the boulder, his binoculars up. His body seemed tight. Primed. Christen turned her binoculars to see what was in his line of sight and found one of the dust clouds she'd wondered about earlier.

"Goats, northeast," his voice came over the radio.

"Copy," someone said back. Both operators' voices had a decided "oh-shit" undertone. This meant something to them that it didn't mean to her. Then she thought back to Operation Red Wings. The SEALs arrived at their location in the Kush region when they were discovered by three shepherds, an old man, and two teenagers. The SEALs decided that the locals weren't combatants and let them go, but they knew releasing them meant the Taliban would hear about their team's position. They made the decision. Instead of killing the shepherds, the SEALs retreated. Christen took in the landscape, rethinking what she saw. Hilly. A few trees. A few more boulders. Yeah. Shit. There really was nowhere to retreat from here.

"Do you see anyone out there?" Nick asked, coming to his feet.

"I see dirt in the air. If it makes you feel better, I didn't see anyone in any direction as we were landing. Of course, we weren't very high off the ground."

"Neither did I. Wonder why seeing the goats squeezed their sphincters."

"I hope we never find out. What happened to the SAS guys?"

"Base this is Alpha actual."

Christen couldn't find the guy talking into his radio through her binoculars. It must be one of their customers on the Black

Hawk. She put her finger in the air to hold her conversation with Nick. She wanted to hear this.

"We have line of sight on local herders," he said.

"Alpha Actual, this is Base, copy. Standby."

Christen sent Nick a flat lipped smile and a raised brow. "So, the Brits. What ended up happening? Did back up finally arrive? Four hours is a long time to go hand to hand."

"When the last of the tangoes took off, the SAS hiked five miles toward their base. Some Kurds picked them up and drove them the rest of the way. Two days later, the SAS were all back at work. Of course, I'm not counting the guys that got shot." As he said that, Nick pulled his gun from his holster and pulled back his slide, checking to see if he had a round in the chamber.

Christen tapped her elbow against her Glock. It was reassuring to know it was there on her hip if she needed it. "The Royal Airforce is doing a hell of a job, though, precision strikes even with the buildings packed together the way they are on those narrow streets." She caught Nick's gaze. "Grey was darned lucky that his prison had a wide perimeter. It's definitely not the typical set up in this part of the world."

"You mean the Deltas were lucky. You'd have hovered above the compound, and they'd be trying to work the plasma torch while swinging on a rope ladder, slapping into the wall. That or they'd just have to go down and shoot the guy. I'm betting they couldn't risk his intel getting out. Otherwise, why'd we get sent on that harebrained mission? Fly down the street and count windows. Shit."

"Shooting the guy would be a hell of a bad calling card for the intel community. Would you sign on if you thought someone from your team might show up and kill you by design?"

Nick shrugged. "Dunno. Maybe. I'd appreciate a bullet from a buddy if I were about to be tortured to death." He reached out to adjust the fabric on the peg. "Whatever Grey knows must be epic, or this rescue would never have gone down the way it did. I bet your stunt-flying makes the front page."

"That would be a disaster on so many levels."

They were both quiet for a moment, circulating their own thoughts.

Nick stood and brushed dirt from the knees of his flight suit and hands. "Seriously? Humping sheep?"

"The movie, *13 Hours*."

"Ah, so basically, we were on the same page. Our collective subconscious has figured out this mission is FUBAR."

6

Tuesday, The Dodoma Rock Hotel, Dodoma Tanzania

"GENTLEMEN," General Elliot said once the three Strike Force operators were alone in the room. "We've signed a joint contract to provide the CIA and the Department of the Treasury Office of Intelligence and Analysis offices with our support on an upcoming mission. You will be given the details of the operation that you need at each progression."

"Yes, sir." Strike Force Commander Striker Rheas answered for their team, though he'd be flying home with the rest of their men.

"The first stage is going to require some acting skills and seat-of-the-pants thinking. Our clients have identified a business-man, William Davidson, as a person of interest. We need to get you on his security team."

"He's traveling without security?" Striker asked.

"He has a five-man team with him. A chauffeur, and a man

who watches his back. The other three cover his wife and three of his grown children, all males. To expand that team with two more operators, the CIA is contriving to get the daughter and two of her friends to pay an unexpected visit to dear old dad. Our clients believe that given the time it takes to fly someone in from the US, if our target can find help readily at hand, he might take the bait and hire our guys on."

Blaze posted his forearms on his thighs and leaned in.

"So how do we finagle this?" Gator asked.

"William Davidson has to discover you. It has to be his idea." The general said. "Imagine that you're out and about. Suddenly, you find yourself in a situation where you're separated from your security, but two Americans, who happen to have close protection credentials, jump in, and save the day."

"Impressive," Striker said.

The general's face shifted ever so slightly to show the shadow of a smile. "We hope so. Right now, it's our best opportunity. If this doesn't work out, then the operation will become a shadow detail, and that becomes problematic quickly. The CIA operations officers will stage when an opportunity presents itself. There will be no comms between you two. Nutsbe with Panther Force will be your support while Deep Del Toro is on R&R. You have Nutsbe's direct number." He waited for a "yes, sir" from Blaze and Gator. "You know the security protocols. You can contact Nutsbe for mundane information with a simple phone call. Anything to do with sensitive materials will need to go through encrypted channels. We know for a fact that FVEY has ears on Davidson. While the members of Five Eyes are our allies, we don't need them to be looking over our shoulder on this one."

"Yes, sir," the men said.

"This first stage will take place in Dar es Salaam on the

Tanzanian coast. We have you scheduled to fly there this evening and get your bearings. Tomorrow, according to our intel, the wife and three sons will be going to Zanzibar for the day. If the family follows the protocol that's been in place up until now, that will leave Davidson with his chauffeur/bodyguard and his close protection. My guess is that this is going to go down tomorrow. The family is scheduled to move to their next destination in two days' time, so the window to get you onto their team is a small one. Don't miss it. You won't know the officers, but they'll know you. You're going to have to do surveillance, and when you see things cooking, you need to go in and pull the pot off the stove, do your citizen-hero act."

"Yes, sir," Gator and Blaze said.

"Remember, you're fighting CIA officers. You don't break our client. Play nice. It's an acting job. Handguns are illegal in Tanzania. I doubt they'll flash one around. That doesn't mean if they do, you let them put their sights on you and pull the trigger, so you can block the bullets with your Wonder Woman cuffs. Just last month, some retired librarian was helping the cops in a shoot/don't shoot training scenario, and the cop double tapped her in the chest only to find out he had live ammo. She's dead. I don't need to remind you, we never play around with bullets, even in training."

The general paused, and the men filled in the space with a "Yes, sir."

"You are to behave as if everything is the real deal. Duck the punches—soft taps instead of takedown slugs. Get them on the ground and tied up, or get the executive bundled out the back. I don't know how to advise you. But everyone should be able to brush off the dust and go home without injuries at the end of the day. Clear?"

"Yes, sir." Blaze replied.

"Just follow along, wait for something to go down, run in, and play hero," Gator said. "Then we wait for the job offer. Do we give them a card? Do we negotiate a contract?"

"Give them a card. Announce that you're Iniquus operators. We've booked you into rooms in Davidson's hotel, where he's meeting with the Tanzanian Department of Energy. You can tell them you put your principal on a plane to Europe, and your assignment is over. You're taking a week of R&R before returning to the States. Let them know what hotel you're in. I'm sure they'll be knocking at your door. If all works according to plan, they can sign a close protection contract with us here at Headquarters. We'll just email it over to them to sign and hand back to you. The call from his daughter Christen won't come in until after the staged event."

Blaze shot Gator a grin.

"Once you're in place, you'll get your next step. As always, good luck. Make Iniquus proud." The monitor went dark.

Blaze slapped a hand across Gator's chest. "Fighting in public on foreign soil. This should be well-received by the locals."

"I'm sure if law enforcement gets involved, the CIA will pull you out of whatever jail they stick you in. Don't fight the cops." Striker said.

"You serious, Striker?" Gator raised a brow. "The CIA will come to our rescue? That don't sound plausible."

7

CHRISTEN

Tuesday, The wrong side of the Iraqi-Syrian border

THE TEAM from the Black Hawk were climbing the hill, looking like pack mules. Christen followed after them as they slid under the helicopter camouflage. Their supplies rolled out of the men's arms onto the ground, and they plopped their packs down, then themselves. The heat of the sun was deflected by the reflective quality of their tarp that made a tent over the Little Bird's rotors. It was demonstrably cooler under here. The July heat in Syria was no joke. It felt like it could bore a hole through your hat down into your head and fry the contents of your brain.

Christen looked the men over. One Delta had his arm in a splint and was rigging a triangular bandage to hold it to his chest now that he'd dropped his pack. Christen moved over to give him an assist. Their uniforms had drying bloodstains. White bandaging peeked out of the rips in their BDUs, abrasions, cuts, and bruising on their hands and faces. One guy looked like he'd broken his nose—all in all, a damned good outcome.

Prominator was one hell of a pilot. She knew the Night Stalkers would debrief his landing, so they could all learn from this event. Christen was looking forward to that hot wash where they'd dissect the mission. But now? She wanted to hear what the Deltas had to say about their present situation.

One of the operators from the Black Hawk caught her eye. "Where are Jeopardy, Nitro, and Grey?"

The Deltas hadn't introduced themselves by name. They never did. Sometimes Christen would catch a call name, but, for the most part, they were just "the customer."

"Someone took off in that direction." Christen pointed. A Delta she hadn't met stood next to her. His eyes traveled along her arm and out into the distance as she pointed. "And another took off down by the copse of trees behind the boulder with your PC." Christen used the term for precious cargo, a non-military person that needed rescue or security while moving from Point A to Point B. "My turn," she said, turning her attention to the Delta to her right. "Where's your pilot and co-pilot? Are they okay?"

"They're banged up like the rest of us. They're down with the Black Hawk figuring out if they can call for some parts and get it up in the air again. I'm told you're here instead of in the air because of a fuel problem. You're completely dry?" he asked.

"No, but I don't have enough to get to base. Better that we stick together. Consolidate weapons and manpower."

He nodded.

They didn't call them the silent professionals for nothing.

Moving over to the open door on her bird, he looked the fuel tank over. "I thought these were supposed to withstand handgun fire."

"Not withstand. Resist. Up to a fifty-caliber round. Looks to me like the shooter knew that too. See here? He was aiming for a single target on the tank. He hit it repeatedly, weakening the structure until he finally got some rounds through."

He grimaced. "Good thing it didn't explode like in the movies."

"Impossible," she said. "But you knew that already."

He winked and stretched out his hand for a shake. "T-Rex."

"D-day," she said.

He moved his hand to the fuel container and slid his finger into one of the holes. He ran his hand over the surface, around the sides. "This is it for damage? Maybe we could patch it and haul the fuel from the Black Hawk. Are you running the same kind of fuel through these engines?"

"Same. JP-4. We'd need at least thirty gallons. Forty would be better. Safer."

"Dogs," a whisper came over the radio.

"Crap," would be the nicest of the exclamations that were muttered by the men around her.

Christen could hear the ting ting tinging of bells echoing through the craggy hills. It didn't seem to her like they were coming any closer.

"We've got two five-gallon containers we could siphon into," T-Rex said. "A couple of trips and we can get you, and your co-pilot, Grey, and four of my worst wounded out of here. I'll send Ty with you to be your firepower." He pointed at another giant of a human being. It looked like Ty could scoop up an adversary and eat him for breakfast, no weapons necessary.

Christen looked around T-Rex's broad shoulder at where his team splayed out in the dirt, working with their weapons. "How badly are they injured?" she asked under her breath.

"Walking wounded, they could fight if need be."

"So that leaves you with--"

"Plenty. We'll do fine. Let's figure out--"

"Kid," a man's whisper rose from the radio into the air.

Again, with the curses.

"Who is that?" she asked.

"Jeopardy." T-Rex's shift was microscopic, but his energy brightened, became more intense, focused.

He tapped two men on the shoulder as he walked by. "You're with me. Ty, you figure out how to keep some fuel in this bird. I don't care if someone has to ride back to base with their fingers shoved in there like the Little Dutch Boy with his thumb in the dyke. A fat wad of chewing gum if it comes down to it," he said over his shoulder.

T-Rex and his two men took off down the hill.

Christen looked around. She felt like she should be doing something, but the something she should be doing didn't occur to her. She'd already done everything she could to set up her helicopter for the refueling bladders she expected the rescue crew to bring in from base. She checked her watch. It was thirteen hundred hours. She didn't expect help before twenty-two hundred hours when it would be dark enough to hide the Black Hawks in the night sky. The next nine hours stretched in front of her felt like an eternity. Could they stay hidden until help arrived?

CHRISTEN LAY ON HER STOMACH, peering through her binoculars under a slim space that separated their camouflaging invisibility fabric from the ground. A little girl tipped her head to the side and blinked. Her little brown toes were dusted with grey dirt.

The sandals she wore were too big for her feet. Her eyes were dark and filled with curiosity. "Curiosity killed the cat," tumbled over itself in Christen's brain as she wished the girl would get the wayward goat and go away. The girl tipped her head back, her mouth wide. Christen anticipated a scream. But the child's head dunked forward in a powerful arc as she sneezed violently then wiped her nose on the sleeve of her cotton dress with faded roses dancing around the hem. She adjusted the red bandana—that was folded into a triangle and tied around her cascade of tangled black curls—as she focused once again on the expanse in front of her.

Christen held her breath as she watched the child try to interpret what she was seeing. Christen's mind went back to one of her first interviews when she was applying to the Night Stalkers.

"You're on a mission of vital importance." The colonel had said. "A child stumbles upon your position. What do you do? Do you kill her? Take her prisoner? Or do you let her go?"

Christen had said, "It depends on the circumstances, sir. All are viable options, just not equally so. During a mission, I expect I will weigh the choices and come to the best conclusion I can, given the circumstances." What Christen had thought was: *I'll be in the air. It'll be night. All the kids will be sleeping. This scenario doesn't pertain to me.*

One of the Deltas crouch walked toward her, whispering into his comms—a sniper rifle in his hands. A silencer screwed into place.

If he took that child down, the sound from the suppressed rifle might blow away with the wind. It just as easily might echo off the rocks and throw the rest of the people who were with the herd into a panic. Then the search party. Then the retaliation. This Delta wasn't on the elite team for nothing. He knew all the ramifications of his actions. And all the rules of engagement.

Christen trusted his expertise. But that didn't mean she wasn't feeling the adrenaline. And not the happy rush that she loved so much. This was the crapola kind that came when you think things might be putting you truly at risk of life and limb or watching an innocent get caught up in the event.

They lay there, side by side, she and the Delta, watching the child. In this moment, their fates were intertwined, and Christen didn't even know the guy's name.

Christen wondered what the helicopter looked like from where the girl stood. Did the breeze ripple the fabric, making it look like a portal between the worlds? Did it glisten, somehow, in the intensity of the sunlight, making this space look enchanted? The child looked up at the sky as if she were pondering. She pointed a finger then traced it down to the ground over to the right. That's where the Black Hawk had dropped. But Christen knew the Black Hawk was too far down the hill for it to be in the child's view. The girl turned and faced toward Christen again and scratched at her bandana, pointed at the sky, and traced her finger down until she was pointing just to the left of where her helicopter rested.

That was strange. Maybe this child saw the helicopters land, and she wondered how they had disappeared. If not, why the pointing?

Maybe their camouflaged helicopter didn't look like anything at all from where she stood.

Maybe she just happened to stop there.

Just happened to look in their direction.

Just happened to pause.

The child turned and ran away.

Sigh. Maybe not.

The sniper guy was reporting into his radio, getting his team up to speed.

"Move it," T-Rex growled under his breath. Two of the operators who had been bringing up fuel cans scrambled out under the corner that had been unpegged. They carried an empty five-gallon container with them. T-Rex turned and pointed and emphatic finger at the plastic jug, filled with fuel they'd left behind. "Get that into the funnel. Go."

One man stood holding the funnel steady. Another lifted the forty-pound canister and tipped it slowly.

"Are you ready to go?" This time, T-Rex's finger stabbed the air in front of Christen.

"As soon as we're fueled," she said. This canister was the fourth to go in. Twenty gallons was half of what she needed in place. She wasn't a hundred percent about the holding power of the patch Ty had rigged. Especially as the weight and pressure inside the fuel tank increased.

"Son of a bitch," Jeopardy was back on his comms. "We've been spotted. The girl ran to a man. He pulled her up on his shoulders, and now they're all high-tailing it."

T-Rex adjusted his radiofrequency. "Base this is Alpha Actual…" his voice blurred as he moved from under the hide and down the hill.

Moments later, he was back. "You. You. You. And you." He pointed out certain team members. "Get on board." He pointed at the Little Bird. His finger seemed to be his mode of cutting down on verbal clutter.

A general "Hell no, we won't go" was raised, and T-Rex lifted the corner of his lip in a snarl. The men might have been grumbling under their breath, but they moved to their places.

Grey came panting up under the camouflage, his Delta guardian, Nitro, still gripped the collar of the man's shirt.

T-Rex pointed at Grey then jerked his thumb toward the

Little Bird. And the Nitro guy moved his fistful of cloth toward the heli, jostling Grey to his place.

Grey had lost his other shoe along the way, and his socks hung halfway off his feet like flaccid flippers. *Flaccid flippers*—that alliteration cartwheeled in Christen's brain while she tried to figure out if Grey was under arrest or if they thought he might flee. She didn't remember a PC being manhandled like that before. But, then again, she'd never been in these circumstances before. She was just trying to go with the flow. Be a help, not a hindrance nor a distraction.

Christen had noticed T-Rex's face had clouded when he came back under the tent, a storm brewing in his thoughts. She could guess why. There would be no air support. Her commanders were coldly-calculating when it came to mission assignments. They were already two helicopters, four Night Stalkers, and ten Delta Force operators down, along with one (whatever the heck Grey was) PC.

Base had calculated that Grey's extraction was worth the risk of their teams being deployed into the city for the day-time mission. But now that they had Grey in hand, Christen wondered what Delta orders were in place as far as Grey was concerned. Under such circumstances, would the operators go to extremes to make sure there was zero chance that the PC would ever fall back into the hands of the combatants? It was possible. She couldn't speak to that. Didn't want to consider it. It wasn't her call. The military wasn't a democracy.

She took a good look at Grey sitting facing out of the heli-copter. His body said calm, cool, collected. His eyes said exhausted and hungry. His skin color was a shade that matched his name. He was playing a brave role, but he was scared, or maybe just in shock. Who wouldn't be? Grey was probably dozing on his cot, anticipating who might come knocking on his cell door and what horror awaited him when suddenly a crew of wild men with skeleton face masks showed up outside of his window and pulled him through the broken panes five stories off the ground. That might take a day or two to recover from. And recovery wouldn't start while they were hunkered under a reflective cloth on the wrong side of the enemy line.

Christen reached for her emergency pack, pulled out an MRE, and handed it over to Grey. He took it and blinked vacantly at her.

"Eat," she said.

He sat still as a statue as if the words weren't gelling in his brain.

A Delta bumped Grey with his elbow and lifted his chin, bringing Grey back from Lala Land.

Grey's fingers fumbled to open the box.

Christen moved to inspect the patch that sat like a giant pimple on her fuel tank. It wasn't confidence building. She sent a wry look toward the men, who carefully filled the tank. She wondered how T-Rex saw this playing out. She wished they'd have a powwow and fill her in on the concerns and precautions —a plan.

Yeah, a plan would be good.

The shepherds are running. Christen would pay good money to know for sure the reason why. She checked her watch: only thirteen thirty-five hours – time was at a standstill.

How far would the locals have to run before they got where they were going? Did the shepherds have contact with the city? Would they have heard of the prison exfil and been asked to be on the look-out for anything odd? Surely, whoever had taken down the Black Hawk had seen it going down and knew their general location. Surely, the same people had seen her heli follow them to the ground. Could that, and not the child, be the reason that the shepherds were running? From the shepherds' vantage point, did they see trouble moving into the area?

Just as the thought formed in her mind, she heard Jeopardy's voice over the radio. "We've got insurgents moving into view. Forty – fifty heads. They've got some big ass guns mounted, too. Get that Little Bird the hell out of here."

All in one fluid motion, the Delta reaction machine mobilized. The man tilted the fuel container up, letting the last drop slide in. He tossed the container to the side as he moved to the tent peg. T-Rex grabbed hold of Christen's flight suit as he shoved her toward her seat.

"No man left behind," she yelled.

"Fuck that," he snarled as he half-lifted half-threw her in place. "We're the customers. You're here to provide for our needs. We need you to get our precious cargo and our wounded back to base. As soon as we've got you cleared, you take off. The sooner you're gone, the sooner we can get ourselves squared away. *Capisce*? Strap in and give me a thumbs up."

This feels wrong. This is wrong. Christen grabbed a hunk of T-Rex's uniform in an equal display of power. "The jury-rigged tank isn't going to hold. The patch needs to be welded in place to cover a hole that big. Duct tape and epoxy just aren't going to cut it."

"Watch your gauge and find another place to set down, lady. Anywhere but here. They're about to light us up, or didn't you hear?" He turned his head. "You and you. Get the damned tarp off. Get them cleared for takeoff." He pointed at Nick, who was reaching for a peg. "You, either get in your seat or grab a gun."

Nick sprinted around to the other side and piled in. Snatching at his harness, he strapped down. "Fucking hell," he said under his breath, slamming his helmet into place.

The camouflaging fabric cleared, Christen cranked her

engines. The blades slow whop, whop, whop gained the speed they'd need for lift-off.

Several Delta's lay off in the distance, hips on the ground, shoulders curved above their sniper rifles. The first of their bullets flew. Christen knew each carefully-sighted bang meant a life extinguished. She maneuvered the Little Bird up and away from the noise.

8

GATOR

Tuesday, The Dodoma Rock Hotel, Dodoma Tanzania

"YO, GOOD TIMES," Gator said as he shut the door behind Striker's retreating back.

"I wonder where our end destination's gonna be," Blaze said. "Tanzania isn't exactly known for surfing. Australia? Hawaii? Maybe Thailand?"

"Your phone buzzed when you raised your hand. Drinks at the bar tonight says it was Lynx."

"Some voodoo ESP tell you that?" Blaze asked, pulling his phone from his pocket. "Yup, first round's on me. Lynx sent a text: **This is the house that Jack built**."

Gator turned his phone toward Blaze with the same message. "Funny, our phones were the only ones to get anything when our hands went up."

Blaze gave a full-body shiver. "Damn, I hate it when she does that."

Gator flopped back across the bed and laced his fingers under his head. "No, you don't. You thank your lucky stars she does what she does. Now, what do you think it means?"

"We were talking about Jack being out because of his leg injury just before that text came through. Last time she sent one of her cryptic *knowing* texts it was to Jack while he was clearing the roof on the Philippines ' mission. '**Jack Be Quick. Jack jump**.'"

"Would you have done it?" Gator asked. "Read that text, run to the edge of a three-story building, and jumped?"

"It's not like Jack took the time to think it through. His phone was in his hand with the text still on the screen when he landed. I watched it fly up when he impacted. All I can say is it had to have rung true to some part of his brain. His body just acted. She saved his life. The whole damned building was an inferno by the time his ass hit the car roof. Would I have done it without hesitation like he did? Shit if I know." Blaze leaned his hips into the lowboy and crossed his arms over his chest. "Her *knowings* are always right, but the interpretation in the moment can put it in a different frame than what happens in the long run. Her being right is a given, but only in hindsight. Would I jump?" Blaze shook his head. "I damned well hope I'm never in the position to have to make that call."

"Might as well ask the oracle herself what's going on." Gator pressed the phone icon.

Lynx picked up before Gator heard it ring. "Thank goodness! What the heck are you doing, Gator?"

"You're the one who sent the cryptic text," he said.

"Not that. Before that. Goats? The little girl? The helicopters? Why the hell were you awash in—"

Helicopters? Those black dots he'd visualized were heli-

copters? Huh. "I got you on speakerphone. Blaze is here with me."

"Hey, Lynx. I got your message. We thought you might have some kind of lens that might bring your words into focus."

"Hey, Blaze. I'm willing to try. I was just lying here thinking, and I got the feeling Striker was coming home."

"Affirmative." Blaze said.

"On the physical plane, I got word that Randy was brought in to Suburban, but Panther Force minus Honey was his escort. Before you ask, I've pulled all the strings at my disposal, and I can't get any details beyond 'he's in surgery.' They started operating at zero three hundred hours, which seems like a bad time to begin, but A) every second counts and B) the surgeon and his team are all in from London. They're on Zulu time, so it was eight in the morning for them. They like to stay on their same body clock time and not switch over to Eastern Standard, so they aren't having to acclimate and deal with jet lag when they're doing such precise work."

"Makes good sense," Gator said, resting the phone on his stomach.

"It made me feel good about the team. Out of the box thinkers."

"And Jack?" Blaze asked.

"His leg? Is looking good. Time and physical therapy are doing their work." Lynx replied.

"Noted." Blaze said. "And he's built a house?"

"Oh, yeah. Sorry, my head was on the word legs. No, he didn't literally build a house. His actions precipitated whatever you two are up to."

"Blaze and me, we have a new assignment," Gator said.

"Stateside?"

"No, the team is heading home. We're staying here to fulfill a new contract. Elliot said less than ten days, and we'll be back at HQ, too."

"We get to surf," Blaze added.

"Tough life," Lynx said. "Hey, I have a meeting, and they're expecting me now. Can we talk on a secure line later? I think we need to figure out what you're headed into. My knowing wasn't the full-on body blow I got for Jack. But it wasn't a subtle tickle either."

"Damn," Blaze said.

"Forewarned is forearmed," Lynx said.

"Yeah, just buzz us when you're freed up." Blaze rubbed a hand over his head, making his military-cut auburn hair spring into curls. "We'll make ourselves available. We have a short flight over to Dar es Salaam on the coast around dinner. Other than that, we're cool." Blaze said.

"Gator…" Lynx whispered, then stalled.

Silence filled the room as if Lynx's single word had cast a spell.

Gator blinked.

Everything went dark.

In his mind's eye, he was in a different time and place a flash of sensation, he was falling. The taste of salt was bitter on his tongue. His eyes stung. His feet were leaden, dragging him downward. He was desperate but not for himself. He had to save *her*. He loved her. Would never let her go. Though Gator lay very still on the hotel bed, in his mind, he thrashed at his surroundings, grabbing for her.

This time, he would save her or die trying.

With another blink, he was back in the Tanzanian hotel room, taking a gulp of air.

This time? What the *heck* was that?

Lynx let out a low moan.

"Lynx, is everything okay?" Blaze asked.

Whatever Gator had just experienced, it had come and gone in a nanosecond. That was the weird-assed shit that happened when he got linked with Lynx.

Did he like it? *Hell*, no.

But it had saved his life and the lives of others many a time. And it seemed he needed to save some woman.

His woman.

"Yeah. Sorry. I was distracted by a...Uhm, Gator?" Her voice was somber – filled with foreboding. "You and I, we need to talk."

"Yeah, we do." He needed to know who this woman was. He wasn't in love with anyone. Not even close. Gator scanned through the ladies he spent time with back in D.C., not a single one resonated with the impression he'd formed. Did he even know her? How could he feel this strong of an emotion—this depth of belonging—for a stranger? Gator rubbed his hands over his face to erase the sensation. That splash of knowing had all happened in the blink of an eye, but it left a sense of longing in its wake.

9

GATOR

Tuesday, The Dodoma Rock Hotel, Dodoma Tanzania

AHBOU WAS LAUGHING, his limbs splayed wide as he flew through the air, then dunked beneath the cool water, throwing up a spray as he hit the surface. Gator reached out a long arm and scooped the sputtering boy out of the pool. Ahbou had never seen a swimming pool before. The water where he lived had hippopotamuses and other man-eaters, so he didn't know how to swim. But he seemed to take to the water like a duckling in spring. Ahbou scrambled up Gator's back to stand on his broad shoulders. Gator grasped Ahbou's ankles, lifted him toward the sky, and gave the boy a toss. Ahbou reached his arms out with a shriek of joy and belly-flopped onto the surface.

A tug on the boy's leg brought him back to safety.

Meg sat under a wide umbrella, grinning at the pair. "Ahbou," she called as Gator lifted him for another toss. "The waiter is bringing your lunch. Come on out of there."

Gator wrapped his hands around the boy's narrow waist and propelled him through the water to the side of the pool. "Come on now, kick your feet. That's right." He lifted Ahbou up to where Meg was waiting with an open towel.

"You're a natural around kids, Gator. Do you have children of your own?" Meg asked, enfolding Ahbou in a beach towel and pointing at a chair.

"I'm as single as they come right now." Gator worked to extinguish the strange sensations that fired along his nerves as he said that. Gator waded farther down the pool. "Course that cain't last but too much longer. My mama's already getting ansty and pestering me to get on with it. She won't be happy until she's got her a passel of grandkids to dote on."

Gator jumped out of the water and stood drip drying as a young boy came to talk to Ahbou. Meg smiled and nodded. Ahbou skipped over to the other side of the pool, where the kid had some toy he was showing off.

Meg reached back to grab a towel and tossed it to Gator, then raised her hand to signal Blaze. "Lunch is here," she called to him. "I guess we should properly call it tea since it's so late in the day," she said as Gator pulled out a chair.

Blaze leaned down to kiss Meg's cheek as Gator picked up the newspaper from the table to make room for the plates. He looked down at the front page where she'd drawn devil horns and a goatee on the guy. William Davidson, it said in bold type. It was the name of their mark. *Interesting.* He studied the picture —despite the pen marks—so he could compare it later to the photo Iniquus would send them for identification.

"'Asshat' is strong language for you, Meg." Gator pointed to where she'd scrawled the word across the man's nametag in the picture.

She gave him a tight-lipped smile.

Gator held up the picture for Blaze to see as he pulled a chair to join them.

"Must be a good story behind that," Blaze said. "Thank you for ordering, Meg."

"You're more than welcome. As to the good story — no, not really. Not good. Actually, it could be devastating. To Tanzania. To humanity. To the world."

"So, he's an *apocalyptic* asshat," Gator said, as he scanned through the article in the English translation newspaper. Department of Energy meeting, yup, this was their target. "It says he's in the country to meet with their energy guy. Energy doesn't have anything to do with animal migration, does it? How do you know Davidson?"

"I don't. He may be a perfectly lovely man. But he's trying to get a deal done here that is controversial. It actually ties to you guys in a way."

Gator kept his body language casual and relaxed, but his attention was fixed.

"Tanzania was working with Derek Bowen and Hesston Oil on a project. Tanzania needs money to bring its people into the modern world and provide for their basic needs — food and water." Meg held her hand up to shield her eyes from the sun as she looked at him.

Gator moved to a chair on the other side of the table, so she wasn't uncomfortable.

"Derek Bowen and his wife Anjie – were the victims of a hostage situation in Djibouti that Randy and Rooster were assigned to negotiate and resolve. And they saved the couple, well you already know that." Meg's gaze was fixed with a frown on Ahbou. "Can you imagine that? Derek and Anjie got yanked off their yacht out in the Red Sea. Going about their business. Not hurting anyone. And then their world was turned upside down." She swiped at her eyes.

Gator thought she was probably equating that scene with what she had just gone through with Randy and Honey. They had been on safari, and then all hell broke loose. Her brother had been nearly killed. She and Honey were taken hostage.

Blaze reached over and covered her hand with his. They sat in silence while she took a moment to get hold of herself.

Meg tucked her hair behind her ears, and with a little thank you smile to Blaze, she continued. "Hesston wanted to drill for oil off the shore of Zanzibar. There are environmental risks to the operation, but the Hesston company had pivoted to become a not-for-profit green energy company. They wanted to use the money from off-shore drilling to fund some massive renewable energy projects in East Africa – geothermal, wind, and solar. Now, I'm not sure where those negotiations stand." She reached over and tapped the photo. "I think, reading between the lines, that William Davidson sees an opportunity with the Bowens out of the picture while recovering from their ordeal. Davidson's trying to snake his way into the negotiations."

"William Davidson is an oilman?"

"He's an 'anything to line his pockets' man, from his reputation. Energy; some attachment to military weaponry; and you probably know he was on the board at Omega."

Omega was Iniquus's rival of sorts. They'd had a major upset in the States and now mostly worked overseas ops. Where Iniquus was willing to push the gray envelope on legality to get a job done and keep America safe, Omega was willing to do the truly black stuff. They were the group who showed up on the news with their naked dance parties around their campfires in the Middle East and balls-out swaggering that gave contractors a bad reputation—a reputation that put other teams, like Iniquus's, at risk of targeting and reprisal by the locals. Gator couldn't very well hold that against the locals. Omegas acted like psychopathic animals in the field. And one of their teams had come at Lynx full throttle, risking her life and shooting a bullet into Blaze. Gator swiped his tongue over his teeth. Davidson had ties to Omega. Interesting.

"I think he's also into luxury hotels and apartments," Meg was saying. "I don't know the extent of his enterprises. Right now, I think he's negotiating drilling rights for oil off Zanzibar. Their techniques aren't nearly as environmentally protective as Hesston's would be. But what has me scared is the helium."

Helium?

"Is there a specific reason why you're following Davidson's reputation? You're an animal migration specialist. What's that got to do with Zanzibar?" Blaze snagged a grape and popped it in his mouth. Then reached for the paper Gator held out to him.

"The scientists on the Key Initiative have been worried about Davidson's dealings in this part of the world. As far as my interests go, it's about the Rift Valley, which extends through Tanzania and includes the Ngorongoro Crater and the Serengeti where the animals I'm trying to protect migrate."

"This is about helium, you said?" Gator asked.

"Yeah, do you guys know about the global helium issues?"

"My contact with helium is restricted to birthday parties and sucking up a lungful to sing in a Minnie Mouse voice for my nieces and nephews," Gator grinned. "Sorry. Do we have global helium issues?"

"More so this month than we did last." She handed Gator a napkin and a plate that held a couple of sub sandwiches. "Let me explain."

"Thank you," he said, accepting the plate and digging in with gusto.

"Helium is a big deal. It's one of the most abundant elements in the universe, but it's not all that abundant here on Earth. We don't just use helium to fill up balloons at a kid's birthday party. It's of vital importance to a bunch of industries right now, like making MRIs, fiber optics, and semi-conductors, and if I'm not mistaken, something to do with nuclear energy, too. Lots of high-tech is helium reliant. Governments are also funding research for engines that would use helium gas for fuel cells and transportation technologies. There are major geological surveys being done to see if there is enough supply waiting to be tapped to power human energy needs. One of the benefits of using helium over petroleum is that unlike fossil fuels that take millenniums to create, helium is in constant production."

"That sounds like a win," Blaze said.

"Maybe," Meg's voice was glossed with skepticism. "On Earth, there are only a few key locations where the helium deposits are concentrated enough to harvest them. Most of the helium comes from the United States. If the power source moved from petroleum-based to helium-based, our country would stand to make a lot of money."

"The US?" Blaze leaned back in his chair. "Really? Where is this found?"

"It's mixed in with the natural gas the US produces. When they pull the gas out of the ground, they put it through a process to separate the gases. A little over seventy-five percent of helium comes from the US. It's like a five-billion-dollar a year industry." Christen said, taking her own bite of food. "Big money," she said with her hand over her mouth. "Hence, Davidson's involvement."

Gator let out a low whistle. "B – billion?"

Meg swallowed and grabbed her glass. "B – billion." Meg tilted back some lemonade. "The second biggest supplier is Qatar. Some comes from Russia, I think. And, as it turns out,

Tanzania has an enormous supply of helium. The geologists found large pockets near the volcanoes along the East African Rift Valley. Not only are there deposits of the gas, but there's also a high on-going production of the gas. The heat from Rift Valley volcanoes apparently releases helium deposits from where it's naturally stored inside of the rocks."

"Like fracking?" Gator asked.

"Yes, a little." Meg took another bite, chewed, and swallowed. "But instead of drilling and forcing fluids between the rocks, this is naturally released by the heat."

"And this is bad?" Blaze adjusted his seat farther under the shade of the umbrella out of the sun's glare.

"That depends on your perspective." Meg put her sandwich down, wiped her mouth with her napkin, and tucked it back on her lap. "A lot of people were very excited about the possibilities if the helium that was discovered here in Tanzania went into extraction. Think about the jobs for scientists and mining experts. As they got paid, they'd buy things – housing, clothing, restaurant food. They'd hire maids and mechanics and—gosh, I don't know—teachers for their children. If it was done right, it could be a boon. But there are huge risks. Mining the lands and building the necessary infrastructure interrupts the lifestyles of the indigenous people who live in the areas. It infringes on their ancestral lands. The tensions here are already high." She stopped talking and pursed her lips as if holding back an expletive. "Mining the gas might interrupt some of the businesses that Tanzania has worked to build over the last generations," she continued. "Agribusiness. Tourism. And, of course, there's the safety and well-being of the wildlife. These lands have some of the most diverse and amazing wildlife – remember we're talking about the land around the Ngorongoro Crater and the Serengeti where elephants, lions, and wildebeests live...The eco-system here is fragile and already straining to adapt to the climate changes. Everything could be wiped out. I really, *really* hope the government says 'thanks but no thanks' to extracting the helium. And tells Davidson no on anything he's proposing. Talk about speeding us into the apocalypse...The helium that is 'off gassed'—not the right word, but you can guess what I mean— from the heat is located very near the volcanoes. And the helium in those areas is heavily mixed with other gases, especially carbon dioxide."

"And releasing carbon dioxide into our atmosphere increases the rate of climate change," Gator said.

"Exactly. Up until this point, the Tanzanian government has been working to protect nature and the animals. But if Hesston Oil's contracts are off the table because their executive was kidnapped, and his company now deems the area to be too much of a hot spot to do business, the government needs to get money from somewhere. This is already a big fat political fight. And to make matters worse, right now, there's a distribution problem for helium. Last time there was a hiccough in distribution, the prices doubled. If the prices were to rise with continued distribution issues? It's a no-brainer for signing extraction contracts – that is, if your brain only values power and wealth." She rubbed her hands up and down her thighs in her agitation.

Gator fought to stay connected with their conversation. His sixth sense pulled and tugged, struggling to grab his focus. He was a horse at the derby held back behind the gate, rearing and snorting, ready to race forward. Whatever was suddenly lighting him up, Gator didn't like it none.

He wished he could condense this into a coherent thought to share with Lynx. Even thinking about the sixth sense felt like using a foreign language. He had to use what was available to him in terms of phrases and words to try to get his meaning across, even to himself. Lynx was right. Thinking and talking about stuff from the ether was hard to do because what she called "mundane vocabulary" didn't quite cover the experience.

But mundane was what he needed to be, this sense of urgency to get off the X and back into the fight, the feeling that his team needed him. He knew that just wasn't true. Strike Force was at the airport, boarding their plane to head home to their loved ones. Gator's mission wasn't spooling up until later that evening when he and Blaze flew to Dar es Salaam. Rational-him knew that. But his whole system was lit up in go-mode, pissed as hell that he was penned up. Yet, here he sat poolside under an umbrella listening to Meg talk geo-politics.

He looked up at the cloudless blues sky and thought, Yup, sure looks like a shitstorm a-brewing.

10

CHRISTEN

Tuesday, Forward Operating Base Bara, Iraq

CHRISTEN PACED THE ROOM, wringing her hands in frustration. Back and forth. Back and forth. *Come on!* She screamed in her head. She was rabid to get back in a helicopter, take off, and head out after the Delta operators she'd left out in the hills. The group she'd brought in was in Medical getting a once over – sewn up and patched. Except for Tyler Newcomb. He stood with his back to the wall, his arms crossed over his chest and a look of patience on his face. It didn't fool her. Christen knew he didn't like being grounded any more than she did. She sent him a scowl in return.

"You're pissed. I get it," Ty said. "But your bird was full. There wasn't a damned other thing you could have done by staying back. Our objective was to pull Grey out of his box and get him tucked into bed, safe and sound here on base. Mission accomplished."

It was reasonable. It was kind of him to say. But Christen still felt like shit.

"How come they call you, Ty? I'd think with the last name like Newcomb they'd call you something like 'Nuke'em.'"

"They tried. I didn't like it."

Yeah, it might take someone with a death wish to try to give Ty a label he didn't want to wear.

Ty's head snapped to the right, and he stared at the door. A private poked his head in, looked around, and backed back out of the room.

This was agony.

Christen took up her pacing again. She didn't leave her customers in harm's way. It was against her creed. It rubbed against every fiber of her being. She needed to be part of the rescue crew. Though, as far as she knew, there was none being staged. She checked her watch. The hands didn't seem to move. She needed them to move. She needed the night to descend—the cover of darkness. Then, surely, they'd send her to pull the men out of there.

The private stuck his head back in the door. "I'm looking for Lieutenant Davidson," he said, casting his eyes toward the Delta operator.

Christen stalked toward the private. "That's me." *Please, let this be orders to go.*

"The colonel needs to speak with you, stat."

Christen bunched a fist in the air and yanked it to her side. "Yes!" she shouted victoriously and sent a grin toward Ty.

Ty squinted at her, assessing, as she danced through the doors, feeling jubilant that she was about to get her shackles unlocked. "Where is he?" she asked the private.

"His office, ma'am."

Christen took off at a jog down the hall. At the commander's door, she knocked and waited with her hand on the knob for him to call, "Come in." She pushed the door open and was at his desk in two strides, ready to accept his orders when she came to a screeching halt.

"Lula," she whispered, seeing the woman sitting in the industrial-metal folding chair in front of the colonel's desk.

"Hey there!" Lula smiled and gave her a finger wave.

Well, this was Twilight Zone material. What was Lula doing in her commander's office at the Forward Operating Base in Iraq? Christen's first thought was the there was an emergency at home, and she needed to be told something in person, something terrible. But that thought was quickly rejected. No one comes to the Syrian border in ISIS's backyard to deliver personal information. No one even knew she was here. How did Lula know she was here?

"Surprised to see me?" Her smile widened.

Lula had been her friend since they met in gymnastics camp as little kids. They'd been BFF's all through high school. They were still great friends, but the Internet kind, keeping up on Skype and emails as their lives and jobs took them in different directions. Christen hadn't been in touch with Lula since Christen had deployed on this last assignment. And she had told no one she was leaving the US.

"Come, sit down." Lula patted the seat beside her. "We need to talk."

Yeah, no, this was weird. Christen glanced over at the colonel, peering at her from behind his laced hands, his elbows perched on the desk. He was looking at her as if he was seeing a new side of her—something he hadn't calculated before.

"Colonel, I thought you might be sending me up," Christen said.

"We're working the situation." His words had no actual

meaning. It just told her that this was separate and apart from the Delta operators she'd left behind along with her teammates Smitty and Prominator.

"Lieutenant Davidson?" A woman shifted out of the shadow. She wore khaki pants and a t-shirt, but they weren't military issue. They were upscale outdoors wear. She looked fit and had a no-nonsense gaze. Christen wondered what branch of the government she worked for. She definitely had some kind of military-type training. She had that look in her eye. Christen instantly got the impression that this woman needed something from her. An ask of some kind. And she'd brought Lula along as grease to smooth things along.

The woman held out her hand. "I'm Johnna Red. I work for the government."

CIA? FBI? NSA? As Christen shook hands with Johnna, she wondered if she'd ever know or if she should care who this woman worked for.

"Please, sit. We need to talk," she said in a warm, friendly tone.

Christen glanced again at her commanding officer, then slid onto the folding chair, curling her fingers around the seat. She wanted to jump up and shake the colonel. Why was this happening when their customers' lives were endangered? Why were they sitting in an airconditioned office while her fellow Night Stalkers were out in the hundred-and-ten-degree heat? Limited water. Bullets raining on them. The downed Black Hawk, magnetizing the militants to their location… this was surreal. Christen crossed her legs. Held. Crossed them the other way. Sprang to her feet.

"Sir, Prominator and Smitty!" she gasped.

"This comes from above me, lieutenant. Sit down."

"Yes, sir." Christen folded herself miserably into her seat, her back straight, her shoulders squared, and sent a tight-lipped wide-eyed stare toward Lula to project her thoughts - *This damned well better be good.*

"I know we've come at a bad time," Johnna started. She stopped when Christen raised a single eyebrow in her direction.

"Christen," Lula gathered Christen's hand in hers. "We're here because we need your help. *You* are the only one in the whole world who can help us." Lula's lips twitched into a smile. "Which, as I say it, sounds like some shady movie line." She paused. "But this *is* big. Right now, your country needs you in its service, just not flying planes." She tried on a smile, but Christen wasn't warming to her. Lula shook her head. "You're going to have to trust me. This is important to the big picture, with lives at risk down the line. *Military* lives."

Okay, now Christen was truly and completely confused. But still adamant. "I'm sorry. But no. I have a commitment to my unit. I'm not interested in any other assignment. I'm happy where I am."

Johnna folded her hands in her lap and leaned forward. "We've spoken with the Pentagon and obtained permission for you to work on this project with us. We only anticipate this taking a very short while. Days, not weeks. Then you'll be right back here with your unit."

"You had no right to do that," Christen said evenly and turned to Lula. "What's this got to do with?"

Neither Johnna nor Lula even attempted an answer. Their gazes drifted to the colonel.

It was a compartmentalized secret. "Okay, if not what, then whom? Who are you working for now, Lu?"

"Oh, I do International law, still. My office is in D.C. I work closely with the diplomatic corps and travel on those credentials."

"You're a spook," Christen said.

"Do people even use that term anymore?" Lula asked. "I'm a lawyer who works with the US diplomatic corps—"

"Got it. What could I possibly be able to do that no one else in the *entire* world could do? And the answer is 'no' by the way." She turned toward her colonel. "They can't order me to do this, can they? I'm not in their chain of command."

"Lieutenant, you have a creed you live by."

Christen didn't like the direction he was heading. "I do."

"'Service in the 160th is a calling that few will answer. Our missions are demanding and hard. As you've proven today, they are almost impossible. And yet, you accomplished the impossible. Your only reward for that will be another mission. One that no one else will try.'" He was paraphrasing the Night Stalker creed, which was darned manipulative.

"That's right, sir. And that's why you should order me back out, right now. To finish what I started."

"You're needed elsewhere." His tone was measured. Emotionless.

"With all due respect, sir, this doesn't sound like a mission for the 160th." She turned to Johnna. "Does it have anything to do with flying? Would you be the customer?"

"No," she said simply. Not a syllable of elaboration.

Christen turned around to face her commander. All she could think was that this was stupid. She needed to be going out after Prominator and Smitty. She needed to get to the Delta operators.

"And the second line of your creed says that you are a tested volunteer," the commander said. "The only thing you seek is to safeguard the honor and prestige of our country. You do this by serving the elite special operators of the United States."

"Exactly, sir. And Lula isn't in special ops, and I seriously doubt that Ms. Red is, or she would have introduced herself with her proper military title." Christen stalled. "Unless, of course, she's in their special activities division of the CIA." Christen focused on Johnna. "Shit. You are, aren't you?" Christen turned her head abruptly to her commander. "Excuse my language, sir."

"Very well, then. We're all on the same page. On this mission," Johnna said, "you will not be piloting, though there is a flight involved."

Christen shook her head. Nope. She wasn't going. Her fellow Night Stalkers needed her here. Their customers needed her skills here. She was going to be single-minded until she'd completed the mission she was already on. Then she'd consider branching out.

"Davidson," the colonel barked, pulling Christen's attention to him. "Before you say no again, you will go talk to these women."

Christen felt like she was being bulldozed.

"While it is still your decision, Lieutenant Davidson," the colonel said. "The Pentagon anticipates that you will accept this mission."

Christen rose and snapped to attention. "Yes, sir." She offered a stiff-armed salute, turned on her heels, and exited the office, Lula and Johnna right behind her.

John Grey was walking down the corridor. He stuck a hand out. "Thank you, Lieutenant Davidson, that was some miraculous flying. Kudos."

"Yes, sir," Christen responded, shaking his hand.

His eyes slid to Johnna. "Red," he acknowledged her. Then he nodded at Lula. "White." He cocked his head to the side and let his gaze sweep over the three women. His face didn't change expressions, but his eyes lit with curiosity. He gave them a tired smile, then moved past them to the colonel's door.

"John Grey, Johnna Red." Christen turned. "And let me

guess, you're Johnna White. Does the CIA color code all of its agents? Do you get to choose? I thought Periwinkle was your favorite color, Lu."

"You can stop now. This is inappropriate for the halls." Johnna Red pushed open a door on the right and gestured them in with a tilt of her head. She flicked on the lights.

Christen and Lula moved into the room, and Lula shut the door.

Christen turned on her friend, fury blazing in her eyes. "Lu, what's this got to do with?"

Lula took Christen by the elbow, came up on her toes, and whispered in her ear, "Your dad."

11

CHRISTEN

Tuesday, Forward Operating Base Bara, Iraq

"TOMORROW, in Sri Lanka, the highs will be eighty-five degrees Fahrenheit," the pilot said as he taxied down the runway and lifted the nose into the air. "With a seventy-two percent chance of precipitation. Humidity is eighty-one percent, and winds are coming out of the north at two miles per hour. Our expected flight time is a hair over six hours. Sit back, relax, and enjoy your flight."

"Sri Lanka?" Christen whipped her head around and caught Lula's gaze.

"Surprise!"

"Do CIA missions always include private jets?" Christen clapped a hand over her mouth and sent a look of dismay toward Johnna. "I'm sorry," she whispered. "I'm usually tight-lipped about missions. I am, obviously, adjusting to this. Whatever *this* is."

"*This* is simply the first step. We need you to call your father, and for our next step, Sri Lanka is the most convenient place from which to do it. So we're off to Sri Lanka for our phone call and a day at the spa, then on to Singapore. Really, there are some lovely perks to our job."

"Spa." Christen deadpanned.

Lula leaned forward with a mock look of revulsion. "You've been at the forward operating base for a while now. You don't exactly look like the socialite we need on display. I bet you haven't shaved your legs in weeks."

"There's very little water at the FOB," Christen didn't feel like she should have to defend her looks. It was her *skill sets* that mattered.

"See?" Lula said with *that* smile.

That smile was beginning to chafe at Christen. These weren't smiling times.

"You're scheduled for an all-hands-on-deck makeover. You will be buffed and polished until you shine." Lula prattled on while Christen stewed. "Waxed and dyed. Anything they can possibly do to make you into daddy's little princess."

Christen wrinkled her nose. "Ewww."

"You are going to be stunning. And Johnna and I will be along for the ride – we have to fit the socialite expectations, too. Poor us." Her laughter filled the cabin.

Christen was having trouble shifting gears. "I left without a duffel. What you see is what you get." She had unzipped her flight suit and tied the arms around her waist, revealing an Army-issued t-shirt.

"We'll take care of that in Sri Lanka. Johnna and I did some shopping for you before we came out to pick you up." Lula said. "We used to wear the same size even if I'm a little shorter. Though, I think the military rations are making you a little bloaty." She reached out to pinch Christen's side, and Christen swatted at her.

Nobody at the base gave a rat's ass what she looked like. They cared about her abilities and her character. Was she an asset or a deficit to the team? Period. Christen wasn't in the mood for a girls' pamper party. Her mind was back in the hills with Prominator and Smitty. She wished this could have waited forty-eight hours. She could have helped finish the mission. Her mind could be on the next one. This one. "Is this an agency plane? Can we speak freely?" Christen asked.

"It is. And now that we're off base, we can."

Christen blinked. Who on base would care about this? Who would listen in on them, and how would word ever get out? "Is my dad in trouble? Did he do something wrong?"

Lula reached out and took her hand. A signature Lula gesture. It was her maternal side. Everyone on their gymnastics team had called her "little mama." Lula hadn't much liked it until Christen had pointed out that it was better than be called a mother f*r.

Lula gave her a reassuring smile. "This isn't really about your dad as much as us getting access to some of the people he knows. He's going to have a party on his island this weekend. Everyone is gathering in Singapore. The next day he's scheduled a sight-seeing excursion for his guests on Sumatra, then they'll head over to his island. What happens on that island is of paramount importance. Red and I need access to put our intelligence-gathering tools in place."

"You mean so you can bug the place," Christen said with a frown.

"Among other things," Red nodded.

"We need to be included in all that goes on," Lula continued. "The best way we could figure to do that was to have you call your dad and tell him that you're in Sri Lanka on a stopover on your way with us girls to Singapore. I have some business there for my firm, and we're using that as an excuse for a mini-vacation. We thought we'd like to do some surfing, so we're heading to his island as our jumping-off spot. You're calling because you wanted to let him know about our plans. Ask him if you should call and warn the staff that you're coming."

"That's going to sound fishy," Christen said. "I've never called him like that before. I've only been over to Davidson Realm once, and that was when he was marrying number four – no five, his newest wife, London."

"He doesn't know what you know. He won't have a reason to be suspicious." Lula said. "What you're going to tell him is that we want to stop by his island house and use his boat to go over to the Mentawai Islands for surfing. Tell him you've already arranged to fly into Singapore. Then ask if he could send his helicopter to take us over to his private island, or shall you hire one to take us over?" Lula squeezed Christen's shoulder. "It's going to be easy. We'll practice before you call. You'll be relaxed and confident. It will be fine."

"You don't think that would seem too...I don't know, obvious? I mean, it's quite the coincidence me wanting to go to the island the week he's having a big party over there."

"And why would he think anything nefarious about you using his island?"

"I've never done. It. before."

"But he knows that you and I go on vacations from time to time," Lula cajoled. "He's known me since we were kids. You and your two besties having some fun would fit right into your father's paradigms of our lives."

"Johnna and I are now besties?" Christen quirked an eyebrow.

"Okay, Johnna's my bestie, and we all get along. Does that work better for you?"

"Honestly, none of this is working that great for me. Am I setting my dad up? I mean, if he's breaking the law, that needs to stop. But if I'm acting in a way that might land him in jail, that puts me in a really awkward position. I'm very uncomfortable."

"A crash course in spy work," Johnna said.

Christen's eyebrows raised to her hairline. "Because now I'm a spy?"

"You're an asset," Johnna smiled. "A wonderful, perfectly placed asset. But a little terminology might help you to understand that what you're doing is, in the end, both good for your country and good for your father." Johnna got up, walked to the galley, and started popping open cabinet doors and rustling about as she spoke. "Again, your dad is not the target. We are following the interactions of some foreign players, and an odd number of them happen to be heading to your father's island."

"The perfect storm," Lula smiled, but as she said that, something dark and deadly wracked through Christen's body. It was the feeling she'd gotten on more than one occasion when she thought her helicopter was about to become a fireball.

Lula leaned forward, "Are you okay? You look airsick."

"I'm good, keep going."

Johnna turned with a tray in her hands. "What we need are cocktails." She put the food and drinks on the table between the seats and poured Christen a crystal glass. "A Singapore sling to put you in the right frame of mind." She grinned.

Christen accepted the drink and took a sip. "The perfect storm?" She reminded Johnna.

"We're trying to make the connections between these players. We'd think these people would be at cross-purposes. There must be a reason why they're all gathering together in such a private place. We want to know what that reason is, and we want to see if we can't encourage your father to cooperate with our efforts."

"Your efforts being…"

"I can't put too sharp of a point on that, as you well know. Some things are compartmentalized, and all of it is need-to-know. I'm giving you as much as I can because I want you to feel comfortable with what you're doing. And *I* need to be comfortable that your loyalty is to the United States over all else, even familial ties. Lula assures me that that's true, that we can trust you. Is she right, Christen? Can I trust you?"

"I took an oath that I will uphold. My oath to the constitution and my creed as a Night Stalker are my guides in my conduct and decision making." Her voice was sharp and militarily precise. "It's actually me that might very well not trust you. I think you got Lula in on this gig to manipulate her to manipulate me."

"Well, of course, I did," Johnna laughed. "Good, so we're all on the same page. Trust but verify. Do you want to know more about the spy game, or are you pulling the plug?"

"Listening," Christen said.

"We have a group convening. We want to use you to get in with this group to pick up what we can pick up. And while we're there, we're hoping to gather some intelligence that would help us persuade your dad that he should become an asset, too."

"A cut-out, actually," Lula said.

"You want to find dirt to blackmail him? Isn't that a Russian tactic? Kompromat?" Christen set her cocktail down. She wasn't a big drinker, and it felt like she needed a clear head right now.

"It doesn't have to be compromising information. It could be that we learn he's patriotic and wants to help the US. It could be that we have something he wants, and he'd be willing to trade.

There are lots of ways to encourage him on board without him having to be compromised."

"Cut out. I've heard the term, but I'm not sure I understand what it means. Could I do that instead of getting my dad involved?"

"A cut out is a term for someone who's a conduit for something—that could be a communication or a physical thing," Lula said. "Let's say that Person A wants to get some information to Person C. But it would be a bad idea for Person A to speak or interact directly with Person C. It might be used against them at some point, a court of law, what have you. What you do, in such a case, is find a Person B. Person B knows A and knows C."

"Dear god," Christen breathed out.

"Hang on, it'll get clearer," Lula said. "A has the information sends it to B. B sends it to C. C has to go to court, 'did you ever talk about this with A?' 'No, ma'am.' 'Did you ever meet with A?' 'No, ma'am. We never had any discussion of any kind about this information. I have no idea what A knows or doesn't know about this information. I can tell you for certain, I never interacted with A about this.'"

"Yup. Got it. Cover your ass communications." Christen said.

"And if we wanted to give someone some information that we thought they would act on--in a predictable and helpful-to-us kind of way— "

"It needs to come from a reliable source," Christen said. "And that would be a cut out you sent disinformation through?" Christen pulled her brow together. "My dad works in highly politically charged matters. Would sending false information on to someone then put him in a compromising position? Could there be retaliation? Setting him up for a cup of plutonium tea isn't something I'm willing to do."

"We never said this had anything to do with Russia." Johnna reached for a canape.

"True. Still. Since he has business dealings with Russia, I'd like an answer. You have leverage, don't you? You waited to get me on this plane to Sri Lanka to tell me, so I wouldn't just walk out the door."

"You wouldn't walk out the door. You're a Night Stalker. You would lay down your life for your country," Lula said.

"My life. But you're asking me to compromise my dad. He may be an asshole. Believe me, I have no rose-colored glasses where he's concerned. But he's still my dad. I know things are a little grey in some of his associations and business dealings, but this is more, isn't it?"

"Right now, we're not focused on him."

"Right now. Later, maybe? Especially after his daughter hands you his head on a plate?"

"He put his own head on a plate. International communications were intercepted."

"And he was unmasked? Does that mean you have a FISA warrant?" Christen waited for Lula to nod an affirmation. "FISA court lawyers are meticulous with their attention to detail. Being at the surveillance stage would mean that they had crazy solid footing." Christen huffed out the stale air in her lungs.

"What? Tell me what you're thinking," Lula said.

"Just this morning, before I went to bed, I read a tweet from Senator Lindsay Graham, 'We are a nation of laws, not men.' I thought about that as I lie there trying to fall asleep, how insignificant the individual is in the scope of history. A grain of sand on a beach. But laws? They are what has staying power — no matter the storm that beats at those shores. The power to make me fly half-way around the world to fight and risk everything." Christen focused on Johnna. "My dad's already got his head on the block. Is he going to jail?"

"It's a distinct possibility unless he becomes helpful, in which case, he's working for us instead of against us," Johnna said evenly.

"As a cut-out," Christen frowned. "An asset. A spy. And I'm the one who has to deliver him to you."

12

GATOR

Wednesday, Dar es Salaam, Tanzania

"HERE WE GO. THIS LOOKS PROMISING." Blaze spun the wheel, squeezing their car into the tiny space between two scooters, leaving mere inches past either of their bumpers on a crowded road in Dar es Salaam's upscale shopping district. "Looks like we've got a front-row seat. Are we laying bets? Restaurant or jewelry shop?"

"Restaurant if we're lucky," Gator said, scanning the other storefronts. Yeah, those looked like the only two choices Davidson would make.

Davidson's limo had stopped in the middle of the road, the front door opened, and a man stepped out, adjusting his suit coat.

"It's hard to figure out where to put your tie when you haven't got a neck, just ears, and shoulders." Blaze said. "Kind of makes him look like a giant penis."

"Steroid track marks and a micro-dick is more like it," Gator said.

"You're sounding a little jealous, princess."

They powered their seats back, so they were less visible from the front window. The side windows were heavily tinted, adequately concealing their interior. It wasn't likely this guy would make them.

"Roid rage ain't no joke." Gator released his seatbelt and put a hand on the door handle, ready for action. "We need that on our radar."

"Roger that."

With his head on a swivel, the bodyguard opened the back door to the limousine and used his bulk to hide Davidson.

"Davidson isn't what I was expecting from looking at his photo in the newspaper," Gator said.

Blaze scrolled his phone and held it up to take a picture, and forwarded it to Nutsbe, their support professional at Iniquus. "Up close, he doesn't look like a titan on the world stage. Let's just send a photo to be doubly sure we haven't fucked up."

Five-foot seven-ish, a hundred and fifty pounds, balding head. They hadn't received those details - just the name and a passport photo. From the change in appearance, it must be an old passport photo.

Blaze turned his phone to Gator.

Nutsbe: **That's him.**

"That's him," Blaze said. "No, 'it's go-time.' No, 'saddle up, boys.'"

"Maybe this ain't the plan. Maybe they're still watching and waitin' for an opportunity."

"I can't see how an opportunity's going to get much better than this. The whole family and their security are spending the day in Zanzibar. Davidson's down to two protection professionals. No place to park a behemoth limo like that down here in the city. It's going to split their team. One of them is going to have to circle the block while Davidson eats. It would be safer if they'd convinced the guy to have his lunch back at the hotel."

"Look at this bozo-security. He's feeling the pressure too. He's puffed his feathers out like he's a rooster lookin' for a fight." Gator's eyes lit with amusement, a smile inched across his face. This was gonna be fun.

"I wonder if they teach peacock walking at the Acme Security School," Blaze muttered under his breath as they watched Davidson stride toward the restaurant hidden behind the bulk of his close protection guy.

This was getting better and better. Davidson's security looked like it was all flash and show. The guard used his body language to make sure that all eyes were on him. It was poor tradecraft. It put a bull's eye on their guy's back. And brought too much interest to his principal. In East Africa, with a Rolex on Davidson's wrist and his fat gold rings? Davidson made a mighty fine target. But the body guard's lack of skills would make everything so much easier for Gator and Blaze.

Gator dialed the encrypted line at Iniquus's Panther Force war room, and Nutsbe answered, "Yo, Nutsbe here. You're on speakerphone, but I'm the only one in here."

"Gator and Blaze here. Can you pull us up on GPS? We're looking at a restaurant. No street number on the face. It's to our immediate right."

"Two seconds," Nutsbe said.

"Medium-sized restaurant," Blaze said. "Chances are, if we go in, they'll see our faces. Once we're made, we're made. It's early for lunch. Do you think he has a meeting?"

"He checked his watch twice," Gator told Blaze. "I'm bettin' he's not only expecting someone here, but he's anxious about it, too. Meg's newspaper said he had a meeting today with the Energy guy. This place looks pretty highfalutin." Gator squinted as he peered down the road at a group of men exiting a shop and heading their way. "If he's chatting with someone from the Ministry of Energy, that might make this interesting. Especially if his lunch partner comes with his own security."

"Alright," Nutsbe's voice rose from Gator's phone. "I've got the street up on my screen. We have a ten-minute satellite time delay, so while I have your location, you're not in the picture yet."

"Roger. Stand-by," Gator said.

"This is unusual for a Tanzanian native. Noon until fourteen hundred hours, it's impolite to do business." Blaze adjusted his mirror, keeping eyes on their rear. "They don't do eat and negotiate."

Gator nodded. "Good policy. It ruins the appetite." The group was aiming toward the restaurant. If they were going in for lunch, that might be good concealment to slip in and gather some intel.

"I can't imagine anything ruining your appetite." Blaze laughed as he turned his attention to the front of the restaurant. He blew out a long breath. "Nutsbe." He raised his voice and called toward the phone. "Can we get eyes on the back of this place? Maybe we can sneak in without pulling too much attention our way."

Gator tapped into his phone. "While you're lookin', is there any word from the client? Is this our X?"

"We don't expect to have any word from them until you've been offered jobs. They're taking the hands-off approach in case you mess this up." He had an obvious smile in his voice when he added, "You'll let us know if you land in prison, and we need to drag your asses back to freedom."

"Wilco." Gator whipped his head around, looking for the limo to cruise back around the corner. He had the guy on a timer so they'd have an idea of how wide their window was between passes.

"Hey, speaking of rescuing you from prison, I just heard some crazy-assed story over one of them clandestine student radio programs in Syria. They said a U.S. civilian got rescued by a military helicopter that flew down one of the main streets, hovered beside this guy's fifth-floor prison window, dragged his ass onto the copter, then took off. In the middle of the damned city. In the middle of the damned day. That's some crazy assed shit! Those Delta boys have got balls."

"Ain't got time for that now, bro," Gator shifted in his seat. "I need intel on this place."

Nutsbe's story had him back chomping at the bit. This wasn't the time for galloping into some fray. He felt the same sensations he'd experienced when he was talking to Meg when they were pool-side. He needed to calm those waters. This situation called for a cool head and some finesse.

"Yeah, yeah. I've pulled it up already. I'm in their public safety database, looking at architectural drawings…"

"Everyone make it home from the mission okay? How'd you know it was Deltas out there?" Blaze asked.

"I was handing off some data to Tripwire from our Echo Force. He's in that region on a close protection assignment. He said one of the Night Stalkers got back to base with the PC and five of the Deltas. The other team went down in a Black Hawk. Injuries were minimal, but they needed transport out of there. No word yet on the second crew getting back, and with Tripwire headed stateside, I probably won't ever know unless they have a KIA count on the nightly news. So, I hope I never hear another damned thing. Here we go. I've got what you need. You have the standard set up: reception area, restaurant seating—bathrooms to the back on the right. On the left, there's a short walkway—double door swings into the kitchen to the right. Keep going, and there's outdoor seating, protected by walls on three sides. There's a drop-off and then a road parallel to the one where you're parked."

"How much of a drop-off?" Gator shrugged out of his suit coat and adjusted his tie.

"Enough to give a nice view of the park across the street. Hard to be exact from this image. I'd guess it's too tall for your average Joe to use as egress, or they'd have some kind of gate and stairs or something. Looking at your weather report looks like a nice day to eat outdoors—mid-seventies—especially if you're meeting someone and want to have a quiet conversation," Nutsbe said.

"Here he comes." Blaze shifted in his seat. Just as they had predicted, the limo had pulled around and now showed up in Blaze's rearview mirror.

"Three minutes, twenty-nine seconds," Gator said.

Blaze set the timer on his watch. "After he turns the corner again, why don't you go shoot some video of where Davidson's seated and where he stuck the security Fire Hydrant. Then we can make a plan for how to keep eyes-on, in case this is where the CIA hits the go button?"

"Roger that. Nutsbe, thanks for the intel. Out." Gator touched the button on his phone to end the call, then dialed Blaze's phone with a video call. "Keep the phone on. I'll feed you information." Gator unfolded from the compact car. At six-foot-three with blond hair and golden-tanned skin, he had no way to blend into the Dar es Salaam population. His muscles were, for sure, on the big side. Not crazy big like the human fire hydrant who was guarding Davidson. Those were "for show" muscles that were specially developed for their intimidation factor.

Who would go up against a man with muscles like that?

Truth was, men built like that didn't have a lot of range or flexibility. Their muscles were so big and tight, they couldn't straighten their elbows, which made punching darned hard unless you got right up in their face and let them throw an uppercut or a hook.

But no one was stupid enough to do that.

Gator built practical muscles. The kind of muscles he needed to survive when he was in the hot zone. But here in Tanzania, the body frames were long and thin. There were no wide shoulders and bulging biceps, and that wasn't good. His being so different called undue attention in situations like this one here. Not much he could do about it, he thought as he pulled the brass handle of the carved wooden door. He'd just try to find a shadow and melt into it. Maybe next time he was back in D.C., he'd ask Lynx to give him some lessons on how she was able to stalk people without them ever knowing.

For now, he slid behind that group of men waiting for the host at the front of the restaurant. He sidestepped to the right, next to a potted tree.

It was a jolt to his visual acuity coming in from the mid-day sun. As his vision adjusted, he picked up details. The walls were white. The room was done up in blacks and browns with bright streaks of vivid colors. It had the feel of money and privilege. Men only. They were dressed in well-tailored suits. Gator was wearing a dress shirt and tie. He'd left his suit jacket in his car. Gator hated to fight in a jacket. It held back his range of motion like the Fire Hydrant's excessive steroids would hold him back in any real hand to hand.

Gator scanned for anyone who stood out from the rest like he did. Someone from the CIA. If they did have officers on-site, they'd have to have known Davidson's schedule. Did the officers ask for a meeting? Like Blaze said, Tanzanian's didn't do business over lunch. From noon until two, business meetings were traditionally curtailed. It would make sense then that Davidson would have that time open to meet a non-Tanzanian, someone who said they were American or perhaps European. Nothin' to do about it, though, but wait and see if the CIA hadn't arranged for a surprise party.

Gator hung out in the corner, watching Davidson's security walk around with his mirrored sunglasses and his ear comms dangling in plain view. Amateur hour. The two Americans were being escorted through the restaurant by what must be the host. Gator shifted around to see them heading down the corridor to what Nutsbe had described as the way to the terrace. This was looking more and more like a setup.

Good.

Gator moved in their direction. He'd slip into the bathroom if he caught their attention.

A waiter pushed backward out of the kitchen door with a fully laden tray of dishes. He turned right into the Fire Hydrant, who had taken point.

The dining room erupted with a bang and clatter, the sound of shattering glass and gasps—the shuffle of chairs. People leaped to their feet. Gator had his back to the wall by the men's room. He had his phone to his ear. The camera lens sent the images on to Blaze's phone as Davidson moved back into the restaurant's main dining room.

"Sparky got doused," Gator whispered into his phone that was sending video images out to Blaze.

"With what?"

"Looks like the waiter tipped the food tray—hang on, can you hear them?"

"Nope."

Gator took in the scene.

"You're covered. You need to get changed." Davidson growled, gesturing up and down Security's filthy suit. "I can't have you anywhere near me looking like that. Appearances are everything."

"The primary is pissed," Gator whispered to Blaze. Better and better.

"Call Gibbons to circle around, run out, and change places with him." Davidson gestured toward the front. "He can do security detail while you go back and get cleaned up, then come back and pick us up."

"Sir, I can't do that. I can't leave you without transportation," His words were a bit hard to understand; his accent was thick.

"Fine. Then just change places and sit in the car. This is my only window to take this meeting. I can't let your incompetence mess it up."

"Yes, sir."

"Go on, don't just stand there. You're dripping. I don't want my guys to come in here, see a circus, and get spooked. Everything needs to be calm and cool."

"Yes, sir."

Gator crouched and pretended to tie his shoe, hiding behind the service station that held extra cutlery and napkins. He watched Fire Hydrant move to the front of the restaurant, too busy talking into his cuff like a wannabe Secret Services agent to notice Gator there in the shadow. What a tool. "You gettin' this?"

"Every word. Sounds like it might be go-time," Blaze said. "I'm in play. I'm driving around back."

Gator imagined a CIA operations officer slipping that waiter the equivalent of a year's salary in an envelope to make that accident happen. It felt good. Yeah. This was *Go time.* "Roger that." Gator rose slowly to his feet. A swarm of kitchen workers busily flew about, getting the food and broken glassware off the floor.

"Here he comes, man." Blaze chuckled. "What the hell is on him some kind of stew?"

The screech of tires told Gator that the limo was rounding the corner. If things were going to throw down, this was the micro-moment of opportunity.

13

GATOR

Wednesday, Dar es Salaam, Tanzania

DAVIDSON FOLLOWED the host out the back to the covered terrace. The two were alone. But Gator, looking through the window in the door, saw a single table set for four. Obviously, the patio had been reserved for the meeting. Gator pushed into the corner as the host made his way back inside. Then Gator positioned himself, so he had a clear view of the front and back of the restaurant.

Davidson sat facing away from the door, looking out over the park. He must be used to taking the beta seat, Gator thought. His personal protection team probably insisted on the positions that gave them the view of the room and the exits. Davidson probably didn't realize how his seating choice might put him in danger. Gator turned and watched through the front window as Davidson's chauffer crossed the sidewalk. Gator pushed through the exit to the terrace. He let the door snick closed, then he lifted a metal pole they used to extend the awning and stuck it into the door handle, rendering this door useless until he removed it.

A car screamed to a stop on the road, five feet below them. Gator stood on his toes and looked over the rail.

It wasn't Blaze.

Gator didn't think it would be.

"Here we go. Incoming." Gator whispered into his phone from the shadows. Davidson didn't notice anything awry.

"Roger. I'm pulling up now."

Four men bounded up the hill, grabbed hold of the railing, and swung their legs over the side. Davidson didn't have a clue. He was caught up with whatever he was looking at on his phone.

Gator waited in the doorframe for the move that would make Davidson feel fear -- the thing that would make his adrenaline surge, the heart-stopping moment when he would believe with every fiber that his life was on the line. That terror was key to mission success.

Completely engrossed, Davidson didn't look up until the bald guy behind him slipped a quilted bag over Davidson's head and pulled it down around his shoulders.

Davidson's screams were muffled in the fabric.

The doorknob rattled, there was a thud as someone threw a shoulder into the door, but it held.

Blaze should be in place by now—time to get this show on the road. Gator leaped forward. "Yo, what the heck are you doin'?"

All four men stopped for a split second while they assessed the new player. Davidson flailed ineffectually, yelling, "What is this? Help! Help! Call the police!"

"I think there's been a mistake here. I think you all should leave," Gator said reasonably as Davidson emerged from the sack in time to see two of the CIA operations officers, with grimaces on their faces, go after Gator.

They swung, and he ducked and spun.

They threw punches that he didn't let land. Gator threw his share of soft blows.

Okay, one connected harder than he'd expected, but it was a slow as molasses haymaker that the guy should have shuffled back from.

Davidson was being held in a chokehold by one of the CIA, who was dragging Davidson back toward the railing when Blaze leaped into the fray.

Davidson got free and ran behind Gator, tried the door, missed the fact that it had been jammed, and hid in the corner of the terrace when he couldn't get it open.

Gator turned just as the CIA op swung a wrought iron chair at his head. Gator dropped and rolled. *Whoowie, that one was close!* The chair swung full force into the CIA guy's buddy. That guy was down and was out for the count. Gator grabbed the chair guy by the collar and wrestle him back against the wall, pinning him there. "Hey, sorry about your pal, but that's on you," he said.

The CIA operations officer threw a hook toward Gator's eye.

Gator turned his head just in time for the guy's knuckles to graze his cheekbone. "Dude, that's going to leave a bruise. I think you're getting' yourself a little overheated."

The man swung at him again.

Gator leaned to the side and listened as the guy's knuckles crunched against the cement wall. That was no play punch. This guy was out of control. Gator knew that could happen to the best of people once they got their fight adrenaline flowing. Sometimes the brain just kind of snaps. But it seemed to Gator like it was a good time to take this party to the ground. Gator dove for the guy's knees, dropping him with a football tackle and tied him into a wrestler's knot. He bent down. "Deep breaths. Calm the shit down," he hissed in the CIA operations officer's ear. "We can make this look real without me sending you to the hospital with a broken back." Gator held the man in place while he scanned the scene. Gator spotted Davidson cowered in the corner.

Blaze was fighting two guys.

The guy who got walloped by the chair lay on the ground moaning. So alive. Iniquus may still be able to keep their contract after this stupid stunt was over.

The man under him was screaming out things in a foreign language.

Gator bent in next to the guy's ear. "Nice touch," he said. "But looky here, if you don't settle down a little, I'm going to end up hurting you, and that's not what I want to do here."

The guy spat in Gator's face. "That wasn't called for. All right, I guess it's nighty-night time." Gator flipped the guy over and bent his arm around the guy's neck, burrowing the bone of his forearm against the man's carotid artery. "You're going to have one hell of a hangover in the morning. But you cain't say I didn't warn you." Gator flexed his muscles, squeezing his arm in tighter. "Just a little tip for the rest of your stay here in Tanzania, though," Gator whispered into the writhing man's ear. "You should avoid wearing these clothes again. Blue and black attract the tsetse flies, and if they bite you, you can get African Sleeping Sickness. It's a damned sight worse than what I'm doing to you now."

With the blood flow cut off from his brain, the CIA operations officer passed out.

Gator rolled the man away and jumped to his feet.

Davidson was hunkered in the corner, his arms covering his head.

"Are you hurt, sir?" Gator asked, reaching out a hand toward Davidson to help him up.

"Gator!" Blaze yelled.

Gator swung around to see that his partner was being held by one of the officers, and the other was pummeling Blaze's ribs. Blaze could easily kick this guy in the head and put his lights out. But this was supposed to be a dog and pony show. Blaze didn't have options that wouldn't seriously hurt the two men. If this were happening in any other operation, these guys would be toast.

Gator jumped over the downed officer. He grabbed the guy using his battle buddy as a punching bag, lifted him up by the belt and the back of his collar, and tossed him over the railing.

The three watched as he rolled down to the street.

One lone CIA officer stood arms wide, hands open. His eyebrows stretched to his hairline as he looked between Blaze and Gator. Gator to Blaze. Over to the two men on the ground. This couldn't have been part of the plan. They were all supposed to dust off and go home at the end of the day.

If Blaze and Gator left the officers here, the men would be arrested for attacking Davidson.

No wonder the guy looked like he was in shock.

Blaze came to the same conclusion. He and Gator went over and grabbed the guy who had taken the full swing of the metal chair.

The officer was sitting but groggy.

Gator snagged him under the armpits, Blaze grabbed the cuffs of his pants, and they tottered over to the rail and, as gently as they could, rolled him over. They waited for a moment while he started the slow slide to the bottom. Then they went back for the second guy and repeated the toss. Before the Iniquus men could right themselves, the last man standing from the CIA's side jumped over the rails himself and scooted down to the road to help load everyone up and hightail it out of there.

It wasn't the fabulous movie star choreography that Gator had imagined.

The whole thing was kinda spastic, to tell the truth.

He was glad it wasn't caught on tape. He *hoped* it hadn't been caught on tape. His eyes scanned the area looking for cameras. None visible. Then he remembered Nutsbe had focused a satellite on them. Gator waved toward the sky then swung his head back toward Davidson.

Did he buy it? *That* was all that mattered.

Davidson had his handkerchief out and was wiping his face when Gator slid the metal rod out of the door, so no one would wonder how the door got jammed.

Blaze had turned Davidson away from Gator's actions and was asking him earnestly. "Sir, were you injured?"

"No, I'm fine. I'm…" He ran over to the railings and looked over. "They tried to kidnap me in broad daylight." His face went from tomato red to ghostly gray, giving Gator a scare. He wasn't sure bout Davidson's heart health.

"They knew I'd be here. I was targeted." Davidson rubbed his hands over his face and plopped into a chair. "Targeted!" His skin was shiny with sweat. "Just like Derek and Anjie Bowen were. I can't believe it. I just can't believe it." His fingers pressed against his temples. It looked to Gator like he might have busted some blood vessels in his right eye, but that could have happened before the event.

Gator thought they should probably call in a medic to take a look at this guy.

The door burst open, and there was the food-covered Fire Hydrant and his chauffeuring buddy, hands wide, legs bent like they were going to pounce on someone. Gator had to duck his head to hide his wide grin.

Man, oh man, they are some kinda ridiculous.

Davidson ignored his security staff and focused on the Iniquus operators. "Gentlemen, I am duly impressed. You came to the aid of a stranger. You fought two to one against some very strong and determined men. I am indebted to you." He held out his hand to Gator.

When Gator grasped Davidson's hand, emotions fought through Gator's system. Sensations that belonged to his sixth-sense. This man had a connection to the woman Gator wanted to protect. Needed to keep safe. Yes, someone Gator *must* guard as though his life depended on it — like oxygen and sustenance. That was all he could cull from the sensation. "Gator Aid Rochambeau," he said, trying to smooth over his reaction "My colleague, Blaze MacNamara, from Iniquus."

"William Davidson."

As soon as the man released Gator's hand, the odd sensations subsided.

Davidson turned, reaching for Blaze's hand. "Owner and CEO of Prime Global."

Gator watched Blaze closely, but his battle buddy didn't have the same reaction. Blaze didn't take a body slam like Gator did.

Man, he wanted to have a private talk with Lynx. Gator needed a better handle on what was going on. Whoever this woman was who was hanging in his periphery, teasing his senses, riling his nerves, he wanted to meet her *now*. Waiting for her to show up was a constant adrenaline surge. Whatever *this* was, it felt dangerous as hell.

14

CHRISTEN

Thursday, Private jet flying from Sri Lanka to Singapore

JOHNNA DUG through her bag until she brought out a metal box that required a code. She punched it in, and the lid popped open. "Okay, we're going to train you on a piece of technology," she said, taking her seat then looking up to catch Christen's eye. "You have 20/15 vision." She reached in and pulled out a contact case. "I'm assuming you've never worn contacts before?"

Wow, they read my file thoroughly. Christen focused on the plastic case then sent a quick glance Lula's way. "I've worn them before. In college, I bought some colored contacts just for fun for dates and such."

Lula bumped shoulders with her. "To make yourself alluring for the boys," she crooned. This mishmash of childhood friends and spy-stuff kept Christen off balance. She liked clear delineations – mission mode/non-mission mode. Yes, she got it. Lula was trying to get her in the right frame of mind. But this was not how Christen operated. Lula was playing the besties card a little too forcefully. Christen was here, as requested. She was doing her duty, as required. It didn't mean she liked it. Any of it. Getting spies into her dad's home and being away from her own work? No, this wasn't fun. But if she was giving Lula and Johnna the cold shoulder, this wasn't going to work at all.

Christen wiggled around, trying to relax her muscles, and slapped on a plastic smile that she hoped she could warm up a tad before she had to make that phone call to her father. "Yeah, well, just for fun." She picked up the contact case that Johnna had set before her, popped the lids, and peered at the clear contacts floating in the liquid. "There's technology in these contact lenses?"

"Yes, hang on, let me pull up our technical help." Johnna opened her laptop and pulled up an antenna. After a few taps, Christen heard a ding. Johnna slid a code developer from her pocket and tapped the numbers in. The screen lit up.

Hey! She knew this guy. Christen pushed her face forward, so she was picked up on the camera. "Hey, Nutsbe."

"D-day, fancy seeing you there." He paused. "Uhh, why are you there?"

"I could ask you the same. I thought you were still flying for the air force…"

"Had a mishap. My flying days are behind me. Now I do ground support and live vicariously." He laughed. "Don't scowl. I love my job. It's a sweet gig. I'll recommend it to you when you're finally done risking life and limb."

"Uhm… thanks.?" That didn't sound so good. She wondered what had happened to him. She'd have to ask around when she got back to the base. "If you're involved, it's got to be something cool."

"We're figuring out the contact lenses," Johnna interrupted.

"Have you used contacts before?"

"They were just asking me that. Yes. It's been a while, but I can get them in and out, okay."

"Alright, let me walk you through the technology," Nutsbe jostled his computer around, pulling it closer, so his face took up most of the screen. "You have two contact lenses, but you only need to wear one at a time. As a matter of fact, you *should* only wear one at a time. The other is back up in case you lose one, or it gets damaged." He looked her straight in the eye. "Don't lose these or let them get damaged. Seriously, they're like a bajillion dollars a lens."

"Okay," Christen said with a grimace.

"These are video cameras and can also take still shots if you're focusing on something important like a contract or a photo or... I don't know, a symbol on a building, for example. The camera switches on and off by how you close and open your eyelids. We're going to practice until we know you're comfortable. It would be a shame if you thought that you were taking an impression just to find out you'd turned everything off."

Christen nodded.

"There are sensors that are programmed to detect the length of time you close your eye. It can distinguish blinks and involuntary movements from voluntary movements. And while this technology is new, and few people know about it, you still want your voluntary movements to seamlessly integrate with your facial expressions, so it doesn't look like your sending Morse code messages out."

"Why not just leave it on all the time?" Christen asked. "Is there a problem with memory? Is the memory in the contact? That seems improbable – well, as if any of this seems probable."

"There might be times when you might want a private moment."

Christen wrinkled her brow. "Why?"

"Using the bathroom, having a sexual encounter… private stuff."

"I'm not here to do private stuff. If I go to the damned bathroom, fast forward. You're not a perv. And I'm not here for sexual gratification. I'm on a mission."

"I hear you, D-day. And if you're more comfortable leaving everything on, I'm cool with it. I'm just letting you know you have an option. As to the memory, we're going to give you a bracelet and a phone. They are conduits. They take in and encrypt the information, then send it on immediately. If there's no receptor for any reason, it's still encrypted and hidden beneath other images. It would look like a music video to anyone downloading the data. If someone were to steal either piece of technology, the phone or bracelet, there would be nothing concerning for them to find. Nothing. So that's not a worry for you."

"Got it. But I imagine that it's weird to watch a video with my blinking black dots into the film."

"The software automatically erases the black spots it interprets as blinks. Otherwise, yeah, it would be kind of nauseating. For that same reason, it also corrects for tilted images and can get rid of some of the blur if there's eye gunk on the aperture."

"Ewww." Christen wrinkled her nose.

"Until you've tried to decipher faces through any eye gunk covered video, you can't realize how nice this advancement is. Go wash your hands for me, please, then try them on."

Christen went to the sink and scrubbed herself clean, then gave a flick without using a towel so she wouldn't pick up any lint. Lula and Johnna sat quietly out of the way, letting Nutsbe train Christen one on one. If they sensed that Nutsbe was a calming, equilibrium restoring factor, they were right. When she sat back in her place, Christen scooped up a contact, balancing it on the pad of her finger while she held it to the light. "Ah, this is crazy! Is this for real? I can't see a thing!"

"That's the point. No one can know you have this technology. You, by the way, are the first time we're trying it in the field, though we've played with the technology around Iniquus Headquarters."

"Oh, you're working for Iniquus now? Golden reputation. Great gig."

"Agreed. I'm glad to be here. Glad to be anywhere to tell you the truth."

Christen nodded and wondered what took him out of the military. Nutsbe had lived and breathed the Air Force. He was a fabulous pilot. Christen had always thought he'd do his time then go on a teach at the Air Force Academy or fly with the Thunderbirds.

"Can you go ahead and slip the right eye contact into place?" Nutsbe asked. "You are right eye dominant according to your file."

"Uhm, yeah." Christen glanced around.

Lula got up and fetched a hand mirror, and then held it in place. The airplane hit a pocket of turbulence, and Christen waited for things to smooth out before she pulled her lid back and tilted the contact against her iris.

She blinked, and her eye watered, but it was comfortable, almost imperceptible. "Does this record sound as well?"

"Just the visual," Nutsbe replied. "The sound comes from redundant locations because while the visual is important, the audio is crucial. Red, did you give her the bracelet yet? I need that in place, so I can sync the two."

"Coming up, just a second." Johnna moved over to the black duffel at the other end of the galley.

"Nutsbe, I imagine while we're on this mission that there will be times when my phone isn't in my hand. How far away can I be to gather the contact lens data?"

"I'd try to stay within fifty feet or so. You can swim in these. *Carefully.* They may not be the best look, but if you have to go into the ocean, you don't want to be popping the contact in and out. Try to wear a snorkeling mask or a pair of goggles. Or if it doesn't cause suspicion, just hang out on the beach. If you absolutely must go in the water, make sure your eyes stay closed."

"Wilco."

"These are thirty-day lenses. The one should last the entire mission no problem. And like I said, if you have a problem, you have the backup."

"Wait – a couple of questions."

"Shoot," Nutsbe said as he lifted his coffee mug for a swig.

"If someone gets hold of the lenses, couldn't they tell that they have technology?"

"If they put them under a microscope, yes. But this is cutting edge, and you're going in as yourself to your father's gig, so, no. That's a minuscule possibility."

"Okay, what about sniffing the air for information?"

"Hackers can do that. But they won't know the source of the information they're sniffing, and they won't be able to read it. It's encrypted, you'll remember."

"Encrypted from its point of origin, not at the point of the reception?"

"Affirmative."

"Okay, that's good. But there are places where we're going that there are no cell towers—the island. As I remember it, the mansion has satellites for regular reception, but in stormy weather, it's ham radio, if anything at all. And while this is considered the dry season, climate change has made all kinds of unusual weather patterns pop up. If we lose satellite, for example, what happens then?"

"The phone and the bracelet know what to do. You don't need to worry about it. I don't want to disclose more than is required. But the data is safe and will be passed along."

"Huh," Christen said, completely unsatisfied.

Nutsbe sat still, his eyes focused to his right, and she heard a door close, and a female voice say, "Nutsbe, do you have a second?"

"Grab a cup of coffee, Lynx. I'm almost done here." He focused back on Christen and blinked. "I lost my train of thought. What was I telling you?" he finally asked. "Oh, yeah! Thirty-day lenses, they should last the whole mission without a hitch. Obviously, with this level of technology, we don't want daily rubbing to clean them or daily changes because that would not only be expensive, but it would leave too many opportunities laying around for the bad guys to get hold of this."

Johnna handed Christen something that looked like a fit bit and then a smartphone. "All set up for you." She smiled. "The bracelet works like any exercise information. You can plug it into your phone or computer and find out how many steps you took, your heart rate, and how active your sleep was." After Christen clasped it into place and clamped the safety chain, Johnna gave it a tap. "It should never come off once it's locked into place. You can wear bangles, or what have you, to hide it during more formal events. As fit as you are, this will make sense to everyone. This is your travel phone. Your phone story is: You always grab a throw-away when you travel to a new country. It just makes life easier, and you don't worry about having your everyday phone lost or stolen. You just have your calls forwarded to the new one."

"Is that true?"

"Yes, why? Would you rather that not be true?"

"If I'm playing with bad actors, I'd rather them not have any way to access my personal phone. I don't want any malware to find its way to my phone."

"True. Okay. I'll fix that," Johnna said.

"I can get it from here. Two secs." Nutsbe tapped at his computer. "All clear."

"Fit bracelet and phone. Not a poison lipstick or a dagger pen?"

"Too old school. Here's one more." Johnna uncurled her fingers to reveal what looked like a very expensive ring, of a size and embellishment that Christen would never wear—well, she never wore rings, period— but the style would fit in perfectly with a socialite persona.

"GPS?" Christen guessed.

"Bingo, we have trackers in all three," Nutsbe said.

"You think I'm going to go missing?"

"Not big missing." Lula reached for Christen's hand. "Maybe tiny missing. If Johnna needs to tell you something, and you've wandered into the kitchen for a snack, she can wend her way down to you. Things like that."

"It's got that level of micro-precision?"

Nutsbe grinned. "Let's just say that my company reaches for the stars when it comes to keeping our people safe."

"You're connected to the GIS?" She turned to Lula. "Do you work for the NSA, not CIA?

"I wouldn't be able to tell you if I did, so no need to ask." Lula squeezed her hand and released her contact.

"Huh, that feels strange knowing I'm personally being tracked by a satellite."

"Lucky girl. Okay, we need to get started on your training." Nutsbe said. "Let's try this out. First, I need you to read a few pages of text, so my computers can learn your voice patterns, and then we'll practice with the contacts, and we'll see what we can see."

"Literally."

"Exactly." Nutsbe smiled.

AFTER THEY BROKE their connection with Nutsbe, Lula leaned in. "Are you ready for this, Christen?"

Johnna's eyes were sharp. "It's a big deal. It's important that we understand the dynamics of what goes down this week. We will all be recording, just as you are."

Christen rolled her lips in.

"We're good friends." Lula finished. "We're here for a vacation. Everything is just fine. Besides, we'll have helpers if we need them."

"Why would we need them?"

Johnna shrugged. "The truth? Many of the men who are going to visit with your father are misogynist pricks," she said. "They'll go into private rooms where women are excluded. The difficult part from our point of view will be the places where a man could see and hear where we cannot."

"Like the bathrooms," Christen said.

"You'll see. They'll segregate us. The men from the women. The men will go and have boy talk – the kind of thing that a woman shouldn't worry her pretty little head about."

"I've found that if you keep your mouth shut and don't assert yourself or your thoughts, that they forget you're there," Christen said. "And you get to hear things."

"What kinds of things have you heard?"

"Enough to know I needed to separate myself wheat from the

chaff and head out to do my own thing. It was up to me to figure out who I was and what I was capable of doing. And what I didn't have the slightest interest in doing, like manipulating the masses for fun and profit."

"Do you still think you'll be allowed to just sit and listen now?" Lula asked. "You are a Night Stalker after all."

"Come on, Lu! My being in the military went in one dad-ear and out the other. The last thing he heard and latched on to was a class I was taking at MIT in origami engineering."

"That sounds kind of cool," Johnna said.

"Yeah, it was. I really enjoyed it. I made a few things that I gave my father that Christmas, and now he tells everyone that I'm an artist and fold origami."

"Seriously?" Johnna asked.

"Seriously."

Johnna looked like she was calculating this information into some equation. "You fold origami for a living?"

"Not for a living. He thinks I'm living on my trust fund money. Which I am not. I give my yearly stipends to Fisher House. He thinks I fold origami as part of my artistic life, and he's even told people that my art is in museums."

"Is it?" Lula asked.

"Sort of. Not museums. Museum. And not now. A few years ago, one of my class projects was on display at the MIT Museum."

"That made an impression on him, though," Johnna pressed.

"Yeah, art is an acceptable way for me to spend my time, and my little exhibit gave that art some credibility. It was a narrative he liked, and that's the one that got glued into place. He didn't come to any of my ceremonies with the military – he said it was a phase, and I would quickly grow out of it. And somehow, it all disappeared for him. I've seen no reason to challenge him on the fact. If origami makes him happy and leaves me in peace, whatever, right?"

"This is good." Johnna grinned. "Very good. Better than I could have hoped for. I thought that whenever you were around, the conversations would stop cold, that we'd only be able to pick things up in passing."

"What were you hoping I'd overhear?"

"We don't have a goal in this operation," Johnna said. "There is no beginning, middle, and end. All we're doing is observing a brief moment of time and recording it for future intelligence use."

"And finding a way to get my dad to cooperate by becoming a cut-out."

"Oh, we don't need to do that by coercion. We just need to couch the information in such a way that he will want to pass it on. We need a strategy, though, and strategy comes from understanding and planning. This is merely information gathering for that planning."

"If that's true, then why the hell am I here? I could be back with my unit, helping get Prominator, Smitty, and the Deltas back safe!"

"Because, believe it or not, doing this will save military lives. Hundreds, if not thousands of military lives."

Christen shook her head. "I don't understand."

"Good," Lula said. "It's better that way."

15

Thursday, Iniquus Barracks, Washington D.C.

"**Y**OU'RE out of your mind. Say what?" Lynx adjusted the screen on her computer to better see the guys' faces. She was on a secure video conference with Gator and Blaze, sitting at the marble kitchen bar in Striker's apartment. It was a better place for her to wait – wait for Striker to get in from Africa, wait for an update on their teammate Randy. Being here in the men's barracks on Iniquus's campus made her feel closer to the action. At least she could reach out and help Blaze and Gator if need be.

"Yeah," Gator's full-on grin lit up his face. "We got hired to have this fake fight, see? The goal was to save our mark from the fake kidnappers who were really the good guys." Gator pantomimed the story, smacking his fist into his hand, making the air crack with the sound of impacts. "And this guy's just whaling on me. I thought he'd got pissed because I ducked under the chair he done flung and caught his buddy, knocking him out cold. Turns out the guy with the chair was trying to take me down for the count. He must have thought I was Davidson's security detail."

"Because he was an actual bad guy?" Lynx gasped. "That's crazy!"

"Actual bad guy. An actual kidnapping we thwarted," Blaze said.

There was a knock on the door, and both men swung their attention around.

"Hang on two secs. Gator ordered room service." Blaze moved out of the picture.

"Of course, he did," Lynx said. "How's the food there?"

"It don't fill me up for long." Gator rubbed his hands over his washer board abs.

"It never does. You guys have been non-stop since you left the US. Are you holding up?"

"We're good to go," Gator said, turning his attention toward Blaze.

"Lucky for us, we're in an English-speaking hotel right now, and they have some food with some staying power."

Gator, the gladiator, was all muscle and power and not an ounce of fat on his body. But that body needed constant fueling. Once when he was staying at her house, he'd bought a whole turkey for dinner with all the fixings. Lynx got a leg, and he got the rest of the twenty-pound bird. It didn't even put him into a turkey coma, like she'd warned would happen. Nope, Gator was an eating machine. It was good to know some things didn't change.

Blaze moved back into the line of view with a laden trolley. He settled back in his chair, and Gator shifted the computer out of the way.

"You don't mind, do you, Lynx? We're nigh on starved."

"No, please. Eat."

Blaze lifted the domed lid on his steak and egg breakfast, leaned over with his eyes closed, and breathed in the aroma. "This is so much better than the last seventy-some-odd hours on mostly MREs. You have no idea how much I've been looking forward to this."

"Go on and eat. No need for it to get cold." Lynx pulled her foot up onto the stool and wrapped her arms around her leg, resting her chin on the top of her knee. "There you were. You thought you were dancing with our client to dupe a mark. Instead, you thwarted Davison's kidnapping. What happened to the bad guys?"

"We still thought they were the good guys, so we helped them escape."

Lynx's eyebrows shot toward her hairline. "No, you did not."

Gator raised his right hand in the air. "Swear to god. We got them all over the ledge and down to their car, then went to tend to Davidson and let his security through the door."

She threw her head back and laughed. "I love it."

"Davidson was shaking our hands, asking what we did for a living, asking what we were doing in Tanzania, exactly like the plan said." Blaze was sawing a hunk off his steak. "We were completely in the dark."

"Then we get the phone call," Gator said. "This guy on the phone was Whooo-e! some kinda pissed off." Gator shook his head. "Not at us but at Davidson. He was supposed to go for cocktails where our client had planned the fake attack, but instead, he'd stayed at the hotel and canceled all his plans for the day. The family was back in the hotel with their security teams. They were supposed to take off for their next destination, and Blaze and me were supposed to be on that plane. The guy was ranting. He says we needed to hang tight while they came up with Plan B."

Lynx's face hurt; she was grinning so hard. "And that's when you told them what went down?"

Blaze and Gator folded over, laughing so hard that tears slid down their faces.

Gator dropped his fork back on the plate and rubbed a napkin over his face.

"We had had no idea," Blaze said. "I mean, get this, Lynx. This guy Gator was fighting was so out of control, Gator decides to put him to sleep for a little bit, and as he's crunching down on the guy's neck, he's whispering in the guy's ear, counseling him against wearing blue slacks because of the tsetse flies."

Lynx turned her head and sprayed out the water she'd just chugged. Choking, sputtering, she pounded her fist against her chest, trying to recover. "You're killing me." She coughed. "The bad guys must have been so confused. They must have thought you guys were insane. Or thought you were some kind of badass."

"Badass? Not the way I was punching, they didn't. I barely tapped the guys." Gator said. "Besides, I'm not sure they could understand English. I heard them yelling to each other in a foreign language. I thought it were Russian. Blaze, though, says he'd didn't recognize any of the words."

"But they were returning full blows? Were you hurt?"

"Eh, Blaze got him some bruised ribs. I've got this one on my cheek." He turned and pointed at the purple smudge under his left eye.

"And that didn't cue you in these were real bad guys?"

"Testosterone," Blaze said. "It can warp the mind."

"Sorry," Lynx said and tried again for a sip of water. "I can't relate. But I'll take your word for it. So where does that leave you with this mission?"

"Our client knows we were successful in our part. We saved the Davidson and proved our metal, Davidson took our business cards, and we waited for stage two, which was the daughter and her friends calling to say they were joining us. Davidson hired us, then moved the groups' flight up a day so we'd beat them to the city. We're in our new destination, waiting on their plane to touch down."

"And now that we're here," Blaze said, "We wanted to talk to you about the text message you sent us. 'This is the house that Jack built.'"

"Yeah, funny how many nursery rhymes there are that have to do with Jack. Not our Jack, just the name in general," Lynx gathered her hair into a ponytail to get it out of her face so she could think. She used the elastic she kept on her wrist to twist the strands into a make-do bun.

"You sent the one 'Jack be quick, Jack jump' last time. Do you think it's tied to that mission we were running? Because Jack didn't build that house, Jack was there when the house—well, building—exploded." Blaze said while Gator chewed a bite of toast.

"The unique thing about that *knowing* was that when I sent the text to Jack, he was on a roof and jumped. The building exploded, and he was saved. I thought that was the perfect outcome."

"But it wasn't?" Gator swiped his thumb over his lips as he focused on her.

"It was. He lived. But then I got the same *knowing* again, when Jack was in the hospital after his surgery, getting his knee repaired."

"Wouldn't that mean that – wait, I'm confused," Blaze said.

"Normally, when you have a *knowing* once the issue is resolved, like Jack surviving the building being bombed, it's over. Isn't that right?"

"Well, yeah, but it wasn't over. He had to jump again. This time jumping meant he had to go save Suz. And when he took off after her, flying down to Brazil, that first *knowing* was finally resolved and was replaced with another nursery rhyme. "Jack fell down and broke his crown.""

"How'd that one play out?" Gator asked.

"Jack fell down and broke his crown – well, some guy with a rock bashed it into his head a bunch of times until he passed out."

"Shit," Blaze said.

"Exactly." Lynx's lips pulled thin.

"And now you have another Jack rhyme?" Gator said. "Maybe it has nothing to do with us."

"It most certainly does have to do with you. I got sucked into whatever vortex was swirling around Gator."

Blaze turned sharp eyes on Gator.

Gator returned Blaze's gaze with a nonchalant shrug. "We were in the room waiting for General Elliot to tell us about Randy, and I was riled up pretty good."

Blaze nodded. "I was too. It was claustrophobic. Tension can do that. So Lynx, you were in Gator's energetic field, and you had a *knowing* 'This is the house that Jack built.' Not about Jack but about something that he had set in motion. Am I understanding that right?"

"Yup, And I got the distinct impression it had to do with you and Gator. I sent the text out right away. Now you're telling me that when you two got the texts, you had both just raised your hands for an assignment. You two and only you two."

"I guess that's an affirmation of some kind." Blaze said. "I think it would help to figure out what this is about in advance. We have two different assignments to consider. Jack's work on that assignment for Iniquus and his search for Suz in Paraguay. This being the third connection."

"That was my takeaway impression. Something started by Jack—well—no, not started by Jack but maybe shifted by Jack? No…Maybe something Jack set in motion? Yeah – that last one feels better…When I had the first 'Jack jump' message, you were on a classified mission. Could you tell me a story that would help me hone in? I don't have any clue what part of the world you were in when Jack jumped from the building, let alone what you were doing."

Both men fell silent, and Lynx gave them a moment to figure out a strategy that would let them pass her information without breaking the rules about classified information. She got up from her stool and gathered her laptop. Lynx wandered into the living area with its floor to ceiling glass wall overlooking the Potomac and the city of D.C. beyond and moved toward the couch.

"I'm not sure where to start," Gator said as Lynx settle onto the cool leather surface and lay back with her head resting on the arm. The computer balanced on her stomach.

"We were out on our mission," he said. "I was lying in the ditch, hands over my head, debris falling all around us. Striker comes up on his knees, and he's shaking the chunks off, coughing into his elbow. He says he thought he saw something flying off the roof just before the building blew. We made it to the side of the building, and sure enough, Jack had jumped. Blaze was on that side and got over to him first. We found Jack rolling on the ground. He crushed the car roof in. His phone was on the road. Your text still on the screen."

"Good thing it was a newer model car and was made for absorbing impact," Blaze said. "It saved his life."

"Amen," Lynx breathed out. It had been that close. *Shit.* Even though she knew Jack was fine, the number of close shaves their team had survived over the last year was crazy. She was hoping against hope they could figure out what was going on so she could give these two the edge as they took off on their new mission.

"Alright, I got it," Gator said. "I can tell you this. I was reading an article just the other day that might interest you, Lynx. It said that ISIS looks likes it might be defeated in Syria and Iraq, but the military is waiting for the next extremist groups to pop up."

"Terror?" Hmm. This *knowing* didn't feel like a terror plot. "That doesn't sit right with me. But keep going with the article."

"You know about what went down here in Tanzania with the scientist group getting kidnapped and the hotel being exploded out in Ngorongoro, but have you heard that things like that are popping up in southern India and the Philippines?"

Lynx let the two regions rumble through her system. Had they been in India? No. She came to a sitting position. "The Philippines? I haven't heard about this. What's happening there?"

"If you were following international news, you might have heard about Mindanao in the Southern Philippines," Gator let his vowels play on his tongue and added a little Cajun seasoning to his pronunciations. He spoke in a cadence that conjured starry nights and the lapping of water against the wharf. It had a warm sing-songy quality that made Lynx want to hunker down for a good tale. But this subject had nothing to do with Gator's gentle tone. She razor-focused on the details he was offering her. "Right, yes, they say that was an extremist attack."

"They don't want you to know what was going on. A group seized the city with two-hundred thousand people in it."

"Al Qaeda?"

"No, it was a new group, and the name ain't important. What's important is that the fightin' was under the black flags that represent the Islamic extremists, but we don't know who or what riled 'em up. This shift in tactics – of smaller bands of extremists using terrorist tactics--is a big problem that US special operations forces have been actively fighting. And that's what this article was talking about."

Lynx closed her eyes. Were the guys headed to the Philippines? That felt like the right basic geographical direction… "What did the article conclude?"

"Special Operations Forces are going to have to change their strategies. Right now, the SOF deploys for six-ish months at a time, but command thinks it's gonna go in a different direction. They say the teams are turning over so fast means they can't develop good relationships in the area, they cain't understand the cultures they're working in – languages and nuance and all. It might be that when people sign up to be on special forces, their careers are gonna look real different from now on, that they're gonna be moving to a country and staying there for the long haul--like the diplomatic corps--to knock down the small fires before they become an inferno."

She tipped her head. "And all that's to say…"

"That the article was talking about special operations in the Philippines and that terror was picking up in small unexpected pockets, spreading themselves out for impact like the school attack in Bethesda and the kids that were kidnapped from there and taken down to Paraguay and the Ngorongoro attack on the scientists."

"Got it. And interestingly, it seemed that the terror flag was flown over both events, but it was a false flag – terror was being blamed for what seemed to be some other underlying crime.

Focusing on the terror act created a mask of sorts. At least that's how I'm interpreting the data that's crossed my desk. It's still all under investigation." Okay. They had been doing special work in the Philippines when Jack jumped. She tapped her fingers on her knee. "I thought you said surfing. Is there good surfing over there in the Philippines?

"Dunno. We haven't been told anything – where we're headed from here, I know we're only staying one night in this hotel. Our Iniquus client hasn't even let us the job entails beyond getting on this fellow Davidson's security detail."

Lynx's mind was searching around, seeing which words struck a chord. Thinking about why they'd need operators who could surf.

Suddenly, Lynx's vision went dark.

She felt like she was tumbling down with great velocity.

Down she went down, down. Her eyes popped open to swirls of grey and green. As she spun, she turned her head this way and that, trying to keep the ground in her visual field, working to make her body fold and bend and reconfigure.

She stopped abruptly.

Something tugged on her arm, and she floated upward. A sense of relief tingled from head to toe.

What was this feeling? Exhilaration?

It felt something like joy, but if it were joy, it was a muddled, confused, guilty kind of joy. Lynx expelled the air she'd trapped in her lungs in one big burst, then flung her hands over her head and gasped in the fresh air.

"What the heck are you doing. Lynx!" Gator's face filled the screen as he yelled at her. "What are you doing? Lynx! Stop."

Lynx was so confused. This wasn't anything she'd experienced before. This wasn't a *knowing*. This wasn't even an out of body experience. It was more like a memory or maybe a precognitive something or other.

She lowered her hands and effected a smile to let them know she was okay, but also to give herself a moment to understand what she'd experienced. Lyx was thinking about the guys. Thought about them surfing. Was this the future? That wasn't something she could really do with her sixth sense. Her skills came in gathering real-time information from a distance, and weird cryptic words—*knowings*—that gave her cautionary information for what lay ahead, like the yellow diamond-shaped street signs that warned that it was slippery when wet.

In that brief moment, she'd been a puppet. It didn't feel like real-time, though. It felt like she was reading a book and flipped forward a few chapters to check on the trajectory of the story.

This was centered on Gator. Blaze wasn't in that energetic field. But someone else was. A woman. And when she reached toward that energetic field for some kind of understanding, Lynx felt lives at risk.

Wow.

Lynx stared at the floor between her feet.

Wow.

It was the only thought she could conjure as she was swept up in waves of terror. And then it was gone. Poof. Leaving behind a wake of exhaustion and grief.

She could still hear Gator calling to her. "Sorry," she said sheepishly. "I was…huh, I don't know what I was, that was weird."

What was that? Who was that?

It had something to do with…Nope. Gone. The sensation was gone.

Lynx couldn't tell Gator what she'd experienced. Whatever that was about, it had to do with an ebbing of power and ability, the fading will to fight. Like being caught in a riptide and slowly exhausting…

She couldn't plant that seed. A seed of doubt bloomed and grew with deep roots, almost impossible to completely destroy. That, and that alone, could be the difference between surviving a situation and death.

Death. Huh.

Whew!

Death.

No. She couldn't say a word about this to the guys.

16

CHRISTEN

Thursday, Singapore

"THIS IS KIND OF UNEXPECTED." Lula stepped out of the taxi and waited under the portico near the front of their hotel, Raffles in Singapore. Turn-of-the-century British architecture, amidst older oriental designed architecture and futuristic modern skyscrapers.

Christen slid across the seat and reached her freshly pedicured foot, in the gold sandal Johnna had picked out, onto the pavement. She looked up at the white edifice with its embellishments that looked like piped icing. "What? That you'd be staying in a hotel that looks like wedding cake?"

True to what Johnna and Lula had threatened, a team of women had tsk-tsked and scrunched their noses as they had whipped off her towel, leaving her standing naked and under their scrutiny in the Sri Lankan spa. They had looked her over and made notes on their pad. Then she was hustled from one room to another. They smoothed on their hot wax, then ripped with abandon — her underarms, her legs, her bikini area was almost child-like now, and Christen didn't like it. She thought she looked like a plucked chicken. Even though she understood the necessity of the procedure after she saw the tiny bikini Lula had bought for her, she still imagined the discomfort of regrowth when she was under the hundred-plus-degree sun back with her unit in Iraq. She'd be back soon. And then she'd know how the Grey mission had ended. That mission clawed at her insides.

Christen couldn't say the spa had been completely awful. They'd cooled her skin with tonics and soothed and buffed her until she glowed. They polished her toenails and her fingernails. They dyed her brows that had bleached in the sun and tinted her eyelashes black, so she would look made up even if she was swimming with no makeup at all--which was what she preferred anyway--and would make the spy lenses easier to deal with without mascara flakes to worry about. Her hair was even styled and highlighted so that her pixie "whatever, just get it out of my eyes" cut looked fun, feminine, and flattering. Then they had gone after her with the makeup that she hated. Light, natural, but ultra-feminine. A pale rosy pink for her lips that looked nice with her tanned and freckled skin and her auburn hair. Alright, being feminine felt nice. Feeling attractive was an okay change of pace.

She wore a loose muumuu-styled dress. Its white color and filmy weight was comfortable in the heat and humidity of the Singapore early-morning sun. The three women had purchased Indian flower garlands after they'd made their way through customs at the airport. The ropes of petals draped to their waists smelled headily of the flowers' perfume. "Lula, this is so ridiculous." She squeezed her friend's elbow as a stab of guilt hit her. "You all don't really need me here. I could have just called my dad and said you wanted to come. I can't be here feasting and drinking while my unit's in harm's way. This is so wrong."

"No drinking. You can enjoy the food, though," Lula said.

Christen sent her a death glare.

"I'm sure that phone call would have gotten me in. Your dad loves me." She gave Christen a nudge. "It might even have gotten Johnna a ticket to the party. But we wouldn't have been able to get the others in."

"You said that before. What others?" A bee had found her flower garland. "Look at me, you've got me done up like a freaking arranged-marriage bride like you're leading me in to meet my groom for the first time. I feel like an idiot." Christen frowned. "And unexpectedly nervous," she said under her breath.

"Are you really nervous?" Johnna asked as she watched the bellboys gathering their luggage from the back of their limo. Christen's cases were new and filled with clothes that still had their tags on them. She couldn't very well go in and be the trust fund socialite with an army duffel, camo BDUs, and flight boots.

"I've got an eye twitch," Christen said. "Now, what others?"

"Helpers. We're a team of five," Lula whispered into her ear as she pretended to rearrange Christen's garland. She ran her hand down Christen's arm and checked that she was wearing her recording device hidden under a dozen cloisonné bangles. "You're all set. All we do is look around. Hang out near deep conversations. And pretend like we're on vacation."

"From folding origami," Johnna grinned. "Let your poor fingers heal from the paper cuts." Johnna wore auburn and gold. She had gleaming black hair that fell in soft waves just past her boobs and moss-green eyes that tilted up at the corners reminding Christen of a book cover she once saw of a woman who shape-shifted into a wolf. Or maybe Christen was just picking up wolf-energy around Johnna. "Here we go." Johnna nudged her. "I see your dad, come on."

The bellboy pulled his trolley politely behind the women. The doorman held the door wide as he welcomed them. Christen's dad turned a broad smile her way. "Here's my little firefly."

Huh, he hadn't called her that since she was like five.

"Hi, Dad." Christen gave her father a hug. And leaned in to give her step-mother an air kiss on each cheek. They were probably the same age. It was weird.

"Dad, you know Lula LaRoe," Christen gestured, and Lula finger waved. "This is our friend Johnna Red. My dad, William, my step-mom, London."

"I'm glad you arrived when you did. London wants to go shopping." He sent a doting smile toward his wife before turning back to Christen. "Our other guests are doing as they wish today. I had left a word for you with the concierge had we missed you. We'll have cocktails and a formal dinner tonight. Do you girls have what you need? Shall London pick up evening wear while we're out?"

The concierge sidled over and handed each of the women a key card for rooms that were side by side, bowing to each. "Please allow me to assist you, should you have any question or need." And then he slid away. The bellhop waited patiently to the side, his white-gloved hands on the luggage trolley.

"We have what we need, thanks, Dad. See you tonight." Christen waggled her card. She was obviously being disinvited from joining them, so no sleuthing there. She wondered if she couldn't devise a way to learn the names and whereabouts of the others in their party, ask the concierge for a list, maybe they could "happen on" some of them before that evening.

"Before I go—now, bug, I know you're going to groan, but please, be an adult about this—here is your security team." Her dad opened his hand, and two of the four men who stood in the shadows in dark suits stepped forward.

Holy shit!

Holy shit!

Holy *shit!*

As her eyes caught and held on the taller of the two, the ground seemed to shift under her feet. Christen had to reach out and grab Lula's elbow. Energy snapped and sizzled as it arched between them, leaving her feeling weirdly effervescent like bubbles from a children's wand or the seeds being blown from a dandelion. Like she'd lost the substance of her body. There she was, floating in space. This was almost the same feeling as when her helicopter suddenly plunged into the turbulence, and she was momentarily weightless, hanging in space, only it sustained as the seconds ticked by. She stared into the deep brown eyes of the blond-headed guy in his perfectly tailored suit.

This was, by far, the weirdest sensation of her life.

She thought about her last mission, when she desperately wanted to look over and see Grey being pulled from the window like a baby emerging into the hands of three very gruff midwives, but she'd found a way to abstain, to keep her focus on the dials. That's what she needed to do now, get her focus on the dials, away from the brown eyes. The brown eyes were absorbing her—no wrong word.

There were no words.

Beyond weird, this was…breathtaking in its strangeness.

Christen had, in fact, stopped breathing. She was the beat of her heart and nothing else.

Is this what it was like – love at first sight?

No. This was *not* what it was like. This wasn't love at first sight, Christen chided herself. This was the heat and the overwhelming scent of her flower garland. It was her strange video-taking contact lens messing with her brain stem, and probably something she ate in Sri Lanka. The elements were all converging on her at once. And her mind was trying to interpret the outcome. Christen brushed her free hand over her forehead. Maybe if she laid down for a few minutes…

"As you and Lula already know, and Johnna may or may not. Money makes for targets, and I protect my own. It happens, believe me, in the blink of an eye. I had one very close shave just recently. If it hadn't been for these two gentlemen, you might not have a dad to hug today."

"What?" Christen forced her head to turn toward her dad. Now that eye contact was broken with the blond-guy, Christen was a whole body again. Solid. "What happened?"

"Bit of a scuffle over in Tanzania. But, all is well." He turned to the two men who stepped forward. Christen allowed herself to look at the second of the two men on her close protection detail. Whatever swamped her system had abated, but she wasn't willing to test the water again with the blond guy, yet. This guy was a little shorter, six feet plus, with copper-red hair that tried to curl despite the close-cut style. His face and stance reminded Christen of a Hyland warrior from the covers of Lula's romance novels.

Okay, she'd take a little peek. Try out her sea legs.

She allowed her gaze to drift to the left and rest on the blond.

Yes, she was fine. This was fine. Her reaction earlier was just a response to all that had been happening. Crazy unfinished missions. Time zones changes. Adrenaline. And being on unsure footing. It was a little acid-trippy, but it was over now.

This guy was six-feet-three or so. He looked like home. Like football and apple pie. He was obviously happy outdoors with his sun-bleached hair—cut very short. He was as all-American as they came. And suddenly, Christen felt homesick and wished she could give him a hug. Yes, that would be like a little taste of home. It had been a long time since she was in the US. Almost seven months of deployment. Christen shook off the desire to walk into his arms and rest her cheek on his chest.

"As long as you ladies are my guests, Gator and Blaze are charged with your security." His voice was stern as if warding off the argument that Christen normally raised. "As I was saying, I've seen these men in action when I was in Tanzania. Quite spectacular, though I hope you never need to see it yourself. I'm leaving you in capable hands." Davidson looked at the men with a special something in his eyes, more than just a compliment. This was his look of high regard and was reserved for a privileged few, like her oldest brother Karl. This was rather remarkable. These must be some of her dad's trusted staff. If that was true, then they were in the "enemy camp," so to speak. Shoot. How were they going to dodge these guys?

Christen had had her share of trying to thwart her dad's security, especially as a teen, but none of those men ever received this level of approbation. She wondered what had happened in Africa. Maybe later today, she could wrangle the story out of them. If she asked, would they tell?

Her dad headed out the door with London. The other two bodyguards followed along.

Christen turned back to their close protection team. Her head back in the game, she had full control of her body.

Full control of the situation.

She was a damned Night Stalker, after all. "Christen," she said. "Lula and Johnna." She gestured toward the others.

"Glad to meet you," the blond said. "I'm Gator, and my partner there is Blaze."

Gator and Blaze had military stamped across their foreheads. From their build to the look of readiness in their eyes--that high level of comfort that only came with understanding you possessed lethal skillsets. Christen presumed these guys retired from special forces roles. She had been working with various customers for the last decade and could spot them a mile away – unless, of course, they were hidden under a ghillie suit or some new-fangled camouflage fabric that made them disappear from sight. That thought brought back the unease Christen felt for leaving her unit. She looked around the luxe and splendor. How dare she be here when others might be in harm's way? She wriggled her knees back and forth to burn off the buzz traveling through her system. This felt so wrong.

"Have you made plans for your day?" Blaze asked.

"I didn't get my exercise in yesterday. I think I'll go for a run," Christen said. Pounding down the street and working up a good sweat might just be what she needed to let go of her last mission and get focused on this one.

"Are you just jogging, or are you going for the full-body workout?" Lula asked. "I need to know what to put on."

Christen tipped her head to the side.

"Go big or go home," Lula raised her eyebrows with a conspiratorial wriggle.

Christen smiled and smacked Lula's high-five. Hehehe, they were about to give the boys a taste of girl power.

"Why don't you get settled and changed," Blaze said. "Gator and I will be waiting outside of your suites when you're ready to run."

Christen caught Blaze's gaze. Not "meet you in the lobby." Her dad had probably told them how much she hated having a shadow. She smiled. "Only if you think you can keep up."

17

CHRISTEN
Thursday, Singapore

OKAY, I'll admit it, Christen told herself as she ran in place to warm up her muscles, then used her stretches to take in the view of the others getting themselves ready to go. *He's revving my motors. Hard.* The close protection team was off-limits.

Way off-limits.

A buff security guard was the reason why her dad's wife, number four, was shaken from the family tree so quickly.

It happens.

Look. Don't touch, was Christen's mantra. Though, she was aware that refrain was gross objectification. Disgusting. Petty. But he was *so* darned cute. All those thoughts about how just close she'd like his protection to be, took Christen by surprise. She was around alpha males on a daily basis. She appreciated their hard bodies and intelligence for what they were – tools to get the job done.

Stop thinking *tools*! *Gah*!

Christen turned deliberately and bent over to put her hands on the ground, tucking her nose against her knees, breathing in a steady five count. The problem with Gator was he touched on all her buttons. He seemed comfortable with his southern-style gentleman's manners – holding the doors and saying, "yes ma'am" with that drawl of his. His voice was soft and warm and reminded her of a summer night on the back porch in the woods, listening to tree frogs. He had sort of a babyface. He probably looked a lot younger than he was. It was the freckles across his nose. It was his ready smile and the warmth in his eyes. Brown. Deep, soft, velvety brown with a twinkle of laughter.

On base, Christen had an "absolutely, no!" policy when it came to dating military men. It could just make things awkward if the relationship didn't work out. And when lives were on the line, there was no room for awkwardness.

She dated civilians back in Kentucky, but it had been several months since she'd had her "Well, I'm off! Have a happy life" conversation with Paul. Paul was okay. But more of a place-holder kind of guy. Her hormones must be racing now because this was the first time she was around men that might be available for a nice conversation over dinner and a tumble for dessert.

On second thought, nah. Neither Gator nor Blaze had an "available" feel to them. She imagined they were both married with babies. Rings weren't a good way to tell. Operators almost never wore their wedding rings on assignment. In a sticky situation, it might give the bad guy leverage.

Off-limits, Christen. This doesn't feel like a mission. But this is indeed a mission and not a swim in the dating pool.

Christen stood, then lunged to the side to stretch her inner thigh muscles. *Muscles. Such nice muscles.* She tried to be circumspect in her ogling. Gator was dressed in running shorts and a tank top, both of which displayed his hard, chiseled muscles. The functional kind that the men on the teams built and none of those stupid stage-muscles that were built for ego's sake.

Christen shifted her feet into warrior pose.

Gator stretched too. An Adonis in running shoes. She caught the tiniest peek at his washboard abs and a goody trail as he lifted his arms over his head and leaned back.

Christen was appalled at the thoughts running through her head. Objectification. She *hated* it when men looked at her like she was a snack cake on a plate, yet here she was licking her lips like Pavlov's dog.

Darned hormones!

I don't want to have sex with him, she tried to talk herself down. That was a lie. She did want to have sex with him. It had been a freaking long time since she'd had sex. Okay, she didn't *just* want to have sex with him. She wanted to get to know him and see why he had such a sweet look in those chocolate brown eyes of his. She wanted to hear his story. She wanted to go on a date. She wanted to be a couple. She wanted…

Christen stood up, startled at the route her mind had just wandered and the speed she got to that thought destination. She'd gone from scolding herself about the hypocrisy of objectification to –

"Hey." Lula sidled up beside her. "Have you been practicing your parkour?" Lula was jogging in place, keeping her heart rate up. "I've been here before on business, and about a kilometer, kilometer-and-a-half up the road, there's a park with some great obstacles. Then another couple of blocks beyond that, there's a series of buildings that are great tests for climbing. Good roofs. I'd say medium risk on the leaps between buildings with a soft landing on the far side. You game?"

"Yup, let's do this. Lead on." Christen was relieved. Parkour was so much better than going for a run. Running, Christen would have continued her inner dialogue. Running, she'd be panting next to Gator's hot, sweaty body, and she'd have to yell at herself about how misaligned her thoughts were to her ethic. Christen wasn't in the mood to have her ethics challenged. It was already a challenge to be here on this "mission" when she should be in the air with her unit. Parkour, unlike jogging, required the same kind of intense concentration that flying her Little Bird needed. And that's what she wanted.

Distraction.

Meditative focus.

Lula swatted Christen's butt, and they took off at their beginning pace. Johnna joined them. They were in tight formation with the same gait. Blaze quickly took the seven o'clock position, and Gator was at two o'clock. His head on a swivel, his eyes traveled across the rooftops and windows. He knew what he was doing. He wasn't just a pretty face. He had the demeanor of a man who'd been to war and was on orange alert, ready and able to jump to red in the blink of an eye—a man of valor.

Nope.

Not going there.

Christen picked up the pace, racing hard for the green space up ahead. She lifted her arms and did a gymnastic's run of flips, cartwheels, and rolls across the grass. As she righted herself, she turned to find Lula planting her feet and coming back to standing.

"Whoop!" Lula yelled, and off they flew. All thoughts of Johnna and their security were left behind.

Lula and Christen had been gymnastics buddies since middle school. They'd both gone to Nationals to compete. In their sophomore year, they'd both had a radical growth spurt and a change of direction. For Christen, it was her new-found love of flying planes. For Lula, it was the decision that she wanted to experience more than gymnastics, which sucked all her time.

They both loved their sport. They just needed to shift it a bit.

They joined a parkour gym, and it had served Christen well. Parkour was a French training discipline that was built on running military obstacle courses. The goal was to get from Point A to Point B in a complex environment in the most efficient way possible. No assistive equipment. If there was a building in the way, you climbed it without ropes. If you needed to get across the roof, you leaped it – no ladders. It was part martial art, part gymnastics routine, part hardcore military exercise, and Christen loved it. Swinging, hanging, vaulting – it was all stuff she did on the mats in her gym. It built flexibility, strength, and stamina. And it took some courage as well as trust in one's ability to get the job done. She credited parkour for placing her at the top in boot camp. Shock and awe, baby! And she was sure it had a lot to do with her making it into the Night Stalkers with her physical and mental abilities and her focused concentration.

Blaze was on the road with Johnna while she and Lula raced and jumped, flipped, and dove over the terrain.

Gator ran beside them. He wasn't even panting. A little sweaty. A big old grin on his face. As she and Lula over/undered, Gator mostly overed. At six feet plus, he couldn't get his body where she and Lula could. He wasn't doing the gymnastics – the handstand pushups on the short columns—he just hurdled the obstacles and kept his head on a swivel as if this was how he went out to protect his clients every day.

They quickly came to the end of the park—Lula lifted her chin toward a court where the balconies jutted out from either side. Christen went first, running full tilt toward the wall, planting her foot and pushing off to twist and grab at the railing on the other side of the alley, yanking her legs up like a frog.

"Hey, now!" she heard Gator calling.

Her feet on the edge of the balcony, she pressed into her heels and threw herself up and out to the next, then the next, then over to the roof. Christen waited up top for Lula to reach her. They high-fived as they caught their breath.

Lula peeked over the edge. "Studdly McStud Muffin has his hands on his hips, and he's looking a bit pissed and a bit impressed."

"Cut the crap, Lula. You can't be angry at men who say shit about a woman's looks and then turn around and give as well as you get."

"True, but just because I think he's a demi-god doesn't mean I don't appreciate his other qualities. He's a good athlete."

"He's a professional. How about we treat him like one?" Christen asked, miffed.

"Uh-huh. I get the picture." She gave Christen a broad wink. "He's all yours."

"He's a *professional*. And so am I. Here on assignment. Doing my thing and getting back to my unit. The sooner, the better."

"Okay, let's get moving then. There's a series of three roofs. Up. Down. Down. And that will put us back on a second-floor roof. Follow along the outside of that third building, on the stone embellishment to the far side, and there's another down roof. Let's meet up there."

After Christen nodded, Lula took off at a run, planted her foot on the roofline, vaulted, tucked and rolled, extended, and was up and running again. Christen followed after her. By the time they'd reached the last roof, she was thoroughly winded.

Lula had her back to the chimney and was gasping for breath. "I'm getting old."

Christen plunked down beside her. "You're not getting old. That would have wiped us out at any age."

"I think I tore something in my back. I need a massage."

Christen hammer-fisted her thigh muscles to stop their quivering. "Is this the kind of thing you get to do with your new gig?" she asked Lula. "Play Spiderwoman?"

"Not at all. This is what I do for fun and exercise, and just in case I need to pull some ninja disappearing skills from my bag of tricks. What I do for a living is make friends."

"Like--what do they call them--like a honey pot?"

"Honey pots have sex to gain access to secrets. I've never taken things that far before, so no. I think you'd be good at what I do. If there ever comes a time when you need a change of pace, I want you to let me know."

"I'd be moving from one man's world to another. Ground-breaking can be back-breaking," Christen said.

"True. But you'd be surprised. Women, in my opinion, are genetically structured for my kind of work."

Christen raised a brow.

"I was at a friend's house last week, a non-industry friend, mind you. And her husband comes in and confronts her with a shoebox. Brand new shoes in it. He rips off the lid, holds them up. 'Louboutins?' Venom in his words. This was going to be war. But she just says, 'psh, I wish.' And she pulls them out of his hands and tucks them back in their box. 'I got these from some street hawker peddling knockoffs for twenty bucks. They'll probably give me horrendous blisters, but *you* said I couldn't have real shoes."

"They were Louboutins?"

"Hell yeah, they were Louboutins. She'd just bought them that morning and paid full price."

"Your friend is a good liar, then. How do you trust her?"

"I don't challenge her on the price of shoes, for one. Look, I'm just pointing out that women have more synapses in their brains, more memory banks, better-applied imaginations."

"Wow, that's a broad paintbrush you're painting with."

"The head of Mossad—Israel's intelligence agency—was talking about women agents just last week. He was praising the women agents, setting them apart as having a clear advantage in secret warfare because of our ability to multi-task, whereas men's brains compartmentalize and have them doing one thing at a time. That's science. He said that we're also better at role-playing and that we're better at regulating our egos, so we can accomplish a goal."

"Okay," Christen stretched her legs out flat despite the pebbles on the roof and folded over into a stretch. "I don't disagree."

"And then women also have a special gift for deciphering situations, which makes sense in the whole 'cavewoman trying to protect the children while Og is off beating up mastodons' scenario. The Mossad director also said that tests show women are superior to men in spatial awareness, understanding territory, and navigation. Which probably makes us better at parkour since we understand how we fit into a space. Probably why you can fly so fast at such low altitudes." Lula rubbed her lower back. "But, again, that's the cavewoman survivalist in us – we had to know where to go to gather and how to get back to the cave."

"Willingness to stop and ask directions instead of ego saying I can handle it; I'll figure it out?"

"Bingo." Lula tapped her nose.

"Speaking of which, I wonder what Gator did after we climbed our way up the wall."

"He's probably kicking rocks."

"You don't think he's trying to get up here?" Christen asked.

"He stepped out a few paces and watched us get onto this roof. I waved at him when I was on the side of the building shuffle-footing over here. He had his hands on his hips, staring up at me."

Christen sat back up. "Okay. He knows we're here."

"Yup. Just waiting for us to come back down."

"I'm assuming you've had no honey-pot rolls with fat men and bad breath. Tell me, do you get to drive backward at a hundred miles an hour using only your rear mirrors?"

"You're making assumptions about my employer. But no. I've *trained* to do it. I've never *had* to. You have all the technical skillsets in place to do my kind of work. My job, though, is about people skills. Like I said, I make friends for a living. I figure out their motivations, their vulnerabilities. I think of myself as a nurturer. Just like any good mother, I train my assets, and I look out for their security. I mean, these folks aren't, as a rule, the sharpest tools in the toolbox. I have to make sure they don't stupid themselves into an early grave. Not good for them. Not good for me. I'd have to find new assets to take their place, and that's time-consuming. I really like what I'm doing. Do you like what you're doing?"

"I hate what I'm doing. I love being a Night Stalker."

"Ah, I see what you did there. We'll have you back on your base in a few days." She came up to a squat with her hands on her low back. "How'd you get the callsign D-Day?"

Christen shot her an incredulous look. "It's my birthday."

"Sorry I didn't put two and two together. I like it. It's pretty darned cool."

Christen followed Lula's gaze as she focused on the horizon, where the sky and the water exchanged a shade of blue.

"I get what you're saying about wanting to be back with your unit," Lula said. "We pulled you out of your element. I'm sorry. I *do* get it. I like my job. I like my life. I wouldn't change a thing." She glanced at Christen. "I'd be pissed if anyone got in my way. You go, girl."

"Every day, in every way." Christen was getting antsy. She imagined that Gator wasn't too pleased not having eyes on them. She stood and brushed the gravel off her butt. She moved over to the edge. There he was, arms crossed over his chest, eyes scanning the roof. She waved and pointed a finger toward their exit route. He lifted a hand in response.

Christen looked over at the edge and planned her descent, then walked to the far side of the building. "See you below," she said. Pushing hard off the balls of her feet, Christen did the powerful driving run that she'd learned for her mat routines. Sucking in a lungful, she held it as she sprang into the air, tucked and rolled, came horizontal, and corkscrewed until she saw the ground. She dropped her hands to spring end over end, dispelling energy, so when she finally stopped, she wouldn't hurt herself.

When she landed at the top of the hill, she tucked and somersaulted down until her feet hit against Gator's track shoe.

He reached a hand down to pull her to her feet, but the momentum of forward movement along with the sudden unexpected tug sprang her body upward. The air she'd trapped in her lungs was expelled in one big woosh. She flung her hands over her head as she gasped to fill her lungs again. Gator easily trapped her against his body with his other arm. And there they were, eye to eye. Her sweaty, panting body pressed against his. Her feet dangling in the air. Her eyes widened at the shock of the sensations racing through her. Tumbling. Falling hard. She wanted to fight the feelings, but her ability to choose an outcome was ebbing. It was like being caught in a riptide. She was quickly exhausting the energy to fight this. Whatever *this* was.

Gator's eyes twinkled with laughter. "Woo-whee, ma'am, that was some kinda fierce." He gently lowered her until her feet were on solid ground and then held her until she was steady. Which took a good while.

18

CHRISTEN
Thursday, Singapore

THEIR SECURITY HAD GONE off to change for their next destination. They'd be guarding the women over on the beach – this was at Johnna's insistence, the beach part, not the security force part. As far as Christen could tell, Johnna wanted to use this opportunity to convince Gator and Blaze that the women were what they said they were, three chicks on vacation.

Blaze and Gator seemed sharp. Christen wondered if she was up to the task of fooling them. If she didn't fool them, if they suspected something was up, would they report it to her father? Would her father confront her? Then what would she say? "Yeah, Dad, I think you're a traitor and a felon. I'm on the team to bring you down." She didn't think her dad was *actually* a traitor. She thought he was probably playing with some bad guys and maybe stretching the letter of the law a bit far. Maybe turning his head when necessary so a deal would push through.

A charcoal grey hat? Sure, *that* she'd believe.

A black hat? That didn't sit right with her.

No. She didn't think her dad was an out-and-out bad guy, like a Mafioso or something. And her involvement was helping to put her dad on the right side of the law. This was a good thing.

She pulled her bikini and coverup from the dresser drawer. She walked to the bathroom, dragging her exercise tank top over her head. Soft-edged missions aren't my thing, she thought as she adjusted the water for her shower.

Christen wanted a mission where she knew the parameters. She wanted the waypoints mapped. She wanted to know the exact required time down to plus or minus thirty seconds. Not this lingering and hanging about. Not this open-ended nonsense. Seconds. She wanted to be able to check the mission off, "completed," and move on.

After a quick rinse and toweling off, Christen tied her bikini top into place and reached for her cover-up. Yeah, it was killing her not to know the outcome of the mission she left. She couldn't shake her anger at being snapped up this way. It was the lingering pissed-offedness of it all that she was trying to gloss over – but she knew she was doing a bad job.

Christen snagged her beach tote, slipped on her sandals, gave herself a good shake and a good talking to as she went out to join the others.

"That's a funny look. What are you thinking?" Lula asked after the elevator door shut.

"I'm thinking about Gator."

"Mmhmm, I just bet you are," Johnna said with a laugh.

"I saw him holding you at the bottom of the hill," Lula crooned. "All pressed up against those hard muscles."

"Truthfully, it was exactly his muscles that I was thinking about," Christen said evenly. "You don't get a body like that by playing video games in your mom's basement. And you don't' get those kinds of muscles by shooting steroids into your system and curling weights in the gym. Those are muscles that are hard-earned in the field. He was obviously military. I'm just wondering if he wasn't special forces. If maybe he's been a customer at some point in time."

"You recognize him?" There was a danger sign in the way Johnna asked that.

"He seems so familiar," Christen rolled her lips in and concentrated on the *why* of that familiarity. After a moment, she shook her head. "Yeah, it's like I've known him for years. But honestly, I can't place him. All I can come up with was that perhaps I've flown him on a mission or missions, and I'm just not putting two and two together. Our customers rarely tell us their names. Even their code names. And they're usually covered up with beards and night vision. I wonder if Gator—" The elevator door slid open, and Christen stopped talking.

Gator and Blaze stood against the wall, waiting. Both were dressed in pressed khaki slacks. Their black polos stretched tightly around their biceps. As the women exited, they waited patiently and quietly, ready to shadow their principals as they left the hotel.

When she'd consulted with the concierge, Christen discovered that her dad had hired a car and put it at her disposal. Their driver was efficient as he cut through the city traffic and took them across the bridge to Sentosa Island, headed for Tanjong Beach.

As they approached the bridge, their driver tapped on his right signal and changed lanes.

They were quiet in the car. Christen spent the time looking out the window at the great expanse of water, trying to quiet her pulse as her knees brushed inches from Gator's. When they pulled up to the curb, Christen waited, like a good socialite would, for Blaze to jump out of the front seat and come around to open her door and offer her a steadying hand. So absurd.

Gator took point, and Blaze held the door for them as they entered the resort's front access. Both had their heads on a swivel.

What they thought they'd find here was beyond Christen's imagination. But never say never, right?

She flashed the card the Raffle's concierge had handed her – they had some kind of mutual contract going on. The guests from Raffles were allowed onto the private beach, supplied with their own cabana, and a server was dedicated to their comfort. Christen hated the whole idea of that.

It sounded nice in a travel article. Probably for someone who was tasting this kind of life for the first time, it was fabulous. But Christen had grown up in it. A bug on a petri dish. Everything she did could reflect poorly on her father. Embarrass the family. The servants knew that if she wasn't polished perfection, then her dad took it out on the workers – they could even lose their jobs. The help made sure Christen never had a spot of dirt on her. They kept her sitting very still in a perfectly appointed child's room. It. Had. Sucked. And her mom thought so, too. Her mom scooped her up one day when she was not quite nine years old. They walked away from everything – their clothes, her books, and toys. Just left. And built a new life. A lush, well-funded life, but one without the looming help. A maid, a gardener, and a cook – all of whom allowed her to eat peanut butter and jelly sandwiches and drip goop down her front.

When Christen signed up with the army and got to crawl through the dirt and mud, she was as happy as she could be. Eating MREs out of her pack and taking showers outside, yup.

That's who she was. A simple girl who liked simple pleasures. And flying like a bat straight out of hell, of course.

Lula hooked her arm through Christen's and sent her a too-wide grin, reminding her they were friends on vacation. Christen smiled back with a plastic affectation. She hated this glittering world and would do just about anything to get back to the FOB.

They followed along behind their host and arrived at the cabana. There, the lounges were covered with fluffy white towels. A woman in a sarong stood next to a table. "May I help you with sunscreen?" she asked.

Lula said yes and laid down on one of the chairs. The woman moved over and rubbed the sun protection into her skin with the kneading strokes of a massage therapist.

Christen went over and picked up bottles of water from the cooler and took them to Blaze and Gator, where they stood outside of the cabana. She overheard the host, indicating that their property's security was very closely monitored. But please, signal should they have any concerns. He seemed startled when he turned to see the bottles in Christen's hands. "I beg your pardon, madam," he said with a bow, extracting the bottles and turning to distribute them to the men as if this gesture was too much for her. "Shall I bring cocktails?" he asked as he gestured her back to her space.

After the women gave their drink orders, the staff moved away. Christen was reminded how glad she was that she didn't have to put up with this lifestyle. In just days, she'd be back to what she loved--flying-- she encouraged herself.

She went over to the lounge and tried to get comfortable, pulling her Kindle from her bag to read. She flipped through the books on her carousel, and none of them seemed interesting. Gator watched her. *Them.* It was his job to watch. But holy hell. Come on. How was she supposed to ignore him?

She wiggled around uncomfortably.

Lula adjusted the pillow under her head. "What are you wearing tonight, Christen?"

"The blue dress, I guess," she grumped.

"Okay, then I'll wear my green one, so we don't clash."

This was stupid. Is this what socialites said to each other as they lay around and twiddled their thumbs? Christen had made sure, since her and her mom's great escape, that she had kept only the most tenuous of connections to this kind of lifestyle. She was born into this world, but it was still foreign to her.

"I like your bikini. It suits your figure. Is it a Boivin?" Lula tilted her head toward Gator. He was the bodyguard closest to their cabana. She was obviously making small talk for his benefit.

Christen froze. Should she know that designer's name? Christen hadn't thought to check the label. It fit. She put it on. Should she say yes? "Thanks, I like it, too." She'd just play this off. "Did you know that most people think that bikini is based on the word bi meaning two – and because of that, later in France, they came out with monokinis, which meant they'd just wear the bottoms and also the tankini, but that's not right. Bikini has nothing to do with the prefix bi-."

"No?" Lula looked bemused.

"No, Bikini is an atoll in the Marshall Islands where the US tested its nuclear bombs. The designer of the new swimsuit thought his design would create a reaction so explosive that he wanted to name it after an atomic bomb going off, so he named it after the Bikini atoll."

Johnna lifted her glasses and peered over at Christen. "Get out of here. It really doesn't mean two pieces?"

"Nope," Christen smiled as she leaned back on her chaise. "In Marshallese, it means coconut place."

"That's hysterical." Lula chuckled. "I'm going to tell that story at my next cocktail party."

"Tonight?" Christen asked, suddenly worried that she'd need stories to tell, and her stories were mostly classified.

"The crowd your dad invited might not find coconut places as funny as I do."

The waiter wandered into the space. He wore a full wait-staff tuxedo with his pants rolled to the knee and bare feet. A white linen towel draped over his arm. Christen had seen images like this in travel magazines. You could pull your lounge into the water, and they would walk out to serve you. Picturesque, sure. But ridiculously impractical. The waiter left, and their security detail moved out to do a sweep. Or something. How do you guard a cabana on a beach?

"To coconut places," Lula said.

They tapped their paper-umbrella and flower trimmed pineapples together.

"Now that we're alone tell me what happens next?" Christen asked.

"We get back to the hotel in time to get beautified for the evening. Your father has the cocktail reception and the dinner. It will be a perfect time for you to watch," Lula said. "Stand near conversations. We'll need to spread ourselves out a bit, though. And *please* try to remember – we're on vacation. We're enjoying ourselves." She looked over to where Blaze posted himself by a palm tree.

"Enjoy your drinks, ladies." Johnna took a sip from her straw. "No more alcohol for the rest of our stay. You can hold the glass, but that's all."

Christen gave Johnna a salute as Gator made his way toward them and posted at another tree.

"Laugh. We're having fun!" Lula said under her breath.

They all laughed on cue.

Christen knew Gator could hear her from where he stood. He was probably listening, so he could report back to her father. She should say something... Something socialite–sounding. Maybe something to do with an origami show at a gallery. She didn't have a lot to say, though. She'd been away for seven months – almost a full rotation. She hadn't read anything trendy in a while – well, socially trendy. She kept up with geopolitics and the military news.

Maybe, I'm becoming a bit myopic, she thought as she lifted the spray bottle of chilled cucumber water the sun lotion lady had handed each of them. She held it up and looked through the bottle at the warped landscape of imported palm trees and Hawaiian white sand that showed through the glass. For some reason, she had riptides on her mind since Gator caught her in his arms at the end of her parkour run. There, that was the fodder she needed for a story. "I read a newspaper article the other day about this family having a day at the beach down in Panama City, Florida. The kids were out paddling around, then they start screaming their heads off."

"Jellyfish?" Lula guessed.

"God, I hate jellyfish stings. They're the worst, aren't they?" Johnna tipped her chin up and adjusted her sunglasses, looking absolutely comfortable with her surroundings. "And who carries ammonia with them to the beach?"

"Find a random guy to pee on you." Lula laughed. "There's bound to be one guy in the crowd that's into golden showers." She turned to Christen and popped her eyebrows a few times, then turned to squint back at the guys, lifting her voice so it would carry. "I bet Blaze would come to your rescue if you asked nicely."

"No doubt," Christen deadpanned as she watched Blaze turn

his head their way, then turn away again with a grin. "I got stung once by a sea jelly—that's what they're calling them now, I'm told—turns out I'm agonizingly allergic. I ended up in the emergency room. The pee, ammonia, and meat tenderizer home remedies are all bogus. I learned that from my sad personal experience."

Lula wrinkled her nose. "You let someone pee on you? Girl! That's just disgusting."

"I was desperate!" Christen spritzed Lula with her spray bottle.

Johnna lifted her sunglasses to look at Christen. "Then, if none of that works, what do you do?"

"Go see a doctor." Lula said. "Go back. Why were the kids screaming?"

Christen sprayed some of the cucumber stuff on her own face. It was nice. Minty. And it was refreshing, especially with the gentle breeze coming up off the water. It was only eighty-three degrees that day. But the humidity was also eighty-three.

"They got snagged in a riptide," she said, settling back. "The adults all go rushing out to save them."

"Swam out to the riptide?" Lula asked. "That's not a good strategy."

Christen wiggled her hips to get comfortable. "Yah think?"

"They get caught too?" Johnna asked.

"Of course, they did," Lula answered. "The ocean is a mother fucker. You don't mess with that mother."

"Amen to that," Christen said.

"Did they all die? The family?"

Christen's eyes were closed. Her hands resting by her sides. A little smile played over her lips. "Craziest rescue you can imagine."

"I dunno, I can imagine some pretty crazy ways to save someone," Lula said.

"The people on the beach lined up, eighty of them, and made a human chain out into the ocean. Then, each of the family members crawled their way up the chain to get their feet under them. Not a single person drowned."

"There must have been a Canadian on the beach," Johnna said.

"Why do you say that?" Lula's voice was a murmur like she was falling asleep under the warmth of the sun. Despite their day at the spa, they'd been traveling for days now, getting from their separate destinations to the convergence here in Singapore. Time zone changes wore at the body.

"It's one of the methods you use to get someone out of the water if they fall through the ice," Johnna said. "If you can't talk them out on their own, and you don't have a rope or a canoe or something to haul out there, you make a human chain, so you're dispersing the weight across the ice. And as a bonus, everyone can haul you up if you fall in with the victim. Of course, on ice, you're lying down, grabbing at each other ankles."

"Interesting," Christen said, shifting around. The chaise was comfortable enough. But she was uncomfortable in her skin. "Okay, I vote that there was a Canadian on the beach. Though a Canadian in Florida in July might stretch the imagination a bit." While they were talking, Christen was considering Blaze and Gator. Well, Gator. She didn't know squat about him. Could he be one of the guys Johnna and Lula were after? Was he privy to the bad dealings her father had gotten mixed up in? Was he complicit? That thought made her stomach churn.

Christen had read about women who did undercover jobs, how they developed relationships to get the needed information. They often fell in love with the bad guys and suffered greatly when they had to bring charges against them. Christen couldn't allow herself to get caught in that net. That Gator had somehow got fixed on her radar went against both her personal and professional morals. She absolutely would *not* allow herself to give in to these ridiculous sensations. If only he would move a little farther out of her sight-line, so she wasn't watching him from under her lashes....

"Can you hand me another bottle of water?" Lula asked.

Christen reached into the cooler. "There's only a few in here. We'll have to let the waiter know," she said, stretching a bottle over to Johnna, then one over to Lula. "Can you see the guys' bottles? Do they need more, too?"

"Quarter bottle each." Lula raised her voice and hailed the guys with her arm. "Hey, come into the shade and get some more water." Lula was her usual little mama self.

Christen watched while Gator did another scan of the horizon, then walked through the sand toward them, his muscles gleaming under a sheen of sweat. A wave of desire lashed through Christen's body. She exhaled, slowly letting that tide recede. She had been trained to deal with emotions. They get in the way of a mission. And she had never allowed that before. She would not allow it now.

Johnna was checking her phone. She stopped when Blaze reached for the bottle Lula held out to him. "Blaze, that's a nick-name, isn't it?" she asked.

"Call name from my military days, yes, ma'am."

"Christen and I were just talking about military monikers this morning, weren't we, Christen?" Lula asked. When Christen opened her mouth to answer, Lula cut her off. "What branch of the military was this?"

"Navy, ma'am."

Lula pushed her sunglasses to the top of her head. "And what did you do for the Navy?"

"I was a SEAL operator, ma'am."

"And now you do close protection?" Lula's voice was incredulous.

"When they say join the Navy see the world, they weren't exactly talking about places like Singapore. Now that I'm retired, I'm enjoying visiting more scenic spots."

"You were in the military, too?" Johnna asked, turning to Gator.

"Yes, ma'am. Marines."

"And what was your job there?"

"I was a Marine Raider, ma'am. Mostly my job was to find people who didn't want to be found and make sure they got into the right hands."

Johnna nodded appreciatively. "And your call name, Gator, is there a story behind it?"

"Oh, no ma'am Gator ain't my call name. It's my given name. Gator Aid."

"Aid. Is that A-i-d or A-d-e?" Johnna asked.

"Gator Aid? That sounds like a long drink of something cool and sweet on a very hot day," Lula said in a flirtatious voice as she glanced back at Christen.

"Yes, Ma'am," he said to Lula before turning to Johnna. "A-i-d, ma'am."

"That must be an old joke," Lula turned back to him with a smile. "But seriously, you're not pulling my leg? That's really your name?"

Johnna tilted her head. "Your mother named you Gator with a last name like Aid?"

Gator smiled his wide smile that was kind of sweet and very wholesome. The wholesome image probably came from his lopsided grin, which had a humbleness to it. Or the merriment that danced in his dark eyes, Christen thought. Or maybe that shadow of a bruise on his left cheekbone that looked like he got into it in the schoolyard or maybe got into some trouble running through the woods. But then his body had nothing to do with sweet or wholesome. Gator's body said fu— Gator caught her eye just as Christen formulated that thought. Her face flamed red. *Shit.*

His gaze shifted calmly back to Johnna's "Yes ma'am. My momma's got a wicked sense of humor. A natural-born story-teller, too."

"Have you got brothers and sisters?" Lula asked. "Did they get great names like yours?"

"I guess that depends on your point of view, ma'am. My oldest sister's name is Medic 'cause that's what my dad did for the Army, and my momma, she was right proud of him. Then there was me. I was born with my first two teeth already in and bit her straight off. After me came the twins, Deck and Marmal. Though, now that he's grown, Marmal likes to be called Mark. And then there's the baby, Seren. But she's twenty-two now. So we cain't really call her the baby no more."

The three women had turned his way and were staring. Their lips moved as they processed through each name in their minds.

Christen blinked. *Marmal Aid?*

Lula doubled over. "Good one." She snorted. "Oh my god, that was so awesome!"

"Ma'am?" Gator asked in all sincerity, looking confused.

Christen was horrified that Lula was laughing at Gator's family's names. She sent him a wide-eyed look, not sure what to say to apologize for her friend.

Gator sent her a wink, and she had a rush of *whew*! She needed to get cooled off. Like *now*.

His gaze traveled down her body and stopped at her thigh. The laughter fell off, and his eyes filled with concern. He brought his gaze up to hers. "That's an unusual place for a burn, ma'am. An unusual shape."

Christen looked down at the red mark that had blistered. She remembered that just a couple of days ago, she was in a completely different world — one where plasma torches threw blazing hot metal shards her way, and her job looked nothing like lying about on a chaise lounge sipping a brunch cocktail. She didn't want to be here. Not in any way, shape, or form. And she didn't want Gator's concern because when he looked at her with tenderness, it did crazy things to her heart.

"Swim break," she called and jogged toward the shoreline. She dove into the dark waters of the strait and pulled hard in a breaststroke, propelling herself away. Gator was going to be a major distraction to her mission, she concluded once again. If she *let* him. She came up for air, took a gulp, and went deeper into the cool sea. She could work past this. She'd use the skills she'd built during her years up in the helicopter. If she could keep her attention on task while the Deltas were pulling a man from his jail cell onto her helicopter, she could do this. She could - she *would* keep her eye on her gauges, her hand steady on the stick. Then she'd get back to her unit where she belonged.

19

LYNX

Thursday, Panther Force War Room, Iniquus Headquarters

"**I** WONDER if we should be worried about Gator's role?" Nutsbe scowled as he fast-forwarded through the video that had been sent over the encrypted channel to Iniquus Headquarters. This particular information had come from Christen Davidson's contact lenses. "She has her eye on him all the time. And I mean *all* the time. It's almost like he's the person of interest, and she's doing surveillance."

"Did you get anything back from the Dar es Salaam incident?" Lynx asked, ignoring what she was sure was Nutsbe's misinterpretation of the situation.

Lynx and Nutsbe each clutched a mug of coffee. Black. High-test. Both felt more than a little groggy sitting at the computer here in the Panther Force war room. While it was cocktail-hour in Singapore, it was twelve hours earlier in D.C. Nutsbe and Lynx had been working non-stop to develop a theory about who had come after William Davidson in Tanzania. The attack didn't have any of the signatures of what had happened to Derek Bowman and his wife. Meg Finley had drawn the conclusion that both Davidson and Bowman were going after the Tanzanian oil contract, though their motivations were night and day.

On the afternoon that Gator and Blaze saved William Davidson, the satellite imaging, at Nutsbe's direction, had zoomed in on the attack. Nutsbe had sent that data on to the CIA who was replicating Iniquus's attempts to identify the attackers. The CIA computers were tasked and churning but had yet to spit out any names. Here at Iniquus, Nutsbe had qualified the computer search parameters with three specific filters: those images as they pertained to William Davidson, to the former USSR countries, or to helium. When they got hold of a roster of party-goer names, Nutsbe added those in, as well.

Lynx and Nutsbe agreed that the Davidson attack had to have been spurred by someone in the know – or how would the attackers be aware that there was a private meeting planned on that particular terrace at that exact time?

"It would be nice to know who was supposed to have joined Davidson out there at the lone table." Lynx took another sip from her mug. "Gator said there were four place settings. Three more people were expected."

"I'll see what I can do about accessing Davidson's laptop. See if I can't scrounge around and find any information about that meeting."

Nutsbe pressed a button, and once again, they were scrolling through the images from Christen's day.

Lynx startled when Nutsbe's computer dinged on full volume. As her body jerked, she sloshed coffee onto the desk. "Sorry about that," Nutsbe said, adjusting the volume.

"My fault." Lynx jumped up to grab a towel while Nutsbe clicked on the secured satellite feed they had been waiting for, initiated by Johnna Red. As Lynx scampered back to clean up her mess, she found herself face to face with Red.

Lynx was finally able to put a name to the face, even if it was a cover name.

Red was a lot younger than Lynx had expected. A lot softer looking than she'd imagined.

Lynx only knew Red by voice from being the foreign contact on a case she had worked a couple of months before; it had to do with conflict relics moving out of Syria.

In May, Red had been in Jordan working on a case to do with illegally funding ISIS groups in Syria.

Was that somehow tied in with this?

Lynx would have to process that information and see how it added to the rest of the intelligence. Could be it connected, could be that casework was completely separate from this case. No conclusions to be drawn until there was hard evidence. Lynx drew a thought bubble on her paper and jotted a few words.

While Nutsbe and Red checked the various data systems they had running, Lynx sat quietly, thinking. Red was pretty in a subtle way – not someone who would over-attract attention. But certainly, someone whom a man would try to impress with his knowledge and contacts. At a glance, Red wasn't just attractive but obviously intelligent, well-educated, and graceful with a timbre of voice that could flip from the no-nonsense tone she was using now to the carefree jaded socialite she was play-acting. A chameleon. For sure, Red was the kind of woman any man would want on his arm, which was an important component —as far as Lynx could tell—to this data collection mission. Lynx knew from personal experience in the field that this was the key to get into many a door and out of many a fix without raising any suspicions. If you've got it, use it – all in the name of American safety and security, of course.

Nutsbe had said that this was a joint contract, CIA and Department of the Treasury Office of Intelligence and Analysis.

Red was CIA.

The other woman, Lula LaRoe, maybe she was from the Treasury, maybe not. But that Treasury piece made Lynx think that this case, coupled with the case Red had been involved with, had something to do with financing US enemies, maybe even terror groups like Hezbollah.

Lynx drew more thought bubbles, noted different questions and directions where she could look. Hezbollah did have a bromance of sorts with Qatar.

And Qatar had shown up in Lynx's research about helium. Not that helium was a given part of the equation either. At this point, Lynx was grabbing at straws. One thing for sure, though, was that Qatar had a player on Davidson party's guest list, a close relative to the royal family no less.

Still, it seemed an odd stretch that Red would be working on something that started in Tanzania. And the information that Meg had fed the guys about helium very well could be just an interesting note in the global energy symphony (or cacophony, depending on your point of view). Davidson worked in energy… She drummed her fingertips on the desk as she let the information perk.

"Red, I was just saying to Lynx, I think we have a problem."

Lynx brought her attention fully forward.

Red brushed her hair back over her shoulder. "With the feed?"

"No. That's fine. We've gone through the visual data from the point where you three put in your lenses on the airplane after landing in Singapore up until now. You all haven't turned on the audio yet."

"We will as we head down to the party."

"Noted," Nutsbe said. "My concern is that you wanted to keep Christen in the dark about the identities of her teammates, Gator and Blaze. From watching her contact feed, I think Christen's spotted an anomaly and is tracking them, well, Gator at least. Do you think that she'll inform her father?"

"No," Red said.

"To which part are you saying no?" Nutsbe asked. "Don't get me wrong, I know Christen. She's a patriot. But if she doesn't understand the role Gator's playing, she may think that her dad needs a heads up about him. Something's caught her eye. Her focus rarely moves off him for long."

Lynx sent Nutsbe a side-eye. Was he kidding?

Red seemed to move through the same thought process holding her eyebrows high as she blinked – pure incredulity.

"I think she needs to be read into this part of the mission." Nutsbe pushed.

"Thank you for the information," Red said, her face now painted with neutral emotions. "I'll pay close attention to the situation. I'm sure if she was to bring concerns to anyone, she would start with either Lula or me." Red gave him a thin-lipped smile. "Christen's not an actor. This mission isn't her bailiwick, and she's struggling. She's straight forward and honest in her presentation. To make this work, she needs to be slightly perturbed that she's being followed around by security. She needs to try to get away from them when she can. When she does, Blaze and Gator need to bring it to Davidson's attention, as I told Blaze and Gator earlier. We understand from Lula that having a close protection team was a major issue between her and her father, and ultimately the reason why Christen stays away from traveling with her dad. In the last few years, Christen only shows up when she can meet them and leave of her own volition, with*out* the security detail. She tells Lula that close protection makes her feel like a prisoner. It would look peculiar if suddenly she was okay with a protection detail. Resentment needs to show up in her eyes and her body language."

"I get it," Nutsbe said. "But she slipped her detail at the hotel and headed out the side door following two of her father's guests and hung out on the bench while they smoked. Gator and Blaze are trying to keep tabs on you three women, all at once. When you three disperse between several rooms, as you did when you came back from the beach, it gives Christen a chance to slip out. If we didn't have her on tracker and camera, we could have lost her quickly. A bag over her head—like what happened to Davidson in Tanzania—and her jewelry removed, Christen could easily be magicked away."

"Our concern is," Lynx said, leaning forward, "that Gator and Blaze thwarted a real-life kidnapping attempt on William Davidson. We have no idea who was involved. We believe, however, that the kidnappers have or had unique access to William Davidson's schedule. If the bad actors followed Davidson's itinerary, they could very well be in Singapore now. Christen could conceivably be a target along with Davidson himself and his other family members. The family's ongoing safety allows your mission to play itself out. Your mission's success depends on Christen's safety. While the others in the family enjoy having their protection in place. Christen is averse."

Red nodded as she took the information in. "I see your point."

"Iniquus would be more comfortable, given the changed dynamic," Lynx said, "if your organization could come to some understanding with Christen about accepting her security detail.

Gator was fine with Lula running parkour with Christen up until the point where they hit the roofs. Once they were out of sight and were in danger-mode with all that flipping between high rises, he wasn't as comfortable with the arrangement," Lynx said.

"Understood. I had Lula egg that scenario on. I thought it was a good way to make a distinction between our team and the Iniquus team, so Christen would keep your guys at arm's length. And your men could prove their loyalty by bringing that event to her father's attention, which they did as requested. Look, Christen's a team player to her bones. Any sign of the five of us being teammates would send up flares for her dad and possibly the others. But I do get your point. We can work to calm down the us/them dynamic." Johnna turned her head toward the door as her cell phone buzzed. "Hang on, I think that's one of your guys." As she walked to the door, Lynx watched Red swipe her cell phone screen to read the text.

"Blaze has eyes on Lula and Christen. You needed one of us?" That was Gator's voice.

"I have your Iniquus support team on a video feed." Red's voice sounded muffled with the distance. "I'll leave you to talk with them. I'm going outside to take this call. I'll just be a minute."

They could hear the click as the door shut.

20

LYNX

Thursday, Panther Force war room, Iniquus Headquarters

GATOR STEPPED FORWARD. "YO," he said with an easy smile as he settled into the place Red had just vacated.

"That was quick," Lynx smiled. "Red said she just texted you – it couldn't be more than three minutes ago."

"The clients are housed at the hotel across the street. Red has this room for communications. No chance of it being wired."

"They're pulling out all the stops," she said.

"Seems so. But look, Blaze and me, we're kind of in the dark about things here. We got hired on and told that we're to keep an eye on Johnna, Lula, Christen, and *things*. It would sure help to know how they defined *things*. Is Red going to read me into the program now?"

"I hope so," Lynx said. "She's going to get you equipped, that much I know. They're using those new image-recording contact lenses you've tried here at Headquarters. You and Blaze will need to be focusing on the comings and goings at the different events. They're particularly interested in who is having a quiet tête-à-tête in the corners and what players are obviously avoiding being seen together."

"Roger that."

"You'll be given watches that record sound. And throw away phones that encrypt both the visuals from your contact lenses and the audio from the watches to send them our way," Nutsbe added.

"We knew Red was the contractor. Who are the other women?" Gator leaned forward to post his elbows on his knee, wrapping his fingers around his wrist. Focused. Comfortable. A wall against the enemy. "Do you know why the two of them were on top of that roof for so long? I mean, it wasn't what I was expecting from a lawyer and an artist."

"An artist?" Nutsbe asked.

"Davidson's daughter, Christen, is a paper artist. She folds origami for gallery shows."

Nutsbe scowled. "Who told you that? Is that what Red's saying?"

"No," Gator tipped his head to the side, his brow furrowed. "That's what her dad said when he hired Blaze and me on."

"Yeah, let me set you straight there, brother. I know Christen Davidson personally. She goes by the call sign D-day."

"More." Gator leaned closer to the screen, and Lynx saw an eagerness in his eyes she'd never seen there before. It seemed Gator and Christen had sparked the same interest in each other. As she thought that, she momentarily became both weightless as if floating and compressed by an enormous force. She held her breath, knowing there was no air to breathe. Terror swam through her body. Desperation. Then she found the air again and sucked in a deep lungful.

"Hey, you okay?" Gator asked.

Lynx took a minute to catch her breath, so she knew she could speak. She didn't like it when she picked up sixth sense information in such a physical way under the best of circumstances. But certainly, she didn't want to do it while she was here in front of Nutsbe and especially not if she was in front of a client. She pounded a fist against her chest. "I swallowed, and it went down the wrong tube."

He nodded, looking unconvinced.

"Before I forget, you and I need some time to have a chat. I have some Strike Force information to pass you that I was *just* thinking about," Lynx said, feeling Nutsbe eyeing her with curiosity.

Gator scratched his hand over his chin and considered her. "I'm guessing it's about the last time Blaze, you, and me were talking about Jack's mission load."

"Yes, exactly, that's the subject matter. As I was saying, we need to chat when I'm sure Red won't come through the door."

"Roger that. I'll get with you ASAP. I can call tonight after the clients go to bed. For right now, Nutsbe, you know Christen as D-day?"

"Honey knows her too," Nutsbe used Rooster Honig's call name. "D-day flies for the 160th. He's been her customer five or six times. She likes to fly MH-6 Little Birds into dangerous places at absurd elevations. I'm talkin' like eight-ten feet from the terrain at crazy speeds. She's got a pair of titanium-plated steel balls, man. Honey said that he never had an uncomfortable second when he was flying with her. Pure professionalism. Skills of a Zen master. She's rock solid, but not CIA or a paper artist. She's a Night Stalker."

"Serious?" Gator said. "Damn." He sat back. "And why are

we here protecting a CIA operations officer and a Night Stalker? Is this about Lula?"

"Lula LaRoe is the childhood friend of Christen Davidson and the legal name for Johnna White," Nutsbe said.

Well, there was news Nutsbe hadn't shared before. Lula wasn't with the Treasury.

"CIA, huh? Okay, again, why are me and Blaze here? These women have the skills they need. None of them are wilting daisies."

"Right, well, they're using Christen as a point of entry into this party. But three women may not have access to all the places where a man might talk – locker room, bathroom, men's lounge. They needed two male operators with close protection skillsets, and they needed Davidson to buy into the scenario. Those men needed to come from a known private security company. Iniquus could fill that bill."

"Okay. And it makes sense to use Christen as an asset. I'd never have guessed she was a special operator," Gator said. "That's not how she comes off when she's around her friends – well, Red isn't her friend. Let's just say Christen seems comfortable settin' in the lap of luxury. Socialite. Designer clothes that she wears like a second skin. Well, until you go out jogging with her and Lula, and they turn it into some crazy movie-scene stunt devils."

"Yeah, Blaze told us she went hard-core parkour on your ass," Nutsbe chuckled, "and that you kept up fine until they hit the walls with their 'gravity has no power here' act. The file says D-day took that up after she decided gymnastics wasn't for her. Guess she needed more adrenaline in her life. She took up flying in high school. Honey was in here earlier when we were running the video we downloaded from her contact lens. He said parkour was D-day's workout routine on base, and none of the men would try it."

"Not Honey anyways," Lynx's smile drew wide. "At six-foot-eight, it's kind of hard to tuck and roll."

"D-day the Amazon princess," Gator grinned, his eyes warmed with affection.

Lynx had never seen that before. In the years she'd known Gator, he'd dated lots of women. He'd even had had a long-term relationship with a woman named Amy. But Amy was pushing for marriage and babies, and Gator was emphatically married to his job. When Lynx and Gator had talked about Amy, there was sometimes laughter in his eyes, affection; he cared about her. But this seemed different.

Lynx thought back to the day that she went out on assignment with their teammate Deep Del Toro as her back up. He'd walked into the art gallery where she was interviewing a witness, and he was gobsmacked. Pow. She had watched the very instant Cupid sent out a double arrowed shot at both Lacey and Deep, hitting them straight through the hearts. Like the birth of a child or being present at a death, it was an intensely sacred moment—a privilege to witness.

Gator didn't look gobsmacked – that word seemed to describe a new sensation that threw you for a loop.

This seemed more...more....

More what?

More long-lived.

More assured.

Older, maybe.

Though, obviously, they were just meeting.

More – primal-beast energy. A smile tickled her lips when she thought that. But yeah, there was something there in that thought. In those words. Something more threatening —"I will rip you limb from limb if you dare to hurt her." As those words bubbled into her thoughts, any lightness was extinguished from her meandering ideas. A threat lay camouflaged in the horizon.

Since Lynx had met Gator, sometimes, when she looked at him, she picked up the whole gladiator vibe. Sometimes it was Viking energy. *Hammer to the North!* A mighty anvil held aloft. A thunderous roar. Yeah, that was definitely the energy she felt swirling around Gator when Christen was in the picture. Christen was his, and he would protect her to the death. Lynx looked at smiling Gator. Focused Gator. Cute, funny, soft-hearted Gator. The visual and the energy didn't match up very well. "Something evil this way comes," not a knowing, just a whisper through her brain. Why the witches from Macbeth suddenly popped into her mind, Lynx was afraid to guess. But yes, this energy—that she was trying, and failing, to define—felt prophetic. She and Gator had been swimming in it since the hotel room in Tanzania before they took on this mission.

And then came a real *knowing*. A full body slam of a *knowing*. This is the house that Jack built.

She knew those thoughts had flooded her system in less time than it took for her to snap her fingers because Nutsbe was correcting Gator's last quip, "Not an Amazon princess. A decorated war hero."

"Yeah, sorry." Gator lay his hand on his chest. "That didn't come out the way I meant. I have mad respect for her skills. Not just the parkour but a Night Stalker? Whooeee!" He paused, a little smile twitching the corners of his mouth, his eyes looking introspective, then he focused back on the screen. "Oh, hey, you said Honey was feeding you information. The team's home?"

"Safe and sound." Lynx forced a smile. "Randy is out of ICU and is in stable condition. They're running neurological tests on him later today, but coming out of anesthesia, he had sensation in all his toes. That's a good sign."

"Whew! Thank you for sayin'. I'd like to be kept up on all that." Gator adjusted the screen and glanced toward the door. "Okay, I've got a small window here. Let's talk about the mission. You've joined the effort, Lynx?"

"I've been added to your team because of the information you handed us about helium. That was an angle that no one had considered."

There was a tap at the door. Gator turned his head and gave a nod.

Lynx could hear the door snick shut, and then Red showed up on the computer screen as she squished in next to Gator.

"I was just about to share some information about helium," Lynx said.

Red reached behind her and grabbed a pillow from the top of the bed she and Gator were sitting on. She hugged it to her, rolling forward until her forearms resting on her thighs, mirroring Gator. She looked like a girl at a slumber party, ready to listen to a ghost story.

"Gator had mentioned to us that Meg Finley had made a connection between William Davidson being in Tanzania and helium," Lynx began.

"Our intelligence said Davidson was in Dar es Salaam to negotiate a contract for natural gas and offshore drilling now that negotiations between the Tanzanian government and Hesston Oil were interrupted over the kidnapping of Derek Bowman."

Gator swiveled toward Red. "Meg says that the helium and natural gas are mixed together and processed to separate them. A contract for natural gas would be a contract for helium."

Red tilted her head, "And Meg's job is…"

"Animal migration, ma'am. But that don't mean she don't

know what she's talking about. She's researched this because this would impact the animals she's studying."

"Our research has shown the same information," Lynx said. Nutsbe scooted to the side so Lynx's face could be center screen. "The US is the biggest producer - a four-point-seven-billion-dollar industry. Asia's booming manufacturing is driving up the competition for a finite resource. As US reserves are dwindling, the emerging markets are importing more and more of the helium from Qatar."

"Who else is involved?" Red asked.

"Russia, and to a much lesser extent, Algiers, Canada, and China. But those last three are minuscule in the global market. For the big hitter, we're looking at US, Russia, and Qatar," Lynx said.

"Meg told Blaze and me that there was a problem with distribution, and she was afraid it would force prices up so that Tanzania would find the market too hot to pass up. You got anything on that?" Gator asked.

"Yes," Lynx said, "Hang on. Nutsbe, can you hand me that page?"

Nutsbe gathered a piece of paper filled with colored thought bubbles of information and held it up. When she nodded, he passed it over to her.

Lynx looked over her notes. "This started with Saudi Arabia et al., jumping on Qatar for their involvement with funding terror. The Qatari ports have been closed. There's nothing coming or going out of there. Businesses are relying on their helium reserves to continue with manufacturing items that require that element — MRI machines and what have you. The US can't make up for the amount of product that's being withheld from the worldwide industry." She put her paper down. "If this keeps up, there will be a fight for the limited supply. And prices will go up. The longer this continues, the higher the prices can go until the market gives way with businesses unable to produce because of lost profit margins. The disruption in the helium market squeezes a bunch of important industries and can set off a wave of global repercussions."

"We need to figure out what individuals would benefit from this spike," Red said. "If this has anything to do with this group Davidson's gathered, it would be an interesting twist, for sure. And one not readily obvious. Let's keep that hypothesis in play. There is no Tanzanian on the guest list. There is a Qatari, a Sheik from Saudi Arabia. William and Karl Davidson are American. No Russians, but we do have someone from Slovakia with ties to Russia. His name is Gregor Zoric, nicknamed Medved'. We've had our eye on him for a while. Medved' has connections with Russian oligarch families. He likes to play in my neck of the woods."

"With Hezbollah and Hamas?" Lynx asked.

"I'm sorry," Red said sternly. "Why would you suggest that?"

"I worked the Sophia Abadi case – Sophia Abadi-Ackerman, she's newly married. But you would know that since you're still her handler." Lynx didn't know why she wanted to wrestle some power away from Red. Lynx was kicking herself for the weird dynamic she just introduced.

"Zoric," Gator said. "We've had a brush with the Zoric family in D.C. They're a crime family with ties to terrorism."

"Exactly." Red nodded. "Gregor's the head of one branch of that family. As I was saying, he likes to hang out with Russian oligarchs and live large. From our reports, I can say he hasn't got much of a soul."

"Psychopathic kind of soulless?" Gator turned a sharp gaze

on Red. "This makes a big difference in terms of preparing for and providing security."

"That's what our psychiatrists have indicated, yes."

"And he's Slovakian?" he asked.

"That's right," Red tilted her head, asking for more information.

"Kind of interesting. When Blaze and me were saving William Davidson in what we thought was a pretend fight--"

"Ha!" Nustbe snorted. "I still can't believe you were fake fighting in a real fight that turned out to be the wrong fight."

Gator sent him a grin. "I reckon those guys think we're pathetic fighters. I mean, my punches were coming in like I was a hundred-year-old grandpa on his sleep meds. I honestly didn't know what to think when it was going down."

"Classic, man." Nutsbe grinned. "That fight's now an Iniquus legend."

Red gave Gator a playful bump of her elbow. "Langley legend, too."

Gator dipped his head bashfully. "I bring it up 'cause the guy I was putting to sleep was talking in a foreign language. At the time, I thought it was icing on the cake for the officer to be speaking in Russian, but when I talked to Blaze about it, he said he didn't recognize any of the words. Blaze did say he thought it was in the Slovic language family. It sounded similar. Mind you, Blaze's Russian is conversational, not fluent."

"Russia wanting to stop Davidson from a helium deal with Tanzania wouldn't make any sense. His oil company holds Russian contracts. They rub each other's backs to get the Russian oil on to the markets with the current NATO sanctions in place. And like I said, the Zoric family isn't part of the oligarchy, but they have firm ties. I think trying to tie Zoric to the attempted kidnapping attempt on Davidson isn't reasonable."

"Noted. I'll research that angle further," Lynx said. "But as I was telling Gator, all of the members of this business party have a helium connection save one. You have two Japanese businessmen from a shipping company which transports helium. There are three Chinese and one man from India. Those four are all involved in industries that require helium for production. Then there is Gregor Zoric, who is connected to Russian energy, Nadir al-Attiyah, the Qatari man who is connected to the royal family and heavily involved in their helium production and distribution, and William and Karl Davidson. The only businessman I can't link in is the Saudi sheik. I have no idea why he's there. But again, he's well tied into the Saudi royal family tree. Those are the eleven businessmen at the meeting."

"Lots of players. Lots of power. Lots of money on the table." Red checked her watch. "Gator, you and I need to go get spiffed up. It's almost time for dinner, and you have a damsel who needs your protection."

Gator stood. "Lynx, I'll get back in touch with you after our clients have gone to bed."

"Everyone's good?" Red asked. She stood and threw the pillow up toward the top of the bed. "Now, we get to meet the gentlemen in the world of helium." She elbowed Gator. "Sounds like a gas!"

21

CHRISTEN

Thursday, Reception, Raffles Hotel, Singapore

HER BROTHER KARL lifted his drink toward Christen in a kind of a salute. "How do you like living in Kentucky?" He sounded like he wasn't sure how to make small talk with her. They had almost nothing in common. They never did, even when her mom was still married to their dad.

"It's fine. There are some beautiful national forests, wonderful waterways to explore." Christen hoped someone would come over and join them to expand the conversation. It was odd for Karl to come to speak to her alone like this. She couldn't remember that ever happening before. Normally she was "my half-sister, Christen," and then the conversation would move on to yachting or what have you, something that had nothing to do with her scope of the world, and therefore, there was nothing she could add. And typically, nothing she wanted to take away either. But her mission was to gather what intelligence she could, and so she actually needed to be the proverbial fly on the wall and listen to the men interact.

She glanced around the room. Blaze stood by the door, Gator stood cattycorner. Johnna was talking to London, and she couldn't find Lula.

"Horse country, too," Karl said. "I just bought Mimi a stallion from near there, outside of Nashville."

Mimi was Karl's fiancée. Mimi looked like a horse, but that was Christen thinking like a brat.

"You live just north of there, don't you? Near Fort Campbell? A lot of special forces operators out your direction," Karl said. "I bet you enjoy that." He lifted the corner of his mouth in a smirk.

Christen blinked. Surely, Karl wasn't on the Christen-folds-origami bandwagon. Surely, he remembered she served in the US military and was special forces herself. "A few." Okay, her tone was a little too sarcastic. She cleared her throat and tried again. "The ones I know are nice."

"Nice? I bet you don't say that to their faces. It's like calling them Nancy-boys. It would hurt their poor feelings." He tipped down some scotch and pointed at her with the glass in his hand. "I imagine they're all peacocks walking about town with their chests puffed out. I bet the muscle that gets the most exercise is their ego." He shook his head. "Ridiculous. I mean, given the technology we have today, how hard can their job be? How can they possibly be losing the war to a bunch of uneducated goat herders?" He reached over to grab a canape from the doily-covered silver tray a waiter was circulating. Karl ate it in one bite and spoke with his mouth full. "And yet all these years later…"

Christen closed her eyes and reached for her training to contain her emotions.

She remembered the heard of goats in Syria, the Deltas as

they lay in the dust, getting ready to fight for their lives while she abandoned them in her helicopter.

When she popped her eyelids open, Gator was in her line of sight and caught her gaze. She imagined he was sending her mental waves of support. Seeing Gator and knowing he'd served as a Marine Raider and was now protecting her scumbag of a brother, who had the *gall* to speak derisively of the sacrifices the military made, Every. Single. Day. pissed Christen off even more. "Can I tell you a secret?" Christen asked, leaning in with a conspiratorial whisper.

Karl gave her a wicked smile and a nod.

"They shit themselves when they're on their missions," she said under her breath.

Karl flung his head back and laughed heartily; he came up sputtering. "Scared, huh?"

"Probably. But that's not why they shit themselves. They shit themselves because they're eating whatever the fuck they can find to eat in some of the filthiest places imaginable with flies landing and defecating on their food, leaving microbes that turn into illnesses that twist their bowls into knots."

Karl pulled back. His grin dropped off and was replaced with a look of disgust. He swiped at his mouth.

Christen reached up and grabbed Karl's lapel, and pulled him back in close. "But that doesn't stop them. Even though their bowels are cramping, and they're feverish, and just want a clean bathroom and some time, they don't get that. Once their mission is in go-mode, they stop for nothing. Not even to pull down their pants and get some relief. If they need to shit, they shit. And if their bowels won't hold while they're running from house to house, then they shit as they run. And they change when they get back. Hopefully safe and sound. But not always. They don't always make it out alive or whole. They put their god-damned lives on the god-damned line so people like you can stand around at cocktail parties and talk with your crappy privileged-class superiority about how little it takes in terms of bravery and skill to go to war and protect our nation." She pushed higher on her toes, so she could hiss right into his ear. "You should be ashamed, you pathetic never-served asswipe."

Christen released Karl's lapel when she felt a hand brush down her back.

"Hey, Karl, remember me? I'm Lula LaRoe. We met when you came to see Christen winning her gymnastics medals at Nationals." She grinned her happy, friendly grin but continued to pet Christen, trying to calm her.

"Oh, uh, yes. Lula. Lovely that you could join us this weekend."

Christen patted her hand over Karl's dinner jacket to smooth the wrinkles from where she'd gripped it. "Karl was asking about Kentucky. Such a beautiful state. Absolutely lovely. He's bought a new horse from just south of me. Where are you stabling your horse?"

Karl seemed thrown by her sudden shift. "Oh – uh, Mimi. Mimi has him at her Virginia home along the James."

"She wasn't able to join you for your dad's gathering?" Lula asked.

"Well, no. I had brought these businessmen together, well, we. Father and I had planned a business gathering, and so we had just invited the men."

Christen thought her head would explode. That last sentence was her existence within the family. The men did the business. The women were the coffee tables, something to put your feet up on to relax. The paintings on the walls to be discussed, "look at the lines and coloring, isn't she beautiful?" The whirlygigs in the garden adding movement, something whimsical to smile at and nod. Females, in the Davidson world, were not actual sentient, intellectual beings. They were there for the pleasure they could provide. Quietly.

"London came." Christen pointed out.

"She's only with us for the day. Father wished to see her. She'll stay here in Singapore with the twins and go shopping while we go on with our meetings."

Father – not Dad. It sounded so fake to Christen's ears. Cold. And distant.

"I understand that now you girls will be coming along on our adventure tomorrow to see the orangutans."

"Women," Christen said. "We *women* will be joining in. That's right." But her words were lost as Karl turned toward the man dressed in his calf-length white shirt over a loose pair of pants. He wore the traditional red and white *gutra* secured with a black rope on his head. The cloth was folded back on either side in the style specific to the men of Qatar. He reached out to hold Karl's hand. A distinctly Arabic act of male affection that Christen was surprised Karl allowed.

"Orangutans," the man said. "No. No orangutans. It deeply saddens me, but I have heard from your security that our plans have been changed."

"Nadir al-Attiyah, of Qatar, my half-sister Christen, her friend Lula LaRoe."

Christen placed her hand over her heart. *"Assalam ualaikum."*

"Walaikum Assalam." Nadir returned the gesture. "You speak Arabic?"

"Only a little bit. I've been to Qatar. It's truly beautiful," she said with a smile. Maybe here was a place she could gather information.

Lula stepped on her toes. It felt like an on-purpose stepping, too. Christen bet Lula was rethinking her recommendation that Christen might find future employment in whatever alphabet organization Lula worked for. (Christen was still betting it was the CIA.)

"I haven't heard anything about a change of plans," Karl turned his shoulder, physically blocking Christen from Nadir. "I planned that event solely with your interests in mind." Karl seemed agitated. "Who told you this about the orangutans?"

"Your father did." Nadir spoke excellent English with a generic American accent.

Taro Eto was walking past. Christen knew him from the photos and names that Johnna had gone over with them before they'd come down to the reception room. "No orangutans," he said, stopping. No one bothered to introduce him to the others in the group, but he seemed indifferent to the women's presence anyway. "There are bandits in the woods. We will go on a tour of an ancient village. Maybe we see orangutan in the wild."

"Father." Karl reached toward his distracted father as he walked by with Gregor Zoric. "The visit to the refuge was called off?"

"The head of my security team deemed it too dangerous."

Christen followed Karl's angry gaze over to a neckless security guard. The man blushed beet red, and did a sweep of the room, then talked into his cuff like a wannabe secret service agent in the movies. Not even real-world secret service agents did that crap.

"I'm sure you'll enjoy your tour, though," her dad said. "I've made sure with your tour guide that there will be ample opportunities to take some wonderful adventure photographs. And the surfing beaches where you will spend the next day are spectacular." He tapped Karl's arm, and Karl dropped his hand to his side. William Davidson turned his attention to Taro. "It will be your only opportunity on this trip to enjoy the beaches. I'm still developing those on my own island. Another year will see them done and lovely." He sent them a wan smile, and Christen thought she could see a headache thudding at his temples. "Excuse me," he said and walked off before anyone could say anything in reply. Lula followed him. She didn't bother to say good-bye. No one but Christen seemed to notice she'd left their conversation circle.

"I have researched the waters of this area. We must be very careful swimming in the waters," Gregor sent a poignant look toward Karl and then a surreptitious glance her way. His English was thick and halting.

"The surf can be strong, but certainly the water is no more dangerous than any other," Christen said. She was ignored.

"However," Gregor said, "once apprised, once aware, one can work to avoid issues." Again with the poignant stare toward Karl. This guy wasn't exactly subtle. Maybe it was cultural, and she was misinterpreting. They had professionals at Langley who could decide. Her job was to look while looking pretty.

"There is actually a very interesting creature to be on guard for, the sea wasp."

"Sea wasp?" Nadir asked. "I've never heard of this. An insect on open water?"

"The name hides the truth. A sea wasp is actually a box jelly-fish and is known to be the most poisonous animal on our planet." Gregor drained his tumbler then lifted his glass in the air. Within seconds a waiter took it from him, asking if he'd like another.

"Here? In the waters where we're to swim?" Nadir pulled his head back and tucked his chin.

"The strong venom." Gregor snapped his fingers. "It can kill its prey in a matter of seconds."

"Oh, but its prey would be shrimp and fish. Things that are easily caught by such a predator," Christen said. "Small animals."

The men all swung their heads to look at her, then turned back to Gregor.

"I have read that the venom can cause issues with the skin cells, with the nervous system, with the heart. Very painful. And since this may cause shock or heart failure instantly, if the victim is stung, people usually drown before they can reach the shore. They die a painful death alone in the water." A slow smile seemed to want to stretch Gregor's lips, but there was no movement.

"If they die alone in the water, how do we know they experienced pain?" Christen asked.

No one answered her.

"If you survive the sea wasp attack," he continued, "—*if* —you will be marked for life. The scarring will tattoo your skin."

"Well, at least that'll make a great bar story," Christen told the air, knowing no one was paying the least attention to her. She swirled her tumbler of bourbon, ordered because she hated the taste and wouldn't be tempted to sip it. She was tempted, anyway —anything to take the edge off. Christen considered the story that Gregor was sharing and what import it might have. She'd surfed these waters maybe a half-dozen times, and she'd never heard of this thing before, the sea wasp. She wondered if it wasn't some made-up crap. She'd Google it later.

"How does one recognize this sea wasp from a regular jellyfish?" Nadir asked. "Should we just assume any jellyfish we see are lethal?"

"They, like the others, are transparent, but with a light blue coloration. Two dozen or so tentacles. Each tentacle is three meters in length, growing from the underbelly, providing thousands of cells to sting the victim." Gregor caught Karl's gaze. "The sea wasp does not sting when it touches its prey. Rather, when the sea wasp senses the chemicals of the prey's skin, the wasp then sends the poison and kills the prey. And the targets are instantly dead in the water."

Was that weird to say? From Karl's narrowed eyes and hard stare, he was getting some message loud and clear. Christen hoped that those in the know who were hearing this cryptic back and forth were able to find the metaphor. It was lost on her. But that's not why she was on this mission. She was tasked with picking up this kind of information. It was someone else's job to sift it and find the nugget of interesting information. She was on task, she reminded herself – though this was nothing like the kind of mission she liked to be on. She was helping. Maybe.

22

LYNX

Thursday, Striker's Apartment, Iniquus Men's Barracks

GATOR CANTED his head as he peered at the computer screen. "You look tired."

Lynx answered with a loud yawn. She stretched her arms over her head then gave herself a shake. "Oh, you know how these things go. I'll sleep when you sleep. But you're twelve hours ahead, and I jumped on this bandwagon already in motion. I need my clock to catch up with yours, that's all. How'd it go tonight? Christen's a bit out of her comfort zone. Did she fare okay?"

"As far as the fitting in, she did fine. She seems comfortable enough in this situation. It was a strange dynamic. The dad and oldest brother Karl seemed to engage with her, the step-mom and other siblings ignored her completely. She doesn't seem to enjoy her family. Now I know who she is, flying as a Night Stalker and all. I'm confused on why her dad tells everyone she's an artist? That don't make sense."

"Her dad knows what she does. Her dad doesn't accept it. Those are two different things. You get that, Gator."

"You don't think that's some kinda crazy? I'm being serious. Could he have dementia or something?"

"He doesn't want to think his little girl is in harm's way. This is easier for him, I'm guessing. I can try to get hold of his medical records if you'd like. It could be that they've already gathered that information, and it's in the file at Langley. If not, once he gets on his island and laws don't apply, Nutsbe can hack his laptop and see if there isn't information on his hard drive."

"I'd appreciate that. Yeah, I'd like to know. It's got to be something. He's either disoriented, or he's got a lot on his mind. Sometimes when he was speaking, he'd just drift off message or changes the sentence mid-thought. He's doing something and then just wanders away. I don't know him well enough to know if that's his normal behavior. I can't ask Christen either. I'm still playing on the bad-guy team, as far as she knows. He could be distracted, but usually, when there's a big deal going down, folks get laser-focused."

"What's going on besides there being something off in his concentration? What kind of character are we looking at?"

"Narcissistic. Needy. Surrounds himself with yes men. Likes the sound of his own voice. The brother Karl seems cut from the same pattern. The other two brothers, I don't know that they're rowing with both oars. Christen definitely won the gene lottery."

"Intelligence. Character. Skills. Yes, I'm impressed with her. From our research, it looks like Karl is being groomed to take his father's place, and the younger siblings look like they're being groomed to enjoy their trust funds."

"That seems about right." He moved the computer onto the bed and shoved himself so he could lay back.

The energy Lynx felt swirling around Gator was intense. For her, it had been an underlying hum of urgency and danger. She knew it was connected to him. She couldn't block it if she wanted to. And she didn't want to. She wanted to keep her fingers on the pulse of whatever was happening for him. It was coming. It was big. The fight of this lifetime. *This?* That was an odd word to insert. Not the fight of *a* lifetime. This. *This?* Huh. Not outside of Lynx's paradigms. Not inside either. Spyder, her mentor, believed in a soul's evolution through various lives. It had been part of the teachings she was exposed to in her varied educational career. That had felt like more of an intellectual game. A philosopher's enigma. And this felt concrete. Whew! That was a lot to take in. Should she discuss this with Gator? Was it better for it to play out? "Let's go back to Christen and her dad. How do they get along?"

"She's quiet. Mostly just listens. I don't know if that's her natural personality, if it's the mission, or if it's the dynamic she falls into in these situations. She comes off as a socialite who knows her place in the old-boy world. Which, with the men coming in from these countries, makes sense. But the dad and the daughter? Night and day, them two. Were you listening in real-time while we were at the party?"

"I was. Sounds like you've got an interesting excursion tomorrow."

"William Davidson's hanging back. Johnna White, well, Lula, made some excuse to hang with him. She'll be our only eyes and ears. It seems to me his staying back is important. I'm glad someone from our team will have a chance to figure out why. The wife, London, and two of the kids have a spa day. William Davidson isn't scheduled to join them for that."

"Langley has an X on William Davidsons back. There will be little he can do without their knowledge. I'm told White will have backup teams from the area if need be."

"Okay. He's keeping his chauffer and one security guard with him. He's specified one for White. I'm not sure if that's to keep her safe or keep eyes on her. It seems an odd choice, is all. There will be fourteen guests and five security team members heading out on their field trip."

"Noted. I'll pass that along."

"There was an argument about bringing all the security teams that travel with the other guests, but the yacht just can't accommodate those numbers even with William Davidson and Lula hanging back. We had a security meeting. The Fire Hydrant's name is Daniel, and he's in charge. He's focused on Karl. The rest of us will focus on the others."

She scrawled those notes on her paper. "I'll make sure everyone's aware."

"I know you have all this from the tapes, but I'm touching on the points of interest, so you aren't losing them in the hours of small talk."

"Appreciated." Lynx had her notes out and was checking the information Gator was handing her against the details she had gleaned from surveillance.

"We're scheduled to take a private jet to Sumatra to do some hiking, and they're setting up lunch at one of the villages. I sent you the waypoints for our trek. I'd like you to check out the area and let me know what we might run into, threat-wise. Check the terrain and wildlife too. These guys don't look like they're out in nature much. Or at the gym. Blaze and me might end up piggybacking these guys around. I don't think they know what they're getting themselves into. The heat and humidity. We need to be ready with the right equipment, best we can put together from what their normal security team has on hand."

"Wilco, I'll hand that off to Nutsbe. We'll have a full report up for you before you head out. What time are you leaving?"

"Zero seven hundred hours our time.

"Yeah, we have plenty of time to get this together for you. You're meeting the Davidson yacht according to the plan you sent us. Is there a dock? I'm looking at the satellite image of the area, and I don't see anything."

"They're going to be sending a dingy to shore, and we'll help get everyone transferred over. They're heading to an island for dinner. Swimming and enjoying the beach the next day. That's where the surfing skills will come in. We may have to pull someone out of the drink. After dinner, we'll set off for the Davidson island, where they'll have the rest of their business retreat. That's when I hope to pick up some good intelligence."

"It'll be interesting to have eyes and ears on the island. I hope your comms are good there. We'll probably have some blackout time until you get back on the mainland."

"That's what I figure." Gator's voice faded off. He swiped a hand over his eyes.

He suddenly looked exhausted, like the weight of the world was resting on his shoulders. Lynx felt fiercely protective. The ferocity was actually kind of stunning. She wanted to hand-to-hand battle anything that made Gator look the way he did. "Can we take a second and talk about the elephant in the room?"

Gator laced his hands and posted them behind his head. "The sixth sense crap I've been wading through?"

"Wading through? It's like a full-blown hurricane. I can hardly stand it, and I'm just checking in on you."

"Sucks for sure. Near as I can tell, this has to do with Christen."

"You feel like you've known her all your life. What else are you feeling?"

"A personal connection. And it's rough. I have to keep constant vigilance."

"Because…"

"Aww now, don't make me say this. I'll sound like a moron."

"Gator, I've been wearing you like a coat since this assignment started. I know what I'm feeling. I need to get some affirmations from you that what I'm getting is what you're getting."

"Shit, Lynx." He pulled his hands down until they rested over his eyes. "Excuse my language."

Lynx waited.

"I don't have the words for this." He pulled his hand away and looked her straight in the eye, then popped his brow. "A storyteller who's all out of words."

"It cuts too close. Let me try. You feel like you have the right to touch her. That she belongs in your arms and in your bed."

"Lynx, that's uh—" Gator pushed up to a sitting position, leaning forward, a rare frown on his face.

"Not in a fun roll kind of way. It feels like you've already made a commitment to her, and there's a constant confusion on your part that she isn't acknowledging the same level of connection. And the worst part about it is there's a storm of some kind brewing. Something bad. Life-threatening. And you need her to understand your connection one to the other, or you may not make it through."

Lynx stopped talking.

Gator sat very still.

Time passed.

"Yeah, if I were gonna tell it and be truthful to you and me both. That there puts it in a nutshell. Craziest thing I've ever felt.

Overwhelming. I thought the level of energy that was zapping me was bad back in Tanzania when we were crowded into the hotel room getting the assignment. But that were just a tickle compared to what I'm getting now that Christen and me have met. I have to keep a sharp awareness. It's true that it feels like I've known her all my life. This charade feels like I'm wearing someone else's clothes around her. And since you said you've been wearing me all day, I know you know what I'm talkin' about." He lay his hand on his heart. "I'm sorry I'm in your space, Lynx. It's not something I'm doing on purpose." He took in a deep breath and let it out. "Is there anything I can do to bring you some relief?" He shifted around, worried lines crisscrossing his forehead. "Maybe some way for you to turn off our connection, so I'm not bothering you?

"You a bother?" Lynx swished a hand through the air like she was erasing the idea. "If I'm wearing you energetically, it means I'm invested in this outcome. I'm glad to be here and doing what I can. You live in my heart Gator. You know that."

Gator rolled his lips in and nodded.

"And could I if I wanted to? No. And can I tell you how to turn down the volume on what you're experiencing? No. It is what it is."

"The pieces – the flashes – they don't fit together to give me anything actionable. I feel like I should be battling this out. But there's no enemy to go after. None that I'm aware of anyway. And I'm gonna tell you, though I know you already know, something bad's coming. Being out on Davidson's Realm where we're headed, without backup or egress and poor comms? It's got me scared."

"You?" Lynx scoffed. "You're one of the bravest men I know. Striker owes his life to your strength and bravery. Time after time, Gator, you've been there for your team and me.

You've got this. Whatever *this* is. And you've got me." Lynx's eyes glazed over with tears, her face turned pink with emotion.

She felt it too.

She *knew* he was right.

This was the end game.

"Thank you." Gator gave himself a shake and a stretch as if coming awake. "The quicker I can figure this out, get the case sewn up, the quicker I can get D-day back in the skies where she belongs. And get me home. Make all these emotions go away. I'm pretty much hatin' this."

23

GATOR

Thursday, Raffles Hotel, Singapore

A TATTOO SOUNDED at the hotel room door. Gator lifted his chin to Lynx then went to open it.

"Hey man," Blaze said as he moved into the room and shot a glance at the computer. "Hey, Lynx. I just got my last person tucked into bed. Sorry I'm late."

"No worries. Gator gave me the rundown on what's going on for the next two days before you get back on the island. We'll do our best to keep our communications open. I was about to share some puzzle pieces I've identified from conversations thus far."

"Okay, shoot," Blaze pushed the computer over to make space on the bed and flopped down, scrunching a pillow under his head.

Gator pulled up a chair, spun it around, and sat on it backward. He crisscrossed his arms over the back and let his chin rest on his forearms. Gator was relieved Blaze had come when he did and interrupted his discussion with Lynx, as cowardly as it felt to admit that.

Gator had dealt in the ether before. Mainly as an observer. Lynx could do some scary-assed shit with her psychic abilities. Gator hated to watch her when she went behind the "Veil," as she called it. She could meld with and become one with a victim, trying to figure out what was going on and how to get help onto the scene.

He'd stood by and watched her take the punishment while she saved life afterlife. It weren't how he was raised. No man worth his salt would let a woman face a physical assault while he stood idly by, twiddling his thumbs. And that was what it had been.

Lynx seemed okay dealing with her sixth sense. Gator *hated* it. Hated the sensations. Hated the distraction. But most of all, right then, he hated that they'd both concluded that all this psychic noise had to do with Christen Davidson. Knowing danger was focused on Christen did crazy things to his insides. Just talking about it, and the volume got turned up in his own body. For relief's sake—since there was no good coming of just talking—Gator was glad Blaze came in to serve as a buffer.

Lynx flipped through the pages in her hand and then stopped, her eye tracking from top to bottom. "I have a connection for you – Medved' means bear in Slovac." She looked back up at them. "That's the Gregor Zoric guy's nickname. The Zorics are a dangerous and powerful family. You know about the branch of the Zoric family that went after Lacey Stuart when Deep was trying to protect her from the Zoric assassins here in D.C. But you've been on assignment since Jack jumped off the roof."

"You made a Jack connection to Gregor?" Gator asked.

"Maybe. You know the story of how Jack went after Suz and hooked up with the Mossad unit in Brazil and Paraguay. Did you also know that when the Mossad took down the extremist's camp, they discovered it was a group of Slovakians who were helping to fund the terrorists and run that training camp? Since then, several of our intelligence communities have been talking to Jack, including NSA, CIA, FBI, and interestingly, the treasury. The CIA and the Treasury happen to be our clients – they've made a connection between money laundering, offshore banking, and activities down in Paraguay. They're trying to make the connection between Medved' Zoric and the Paraguayan kidnapping."

"And you think Gregor Zoric might be that Medved' Zoric from Paraguay?" Blaze asked.

Lynx tilted her head back and forth as if weighing the idea. "Seems like we keep playing in the Zoric's back yard. I'm going to call Special Agent Steve Finley and see if he's willing to weigh in. Right now, we know for a fact that the Zorics are connected to Iran and Hezbollah and so Syria. Voila! I think that's the Johnna Red connection." She paused, looking up from her notes. "Speculation. Grain of salt."

Both men nodded.

"Money to fund extremist activity is absolutely funneled to Hezbollah, through the Zoric connection. And drugs and artwork are funneled back their way. These are business and economic considerations not driven by any religious connection, except where they find it useful as a tool."

Gator shook his head. "Wait. That makes no sense what you were sayin'. It was an al Qaeda cell in Paraguay. Why was a Hezbollah sympathizer helping al Qaeda?"

"In Paraguay? That's a very good question. We don't know for sure what the terrorists' affiliation was. They were operating under a black flag. Does that sound a little like something that you were telling me about in the Philippine article?

That small groups were fighting unaffiliated but under a black flag?"

"Shit," Blaze muttered.

"The Mossad and CIA are sharing the documentation that the Mossad gathered from the Paraguayan camp, but it's need-to-know. And we really have no need, outside of curiosity, to know. Al Qaeda was a guess based on the historical association that Osama bin Laden had in Paraguay, not from any concrete evidence."

"Okay. Got it. Why are you bringing this up?" Gator asked.

"Suz and Jack both said in their hot wash that the guy who was being reported to over the satellite phone was called the Bear. Also, a note was intercepted that was being sent out from the Tanzanian prison camp the scientists were held in along with Meg Finley and Honey Honig. It mentioned Medved' which, again, is Slovac for bear. Unfortunately, since Honey neutralized Momo Bourhan and his men, we have no new information and no one to interrogate."

"You think the guy here might be the same bear? I'd imagine that were kinda common as a nickname over in that part of the world." Gator rubbed a hand over his jaw.

"I agree a thousand percent. I'm laying my thoughts out there in case it bubbled any connections or memories you guys had from Jack's last mission. I'm keeping an open mind."

"Gotcha. Grain of salt." Blaze said.

"What else do you know about Russia and helium?" Gator asked.

Lynx reached for a pad of paper. "Let's see, just ticking down some of my notes: Russia may be able to help the global markets catch up on their requirements because its gas reserves hold a higher proportion of helium, and the fields are close to Asian markets. Uhm... Davidson's on the records for helping to push

US laws concerning the federal helium reserve, located in Amarillo, Texas, his home town. It's the only strategic reserve of helium in the world. It's also the main reason why the U.S. is the top global helium supplier. The government began privatizing its helium reserve in the 1990s. That's when Congress decided private-sector demand for the gas had exceeded federal demand. They passed a bill to share public helium with private companies. The Department of Interior generates revenue from that sale of helium."

"Davidson was involved in lobbying for that bill?"

"Yup. He's been in the helium game for a while."

"And we're sure this is about helium."

"Nope. But I've been trying to put the puzzle pieces of people at the party together, and that's the only configuration that makes any sense right now. Think of it as a hypothesis."

"But why?" Blaze asked. "William Davidson's looking like both the victim and the villain here. Which do you think it is? Did the CIA tell you? Is he an asset or a target?"

"You know what I know," Lynx said. "For some reason, they think it's best to keep us in the dark. We're eyes and ears. We're meant to gather data. And I'm putting it through the helium filter to see if it shines things in a new light."

Blaze tightened his jaw. "Just between you, me, and the lamp post, that feels like a damned dangerous plan of action. I've had a cold tickle on the back of my neck since the hotel room in Tanzania. I couldn't tell you why, but this mission has FUBAR written all over it."

24

CHRISTEN

Friday, Raffles Hotel, Singapore

"**MY DAD'S NOT GOING?**" Christen sat on the bed, tugging on her hiking boot.

"No, I was talking with London last night at the cocktail party. She's very excited. She's here because her pee strip says she's ovulating." Johnna sent Christen a catty look, biting her lip to suppress the smile that twitched at the corners of her mouth.

"She said that?" Christen held up her hand to halt Johnna's answer. "TMI."

"London wants a baby. She thinks they made one yesterday, but she wanted to go ahead and continue to do the deed for the whole time the strip says she's ripe—her words—so she's sure that it takes."

"Uh, okay. Thanks for that nauseating visual. The end result is we're going to go on our little field trip, and Dad's going to stay back and boink wife number five to see if he can make another kid. Awesome. Where does that leave the mission?"

"The mission is a go. We're reconfiguring." Johnna moved over to the window and looked out. "You have a better view on this side of the building." She turned back. "I have a question about your dad." She let the curtain fall back into place. "Has he been ill?"

"Not that I've been told." Christen's brows furrowed. "Why? What did you hear?"

"He told Daniel and Karl that he's staying back to take a call from his doctor. Which is interesting. Either he's taking a call from his doctor, or he didn't want them to know he's seeding the next generation. Or both."

Christen reached for her other boot. "Daniel's the guy that looks like a fire hydrant? No neck? Lots of flash and show? Never speaks unless he's off in some corner chatting into his shirt cuff?"

"He's the one." Johnna pulled out a chair and sat down.

"Needing to stay back for a doctor's call sounds serious on the surface. My bet is that he never planned to go on the hike whether London showed up in heat or not," Christen said, not ever imagining a sentence like that would spill from her lips or those thoughts form in that configuration. "I can't see him hiking through the forest in high humidity. He's not really a jump on a surfboard kind of guy."

"Are *any* of these men?" Johnna was dressed in clothes specifically made for hiking in these conditions, loose, light, water-resistant, but breathable. The cloth was designed to protect against brambles and was chemically treated to keep away the bugs. She'd brought similar clothes for Christen, so they were both dressed to be as comfortable as possible.

Hiking in new boots, though, Christen thought, was going to suck. "Yeah, these guys are going to be complaining turtles."

"Complaining turtles," Johnna snorted. "That's so accurate."

"Karl told me they'd have a staff photographer who's going along." Christen looped a double knot in her laces. "I believe the goal is to take interesting photos of them doing manly things in exotic places – the kinds of carefully-staged self-deprecating photos that can be used in board meetings to tell a parable of their machoness. Sort of like Putin riding horseback with his shirt off and doing judo on grizzly bears."

"With his shirt off."

"And his saggy man titties. Seriously. What is wrong with people?" Christen stood, now fully dressed. "I'm just saying this out loud now; I will not be fireman-carrying anyone out of the rainforest. Security had better be bringing plenty of folding stretchers."

Johnna stood in front of the mirror and re-tucked her t-shirt. "Back to my question. Do you think your father is actually talking to a doctor?"

"He's never spoken to me about the state of his health," Christen said, thinking just how weird it was to have a parent who was so distant when her other one—her mom and she—were so close. Christen and her mom shared everything. Except for this mission. No, this one Christen would not get to tell her mom about, and she could let go of the guilt about that too. This mission was classified.

"We'll know soon enough. We've got their phones and rooms bugged. Lula is staying back to track him. She told him she had her meeting today and asked to join him in the helicopter when he goes to his island where she'll connect with us."

"He agreed to that?"

"Yup."

"So it's just us."

"Yup."

There was a knock on the door, and Christen opened it to the bellhop. She stepped back to allow him in, then pointed. "These two bags go with those being gathered for the William Davidson party. This smaller case will go with me in the car." She handed over her key card.

"Very good, madam." He bowed as she walked out of the room to find Blaze standing guard. His back to the wall. Christen looked around to see if Gator was there, wondering if he would still be tasked with Johnna and her safety or if he would be reassigned now that her father and Lula were staying back.

Christen was surprised that the idea of Gator not going along affected her so strongly. She would have thought she'd welcome the distance. As the three took the elevator down, disappointment flooded her system and pulled down the corners of her mouth. She purposefully set those thoughts aside by conjuring her friends Prominator and Smitty. Were they back on base and okay? Were the Deltas? She sent a little prayer their way.

When the elevator doors opened, the three were directed to a waiting limousine that would take them to the airport and their short flight to a private runway in Tarutung, North Sumatra, just south of Orangutan Haven. From there, they would take Jeeps to the east and their trailhead. They had a ten-kilometer hike into the rainforest, stopping for a catered lunch in the headhunters' village before continuing another four kilometers to the yacht. She wondered if Blaze wanted to lay bets with her on the party's ability to get back out to the yacht on their own power.

Daniel was standing extremely close to Gregor Zoric. That Daniel was speaking to a human and not his shirt cuff was remarkable, and Christen did her calculated blink to take a picture of the interaction and then another to turn her video back on. At least she thought that was what she was doing. Hard to tell. A little more practice might have been good.

Blaze directed the women to a limo with the door standing open. He peeked in then opened his hand to indicate they should enter. Christen climbed in first and swiveled into her seat, where she located her safety belt. Johnna followed her in. Blaze stood protectively blocking their open door, scanning three-sixty.

Still no Gator.

Karl, an extremely taciturn Indian man, and Nadir climbed in. Blaze made a final sweep then sat in the seat next to Johnna. With a tap on the partitioning glass, they were off.

Right away, Nadir caught Karl's eye. "You read the news this morning?"

Karl tipped his head to the side, inviting more information.

"Bowman was found by American mercenaries and was rescued from Djibouti."

The atmosphere in the car changed. Everyone, save her and the Indian guy, had gone still and focused. This name meant something important not just to Johnna but the Blaze guy and Karl.

"They're alive?" There was incredulity in Karl's voice. And he'd said "they." Nadir had said Bowman, a single name.

Christen used the window as a reflective surface to see the interior and to give herself a look of preoccupation.

"Both, yes, the husband and wife were taken to an American army hospital in Europe, and now they are home and released from their hospital in the states. They have been interviewed by the CIA and FBI, according to the paper, and were cooperating fully in trying to find the perpetrators. Bowman's political connections will see that this is pursued. His business relations will insist on a conclusion to the case." Nadir shot a look around the car's occupants to find everyone otherwise engaged. He lifted his voice a little. "This is, of course, very good news for the international business community. Executives need to feel safe traveling the world. We are, after all, in a global marketplace."

"What do you think this means in terms of the oil deal? Is he returning to Tanzania to develop a deal from Hesston Oil?"

"The article says he's decided to retire after this incident. Indeed, I believe this incident has cleared the playing fields."

In the window's reflection, Christen caught the smile that flashed across Nadir's face. She longed to pull out her phone and start an Internet search.

"My father had a lunch appointment on the last day we were in Dar es Salaam, Tanzania. He was supposed to meet with three members of the Tanzanian Energy department." They were back to speaking in hushed tones. But the car wasn't that big. It wasn't like Christen couldn't hear – or they weren't being picked up on the audio-recording devices that both she and Johnna had on.

"Lunch?"

"It was a private, friendly get together. No official business was to be discussed."

Nadir gave a nod of understanding.

"My father was jumped by four men and saved by his security team."

Again, Nadir made a sweep of the car's occupants before responding. "Do you know the names of the men he was meeting with?"

"He's still trying to find the right players, the right pressure points," Karl said cryptically.

"Momo Burhan was not at that meeting, I can assure you," Nadir responded.

"How exactly do you know that?"

"He is dead."

"Momo's dead?" Karl leaned forward and twisted his body toward Nadir. "How? When? Wait, how do you know that?"

Nadir offered a closed-lipped smile and tipped his head back, considered Karl as he looked down his nose at him. "Sources," he said. "In terms of your ongoing negotiations, now that the eco-pawn is off the chessboard, we can get some work accomplished."

"The problem with the Bowmans, followed by the attack in Ngorongoro Crater, means that this region will be considered a hot spot. The men who come to work for us will want hazard pay. The cost of business will go up."

"Experts, yes. Of course, these incidents will also affect the local economy as tourism falls away, which means the locals will be desperate for new jobs, and their wages will plummet. It might end up that this works in your economic favor."

"Even if this is so, the businesses will have to be extremely lucrative to follow through," Karl said. "Our continued cooperation is the only way to make this happen. I'm glad you were able to join our little adventure. Thank you for coming."

Nadir touched his hand to his heart. "May we always be friends."

"I never wish us to be enemies." Karl touched his heart in return.

The Indian looked up from his phone. Glanced from Nadir to Karl and back again. "The price of helium is up considerably today. This is very bad news for me. Very bad, indeed."

LYNX

Friday, Panther Force War Room, Iniquus Headquarters

"HEY, WAKE THE HELL UP." Nutsbe had his hand on Lynx's shoulder.

"What?" Her eyes popped open as she was startled awake. Lynx cast her gaze around the room. Confused. Disoriented. "Oh, ha!" Lynx said as she realized she'd fallen asleep in front of the computer. She rubbed her hands over her face. "I'm glad you woke me. I was having a horrible dream."

"Yeah? No, shit. At first, I left you alone 'cause you were just kind of moaning, and I'd hate to wake you up if it was the good kinda dream."

Lynx wrinkled her nose. "Gosh, thanks."

"But when you flipped over to screaming "help!" I assumed you weren't enjoying a roll in the hay."

"Hardly." She tapped at the computer and stared at the screen. "I don't see a signal for the team's comms. The only thing up is GPS. Looks like they've landed in North Sumatra and are driving to their trailhead. Have you talked to anyone?"

"They're off comms right now. I can get them on a satellite phone in an emergency. That's what you were yelling about. Gator and Christen. Turned my damned spine into an icicle the way you said it."

Lynx rolled her lips in and tried not to show any emotion in front of Nutsbe. The stoicism that was part of the Strike Force DNA had a little glitch when it came to her genetic makeup. Lynx wore her heart on her sleeve. Though she tried hard to master her expressions, she wasn't very successful at it.

"That all sounded kinda woo-woo." He did jazz hands as he said it, huffing a strained chuckle like he was forcing it from a very small space. "I believe in it, though. My grandmother always knew when I was doing something bad when I was a kid. If I even started to do something I shouldn't, the phone would ring. Inevitably, it was Nan asking me what the hell I thought I was doing. Straight and narrow, it was for me. Yeah. She died just after I joined up." He sniffed hard. "When my transport got hit, I swear she was kneeling there beside me. She wasn't directing me to the light; she was yelling at me. Cussing me out." He winced and gave a kind of hiccup laugh. "She wasn't a cookie-baking grandma. She was more of the smokin' and boozin' kind." He shook a finger in the air and made his voice craggy. "'It is not your time, young man. Don't you even think about it. Get yourself out of this junk pile and get yourself moving to the north. Move it.' That vision saved my life. Everyone who was with me was dead. I was lying there in shock. I wouldn't have crawled off my X if it hadn't been for her. Wouldn't have gotten far enough away when the second RPG hit the wreckage." He spread his fingers wide and focused on the spaces between them.

Lynx knew this was an anxiety technique. Look and label what you see, move to the next open space. It helped switch the brain to the here and now when it wanted to go relive something horrible.

"Damned if the guy who picked me up didn't say that an old lady in a pink pantsuit had told him where to find me in the trees, but when he turned, she was gone. Why there would be a woman in pink pants in the middle of Afghanistan, he never seemed to question. He said he was afraid she'd set him up for an ambush, so they went in slow. He described her and everything. It was Nan. It was definitely Nan." Nutsbe was nodding at the wall as he told that story. A deep frown now pulled at the corners of his mouth. His eyes were red and moist. "She saved my life."

Lynx put her hand on his shoulder and let him collect himself from that memory.

When he finally turned, Lynx said. "I'm so glad she did. I'm so glad to know you."

"Don't know why I'm thinking about it." He tried to force his frown into a smile. "Funny, I haven't thought about it in a long time. Something about you saying Christen's name…the tone of voice. You're worried. Now, I'm worried."

"Weird dream – it seemed so real." She tried to brush the lingering sensations off. "If you hear from Gator or Blaze. I do need to talk to them, though."

"Sure, yeah, I'll pass that along."

Lynx picked up a pen and tapped it on the desk, thinking. "My mentor, Spyder McGraw, says there are no coincidences."

When Nutsbe looked her way, he'd wrestled his face back to neutral.

"The web of connections is actually small, he said. It's the whole Kevin Bacon distance game."

"I'm not following you, Lynx."

"My saying something in my sleep triggered a specific memory for you. If you follow Spyder's philosophy, then my dream of this specific thing triggered your specific memory. Your specific memory should inform my thoughts and actions."

"Okay, that's basic Carl Jung and the collective unconscious."

"Exactly. And what your story tells me is two-fold. One: Since you mentioned the way I said 'Christen' and you told your grandmother story, we take you out and put D-day in your place. That would tell us she needs to get out of there. She needs to get off her mark. Something bad is heading her way."

Nutsbe dropped his jaw and tilted his head back, thinking. "I can see that train of thought. But what would we communicate to the team? We can't pull Christen out of a mission without something solid."

"Yeah," Lynx grimaced. "I had a dream, and Nutsbe had a memory sounds—"

"Nuts."

"Amen."

"But you said two-fold." Nutsbe pointed out.

"That's the 'six degrees of separation from Kevin Bacon' game. Though, I'm not seeing six degrees. I see one, maybe two degrees of separation from Gregor Zoric. We just dealt with the Zoric family. First, in February with Lacey Stuart when the Zoric family was using her to raise money to fund terrorist groups. Second time they showed up on our screen was when they were implementing terror at Suz Malloy's elementary school and dragged her down to Paraguay. Does that seem like too big of a happenstance? And here they are again. The Zorics." Lynx scraped her teeth over her upper lip. "Feels that way to me, too big of a happenstance. I think this falls into the Jung theory – the same story told around the world." Her voice drifted off as she gazed at her lap, letting her thought percolate.

"I've got one to add to your theory."

Lynx turned curious eyes toward Nutsbe. "Shoot."

"On the voice recording, Nadir was talking about the Bowmans being saved and Derek Bowman retiring from Hesston Oil."

"Okay."

"Yeah, well, he was talking to Karl about Momo Bourhan."

"No kidding? Wow. In what context?"

"Karl was referring to the lunch meeting—the one where Gator and Blaze saved the day—Nadir was saying that Momo didn't go to a lunch meeting with William Davidson because he's dead."

"Yeah, he is." Honey had made sure of it in order to save Meg and the other scientists.

"Karl seemed to have the expectation that Momo would be there and was completely surprised by the news of his death."

"How would Nadir know Momo was dead? I don't think the Tanzanian government officially identified the terrorists yet."

"Karl asked the same thing – Nadir said, 'sources.' And then he said the eco-pawn is off the chessboard, we can get some work accomplished."

"Eco-pawn, that's not Momo. That's Derek Bowman and his retirement."

"That's how I read it. And now we have the confluence of the Zorics and Momo. What do they have in common?"

"Terror." She picked up her phone and pushed number four on her speed dial.

"Jack here."

"Lynx here. Two quick questions. Down in Paraguay, on your mission, you had an asset who gave up the name of the person who ordered the kidnapping of the children. Who was it?"

"That was the mutterings of a dying man, Lynx. You know how the brain functions when you're dying. It's not like in the movies where there's a moment of conviction, one last beautiful chance to right this life's wrongs. It's a muddled chemical mush."

"Still. Humor me."

"Gregor Zoric."

"And there was a code name that your prisoner gave up. The name of the guy who wanted a video of the boys, what was that name?"

"The Bear."

"K, thanks. Did I wake you?"

"I was just drifting off. Do you need me down there? Are you on Gregor Zoric's trail?" Jack sounded wide awake, champing at the bit.

"We have a Gregor Zoric on our radar screen. I'm compiling data. If I get anything interesting. I'll make sure you know. Thank you. Good night. Sorry to wake you." She tapped the phone off and took a moment to jot the information on her sheet. "You know what I need?"

Nutsbe pushed back in his seat. "Looks like you've got your nose to the ground. Warning though, this could be two different people. Several different people."

"Exactly. See?" She smiled. "Same wavelength. I need to talk to Steve Finley at the FBI."

"Meg's brother? You think she might be tied into this because of Momo's attack in Ngorongoro?"

"No, this doesn't have anything to do with Meg. We have two interesting ties here. Momo's name being on Nadir's lips and a member of the Zoric family. Steve Finley was investigating the

Zoric case. He's in the terror unit and may very well know who Gregor Zoric is and the role he might be playing in this bizarre weekend party." She pulled out her phone as she stood. "It's starting to feel a little bit like the set-up for a game of Clue."

"Well, if Miss Scarlet and Mrs. White were Johnna Red and Johnna White, you might be on to something. Hopefully with no body to be found in the parlor with a candlestick holder at the end of this."

"Amen to that. I'm going to head over to my office to call. I'll let you know if I come up with anything interesting."

"Cool. I'll work on the data that came in this morning from the team. See if anything else interesting happened on the way to the trailhead."

"THIS IS URGENT, but it's not an emergency," Lynx said into her phone as she walked into her Puzzle Room on the Strike Force corridor. "I can talk to you about this in the morning." She flicked on the lights and smiled over to her Dobermans, Beetle and Bella, curled up on their beds, watching her with uplifted brows.

"This is fine." Steve Finley said. "I may have to leap off at any second, though. We have an event playing out, and I'm waiting for an update. Until then, I was twiddling my thumbs."

Lynx sidled over to the other side of the room. She plopped down with the dogs. Beetle shifted until her head was in Lynx's lap, then rolled over until she was belly up. "Gregor Zoric," Lynx cut right to the chase. "What do you know about him?"

"Malicious asshole."

"Well," Lynx laughed. "That was succinct."

"He's got a starring role in the Zoric family. He's ingratiated himself with the Russian oligarchs. He likes to live large. He's a genius-level IQ, manipulative as hell, and he doesn't give a fu* – ehm fig about anyone but himself. His power. His money. His ego. He's also vicious and doesn't mind inflicting pain in any form or variety to get what he wants. He kills with the same emotional investment as I have when I blow my nose."

"Crap."

"You're not playing with Gregor, are you?" She heard him tapping at his computer keys. "I have him in Singapore, and you're calling me from D.C., so at least there's some space between you."

"My sources say he's in North Sumatra right now headed to William Davidson's private island, Davidson Realm."

"Where's that?"

"The west side of Sumatra in the international waters of the Indian Ocean. He's there for a business retreat."

"Interesting. Do you know the subject of the retreat?" Steve asked.

"First, Medved'. That ring a bell?"

"That's Gregor's nickname. It means the bear."

"Okay, next. The Levinski kids/Suz Molloy kidnapping in Paraguay. There was a player named the Bear who was on the other end of a satellite phone conversation when our operator Jack McCullen saved the hostages. There was also a man who was involved in Hezbollah financing, who was operating in Paraguay named Gregor Zoric" Lynx was met with a silence that felt thick with thought. She was on the right track. She knew it. "I know the FBI is investigating the Levinski kidnapping case. I know you are the Zoric expert. Can I send you a picture? Could you confirm if these three players: Gregor Zoric, who was mentioned as a financier, Medved', the bear, who was mentioned as part of the kidnapping plot, and this Gregor whom we're watching are actually the same player?"

Lynx was met with that thick silence again. She tapped her computer and sent the picture over to Steve. Lynx could hear the ping of his computer as the picture landed in his mailbox.

"I'm looking for a yes, or a no. In return, I'll give you a heads up on what he's up to in the Indian Ocean."

"Yes," he said.

"Yes…?"

"All three are the same. Now, why is he in your crosshairs?"

"Not cross-hairs. He's on my radar. Why? I don't know. He's the guest of William and Karl Davidson. The Davidsons were in Tanzania talking to the energy department just prior to this trip. Helium has come up as a possible subject matter."

Steve said nothing.

"My understanding is that Gregor has ties to Russian energy resources, and Davidson has energy contracts with the Russian government."

"Okay," Steve said, "and where does all that lead?"

"To crazy town. These are all just pieces in the puzzle: a little bit of blue seems to fit together with another piece that has some green. I have no idea what the picture looks like. I can say that if your description of Gregor Zoric is accurate, then he could easily manipulate the Davidson men. Blaze and Gator are saying the Davidson men are palpably narcissistic and greedy. Dangle a little cash, stroke their egos…"

"Helium. That's interesting, actually. I was talking to—" There was a knock at his door and a conversation that was muffled and unintelligible. Steve came back on the line. "That's me. I've got to go. I'll run this by some folks see if I can't dredge up something to help."

"Luck!" Lynx called as the line went dead.

26

GATOR

Friday, The Trailhead, North Sumatra

"IS IT SAFE HERE?" It was the Japanese guy, Taro Eto.

The group that held all the Davidson party-goers--except for Papa Bear Davidson—had all arrived on the same privately charted jet.

Then the group had split up, again.

After the men in the party had been bounced and jostled over the backroads to the trailhead and the sun had risen higher in the sky, several of their group had decided to stick with the driver and luggage as they headed down to the coastline. From there, the walk to the yacht mooring was a mere three kilometers. Daniel, the head of their security detail, had warned them that they could only offer these guys one bodyguard. The men seemed to think that was just fine.

Their expedition group was down to eight businessmen, two women, and four bodyguards – him, Blaze, Daniel, and Ralph.

They had a guide and a photographer, but how this photographer was going to take pictures of great men doing great things out here in the forest was beyond Gator.

These titans of industry already looked like they were melting, and that was the photoshoot of them smiling and waving as they got off the plane and loaded into their jeeps.

"I heard that there was unrest," the East Indian said. He seemed to know Taro - they grouped together frequently. Gator made sure to blink and take still-shots of them interacting.

"The bandits are near the orangutan sanctuary, in north," the guide said as if this should quell any concern.

"So it's safe here?" Taro pushed.

The guide shrugged. "Safe enough."

"*Enough*?" Taro turned to his friend. "What does that mean?"

Gator shook his head. They were barely into the tree line. This was gonna be fun.

The guide stopped and pointed at a leaf. The photographer hustled forward and took a picture.

"What is that?" Taro asked.

"They call it poison leech," the guide explained.

A poison leech. Gator made sure to get eyes on it, so he could recognize it along their walk.

Christen pulled her arms in tight to her chest. Their bodies brushed as she moved past Gator. He sucked in a breath to help him brace against the emotions raging through him at that moment. If he could just hold her to his heart, just for a moment, he might find some respite from the storm she'd kicked up in his system.

Nadir hustled toward the guide. "I want to see the orangutans in the wild. Is it possible that there are some that live in these trees?"

"Not here. North," the guide said.

At least he pointed due north when he said it. That gave Gator a little comfort that he knew where he was going. Gator had his GPS zipped into his thigh pocket. This trail was already in the downloadable maps – it wasn't like they were bushwhacking. It wasn't a wide, well-worn trail, but it was in pretty good condition.

"Where the bandits are?" Taro was asking.

Nervous little fucker.

"Yes," the guide replied patiently.

"Are we staying near here tonight?" Taro asked.

"Too dangerous at night. You go way out in the water for to be safe," the guide said.

Then they walked in silence.

About two kilometers in, Blaze asked if everyone was hydrating. They all wore backpacks with the survival ten. An emergency tent, fire-starting equipment, a space blanket...most importantly, everyone had a camelback water bladder and a hose to suck from. As Blaze asked the question, the hikers dutifully put their hoses in their mouths and took a few swallows.

"I'm going to keep reminding you," Blaze said. "In the humidity, your body has to work harder to cool you down. There's no evaporation to help you out. Drinking is very important."

Gregor, Karl, and Nadir had clustered together. Christen and Red had inserted themselves near their group. Gator walked just behind them. Taro and the Indian guy hiked right behind him budged up tight, sometimes stepping on his heels. Gator needed to get this Indian guy's name. He kept listening for it in conversations...Neither he nor Blaze was issued the usual headshots and roster of names at the beginning of the mission. It seemed Daniel liked to hold his cards tight to his chest. Odd. Unprofessional. But that had been Gator's take on the guy since he'd first seen him step out of the limo in Dar es Salaam.

"I knew this woman once," Red gave Christen a nudge and a significant look that was lost on Karl, Nadir, and Gregor.

Gator wanted Gregor to be nowhere near Christen, though he knew it was Christen and Red's job to get in close.

"She was a numbers cruncher at my office," Johnna said with a lazy tone of shooting the shit. "One day, I was in the break-room, and she was all done up, a fresh manicure, new highlights, new outfit. I asked if she was having a job interview or some-thing special that day, and she said she was celebrating. I asked what she was celebrating, and she said, 'water.'" Red picked up her hose, took a few swallows, then flipped the nozzle off and let it drop over her shoulder.

Christen caught Gator's gaze for a long moment. She murmured. "Well, that was an unexpected response. Water." Red put her hand on Christen's elbow and leaned in to whisper. "You have a little drool, just there on the side of your mouth." She wiggled her finger on the corner of her lips to indicate where.

"Funny," Christen said, and her face flamed pink. She sent an embarrassed glance his way, and Gator grinned in response.

Red had noticed that there were sparks flying, too. But then he remembered his talk with Lynx, and the grin fell off. This was no time for flirtin'. His practiced eye swept the foliage for any sign of danger.

"Seriously," Red kept talking as if nothing else were happen-ing. "She said she was crying into her pillow one night, stressed to the max because she couldn't make ends meet. She tried to figure out what she could change, so she had money in the bank at the end of the month, and she decided that one of the best things she could do for herself was to drink more water. And by that, I mean nothing else *ever*, only tap water."

"Water only?" Karl asked. "How in the world would that help anything? A good stiff drink might do her better."

"I can see that as a strategy," Christen said. "If she got a five-dollar coffee every morning, that's a hundred and fifty dollars a month right there. If she skipped a soda at lunch, say two dollars a day, that's another sixty bucks."

"Yup. And she didn't swerve even if someone else was buying, or it was there for free because she thought then she might just say, 'Well, I'll just have this one cocktail with my friends, I deserve it after a long day like today.'"

"Do the math," Christen said. "Two cocktails on a Friday night, two on a Saturday night. A bottle of wine to sip while cooking during the week that's another fifty bucks a week. She's up to four hundred and ten dollars. Add orange juice at breakfast and random other drinks... Yeah, I could see how she might be drinking down five or six thousand dollars a year."

"Exactly." Johnna took another sip of water and raised her chin toward Christen, reminding her to keep drinking. Christen took a few sips while Red continued. "That was what she calculated, but she said that the savings were more than that. When she stopped drinking alcohol, she stopped going out with her drinking pals, who talked each other into dinner out and getting the desert. When she stopped drinking alcohol, she stopped buying weed. No weed, no munchies, and no midnight calls to the pizza delivery guy."

Nadir had a bemused smile on his lips. Gregor was considering the women with a hard-calculating stare. Gator was worried that the women weren't pulling off their cover story and that Gregor might be guessing that these two fit, intelligent women weren't who they said they were.

"No bail money, no attorney and court fees," Christen said.

"I hadn't figured those numbers in." Red snapped a branch

and threw it out of the pathway. "When she stopped drinking the coffee, she stopped going to the coffee shop. She wasn't tempted by the smell of blueberry muffins. She said in the first month of drinking only water, she had an extra seven hundred dollars in the bank."

"No way," Karl said.

"Way. She also lost ten pounds without even trying. I couldn't tell the difference, but she could, and that's what counts. She spent some of that savings to reward herself, and now she's got some money in the bank and is much happier. Water can giveth, and water can taketh away, depending on her mood."

"Amen,," Christen said, then she twitched as if a shiver were running down her back.

After that, the walk was silent.

Blaze walked point up the path, with his GPS in hand, talking with the guide. Gator looked back to see Ralph behind his two timid shadows, then three other businessmen, and then Daniel was a speck in the distance taking up the rear. The farther they walked, the more their group was spreading out as those with more athletic ability kept a quicker pace. Gator didn't like that they were so far apart. But there was little he could do about it.

The heat was oppressive, and Gator noticed that almost everyone was wearing new footwear. He wondered if they had broken their boots in properly or if everyone was getting massive blisters. They weren't complaining, though. That was good.

"Drink," Blaze called.

27

GATOR

Friday, Rainforest, North Sumatra

THEY CAME AROUND A BEND, and the tree branches opened up. They found themselves in a massive clearing. Homes were built in neat rows and topped with boat-shaped roofs. It looked more like a shipyard than a village. As the group huddled around their guide, he described the architecture and how it served the villagers well during the rainy season. Many of the homes were hundreds of years old, he explained, and were still used by the same families today.

"Now, gentlemen." The guide failed to address the women, or maybe his English was poor enough that he thought that the term was inclusive. "I know you're here to take fabulous pictures. Mr. Davidson, your host, told me that he had planned to have you pictured with the orangutan. As this is not possible. I have produced an even better photographic opportunity for you." He sounded like a carnival huckster to Gator. "I will be introducing you to the village holy man. He is of the Christian faith, but as those who came before him, he blends his Christianity with the beliefs of his ancestors."

There was a general discomfort in the group. People shifted from foot to foot.

"Yes," he chuckled. "I see that you've been told that these villagers were once head hunters, and they ate their enemies. But thankfully, this is not on the menu today since you have provided your own caterer."

There was a bit of nervous laughter amongst the men.

"Today, we will meet with the holy man. He will prepare you, then we will walk on the burning embers! What wonderful pictures of you walking bravely across the hot coals!"

Hot coals. *What?*

"After this, we will show you our warriors as they dance and leap the boulder." He turned to Karl. "You say boulder?" He pointed to the large rock in the middle of the open space. It was about shoulder height to an average man.

"Boulder works," Karl said.

"And they will jump this for the video." He nodded at the photographer, who nodded in return. "Then you will leap over the boulder for photo opportunity. Before you leap, you eat. American chef is there behind the houses preparing your meal. All food you know and enjoy. I promise you, no cannibal meat." He grinned broadly as if this were a great joke.

No one in the party seemed to think it was funny.

A couple of them pulled out their phones to see if they had a signal and looked up at the cloud-covered sky.

The guide saw this and misinterpreted it. "Unusual day. The weather is changing. We think maybe a storm later. Not now, though. Tonight. This is new. This weather. Climate change."

That last bit didn't seem to go over well with these men.

They weren't in the business of worrying about climate change. They were—as far as Gator could tell—petroleum giants. Either producers or consumers.

The guide opened his hand toward the end of the row of houses and set off.

Gator was unsettled. There was a weird vibration about this place. He'd felt that way in some places in the Middle East. A shimmer of something. An accumulation of undefined energy. It raised his hackles. He sidled toward Blaze.

"They're going to walk on hot coals?" Blaze said under his breath. "We can't medevac out of here."

"My guess is one guy steps in, burns his foot, screams to high heaven, and there ain't no other takers on the opportunity. We have burn bandages enough for that in our first aid kits. We can take turns fireman carrying him outa here." His gaze scanned over the group. "Maybe we can get a little one to go first."

Blaze shifted his focus over to the group. "Keep Gregor away. I'm not sure how we'd wrangle him down a path." Blaze slapped a hand on Gator's shoulder. They moved behind the group where they were listening to the holy man explain his ancestral beliefs, his words being translated by their guide.

Gator moved into the woods and scanned for anything that needed his attention, lifting his feet high as he made his way through the foliage. Blaze stood to the side of their group and caught his eye. All was well there. Gator increased the distance and made another sweep.

When he got back to the group, they were seated on benches that had been carved out of logs and had been worn over time to a satin finish. The holy man raised his stick, and the sounds around them stopped. The birds, the insects, the frog calls stopped. What had been a loud buzz of ambient noise became eerily silent. Gator was instantly focused. This weren't normal.

The holy man called to the sky then threw fists full of herbs on the fire. A shower of sparks flew up, making everyone gasp. The photographer was snapping his pictures of the show. Gator caught Blaze's eye. Blaze gave him a one-sided smile. *Look at this show*, it said to Gator. But Gator was on alert. The bugs didn't stop humming all in accord for nothin'. He'd seen the power of magic on dark nights in the bayou where voodoo was a way of life. There was strength in this holy man's incantations.

Smoke billowed and cloaked their group. The air was still, and the humidity high. It held the thick cloud in place, stinging their eyes, making them cough.

More herbs, more sparks, more smiles on the faces of the group.

Even nervous-as-shit Taro was smiling.

The holy man stamped his walking stick into the ground three times and swirled his hand in the air as he called out what sounded to Gator's ear like an invocation. Gator watched as the faces of those around the fire slackened. He wondered what plants had been thrown on the flames. He sent a glance toward Blaze to get his gut check of the situation. Blaze was leaning back against the tree trunk, looking drunk on the experience.

Eyes shut.

The same slackness about his face.

Gator looked at the other two guards, the guide, and the photographer guy. They had succumbed to the smoke and the chant. Gator was the only one standing on his own two feet. The only one with his eyes open. He was afraid to step closer and breathe the fumes. He wondered if this was all part of the preparation for the fire walking. Truth be told, he didn't know what to make of this.

Whooeee, I have seen some strange Voodoo shit. But this

here takes the cake. His thoughts seemed to have physical density, and they wended their way over to the holy man.

The holy man turned toward Gator. And though his mouth didn't move, Gator heard, "Welcome."

Without forethought, Gator pressed his hands together over his heart and bowed.

"This is but a dream." The holy man held his arms wide. "We live through thousands of dreams in this life-time. We live through thousands of lives in our soul time. We enter one life with birth and return to the whole with death. As the water comes from the sea and falls again into the sea. From the sea. To the sea. Dreams of our lives are like our lives in one life."

The words were like a dance. A spell. They swirled around Gator. Making sense. Not making sense. Gator needed to make a sweep, needed to make sure the area remained safe. He needed to check pulse points and respiration on the group to make sure they were dealing okay with the drugs that filled the air. But he couldn't move from where he stood, his eyes locked on the holy man. Gator had never met anyone this powerful before. Formidable. Gator wasn't afraid. Perplexed? Yes. Curious? Definitely. But he felt nothing malevolent here.

"What brought you to this place at this time?" The question came on the wind moving from the holy man's mind to his. The man hadn't opened his mouth; he couldn't speak English if he did. But Gator knew the question was posed. It was the kind of question that Lynx would ask. She didn't believe that anything happened by chance. She thought that people moved in and out of our lives, purposefully. She'd say that Gator's being here now and having this experience now was a gift that would serve him. He could almost hear her whispering those words. But it was just the wind, he told himself.

Gator had no answer as to why he was in this place or why

this time. But it made perfect sense in the grand scheme of energetic shit-storm he'd been living through that this was happening. Why not throw a little shamanic-voodoo-Sumatran holy man hallucination into the mix? Man, Lynx was going to laugh when he told her about this.

The holy man rested both hands on his staff. "You have walked the Earth many lifetimes. You have been accompanied by two women. One is a woman who has fought beside you and been your bosom friend – I see her as a wild cat, her spirit animal. She is your great friend. And you think of her now."

Shit.

The holy man lifted his arm, the sun-faded red cloth of his cloak draped and rippled in the now turbulent air. "You came for her."

When he pointed to Christen, a dragon breathed fire through Gator's system.

This guy needed to drop his arm and leave Christen the hell out of this.

The holy man smiled. "This is the woman who has fought beside you and loved you in every lifetime. And always tragically. You recognized her immediately when she walked into the room. You claimed her as yours the second your eyes met. You knew you loved her when she touched your arm. And you felt the fear."

"Yes," he said it without words but knew the holy man heard him. Everything the man had said was true: How he felt. What happened in the hotel lobby.

"It clawed at your stomach. It felt like you could not survive it. It growled like a monster through your system."

"Yes." Gator wanted to take a step closer. To get between Christen and this man. Not out of fear but out of...habit. Huh. That was an odd thought. He really hadn't known Christen long enough to have developed a habit. Gator couldn't move, couldn't get off the X.

"I see your heart. You don't believe in a soul's journey. You think this is your one opportunity. One life and then the after-life, either heaven or hell."

"That was the way I was raised, yes, sir."

"I wish to help you to understand. Each lifetime is rolled one over the other. Many lifetimes, always the same. And this life-time, too, unless you decide to break the agreement."

"Whoa there, what agreement – an agreement I made in a different lifetime?" The holy man's words weren't the linear black and white kind Gator liked. They were swirls or color, and Gator was having trouble making sense of it all. "Sir, that's not what I believe happens. I don't believe in reincarnation. If that's what you're sayin' to me."

"You believe in the Ten Commandments, Thou shalt not kill?"

Gator said nothing.

"And yet you have, and you do, and you will kill. There are no stipulations in that commandment – it does not say thou shalt not kill unless your president requires it. Thou shalt not kill unless you are protecting someone else. It simply says thou shalt not kill, and so you have decided that within that law, there is room to maneuver. You believe in the commandment, and yet, you also know there is another reality. I am not asking you to change your belief system, but if you wish her to live, you must consider that there is more than meets the eye."

And with that, he slammed his rod into the ground, and the Earth shook beneath Gator's feet, the air ocellated.

"You are on a journey. Fly." Again, he raised his staff over his head and brought it down onto the ground with a bang that was too loud for wood against soil. The bang blew outward in circles like the blast from an IED shocking the air. It blew through Gator, breaking him into particles that hovered and crowded like a swarm of bees. Then he came back together. This must be a dream. Those herbs that guy was throwing on the fire must be some kind of powerful hallucinogenic.

In his drug-induced dream, Gator was at the gate of a castle, dressed in heavy armor. His horse snorted and stomped the ground beside him. "I *will* keep you safe," he promised the black-haired woman. She was tiny and delicate; her face was pale with fear. Though it looked nothing like Christen, this was Christen. She rose up on her toes and pressed a kiss against his lips, He desperately wanted to feel her in his arms, but the suit of armor made contact impossible.

"I will love you forever," she whispered, her eyes feverish with dread.

And with those words, the air spun, and Gator was watching —as if fast-forwarding through a film—a mighty battle where their forces were overcome, and he was taken prisoner.

The castle gate was breached. Before their eyes, the women and children were slaughtered. Gator opened his mouth to scream as he saw the broad sword slice through Christen's raven hair, her delicate neck. Gator fell to his knees in anguish.

Bang went the staff

Gator knelt on a pelt thrown on the dirt floor of a round hut. He was dipping a piece of leather into the herbed water and squeezing it in his fist. He pressed the tincture to a woman's head. Christen. She had the dark skin of an African woman, a flatter, wider face—the same feverish, frightened eyes.

"Don't leave me. Please don't leave me," Gator whispered, as her eyelids slid closed.

"I will love you forever," she whispered.

Gator was on his knees on the edge of the Sumatran rainforest, gasping at the pain that wracked his body as he realized that Christen, in that moment, had died. He wasn't sure he could endure this level of agony. His eyes sought those of the holy man, begging for relief. It was like nothing he'd ever experienced.

Nothing he could have even imagined.

The holy man banged his staff into the ground.

Gator crouched in the corner of the alley, his body shielding someone else's. Gator knew it was Christen without even seeing her. Her body trembled against his. The snarls and barks of the dogs echoed off the stone walls.

"Here they are. That's her. *Schnell!*"

Gator saw a man holding back his enraged German shepherds. Another man in an SS uniform stalked toward them. "Yes, here she is." He called over his shoulder. "The leader of the Resistance? If the resistance is made of such as you. We will have them all corralled by morning. It will be very hard to resist from where you're going. Stand up."

Gator pushed to his feet, pulling Christen up beside him, tucking her behind him though she didn't want him to. How could he protect her? How could he save her? The SS were soulless when it came to torturing their captives for information. Gator's eyes scanned the alleyway, up the walls to the roofline, looking for any route for her escape. Christen pulled him around to look him in the eye. "I'm sorry," she breathed out. She pressed a kiss onto his lips. Gator shook his head. *Don't say it. Please don't say it.*

"I will love you forever." She said it without emotion. It was matter of fact. It felt cold next to the heat of his horror. She turned and ran directly toward the SS officer. He lifted his sidearm and bang. Christen dropped. Dead.

Bang went the Shaman's rod.

Gator needed him to stop, for this to stop. All the agony over all these lives was churning through his system. It consumed him. Flooded his cells. Made them shriek with the pain of his losses.

Lynx help me – it was an involuntary cry of desperation as the wind picked up and the air wavered again to take him to a new scene.

They stood in front of a horse. Gator crouched, hands spread wide. He looked down at the rattler, coiled, noisily warning its intent to strike. "Don't move," he exhaled, trying not to disturb the air and rile the snake any more.

He raised his eyes to Christen, in her long dress and straw hat. As he did, her gaze met his. "I will love you—" and though he shook his head and waved off her words, she uttered them anyway—"forever."

There was a sudden movement - a blast—a scream. Gator turned to see Lynx rushing forward with a shotgun in her hand. The snake lay dead. Relief flooded Gator's body. "Thank you, thank you, thank you," he said until he saw Christen lying on the ground, her hand gripping her neck.

She'd been bit.

Lynx looked up. "I couldn't get to her. I'm so sorry." She raised her gun. "Don't move. Behind you," she yelled. Bang went the shotgun.

Bang went the rod.

How long was this going to go on? Surely, that was enough. He saw the pattern. He got the message. Let this end.

"Lynx," Gator hollered. He lay on the precipice, his right arm over the edge. He gripped a wrist. He knew it was Christen. He knew that the ground had given way. Lynx ran forward and grabbed at his belt, held him steady, kept him from sliding forward. They were stuck there. Gator could not make any move that didn't make the ground under him crackle, and the rocks slide. He couldn't haul Christen up. He couldn't let her go. And Lynx couldn't let go of his belt, or he'd just slide over the edge. They were at an impasse.

Had been an impasse for a long time.

They panted and exerted. Every once in a while, one of them called out for help. The ligaments and sinew of Gator's shoulder were giving way. He felt them tearing. Extraordinary pain shot up his arm, begging him to release his hand and find relief. But Christen was hanging there, her feet dangling mid-air. If he released her wrist, she would fall to her death. A scream of anguish ripped from his throat. This was agony. This was torture. Stalemated, he tried again to flex what was left of his muscles and bring her up. As he did, more of the cliffside slipped away.

"Let go," she called as her fingers released from his wrist. "Let me go. It's okay."

"No!" he bellowed.

Lynx grabbed tighter to his belt and tried to crawl backward. Her heels dug into the friable dirt.

"Let me go. It's okay. This will not end my love for you. I will love you forever."

He felt her fingers slide from his hand.

And she was gone.

And he was nothing.

Not a sensation. Not a body. Not a thought, nor care, nor a soul.

He was absolutely *nothing* without her.

Gator managed to lock his eyes on the holy man. "Let me go. Stop this. I can't…" he whispered. "I understand."

The holy man was a statue. Still. Silent. Unconvinced.

"The cycle has to be broken," Gator panted out. "We found each other again. Even my friend Lynx can't save us from…*this*, no matter how hard she'd try. No matter how hard I'd try. I've felt this from the beginning. From seeing her walk through the door. My connection. The depth of my love. I knew it was too good to be true. I get it." Gator climbed back to his feet. He stood like a soldier. "I'm on this mission for a few more days, sir."

The holy man cast his gaze toward Christen in her trance. Gator wished this was just a bad trip on some exotic smoke. But it all rang true. From Tanzania until now, this all made sense to him.

"Please. I can't leave this assignment for a few more days. Then I'll never see her again. Never talk to her again. She doesn't love me. She's never said a word to me outside of my role on her security team. I'll leave. I'll be out of her life. I'll make sure of it." He'd seen Christen looking at him, the feelings that swirled through his own system: curiosity, confusion, a connection had been reflected back at him when he'd caught her gaze. He had to go before she gave voice to those feelings. Gator knew he could never tell her how he felt. And he knew as sure as he knew the sun would set and night would fall, that she was the only one for him. He'd walk the rest of this life alone. "Can you help her? Help her stay safe through these next few days until I can go?" It was a huge price to pay, to leave her, to never see her again. But Gator was willing to pay any price to protect Christen.

As those thoughts formed, the holy man slammed his stick into the ground.

All eyes blinked open. Gator stood under the tree.

Shell-shocked.

Bereaved.

Determined.

28

CHRISTEN

Friday, The Rainforest, North Sumatra

FROM HER PLACE on the log between Taro and Karl, Christen watched the dance of sunlight filtering through green leaves. She felt the oppressive heat, the weight of the humidity. She had been floating in perfection, and coming back into her body–so to speak—made her hyper-aware of the heaviness of the air as it pushed and pressed against her.

The first thing she did once her vision cleared was search out Gator.

He stood with a look on his face that she instantly recognized. This was the combat-ready face, the ready to go, ready to fight, ready to die look of her customers when she taxied them to their missions. It was the look T-Rex wore when she lifted up into the Syrian air, leaving him behind to face the onslaught.

She shifted to follow Gator's line of sight. His focus was on the holy man. She turned to see what Blaze was doing. Did he sense a threat, too? Blaze and Gator seemed to go together like battle buddies. They seemed separate and apart from Daniel and the others.

Blaze seemed fine. There was no strain of muscle under his skin. Blaze turned to catch her eye, and she, in turn, tipped her head toward Gator. Maybe Blaze needed a heads-up that something wasn't right.

Blaze made his way around the periphery to whisper in Gator's ear.

The others in their party were coming to.

Karl looked like he'd been sucking lemons. Something about his trance-journey must not have gone so well for him.

The guide moved into the clearing. "All is well? Come come. We will take a walk through the fire."

The group stood and jostled hesitantly after him, pooling up like a school of fish – not a one of them wanted to take the lead. They came to a picturesque clearing just to the side and behind one of the houses. An ancient mound of craniums formed a macabre wall on the edge of the rainforest. In front of the wall was a long pit filled with coals. Reds and oranges glowed from the embers. Flashes of yellow as a flame–here then there—gathered enough fuel to lick at the air that wavered with heat.

"You are little lady," the guide said to her. "You show big manly men how this is done."

Christen wasn't interested. There was no way in this world she was going to walk through a pit of burning coals. He took her gently by the arm and lead her over to a place at the top of the fire pit. She was willing to walk over and give it a closer look, but that was about it. Christen could feel Gator swelling in size—as if he wasn't a giant of a man already. She could feel his agitation. When the guide stopped, Christen had to hold back the laughter.

"Okay, sure," she said. "I'll walk on your coals." She plopped down on the ground and pulled off her boots and socks, rolled up her pants to the knees. Christen saw out of the corner of her eye as Gator sent a command to Johnna. A special forces trick of speaking without speaking. Johnna nodded and scurried over to her as Christen stood.

Johnna got to her side just before Christen took the first step, looked down, and saw the truth. The ground was uneven. There was a slight hill of embers that hid the fact that there was a dirt path down the center of the pit. If you didn't fall, you wouldn't be burned.

Johnna gave Christen a dramatic hug and good-luck, then stepped back.

Gator was outraged.

It was kind of comical.

The photographer lay on the ground where he was sure to get a shot that looked exactly like she was walking on coals. As she started across, Gator raced for the other end. Christen guessed it was to grab her up when her feet caught fire. When he saw the path, he leaned over and put his hands on his knees, panting.

Christen walked slowly, her eyes only half-opened, as if in a trance – the other men still hadn't figured out the optical illusion. She wanted to see if any of them would pee themselves, thinking they'd have to man up and do this. *Karl, I'm thinking of you, asswipe.* As she emerged from the other side. Gator shook his head at her and stood. She held up her hands like a gymnast taking in the cheering crowds, turned, and waved, then dropped her hands and loped off to get her shoes and socks.

Johnna was next, and then the men. Having the women go first meant that they'd either have to participate or look like a wimp in front of the others.

Not a one of those who walked down the path gave any indication to the others that it was safe and painless. One guy, Nadir, even got up on his toes about midway through and started yelling, "Yowch. Yowch. Ayah!" as he hopped and skipped all the way to the end. That stoked Taro but good. The last one to go, he was a quivering mass of jelly by the time he got to his turn. Christen thought he might start crying with relief when he saw the clear pathway.

Lunch was next, and it was light and refreshing with succulent fruits and salty foods to help them endure the heat. Gator stood at the periphery – feet set wide, his arms crossed over his chest, hawk-eyed as he watched, making sure they were secure. But he hadn't caught her eye since she was on the firewalk.

She wondered if she'd pissed him off.

A mother approached Gator with a crying baby and was talking to him, trying to hand him the infant.

Gator signaled the guide over.

Christen scooted closer so she could hear what was going on.

"Mother wants son to be a strong warrior. She ask you to bless the child."

"What?" Gator's brows drew together, his hands up, he took a step back as if to give himself some room to understand the situation.

"Bless the child. Take him from her hands and blow on his face to offer the spirit of the warrior."

Gator looked so utterly self-conscious and bashful. The villagers paused what they were doing to watch. They probably thought this was an honor for him, a distinction, but Gator turned pink with modest embarrassment. So damned cute.

The holy man came and put his hand on the mother's shoulder. Christen could see that Gator couldn't think of a way out of this scenario that wasn't offensive. Gator smiled at the mother and gently gathered the baby. Tucking the infant into the crook of his arm, Gator rubbed the little guy's tummy and talked to him with a melodic tone. His Cajun accent was thicker than usual, blending French and English words. The baby hushed and stared back at Gator. Then Gator lifted the baby and lay him over his massive shoulder. The baby wriggled over until he found a spot where he was pressed against Gator's neck and sucked on its fist as he shut his eyes. One massive hand covered the tiny bottom, keeping him in place.

The mother smiled widely, nodding, and bowing her pleasure. When she scooted away, the holy man indicated a place on the bench. Gator swung his head and checked three-sixty before he sat down. The mother came back with a lunch plate for Gator and bowed as she handed it to him.

Gator ate one-handed. His energy had shifted.

The baby had soothed him.

Whatever was riling him up after their meditation had now eased its sharpness, and Gator looked like Gator again. A little smile playing across his lips as he took a bite of panini.

Christen tilted her head as she watched, thinking, he looks like a dad.

I wonder if he has kids. I bet he's great with them if he does.

Johnna kicked Christen's boot, "Stop gawking. Eat your lunch."

THE SHOW that the village men put on after they ate was a wild display of ancient dance moves designed to develop endurance and strength. The young warriors in their loincloths and brightly colored beads lined up and ran at the boulder, leaping it and landing in a sandpit that protected their legs and ankles. Christen itched to try it., The boulder was kind of high to get over without touching it like, a gymnastic vaulting horse, but she thought she could do it.

True to the guide's earlier explanation, they had another photo op – again, it was contrived for excellent photos. The reality was, they'd pushed a platform up to the boulder, and the men weren't actually leaping the stone as much as they were jumping down into the sandpit. Christen demurred. That wasn't any fun.

The hike out, following the festivities, found a whole lot less grumbling under the breath. The men were obviously tired, but they seemed to have had a good time. And they had delighted on seeing how brave and strong they looked in the images the photographer had scrolled through for them to review.

Christen saw this day for what it was. A shared experience where they'd felt a little fear, had a laugh, had an adventure, struggled together. It was the kind of thing that corporate boards liked to do to make the team cohesive before they sat down and hashed through a mutual issue. Negotiations were much more successful once you see each other as comrades and allies instead of stiff-shirted individuals fighting for personal goals. Now, Christen thought, these men would start opening up and sharing. Now, the quiet conversations would be of the most interest to the US government. And they were talking. Unlike earlier that day, when everyone sort of grumped down the trail, silently suffering.

The Daniel guy had taken point. Three men then Blaze. She was in the group with Gregor Zoric, and he was talking to the man from Saudi Arabia and the one from Qatar. They were aware that she was near, and they had switched to Arabic to exclude her from their conversation. Christen spoke Arabic. Not perfect Arabic, but she read the papers and listened to the news every day – if they spoke in metaphors, she'd be lost, but if they were using basic language, she could follow along just fine. And it really didn't matter either way. This was all getting sent back to Nutsbe and the US government, and they'd get it translated easily enough.

This spy stuff was boring.

Christen glanced back over the line of people. Johnna was walking near another group that included Karl, and Christen knew that she was there to pick up that conversation. Then a few more of their group walked with the other guard, Ralph, and somewhere at the back, where she couldn't see him, Gator was the caboose. Christen felt antsy that she didn't have him in sight. She hadn't seen him since he'd handed off the baby to the grateful mother when the infant woke and was hungry.

Christen thought he looked sad when his baby fix was over.

The softy.

She smiled to herself as she walked along.

She only kept a light attention on the topic du jour. Qatar was not producing their own food. A closed border between Saudi Arabia and Qatar was causing hardship for the Qatari people who needed access to food. That was problematic. It put pressure on at home. They talked about scuba gear and satellites and the use of helium...how dependent the modern world was on the supply.

They took a few steps in silence, then Nadir turned to Gregor. "The sanctions bill died in the US Senate committee, as we knew it would after we lost our leverage. I'm not sure how to work around this obstacle. But we'll have to find a way."

"Yes," Gregor said. "A very surprising turn of events. If my instructions had been followed to the letter, all would have gone as planned. The persons who made the decisions to kidnap the young teacher from Maryland have been punished. Properly. Everyone has been reminded that they will act in concert with my wishes." A few more silent steps, then under his breath, "I will think this through." Louder, "I have the means of acquiring a new person to take the place as head of the Senate committee. If we all agree that that is the step that needs to be taken, my people can have the barrier removed from the stage. A new committee leader might then bring up the legislation for consideration once again. We could see how much pressure we can put in place. The Russian government has a deep file of kompromat to assist us."

Kompromat was a Russian word, not Arabic. The whole conversation was cryptic as hell. At least to her. Gregor wasn't a fabulous Arabic speaker - his verb conjugations and his noun pronunciations needed work. She was picking up a good fifty percent of what she thought he was saying. Happily, someone else was tasked with unraveling that puzzle of information. Other than recording that last bit of conversation, Christen couldn't figure out why she was here. The other stuff about Qatar's food problem and the pressures between the Qatari and Saudi border was reported in the newspapers; the information everyone who cared to know knew.

The men walked along silently when suddenly Gregor said something that loosely translated to," If we're going to make this work, we'll need a new Momo."

That got her attention, but she tried to be a good spy and go along looking at her surroundings as if she couldn't care less what they were saying.

He tapped the elbow of the Saudi guy. "Do you know someone who has a team to get the job done?"

"Properly?" Nadir added. "Momo's activities failed three times in a row. He was not the professional he led us to believe he was."

Well, now the guy is supposed to be dead, so it was a little late to place blame, Christen thought. She wondered what country a name like Momo came from.

"I do. I'll handle it," the Saudi replied.

Christen wondered what job they needed filling that would be shared amongst the three. She wasn't deeply curious. On the surface, this conversation was dull. Really, Christen couldn't even conjure a scenario where any of this was relevant.

Lula was definitely wrong about asking her to think about a possible career change. Christen was a pilot, full stop. She'd leave this kind of day to people like Johnna and Lula.

The only bright spot in this whole crappity mission was that she'd met Gator.

Finally.

29

CHRISTEN

Friday, The water's edge, North Sumatra

"I'M GETTING an eye tic from this damned contact lens," Christen told the water as it lapped at the rock under her feet. They had reached the shore, and she was waiting for her turn to be shuttled to the yacht. The crew stood on the deck, holding a salute, in their snazzy white uniforms. The water was choppy and dark. Ominous clouds continued to gather. Maybe on the other side of the islands, they'd find a little sun. If she had to be here, she might as well have a little fun surfing. Then she reminded herself that Nutsbe had said not to go into the water and lose the bajillion dollar contact lens.

Gator had been with the first group that was ferried over to the yacht. Once he clambered on board, she could vaguely see that he was conferring with the security guard who had escorted the wimpy guys directly to the boat. Probably counting heads…

"Parts of this job suck," Johnna said under her breath as she fanned herself with her hand.

"Parts?"

"Different strokes for different folks." They were standing well away from any listening ears. "While we're boarding and getting settled, our team will be quietly placing listening equipment around in the various cabins and public areas. The comms will pick up the conversations and store or transfer them, depending on the satellite connection."

"Won't that be a great big mess?"

"Each device is set to a different frequency, so they're not all on the same channel. The software can clear out auditory debris, waves, wind, what have you. You could cut down on some of that by not sighing so loudly and lessening the mumbling under your breath part."

"I am not doing that," Christen said. "Okay, I'm not doing it that much."

Johnna smiled. "Hang in there. We're two days down, three days to go. When the party breaks up, you'll be back to your unit."

"Thank god."

"I got in touch with Grey. Thank you, by the way, for what you did to save him. That was some damned miraculous air artistry."

Christen froze. Was Grey able to pass on some intel?

" I told him you were agitated and distracted by the mission you left incomplete."

Christen reached out and gripped Johnna's arm.

"He said they had to explode the Black Hawk, but everyone got pulled out of the hills. Two wounded, neither of those operators were at risk of life or limb."

"And my guys?"

"Smitty and Prominator had some wounds from the crash. Other than that, they're fine. Now, I want you to focus. The boat is a nice tight space. We like that. We want to make sure to see who talks to whom and for how long. Eyes open and recording. If you think they're in a space where they won't be recorded, try to hang out there. If you think your presence is causing an issue, leave your phone behind and go elsewhere. Okay?"

"Got it."

"Good. We're up." Johnna smiled and walked toward the dingy, accepting Blaze's hand as she stepped in.

AFTER CHANGING into a bikini top and a sarong skirt, Christen rejoined the party having their well-deserved celebratory cocktails on the deck. They'd made it through the day. Christen wanted a cocktail, but Johnna had caught her eye and given a slight shake of her head. Christen opted for Perrier and lemon.

She sat down next to Nadir. He was young and looked intelligent. Possibly, he was educated in America, which would make him more open to speaking with a stranger. Christen hoped she could start a conversation with him about what his role was in the group.

"That's an odd place to get a burn," Karl said.

Christen looked down at the white blister that was exposed when the fabric of her wrap slipped to the side. "Occupational hazard."

"You're an artist?" Nadir asked. His gaze fastened on the burn, then they slid up a few inches toward her crotch—*obviously a gentleman of the first caliber.*

She flipped the fabric to better cover herself and said, "I try to be anyway." Normally, she'd move away from a creeper like that. She knew Johnna would think this kind of attention was a win and would milk it for all it was worth. Christen didn't have milking skills. She had shooting skills, though.

"Look!" Taro yelled. He gripped the railing and leaned forward. He was the only one wearing a life vest. "I told you so," he said as he scanned behind him until he found Nadir. "Here, look."

The group moved over to the rail to see what had excited Taro. "Those are sea wasp. See the color? See the boxed shape? See how long the tentacle?"

Karl said, "Aren't you allergic to jellyfish?" and then he grabbed her arm and gave a kind of push-pull to frighten her into thinking she was going over. But as soon as he gripped her arm, her reflex had her grabbing his thumb and twisting it until she had control of his body. This told her that her subconscious still recognized Karl as the enemy of her childhood – the one who enjoyed tormenting her.

And what it told the others who gawked at her move was that she had other skills than folding paper.

Shit.

"You did it!" Johnna laughed and clapped her hands. "Awesome!" She slid over to put her hand on Christen's so Christen would release her grip on Karl. "That totally worked! And we just saw that on the YouTube video. How cool is that?"

"Pretty cool," Christen forced a plastic grin and high fived Johnna.

Attention went back to watching the sea wasps. They were beautiful as they floated about. There was death surrounding their boat. Well, at least she was safe and sound on board.

The captain ahem-ed. "Ladies and gentlemen. I am Captain Baluk. We are now underway toward the island for your swimming and surfing pleasure. The string of islands off the coast of

Sumatra means there is very little wave action here on the mainland. We must round the islands to reach the Indian ocean, and there, there are some spectacular waves. These waves are considered some of the best in the world of surfing because of the good barrel and a right-handed break."

"What's that, the right-handed break?" Nadir asked.

"If I'm surfing with my left foot forward on a right-hander, I'm facing the wave," Christen said, and he nodded his understanding.

"This evening, we will anchor off the coast of our destination," The captain was saying. "You will eat dinner under the stars. And tomorrow will be your day to enjoy the beach. Hopefully, there will be a shift in the weather, and you will have sunshine. While you sleep tomorrow night, we will continue on to Davidson Realm, where you will disembark for brunch. Please let me or the staff know if you have any needs. And if it is in my power, I will see it done."

There was a general murmur of thank yous, The captain bowed and left.

Christen looked up at the sky. She'd been reading weather by observation for decades. This didn't look promising to her. She'd lay good money that by tonight it would be raining hard. Probably all through tomorrow as well. And while conversations would be easier to catch in the confines of the yacht's interior versus the mansion and garden grounds, they should probably skip the day of surf and sand and head back to her dad's island. But then again, that might just be wishful thinking about the rain. She wanted to be one step closer to ridding herself of her cloak and dagger.

30

CHRISTEN

Friday, The Davidson Yacht

"A DANGEROUS DARKENING of the heavens, a sudden hush of the hustle that made life tick; the boats swung drunkenly at their moorings with the crouching breeze stalking its quarry... Then the mighty drums rolled, the boys with their sticks and their bright rat-a-tat-tat, the sound of a thousand heels stomping against the over-pressed earth. The whinny of the horse, the cracking whip of light against the dark, and the gods lifting their fists with a Huzzah! resounding across the hills and echoing long like the moan of a child lost in the shadow of his dreams."

Christen stepped toward the yacht railing and lifted her face to see Gator's eyes. His far-away look reached out over the water. She wondered if he even knew he'd said that aloud or realized she was there. Christen didn't know him as anything other than the affable and capable Marine who watched her back for the last two days. But even still, she could feel that something about the water and sky had gripped him. His face was stone.

"That was Erwin Prath," she said, her tone soft so as not to startle him.

He dragged his attention from the horizon and focused stormy eyes on her. Just that morning, they were warm and laughing. Yes, something had profoundly changed throughout the day.

"Ma'am?"

"You were quoting from the Erwin Prath essay "The End of Days." I can't recite it, but I recognized it."

He'd shifted back to himself, earnest and intelligent. He sent her a smile that made her think the word "wistful," but with an underlying cord of determination, preparation, a girding of the loins, a man ready for battle. Christen looked out over the waters. A storm was brewing, but it seemed to Christen that he'd carried that look in his eye since they'd been in the village. What had changed?

"I was born in a little Cajun cabin on the bayou in Louisiana. It was built by hand by my great grandfather. Water was our life. I could swim long before I could walk. In that house, we were a passel of kids nestled together like a litter of puppies. At night, my mama would read to us. Essays and stories, but mostly poetry because she wanted some peace, and she tried to bore us to sleep." His sweet smile burst into a momentary grin then slid away. "That one I was remembering was one of her favorites."

Christen wanted it back, that grin.

Wanted a moment of happy.

She had seen something in his eyes while he gazed out over the electrified night that made her tremble.

The coming storm.

She remembered the day she'd looked out of the bug-eyed

bubble of her helicopter and seen a desert haboob—the massive storms of dirt, a blinding blizzard of debris—stampede its way toward her. She was charged with the safety of the mission. She'd flown as fast as her Little Bird would take her in the opposite direction, the customers laughing and oblivious in the back. But she knew the storm, like a giant monster, crawled hungrily forward, ever closer, gnashing its teeth. It could very well mean death.

She struggled away from the feeling of foreboding.

"Five children all told?" she asked, reaching for banality, something that didn't make her feel like the world would suddenly implode. Christen hated the feeling of being out of control. She trained her whole life for not just command of the situation but micro-precision. In her gymnastics, in her flying, in her military career. Precision. Control. Here on the water, she felt as minuscule as a star in the far distant heavens with no ability at all to influence their situation.

"Yes, ma'am, three boys, me and the twins, were the filling in the sandwich with sisters on either side."

"You were kidding about their names. Your sisters Medic and Seren."

His lips quirked up. "Yes, ma'am. My sisters are Genevieve and Auralia."

"Your last name isn't really Aid."

"No, ma'am. My name is Jean-Marie Rochambeau. Direct descendent of Jean-Baptiste Comte de Rochambeau. My mama, she said we were of noble birth - kings of our destinies." He stopped and pursed his lips. His gaze became turbulent again.

"I studied about him in history class, your ancestor. A French General who arrived in the American Revolution with enough troops that he helped to defeat the British at Yorktown. Without him, we may not be our own country. We might well still be part of the British Empire."

"Yeah, he done good." Gator reached out and lightly touched her shoulder, let his finger trail slowly down her arm, and slipped his hand around hers. He visibly swallowed.

"It's going to get bad, isn't it?" Christen asked, pulling her gaze from his to look out over the water then back again.

He nodded.

"The captain said he turned around. Do you think we'll make it back to dad's island before it really gets blowing?" She thought again of her little helicopter and how she pressed to stay just ahead of the haboob, landing, jumping out into the debris that abraded her skin, despite her flight suit. She remembered not being able to move forward against its wrath to get to the buildings at the FOB and possible safety. She lay on her stomach, trying to lizard-crawl forward. Her clients, the two SEALS, grabbed her arms on either side and dragged her up. Their heads hunkered together, pressing in to shield her, the men muscled their way through the door. Once inside, Christen dropped to the ground, spent from the effort. The men had their hands on their knees, gulping at the air.

"Thank you, ma'am," one had huffed out.

"Teamwork," she'd said. She was equally indebted to them for getting everyone to safety.

"We still have some time," Gator said. "I talked to the crew. They're full steam ahead. It was a shame that that decision was made so late. We're backtracking now, trying to get back around to the other side of this island. That might be a little calmer. The captain's not heading for your father's island. He's heading slightly southwest of here toward the mainland. He said there's a port he thinks he can make. If the captain aimed for your father's island, it would move us into the storm, not out. He's radioed ahead. The harbor knows we're coming and will make accommodations for us."

"We still have a radio signal then?" She turned her hand and laced her fingers with his and stepped closer, so their bodies aligned. There was peace in their physical connection. She felt perfectly at home standing like this.

He brushed his thumb down the side of her face. Caught in under her chin and tipped her head back. Christen thought he was going to kiss her. She was surprised and pretty darned disappointed when he let his hand drop and stopped himself.

"The mainland has us on radar," he said. "They're tracking our progress. Headquarters has us on satellite, but we don't think that will hold. I know you'll probably feel better when you have the control stick in your hand, but the captain seems to be competent." He unlaced his fingers from hers. But he didn't move away.

Christen pulled her brow together. "You know what I do?"

"That you're a Night Stalker? Yes, ma'am. My buddies Nutsbe Crushed and Honey Honig speak highly of you."

Ah hah! Interesting. "You're an Iniquus operator?" Iniquus was based out of D.C. D.C. was only an hour and a half non-stop flight from Nashville. That wasn't an insurmountable distance. They could see each other when she was back at Fort Campbell.

"Yes, ma'am."

"And you signed on with my father?" Christen forced herself to shift gears. She looked at her feet, processing. He and Blaze must be the other two in their group of five. She wondered how the CIA had finagled them onto her father's employment sheet.

How had they won such admiration from a man, who wasn't exactly known for handing out approbation like bonbons?

How had they won the appreciation that her dad obviously felt?

Huh, a mystery.

And here, Christen had assumed that the other two CIA offi- cers were lurking in the shadows, play-acting at being fellow tourists or perhaps had dressed in staffing uniforms and blended.

"Yes, ma'am, just for this trip. Mr. Davidson needed extra security when you and your friends joined the party."

"I wish you would stop calling me ma'am."

"Yes, ma'am. Protocol."

She nodded.

It meant that there were space and discipline between them.

It was militarily correct.

And probably why he'd stopped himself from following through with that kiss. He was contracted and on duty, and that would be a breach of ethics. And Iniquus operators had a golden reputation for high ethics.

Three more days and they could do what they wanted.

Right now, she wanted to put her cheek against Gator's chest and hear his heartbeat. She knew it was racing. She knew he was mastering adrenaline in his system. She was anyway.

That sense of foreboding.

And the sense of discovery.

Of new lo—

"Christen?" Johnna called.

Gator tap-tapped Christen's back, a release signal as he stepped away from their private bubble. She was bereft at the loss of his touch.

"Christen? Ah. There you are. Cook says the food is ready. Everyone should eat now." Johnna arrived at her side. "Oh, hey, Gator." She sent Christen a side grimace with a "Whoops – sorry to interrupt" dip to her lower lip. "Cook says the storm's going to be brutal – well, he said there's a 'difficult weather cell' moving into our area. He says he won't be able to fix a sit-down meal after this. But if we should grow hungry, he has sandwiches and fruit in the cooler. He didn't look too confident that any of us would want to eat, though. And they're taping barf bags every couple of feet around the interior. I imagine a bout of seasickness in my near future." She turned to Gator. "Do you have any information?"

"Iniquus says the storm formed out of nowhere. It's big and fierce. The captain's aiming for a mainland dock, away from the worst of it. It could be that we can out run it or at least stay out of the main path."

"You don't sound confident."

"I think you need to be prepared for a difficult time, ma'am. The good points are: we're in a yacht of substantial size and power. The captain is used to these waters and has been piloting for decades. And he's as invested as we are in getting to safety."

"That pep talk was awe-inspiring," Johnna deadpanned. "Especially that last sentence."

"Ma'am, I sugar-coated it as best I could while still giving you the information you need."

"That was sugar-coating it?" Johnna's eyes stretched wide. "Shit!"

31

GATOR

Friday, The Davidson Yacht

CHRISTEN DIDN'T LIKE him calling her ma'am. There was no help for that. He had to keep his distance. Before, it was for professional reasons, and now? It might help safeguard her.

Gator was aware that he hadn't called her Christen and promised himself he wouldn't. Christen sounded soft, like a lullaby being hummed and carried away on the summer breeze. Christen was the woman he longed to wrap in his arms and hold against his heart. The woman he wanted to talk to and hear about her life, learn her stories, to tease and tickle, and watch her graceful movements that hid her physical strength. D-day was the warrior who'd come to do her duty. And that was the aspect of her he needed to focus on. Professional and distant.

He'd messed up. Bad. He'd shared personal stories with her, reached for her hand. Let their bodies touch. Damned near kissed her. It set a craving burning through his system.

Catastrophic.

It felt like Katrina on the bayou. He was fifteen years old and biding his time before he could sign with the Marines following in his dad's footsteps into the military when that storm ripped his childhood home from its foundation and tossed it end over end. When the family was finally allowed to return, they'd found it in splinters. It broke his heart to see his mama kneeling in the still damp dirt, hugging a weather-beaten picture of his dad to her chest, the one that was took just before Dad was killed in Iraq. It felt like a miracle to have found it. There wasn't really a whole lot more of anything to find in the debris. There weren't nothin' left from his childhood but the memories he carried with him.

Once Gator became an Iniquus operator and was making good money, he had tried to rebuild what his family had lost. His mama had bought a trailer home, so she could live on the family land. He'd replaced it with a house that was classified to withstand a category five sustained hurricane, had it constructed up on stilts to allow for storm surge. It was modern and beautiful. He wanted to take pride in it. But it weren't the same as their little hand-hewn cabin had been. It lacked a story.

He'd made sure his mama had everything she'd need. All the bells and whistles that might make life easier as her kids all went off to live their lives. Only Auralia, the baby, was still living with her. His mama was proud and grateful, but Gator knew in her heart what she wanted was her old life back. And that, Gator couldn't do nothin' about. She'd was born and raised in a house where her kids were born and raised, and now it was gone. Nothing would be the same again.

Christen was his Katrina. She blew into his life. Upended him. And for the rest of his days, he'd deal with the aftermath and loss.

"There you are," Blaze said. "They've finished eating. The crew's getting everything locked down."

"I just checked in with the captain. It gets rough from here. We have about five more minutes, then everyone needs to be wedged in their bunks with a life preserver and all the pillows we can find." Gator spread his legs until his feet touched either side of the walls here in the hallway of the upper level, his hands pressing out, braced. "What's going on below?"

"Life vests were distributed. We asked everyone to leave their rooms unlocked so we can get to them if there's a problem. Karl had some anti-nausea meds that he distributed. He's suggesting that the staff not take them because they can be sedating."

"Do we want them sedated?" Gator hollered as the wind picked up its howl.

"Your guess is as good as mine."

Gator leaned in to yell into Blaze's ear. "Did Red and D-Day take them?"

"I didn't see. Red was in the head puking, so if she took them, I'm not sure they got into her system. They probably went down the drain with her dinner. I stayed with her and made sure she got tucked in bed nice and tight. D-day came in to see if she was okay, and her eyes were as wide as saucers."

Gator sent him a scowl.

"She's fine," Blaze patted his shoulder, then slapped his hand back to the wall to catch his balance. "Horrified, but fine. She said she was making her way down the hall when the door to Gregor's cabin slapped open. There was Daniel on his knees, giving the big guy a blow job. Gregor was apparently naked and as hairy as a silver-backed gorilla."

A grin spread across Gator's face. "What did she do?"

"Said excuse me and shut the door. She told me she couldn't imagine anyone wanting a sexual experience during this."

"Maybe Gregor needed a little stress relief, something to take the edge off."

"D-day was concerned that one big drop from a wave and taking the edge off was exactly what might happen." Blaze fell into Gator, laughing.

"Oh, man, the visual on that..." The boat tipped precipitously. Gator slammed Blaze into the wall on the other side of the hall as they fell backward. Gator cupped his hand and yelled. "This is getting too much. We need to get below. The captain said he'd use the intercom if we can help. When Daniel's done servicing Gregor, he can tell us if he's changed his strategy on handling the guests and this storm."

"I'm not sure there is a strategy to get through the storm, other than pray."

32

GATOR

Friday, The Davidson Yacht

GATOR WAS WEDGED between the wall and a pipe, holding on for dear life. He had known things were gonna get rough, but nothing he had imagined looked anything like this. It was like they were a toy boat being tossed around a toddler's bathtub—a hyperactive, hyper-destructive toddler's bathtub after he'd scarfed down his Halloween candy.

They'd tip back as they rode a swell then drop weightlessly. Boom! They'd hit the surface. Gator had puked his guts up so many times there wasn't even bile left in his belly. His throat was raw from the acid and from yelling. And the stomach cramps wanted to bend him in two. He was left with dry heaves and the sweats. "Embrace the suck," he whispered.

Something had gone wrong with the electrical system, and they'd lost lights and air conditioning. The air inside the state-rooms had sponged up the water, and he was soaked with sweat and humidity. The boat tipped back, Gator gripped the pipe. He'd duct-taped a flashlight and a radio to his arms so he would have them handy. The illumination from the flashlight just added to the sense of eeriness. He went weightless. The boat crashed down. Its joints moaning and shrieking. Gator's damp grip slipped from the pipe, and he tumbled forward, his momentum stopped by the couch built into the wall.

He grappled with the furniture until he was upright. That one was bad. Well, they were all bad. That one was worse. It had been a while since he'd done rounds. He should check on folks. And though D-day wanted to push into his thoughts, he pushed back just as hard. A few more days. He had to keep her alive a few more days. Then he'd be gone, and she'd be safe.

"Charlie to base."

"Base," Daniel said with his thick accent.

"I'm gonna make rounds of the cabins."

"Copy. Out."

Gator bet he copied and *was* out. Blaze and Gator were the only two security guards providing security. The other three were hunkered in their berths or somewhere. Gator hadn't seen them since Daniel laid down the law for the guests to stay put in their cabins.

"Delta to Charlie," Blaze came over the comms. "I'll take the upper deck and see how the crew are doing. Make sure the captain's still tied in."

"Copy." Gator waited for the next drop and slam. As the boat hit back down in the water, he pawed his way through the room to the hallway. He forced the door open and headed to the first door on the left to check on D-day. D-day had taken the meds and was all but blacked out the last time he'd been in. He'd ripped up some sheets and tied her to the bed like a patient on a medic's stretcher. He made sure she had pillows wedged at her back and front in case she puked, so she couldn't roll over and aspirate the vomit into her lungs and drown.

He made it all the way over to the bed as a swell lifted them up. He knelt beside her, using his flashlight to scan for any problems. Then he was weightless and clinging to the box spring. Then they slammed down. Boom!

He checked her pulse and respiration. Checked the ties to make sure they were tight but not restricting her blood flow. Checked to make sure her life vest was secure.

"Gator," she moaned. He reached out and lay his hand against her cheek. She was too hot. The room was stifling. "Gator."

"I'm here," he said, brushing his thumb over the softness of her cheek. He reached down and felt her arm, clammy with the humidity. She kicked against the restraints. She was wearing a t-shirt and a pair of lace panties.

Gator worked to pull his gaze away from the length of her legs.

"Gator, listen. You're not listening."

"I'm listening." He swallowed down the "ma chérie" that he'd never get to say to her. In his mind, he saw the holy man standing there in the fire circle. "I'll live up to my end of the bargain. You get her through this." He said it out loud. He wanted to make sure he was heard by the holy man, by the saints his mama prayed to every day of her life, to the guides and angels he'd always felt near him, to Jesus Christ, to God Almighty to any benevolent force that would hear him. "Get her through this," he prayed.

"The craziest thing, Gator... Saw you and knew..." she muttered.

Gator crouched closer. "Knew what?" Again, he had to swallow the words that formed naturally on his tongue, "You knew what, ma chérie?" –my cherished one. He put his hand on her forehead. His heart raced.

"Knew that I would love you f—"

Before she could finish, Gator slid his hand over her mouth. She hummed the word behind his palm.

She'd almost said it out loud. Almost cast the spell, or made the contract, or whatever it was that those words did.

Every time.

It was those words and then death.

Her death.

He wouldn't allow that. Not in this lifetime.

This lifetime, he'd break the curse, no matter what it took. No matter what it took away from him.

He forced himself onto unsteady feet.

Merde!

Okay. It was going to be okay. He'd tell Blaze to take point on D-day. He'd stay in the shadows. What was he thinking out on the railing touching her like that?

Did it matter if she was dreaming when she said it? Could she really feel that way?

Merde!

He turned this way and that as if searching for an answer that might lay in the puddles beneath his feet.

He wished the holy man had told him what to do. How to fix this. How to save her.

Gator tumbled himself from the cabin and stood outside her door, panting. He loosened his knees and rode the waves, catching his breath. The hall door banged open, and the wind whipped salted mist across his exposed skin. The hallway was ankle-deep in water from the crashing waves.

He forced himself to the next cabin, then the next and the next.

At the end of the row, all of the guests accounted for, Gator headed back to talk to Blaze and switch positions. As he passed D-day's room, the door stood open. He reached to grab the handle and made a quick sweep of his flashlight before he pulled it closed again.

Her bed was empty. The restraints untied.

He shot the beam of light through the stateroom; she was gone. She'd been drugged and was dreaming. Did she get up and wander? He checked the head. Empty. As he turned to leave, he saw a lifejacket floating near the wall. He picked it up and carried it with him. Fear sizzled over his skin.

The beam from his light slid down the hall. Empty. He moved to Johnna's room to see if D-day had gone down there. He had tied Johnna down like Christen, and she had squirmed her way forward and was puking over the side of her bed. Gator closed her door against the rising water.

He slogged his way down the hall, his hands pressing into the opposite walls, the life vest dangling from his shoulder. He concentrated on staying upright. He made it through the salon, shouting her name. The wind lifted and carried the sound of his voice away.

"Charlie to Delta," he bellowed into the radio.

"Del—co-y, Go ——d." The radio hissed Blaze's voice and static.

"I can't find D-day."

"Read—SSSSsss—two." Blaze let Gator know he couldn't hear him.

"I. Can't. Find. D-day!" Gator yelled.

All he got back was static. Gator ripped the radio from his arm and checked it. It wasn't a maritime radio. Damn thing was destroyed in the saltwater. Gator threw it across the room in frustration, then moved to the doorway that would take him outside and up.

The doors to the salon banged rhythmically against the wall. The wind whipped into the sitting room, but the strength was nothing compared to what was happening outside. Wind gusts, pounding rain, the waves swelled into black walls around them.

Gator flashed his light down one direction, nothing.

Down the other…

Gator focused on two shapes, black against the black night working near the deck.

His first thought was that the crew was trying to get something rigged.

He made his way toward them. Maybe they'd seen D-day.

As he made his way around the curve of the bow, he saw them lift something white.

Then he made out a leg, and his light caught on bright pink nail polish decorating the toes.

Gator ran.

The sheet slipped, and he saw her face, eyes at half-mast.

She was fighting them.

Tiny compared to the two dark figures. Drugged and disoriented.

They pushed her over the side.

"Christen," Gator screamed, and with a running leap, he dove after her into the sea.

33

GATOR

Friday, In the arms of Armageddon

GATOR FLAILED his arms in the direction he thought Christen should be.

Kicked.

Pulled.

He fought against the buoyancy of his life vest and the one looped on his arm.

His flashlight underwater lit mere inches in the murky brew.

The salt stung his eyes as he frantically searched around him.

There!

Below him, he saw a flash of white.

His lungs screamed for air.

His brain tried to force him toward the surface.

He was back in training, in the deep end of the poo,l when his instructors grabbed at his legs and pulled him down when he was on his last few seconds of air. They'd taught him over and over to stay present, to fight for the goal.

His goal was that flick of white.

Another mighty pull of his arm, and he snagged cloth around his index finger, yanked. And she glided into his arms.

Whomp.

The water collapsed over top of him. They were pressed and forced deeper down.

Gator wrapped his arms around Christen's waist and pulled her tightly against his chest. He waited for the life vest to lift them in the right direction. He was so turned and tumbled, if he started swimming, he might be driving them deeper still.

Up they rose.

She dangled lifelessly as he pushed her face toward the sky.

He needed to check to make sure she was breathing, but they were rising up another swell. Gator's battle-tested mind was sharply aware, and he prioritized his actions.

Gator wrapped his legs around Christen, squeezing her in his thighs as he worked to fasten her life vest around her.

He put the edge of her sheet between his teeth and bit down. This sheet might just be the thing that kept them alive. He felt like it was a gift.

–A gift that he'd seen her life vest in the stateroom, a gift that she was wrapped in the sheet, a gift that he'd been there when she was tossed overboard, that he'd found her in the waves, that he had her in his arms. He sent up a prayer of deep thanksgiving.

With shaking hands, he screamed at the clasps that didn't want to fit together. He had seconds before—Boom!

They crashed.

The wave forced them down under the water, deep, deep.

His ears popped.

His lungs screamed.

His arm was shoved up the center of Christen's life vest, keeping them from separating, and he forced her mouth to stay shut, held her nose as best he could, trying to keep any more water out of her lungs.

Up they floated.

He tried to feel for air coming from her nostrils but was confused by the winds that whipped past them. He shoved the sheet into the waist of his tactical pants and then attached the clasps of their vests together one at a time as they rose up another swell.

He slid his arm through her shoulder hole and screamed in her ear, "Deep breath. NOW!" He plugged her nose as the wave crashed and drove them down, down through layers of water. Down past the heated surface, down into the cold beneath.

Up they rose.

He gasped at the air.

Filled his lungs.

Exhaled and filled them again.

He put his hand on Christen's chest, and he could feel her heart beat, could feel her sucking in deep gulps of air. He flipped his arm with the flashlight and saw that her eyes were still closed. "Here we go again," he bellowed.

Boom!

Down they slid.

The next time they reached the air, Christen was panicked and fighting. She was strong. He knew she was strong, but this was adrenaline, strength, and training. This was her limbic system, confused by the drugs, confused by the waterboarding, desperate to get out.

Get free.

Get safe.

She had no idea who Gator was.

She just wanted to survive.

Boom!

They went down, still fighting.

Gator finally wrestled her arms to her side and held her in a bear hug. He wrapped his legs around hers and squeezed to stop her from kneeing him in the groin again. The pain was excruciating, and if he passed out, he didn't give either of them much chance of living through the night.

Up they rose.

"D-day!" he screamed in her ear. "You are a Night Stalker! Night Stalkers don't quit." He felt something in her shift. He tried it again. "D-day! You are a Night Stalker, and you have a creed! Night Stalkers don't quit."

They rose up again on the wave. She didn't strike at him anymore. She wrapped her arms around him and pushed her face forward until her lips were at his ear. "Night Stalkers don't quit."

Boom!

34

LYNX

Friday, The Men's Barack's, Iniquus Campus

"HEY, HEY, HEY." Lynx felt Striker dragging her from her nightmare into his arms. "You're having a bad dream."

"Gator! I have to save Gator and his wife," she pushed the words up from the depth of her nightmare.

"Gator has a wife?" He was brushing the hair from her face, kissing her lips. "Come on now. Wake up. You're dreaming. It's another nightmare. Wake up."

The wave hit. It felt like being in a car crash. She struggled for survival. There was a tangle of arms and legs. Rising up again. Blissful air. She looked up. This next wave was enormous. It was like looking up the side of a skyscraper. It was horrifying. Her mouth dropped open, and she screamed. Screamed loud and long. Screamed, using every last particle of breath in her body.

"Fuck, Lynx, wake up!" Striker was shaking her, trying to

rouse her from her terror. She was aware of him, of her surroundings, but she was out of her body. Too far out to find her way through the nightmare and back to her bed. With another solid shake. She came slamming back home. Her eyes popped open. She pushed herself forward, eyes wide in shock, clinging to Striker's shoulders, chest heaving while she filled her lungs again with oxygen. He tucked her head down in the curve of his neck and combed his fingers through her hair. "You're okay." He crooned as he wrapped his body around her and rocked her in his arms.

It wasn't her. She was fine. Gator. Gator was in danger.

Someone pounded on the door. Striker held her head between his splayed fingers, tipping her face up so he could look her in the eye. He gave her a nod and went to open the door.

Her scream was still ringing in her ears. Of course, someone would come check. She scrambled out of bed and followed Striker into the living room. Jack. Jack looked at her, then turned to whoever was coming up behind him. "Beetle was chewing on the TV remote. Horror film and volume control," he said.

That seemed like a reasonable thing to blame on her dog. It could happen. Beetle and Bella were circling her, sniffing and whining, working her already raw nerves.

Whoever had arrived to save the day slogged on back to bed. She could hear the message being passed along. What did she expect? This was an Iniquus barracks. Every single one of the men who lived here also lived for the opportunity to run into danger.

"What's happening?" Jack asked as he moved into the apartment and shut the door. He was dressed in a pair of gym shorts. He was barefoot and bare-chested but didn't look like he'd been asleep.

"Gator," she said. "I was dreaming about Gator. It was so vivid. He dove over the side of the boat. He's trying to save D-day. They're in the ocean."

"In your dream," Jack said.

"No. No." She gripped at her shirt. "No, I don't think so. No, not in my dream. That's what's happening now. He's just on the other side of the Veil. He's yelling for help. We have to do something."

Her phone buzzed on the counter, making it spin in a circle against the smooth surface. She leaped forward, grabbing it. She swiped a trembling finger over the screen.

"Lynx here," She brushed her hair out of her face and stared into Striker's eyes, listening. "I'm on my way."

Striker and Jack stood with their arms crossed over their chests, feet wide, faces grim.

"The yacht is in a typhoon. They still had intermittent satellite connection on the boat up until about ten minutes ago. The last feed they picked up has the boat in one location and Christen Davidson in another."

"What? What does that mean?" Jack asked.

"She was wearing a ring with a GPS tracker," Lynx explained. "That ring got separated from the boat. One would assume that means Christen is in the water."

"Lynx was screaming from a nightmare that Gator dove in the water going after Christen," Striker said.

"Then they're in the water." Concentration lines crisscrossed Jack's forehead. "Let's get to Headquarters. Get a rescue plan together."

THE THREE OF them burst into the Panther Force war room, where Nutsbe was busy tapping at his computer.

He looked up. "Commander Rheas, I have no communications link to your men."

"Has the CIA been updated?"

"John Black is headed to Langley, and we're expecting a callback."

"Were you able to get in touch with Lula LaRoe? I understand she was eyes and ears on William Davidson. Where are they?" Lynx was over at their whiteboard and was busily drawing dividing lines and posting names.

"William Davidson and Johnna White – Lula—were deposited on Davidson Realm, and the Davidson helicopter returned to Singapore. Once Lula was on the island, communications were scrambled."

"Scrambled?" Jack leaned his six-foot-five frame against the wall, taking it all in. He'd pulled on the Iniquus uniform of digital print camouflage tactical pants, charcoal grey compression shirts, black Vibram-soled work boots. He looked ready to jump into the fray – but the fray was on the other side of the globe.

"My guess is that William Davidson was well aware that this party would catch international intelligence attention, and our Fivey allies would have ships out trying to pick up anything they could." Nutsbe said, "I'm betting he wanted to make sure that what happens in the Realm stays in the Realm."

Lynx moved to another whiteboard and posted that information. The phone on Nutsbe's desk rang. "Please hold for John Black, CIA."

They had all dealt with Black before. They waited silently for him to come on the line.

"Black," he said.

"Sir, this is Nutsbe Crushed, Iniquus Panther Force. You are on speakerphone with Commander Striker Rheas, Strike Force, his second in command, Jack McCullen, and Iniquus puzzler Lynx Sobado."

"Very well. The message I received was that there's been a disruption in communications both with our officers, Johnna White and Johnna Red, and that of our asset Christen Davidson."

"Yes, sir," Nutsbe responded.

"On our end, Langley cannot pull the Paradise Found Yacht up on radio or satellite. We have no means of communicating."

"Nothing here either, sir. I've plotted their course. I'm sending you an image." Nutsbe's finger moved over the keyboard. "This is where we lost data."

"Are we sure that it's still afloat?" Black asked.

"The failure corresponds with reception rather than a transmission. The satellite is no longer functioning in this area."

"Hey, you," Black called to someone in the room with him. "Try another satellite to reach this yacht."

"Sir, none of the satellites are functioning in this area because of the storm," Nutsbe said. "Red and White split up, as I indicated in my report. We believe White is safely on Davidson Realm. Red and Asset Davidson were positioned on a yacht that was due to arrive on that island thirty hours from now. They were caught in an unexpected typhoon. They were making their way to a mainland port when we lost contact."

"They were not in distress when you lost contact?"

"They sent a pan pan at ten pm Zulu time. It was not followed up by a mayday."

"Do we have ships in the area that could get an eye on them?"

"US Naval ships, sir? No. There are none that are close enough to assist."

"Alright, now what's this you say about the asset, Christen Davidson? She's gone overboard?"

"We believe so, sir. She was wearing a micro GPS unit in her ring as well as her communications surveillance band. Both of which pinged on our map in the same spot, but it was in a different spot than the yacht pinged. The ring is on her right hand. She wore the band on her left."

"Why are you giving me that information?"

"It seems unlikely that the ring and band would come off of her and land in the same space in the water unless she was still wearing them. I conclude she went overboard."

"Did you get a visual feed from her contact lenses? Where's her phone?"

"The phone locates with the boat, sir. Negative to any surveillance information. It comes in over the satellite feed – of which we have none right now. But, whatever she saw before going over should be sent to us as soon as there's a break in the clouds. The size of the boat was smaller than the range of her lenses. As long as her phone stays operable, we'll eventually get those images. Of course, we would assume that once she went over, she would have lost her contact lens, and she would quickly be out of range of the phone. If she were alive to see anything."

A chill went through the room. Striker and Jack looked Lynx's way for information. "Sir," Lynx said with conviction. "Christen Davidson is an athlete, a Night Stalker. I believe she's alive. I would like to develop a rescue plan."

"I'll be back in touch," Black said. The phone call ended.

They all stood stalk still for a moment absorbing the information.

"Nutsbe. She's alive. I can feel it in my bones," Lynx said on an exhale.

Nutsbe looked more than skeptical. He shook his head. "I've been watching the damned thing on Red and D-days lenses before we lost contact. It's apocalyptic out there, man. I wasn't laying much hope in the yacht coming through this, let alone a man overboard."

"Was she wearing a life vest?" Jack asked.

"Last I saw? Yes. But these are thirty-foot swells. That's a three-story drop. Jack did that and ended up on the operating room table. Can you imagine dropping like that over and over again for hours on end? I'm telling you. There's no possible way that she survived this."

"That you've ever thought of – that you can imagine," Lynx countered. "Don't give up on her training and her guts. The average human being? I'm right there with you. But Christen Davidson is cut from heroic cloth. She is physically capable of astonishing feats. She's been trained to deal with extreme levels of danger with a focused mind, to process and strategize. She is an elite human being. You know that. You know that first hand. Nutsbe, don't count her out. We need to send rescue."

"No one's heading into this mess. No matter how much we'd pay."

"Yet. But that doesn't mean that we can't get ourselves prepared. Boats will be able to get out before aircraft, I would think. We can start there. They'll know the currents best. But we can try to figure it out. They've probably been pulled pretty far away after all these hours."

"Wait. Whoa. They?" Nutsbe swiveled his chair to face her.

"Remember the story you told me about your grandmother?" She waited for his nod. "Just now, I woke up from a dream—a nightmare--where I saw Christen being thrown into the ocean and Gator Aid Rochambeau diving in after her."

"And they were both still alive?"

Lynx looked at him with a steady gaze.

Nutsbe pulled himself around and reached for the keyboard. "Rescue mission it is!"

35

GATOR
Heck, if I know what day it is or where we are...

THE RAIN STUNG THEIR FACES. It was hard to breathe. There seemed more water than air available in the dark atmosphere that enveloped them. Gator had turned off the flashlight to conserve batteries. It was state of the art tactical equipment, waterproof – but he wasn't sure that meant this kind of waterproof. The waves had calmed. And while they still rose and fell like a rollercoaster at the fair, they were bobbing on the surface. They weren't getting beaten into the depths like before. Gator tried to calculate what time it might be. He'd guess they'd been in the ocean for five or so hours, soon the sun would come up. That would help their morale.

Belly to belly with their clips, keeping them together, it wasn't the perfect configuration. They had banged each other up pretty good as they tumbled hour after hour. It was the entirety of Raider Spirit – the Marine Raiders version of the SEALs hell week—all rolled into one long night. He'd gotten his boots off his feet. At least that protected Christen from slamming up against the hard surface of his soles.

The drug still hadn't worn off Christen. She had struggled against it, but Gator had convinced her to put her head on his shoulder and try to rest.

He thought about Johnna Red. The drug had been absorbed into her body quickly. Blaze had said Karl was passing out medicine, and Red was puking. Blaze thought the time frame was such that, if she had accepted the drugs, she should have puked them back out. But she was in the same daze as Christen had been when Gator ripped the sheets and tied Red to her mattress. It had been hours of rain and wind by that point. It had gotten so bad that the captain had sent out a pan-pan alert, letting area boats know that they were in a state of urgency if not an emergency. It let potential rescuers know they were in distress but didn't require them to stop everything and come to their aid.

Gator wondered if that had turned to a mayday when the crew discovered two people missing from the yacht. Was the US Navy headed their way? There were a lot of *ifs* behind that thought. *If* they had been discovered missing by the yacht crew. And *if* there was a US Navy ship in the area. And *if* anyone besides Blaze would care that they were gone.

Chances of anyone noticing and trying to do something about it—came down to almost zilch. Blaze, he'd be looking for them. Everyone else was drugged except the crew and the security, as far as Gator knew.

Why would Karl pass meds like that? Did he mix them up? Did he think that sleeping through the event would be helpful? What the hell kind of drug would affect Christen like this? It was almost like she was roofied or some such shit. Gator could see

Karl as the kind of guy who would get off on drugging women so he could be in control.

Gator thought back to the boat and wondered who had thrown her over. Whoever those men were, they hadn't taken Karl's pills. Either crew (which made no sense) or security, or guests who were faking the medicinal effects. It wasn't Blaze, him, or Johnna. It was a small playing field. Why, though? Why would someone throw Christen over the side? Who wanted her dead? They'd pulled off her life vest. It wasn't a stunt. They were trying to murder her.

All he had seen was black silhouettes against the inky backdrop. The satellites probably weren't functioning in all this, but Gator still had his watch on his wrist. Even if he died, as long as he was floating in his life vest, the watch should send those last images on to Headquarters. Once the storm was lifted, Iniquus would put two and two together and be on the hunt for them. And he knew Lynx had already sounded the alarm. If she picked up the images of the little girl in the field with the goats and could see better than he could that the black dots the child was watching were helicopters coming down, then Lynx would be living through this with him. Strike Force would be rallied. All hands on deck.

"D-Day?" He needed to stop thinking of her as Christen. Their being in the water made it more important than ever to keep his guard up. He couldn't be tempted to pour out his heart. If she'd finished the words she started in her drugged stupor, it could be—it was possible—that she felt the same way that he did. And those words could mean that they wouldn't live to see their rescue. Or worse, that only he would live to see their rescue. That thought brought back the torture he'd felt under the holy man's spell. The utter horror of living on… "D-day!"

"Hmmm"

"On Tuesday, before you left for this mission. You were deployed to the Middle East. There were two helicopters, One was shot down, one landed. You flew that mission."

She nodded against his shoulder.

"There was a little girl. Red bandana. Roses on the hem of her dress and goats."

She nodded and snuggled closer. "Yes, that's right." She was shivering despite the warmth of the air and water.

Even if the water was warm here, it was still cooler than body temperature, and they both stood a real chance of hypothermia and death.

He'd have to rouse her soon; get her kicking to warm up.

That last nod of her head was the affirmation he needed. He'd connected to her as soon as the mission was a go, and Johnna Red and Lula LaRoe were headed toward D-day's FOB. He sent a message of thanksgiving to the heavens for all of the information, all of the warnings he'd been given. As much as he had hated the experience, it was still a gift. He felt a little better equipped to keep her alive.

But who wanted her dead?

The contact lenses might be their only way of knowing. He had lost his lens the second he hit the water. D-day, too, he was sure. But her eyes had opened when she was lifted when she kicked and tried to get away. Whatever her lens picked up might have even better images on them than his would. Yeah. He wasn't sure if her bracelet or his watch was up to the punishment they'd just endured, but there was a chance.

Gator's jaw trembled with cold, and his teeth rattled.

D-day moaned in his arms.

"Help is on its way," he whispered into her ear. "They know we're in the water. They're coming. We just need to hold on."

"Night Stalkers never give up," she muttered it so quietly, he barely heard. But Gator felt reassured. That must be the mantra that was circulating in her brain. Having that fundamental belief that code was imperative – it had gotten many a Marine and soldier through many an impossible situation.

And if ever there was an impossible situation. This was it.

36

CHRISTEN

Saturday, (maybe?) The waters off the west coast of Sumatra (probably)

IT TOOK A FEW AWKWARD TRIES, but she and Gator had figured out how to lay on their sides and scissor kick and sidestroke without hitting and kicking each other.

They weren't aiming toward anything. They had a vague idea, from where the sun was positioned low in the western sky, hidden by a thick blanket of clouds, that this was the direction of land. It had been a long day in the water.

The waves were still choppy.

She had swallowed down her fair share of saltwater, and Gator had made her stick her finger down her throat and barf it back up. Still, her stomach cramped and seized. The drug had worn off, and Christen assumed that was the source of her killer hangover. Her head was a kettle drum being beat with a staccato constancy.

They had no idea where they were. Grey water filled the bottom of her visual field; the grey sky filled the top.

Three hundred and sixty, there was nothing else to focus on.

They were aiming west toward land. Neither of them had any hope of swimming that far.

They were both dehydrated from vomiting on the yacht and almost twenty-four hours in the saltwater. They had lapped at the freshwater from the rain as best they could, but that had ended.

A blessing and a worry.

Both were low on calories that they'd been burning to stave off hypothermia. Their muscles screamed and cramped from fatigue. This exercise in swimming was supposed to warm their blood up and keep them alive a little longer. Gator was worried because she'd stopped shivering.

Gator swore to her that help was on its way. Swore that he had some kind of psychic connection with some chick back home named Lynx, and she would be tearing up the airwaves getting them help. He told her that Lynx was rabid about protecting those she loved, and nothing that could be done would be left undone.

Christen focused her will on staying alive for that rescue.

They decided to take one thousand strokes and then rest. They agreed to carefully count each one. An occupied mind wouldn't worry about sea wasps or anything else that might be lurking under the churning froth covered waters. An occupied mind wouldn't formulate all kinds of vicious, jealous feelings that Gator must be in love and possibly—probably--married to this woman whom he was so deeply connected to. Maybe he'd even fathered her children.

Oddly, those thoughts seemed every bit as life-threatening as the waves that had crashed over her last night. As if not being ble to love Gator could pummel her into the depths, and she might not resurface.

She didn't know anything about Gator, she argued with herself. Nothing. He'd taken her hand standing on the yacht's deck…But that could be because he was a player. Or it was a weird moment. It might have meant nothing to him. It could have been friendly, and she was interpreting things through her own heart's lens. That moment might have nothing to do with real feelings. Feelings like she'd been wrapped in since they met. She wasn't going to ask him for clarification either. Though, he was right here, his face inches from hers. She needed to stay on mission. Her mission was to survive. Once she was out of the water, she'd face the next test.

Right now, she needed to take stroke number three hundred and thirty-four.

Three hundred and thirty-five.

Three hundred and thirty-six.

"It's going to be dark again soon. They'll call off the search until morning," she said, girding her loins, so to speak. It was going to be a bad ten hours or so. She'd been through worse before.

Ten hours of bad was doable.

"Okay," Gator said. "We can easily make it until morning."

"Agreed," she said.

Three hundred and forty.

Three hundred and forty-one.

"I think I'm hallucinating,"

"Do you see a boat?" he asked, stopping mid-stroke, swinging his head.

She felt the electricity of adrenaline move from his body to hers. He wrapped his arms around her as if to protect her. Then she felt a nudge against her back.

"Shark," she exhaled. She hadn't been hallucinating.

The bump came again.

Gator thrust them deeper into the water. They were cheek to cheek as the massive shark swam straight at them. It suddenly turned and swam off. They pushed against the water to propel them back up to the surface. Christen sucked in a lungful of air. "What just happened."

It took Gator a moment to catch his breath enough to answer. "Guy I knew once told me that sharks hate eye contact, so if you're ever attacked, try and stare 'em down."

"And you believed him?" Christen laughed at the absurdity and her over-tight nerves.

"It worked, didn't it?"

Her face lost the victorious grin. "There are more of them. Look, here they come."

Gator reached into his tactical pants and pulled out the sheet she'd been wrapped in the night before.

"What are you thinking?"

"I'm not sure. Maybe if we get this around us and the fabric is floating out, it'll confuse them." He lifted his hands up as if donning a cape and wrapped the cloth around them, letting it drift. The sharks were still there. They weren't circling. They weren't bumping into them either. Maybe it was working. Or maybe they were just plotting.

Gator and Christen bowed their heads until they touched.

"You're keeping me sane," Gator said. "I couldn't ask to go overboard with a better battle buddy."

"Same," Christen said. But the words hurt. She thought of him as so much more than a comrade in a catastrophe. He didn't feel the same, or he'd have chosen different words. And there was that Lynx, chick. Christen was horrified at the return of those jealous emotions; she really had nothing but gratitude for anyone who might be laboring to pull them out of the water.

Another night. Another night of darkness.

The flashlight wasn't working, and Gator had kept the shiny parts of it to use as a possible signal but let the rest go.

It was extra weight they didn't need.

Tonight would be pitch black.

Sharks. Jellyfish. Cold and fear.

She tipped her head back and, with conviction, shouted. "Night Stalkers *never* give up." And that's when she saw it. "I think I'm hallucinating," she whispered.

"Only one hallucination allowed every thousand strokes. We were at three hundred forty-two when we took the shark break. We still have a few more strokes before we get another hallucination, and then it's my turn." He grinned, but there was little energy to it. She could see in his eyes the toll that this was taking on his mind and body. Same as hers. They were in trouble.

"Okay," she said. She turned her head and rested it on Gator's life jacket and watched the phantom ship chugging toward them. It was the fifth ship that one of them had seen. They'd call out and point. The other would turn and see nothing.

Once, the illusion was so strong, the desire so big, that they both saw a canoe paddled by two boys, and they took out after it. But when they got to the side, it vanished.

This time it was different. This boat had lights. It also made noises. "This is a pretty good hallucination I'm having."

"Copy that," Gator replied.

"I'm going to tell you what I see, and you tell me what you see at the exact same time – let's test the possibility that I might not have gone completely insane."

"Wilco. Count of three. One. Two." The descriptive words that came out of their mouths were almost exactly the same.

"It might be real," Christen said, in shock.

She glanced around, and the shark fins no longer traced through the water. "Quick! Quick! We need to unhitch ourselves so we can spread the sheet, and they can see us."

They both tried, but their shaking waterlogged fingers wouldn't cooperate.

They spread the sheet into the current as best they could, held up a section as high as they could, and yelled their heads off, buoyed by hope.

Bells and commotion told them that they'd been spotted, but the two didn't take a chance that what they were perceiving was their wishful, hopeful brains making up illusions. They continued screaming and waving as they saw two men dive into the water and swim their way. They screamed as the rescuers discovered they'd been locked together and devised a way to haul them back to the boat. They screamed and yelled while they were plucked from the water and hauled onto the deck, while knives cut their lifejackets from around them. They screamed and yelled until the crew said. "We've got you. You're safe."

They clutched at each other, a habit now, while warm blankets were wrapped around their trembling bodies, and water bottles were pushed into their hands. "Just a little sip. Not too much. There. Nope. Stop. Only a tiny bit at a time." And that's when they both finally registered the miracle of their rescue. They were safe. They'd been found. They rolled into each others' arms and sobbed at the enormity of their gratitude.

THE CREW on the aptly named "Fortune's Wheel," a tourist boat run by a seventies-era surfer-dude from New Jersey, were stellar.

"We got the call. They were looking for boats willing to go

out as soon as we deemed it safe. It was still dark last night when I gathered my crew. I told 'em get ready, as soon as it's light we're going to find these two. I believed..." he choked on the end of that sentence and swiped at a tear. "I was supposed to go to a funeral today. My buddy, Larry, he had a heart attack on the water, and they couldn't get him in to medical help fast enough. I surfed with him for decades. A real loss. He loved the water." He stopped, and his focus went inward. "I prayed on it. Prayed to Larry. I told him that I could go to his damned funeral and toss some dirt, or I could get in my boat and go save you. I had a feeling you were alive. I *knew* it. They told me you were both elite soldiers. I've read about what that takes. Yup, I knew you were out there, fighting." He laid his fist on his heart. "I said to Larry, that's what I was going to do, in honor of him. I said, 'Larry, point the way. You can see clear now. You know where they're at. I just need a nudge, see?'"

He looked up as one of his men came in with a tray of mugs filled with hot soup and passed them around. "I was watching the coconuts, and they were pulling hard to the north," he continued. "You two floated almost a hundred kilometers from where they said you went over. How the hell you lived through that... my hats off to you." He raised his mug in their direction.

Christen wasn't sure she had the strength to even get hers to her mouth.

She wanted to sleep, but they wouldn't let her.

They were slowly warming them, slowly hydrating them, and giving them nutrients. They said to do otherwise would shock the body.

"I was heading to where I thought I might intersect with you." He tapped a finger on his chart. "And I swear to god, I felt Larry reach over and adjust my hand on the wheel, turned me a good three degrees. If that adjustment hadn't happened. I never would have seen you. Never."

He stood up and reached into the cabinet and pulled out a bottle of rum and three glasses. "I'm just giving you a drop. It would kill you to take a shot. But I'd like to give a salute to Larry."

"To Larry," they said.

Christen threw back the alcohol. It burned her parched throat to the point she had to stifle a scream behind her fist.

"Drink your soup. Then, I think you two should get some sleep. I'll let you know when we reach the harbor. It'll be a while. Your company, Iniquus, will have an ambulance waiting to take you to the hospital. They want us to take you back to Singapore. They said they need to speak to you as soon as you're able. They also said you aren't to communicate with anyone else until you get up with them. I ain't prying into your business, how or why you found yourself floating in the northern reaches of the Malacca Strait. I'm not asking...." He looked up at them with puppy dog eyes.

Christen thought he should have something to satisfy his curiosity. She turned and looked into Gator's eyes, "Just happened to end up in the wrong place at the wrong time. But thankfully, we were together." And as she said it, Gator slowly closed his eyes and crossed his arms over the bright yellow t-shirt donated by one of the crew. It felt like he was pulling his energy back away from her. It felt like a retreat from a battle he didn't want to win.

37

CHRISTEN
Monday, Singapore

THEY HAD BEEN CLEARED at the hospital. The guys on the boat had done an outstanding job getting them warmed and rehydrated. The doctors said they'd followed protocol to the letter. "Go home. Get some sleep. Give your bodies some time to recover. If you're having trouble sleeping or with anxiety. I encourage you to see a mental health care professional." He shook their hands.

A nurse held out a clipboard, and they each scrawled their signatures across the discharge papers. They were a little lost as they walked out of the hospital room. Gator was wearing board shorts and flip flops that weren't quite his size. She had on a Size XXXL t-shirt that she wore like a trash bag with a pair of flip flops that were way too big. They looked like homeless people. And they were of sorts. No ID, no money, no plan. They were headed for outside, so they could talk. Getting in touch with Iniquus was top of their priority list.

They moved toward the emergency department exit when Johnna rounded the corner. She stopped in her tracks and stared at them. "Holy fucking shit," she said. "It's true." She walked up between them, turned one-eighty, wrapped a hand through each of their arms, and started walking back out the door to a waiting cab.

That was it.

The only thing she said. "Holy fucking shit." Christen thought that summed things up pretty well.

Christen looked her over. She was pale despite her tan. She was cut and bruised but otherwise looked fine.

"Tell me about Blaze," Gator said as she reached for the taxi door handle. He was braced to hear his bad news.

"He's pissed. He took a blow to the head and is being monitored. He ended up with a pretty bad concussion. The doctors won't release him, and your company has ordered him to stay put." She pulled the door wide and brushed her hand through the air to tell them to get in. "I told him you guys were safe and sound. I'm not sure he believed me. But, he'll see for himself soon enough."

Christen scooted to the far side. The marrow of her bones was tired. She couldn't imagine ever feeling energetic again. She thought back to Nick of Time and his story about the SAS going hand to hand for four hours with the militants. They took a day to recoup, then got up and went to work. Yeah, but she was in the water for some twenty-two hours. She probably deserved a little longer recuperation.

They drove in silence.

Christen stared out the window. She'd lived to see another

day. Go figure. She leaned forward to catch Gator's eye and send him a smile. But he didn't turn his head her way. *Huh.*

She wanted to reach for his hand, but he'd crossed his arms over his chest and was tucked in tight. True, he was sitting in the back seat of the cab, and he was a big guy without a lot of space. But still...

When the taxi stopped, it was at a house in an upper-class neighborhood with a tall wall around it and an electrically powered gate. The gate swung open, and the taxi stopped in the drive.

Johnna and Gator both did a sweep to check the area.

Christen figured if she was supposed to have died, she would have done it last night.

She wanted to go in and get the debrief over with.

THERE WAS no one in the place. Though it looked like someone lived there. Johnna gestured to the couch. "I'm sorry. I'm sort of in shock from the events. I was released from the hospital at the same time you were."

Christen leaned forward.

"It was dehydration from vomiting, bruising from the storm, and I wanted to get a tox report on my blood to see what Karl fed us. It certainly wasn't Dramamine like he said it was." She turned to Gator. "I was aware enough to know you lashed me to the bed and that you made rounds to check on things. I will be writing that into my report. Above and beyond. Truly appreciated." She was nodding along with her words. Emphasizing them in a way, her tired voice wasn't able to. "If I'd been left alone to my own devices, I honestly don't think I would have made it through the night. I would have either drowned in my own puke, or I would have been tossed around the cabin like a rag doll. Thank you." She looked from one to the other. "You look like shit. But I'm told you're medically stable."

"Yes," they said simultaneously. They'd slept the whole way to Singapore, but Christen didn't think she'd recover until she'd slept for a week.

"I'm sorry to press you. We think there's a small window. Your team at Iniquus is anxious. I'm not sure they believe you're safe."

She reached over to the laptop and pulled a keystroke randomizer from her pocket, and put the code in. Up on the television in front of them came what looked like a planning room. Four faces pressed forward.

Christen recognized Nutsbe.

"I asked you not to lose the contact lens. You told me I could trust you with it," he said.

She offered him a weak smile in return. She wasn't up to banter.

Gator said, "This is D-day, my swim buddy. D-day, on your left, is Jack McCullen, team second in command, then my commander, Striker Rheas, and that there's Lynx. She's the one I told you about. Lynx—" His voice caught and broke.

"Don't you dare," she said. Emotions caught hold of her face. Her muscles tensed against it, but her skin flamed pink as tears filled her eyes. She brushed her hands over her face as if to rearrange it into the stoicism of the men. She was wholly unsuccessful. "I know. I know all about it. All of it. The rattlesnake. The cliff. The pledge. I know. But right now, you're safe, and so is D-day. So far, so good. We'll figure things out one step at a time."

That was cryptic as hell. But one thing that wasn't a mystery was that these two loved each other deeply. Only, it wasn't the kind of love she'd been afraid they shared. This one felt like a deep accord, a long and intense friendship. Bigger than family. But not his wife. By the way Striker turned to her and rubbed a hand up and down her arm, and the loving gratitude he got in return – that was the committed couple relationship. Christen was relieved. A little.

If Gator would just look at her. He hadn't looked at her since the drink on the boat.

Nutsbe tapped at his computer, and the scene changed: there were whiteboards covered in colored magic marker script behind a table with a row of chairs. Now it looked to Christen like she was attending a business meeting.

"I wanted to share some of the puzzle pieces I've been putting together." Lynx was really young looking, early-twenties, maybe. She had long blond hair and a sweet, girl next door kind of feel to her. In no way did she look like she should have as much power as she obviously held in that room. It made Christen curious.

"The pressing question is what happened on the yacht? Why were Johnna and Christen drugged?" Lynx asked. "Why was Christen thrown into the water? And to get there, I want to start at the widest part of the funnel of activity that ended up with Christen and Gator in the water."

Damned. Every single person in the room was looking at her like she was about to show them the holy grail. Something about this woman had earned their respect—big time.

"Perfect," Johnna said.

"There are four kidnapping/terrorist events that we are looking at prior to the attack on Christen Davidson. One in Paraguay. Steve Finley from the FBI." She stopped and looked at her watch. "I expect him here any second." She looked at the door, then continued. "Steve was able to identify one of the leaders of Paraguayan kidnapping crime as Gregor Zoric, also called Medved', or the Bear. To that end, Christen picked up a conversation in Arabic between Gregor, Nadir, and the sheik, and we translated. Gregor said, 'The sanctions bill died in the US Senate committee, as we knew it would after we lost our leverage.'" Lynx was reading from her board. She turned toward the camera. "The leverage being the students who were kidnapped and the committee leader being their grandfather." She turned back to the board. "Nadir responded, 'I'm not sure how to work around this obstacle. But we'll have to find a way.' Gregor answered, 'Yes. A very surprising turn of events. If my instructions had been followed to the letter, all would have gone as planned. The persons who made the decisions to include the teacher have been punished.'" Lynx let her gaze take in all the listeners. "We believe the teacher he's referring to is Suz Malloy. Okay? That's crime number one, then the Bowman kidnapping is two. Three, the Ngorongoro terror attack and kidnapping the scientists. We'll get to those in a second."

"And four?" Striker asked.

"An attempted kidnapping of William Davidson, Christen's father," Lynx said.

"Wait," Striker said, "I thought he was the person of interest."

"He was," Lynx said, "And he may still be. But we learned some very interesting things from Christen's foray into the spy game."

38

CHRISTEN
Monday, Safe House, Singapore

LYNX LIFTED A FINGER, and a picture filled the screen. "From satellite imagery, these are still shots of the attempted kidnapping of William Davidson.

Christen saw her father hunkered in the corner. Gator was taking a blow to his cheek; that explained his bruise. Blaze was blocking punches from two men, and there was a man on the ground. "Tibor Zoric. Gregor's nephew." She pointed to one of the men near Blaze with his face exposed. Another photo flashed up. Gator had the guy who punched him in a headlock and was putting him out. "Ivan Sworski." She pointed first to the one in the headlock then to the guy on the ground. "Marco Kis, is the guy who's lights-out. The fourth man is, as yet, unidentified."

Well, now Christen understood the warmth that her dad had shown Gator and Blaze. They'd saved him from the attack. Hell of a coincidence, though, that they were near this scene right when they were needed. This stank of a CIA manipulation – but Christen couldn't put her finger on how all of that would have unfurled.

"Gator," Lynx said. "I have some questions about the day that you saved William Davidson from being kidnapped."

Christen's body tensed.

"You're at the restaurant. Blaze sent me the video of you walking in." She nodded at Nutsbe, and Nutsbe brought a screen down, and a video played. It was her father and Daniel in a restaurant. Was she going to see someone trying to hurt her dad? Christen wasn't sure she was up to that at this moment.

Gator sent a quick glance her way. Just enough, it seemed to draw some conclusion, then he watched the action play out on the screen. Daniel got drenched, and her dad was yelling at him.

"It's this part here that I'm interested in. It's hard to tell from the video. Nutsbe, can you play it slowly that part just before the waiter comes out?"

The video played again. "Here," she said. "It looks like he's holding your dad up. Keeping him in the area where you're standing, waiting. Daniel turns his head and sees the waiter with the tray. He steps forward. There. See that? It looks to me like he's flipping the tray onto himself. That he had planned this event. Do it again, please, Nutsbe."

While it played again, Christen could see exactly what Lynx had seen. It looked completely different than when it had played the first time.

"It's interesting," Gator said, "because I blocked the door to keep them from coming through. But the driver and Daniel both knew how to get around back since they had to circle the block over and over. There was no place to park a car that long. They knew Davidson was on a terrace."

"When they couldn't get through the door, at least one of them should have driven around to help their boss," Jack said.

"They didn't get off the X the entire fight. It was me and Blaze and the four kidnappers. Then when the door was unblocked, they popped through like avenging angels."

"And Christen, you observed Daniel engaged in oral sex with Gregor," Lynx said.

Christen felt herself blanch.

"Don't worry, I'm not going to play the video of that one. We have no way of telling what that relationship is about. It could have been a whim. Weird kind of a whim to have with the storm going on. But that's thankfully not where I was focused. It was interesting that your eyes were getting droopy. You were having trouble keeping them open. It means that the drugs were affecting your system. Red was feeling the effects, too. We could see it in her camera lens, but it didn't seem from the video that either Gregor or Daniel was affected. Did you see them take the medications?"

"Gregor, yes. I saw him swallow them," Christen said. "Karl asked security not to take them because they could cause drowsiness."

"Maybe his size stopped them from having the same effect as they had on Christen and Red," Striker suggested.

"Let's let that simmer. We don't have a tox report yet." Lynx said. "D-day, if you don't mind, I have a question for you."

Christen sat still.

"Before your audio was turned on, when you returned to Raffles the day that you spent at the beach, you snuck away from Gator and Blaze and followed Nadir and the Sheik outside. You sat on a bench, and I'm assuming you used the fact that you had not yet been introduced to them to hide that you were eaves-dropping."

"Yes, ma'am."

"Your file says that you are a fluent Arabic speaker. Can you tell us what they said?"

"The Sheik was telling Nadir that Russia had discovered that the US allies in Five Eyes were intercepting comms from Davidson Realm. The Sheik had approached my father with the information, and my father said that he had already set up sophisticated jamming equipment, and there would be nothing they could pick up. It would make things a little difficult for the guests because there would be no communications of any kind. But this would help keep everyone safe. Each guest would be searched for any recording devices. They would be removed and returned at the end of their stay. While uncomfortable in some respects, this should comfort them in others. There could be no spying of any kind while we were there."

"And you brought this to Johnna's attention?"

"She said that wouldn't be a concern with our equipment."

Johnna cleared her throat. "Before we walk any farther into the data, I am just going to take a second and remind everyone that the CIA is an intelligence-gathering community. We don't arrest. That's not our goal. We observe. We document. We get that information to the people with the authority to act. We have observed a pattern emerge on the global playing field that is both interesting and concerning. On this mission, it was our objective to add more data to those observations."

"To that end, I've put together some thoughts," Lynx said and pointed to the whiteboards crowded with information.

There was a ding at Nutsbe's computer. "Incoming. This is from Blaze's comms. He must not be lying in bed, letting the nurses mop his fevered brow. Huh. It needs translation. Did any of you know Karl spoke Russian?"

"I did," Johnna said. "He practices with Daniel. Is that who he's talking to?"

"I don't know. Here we go. The computer has it worked out." He tapped a key, and they heard Karl say, "This problem is monumental. Your family has been fucking this up. Fucking this up. Fucking *this* up. The entire Virginia bunch are arrested on trafficking charges in D.C.."

Nutsbe stopped the tape and said, "There was a major arrest of the Zoric family members in D.C. last February." He tapped the computer to continue the robotic voice of the translation software.

"Which meant the team didn't have the manpower to support the attack on the school," Karl said. "They get nutso-crazy and decide to kidnap a school teacher who was engaged to a fucking American G.I. Joe. Your camp in Paraguay is destroyed. All the men who were training for our assignments are fucking panther food down there. Then I find out that the Bowmans were rescued. That was supposed to go on for months. Months of angst and hand ringing. The scientists who were kidnapped out of the Ngorongoro hotel, which was supposed to go on for months, to create the fear that we needed. We *need* people to be terrified. Terror creates pathways to wealth. You put too much trust in Momo. Momo was supposed to take my father. Dad was supposed to die without his damned chemo. The horror of knowing a man was out there without his meds, living in a hovel...sympathy was supposed to be on my side. Political good-will should have been on *my* side. But *fuck*, Momo gets himself killed, and you send in the clown squad to pick up my father."

Nutsbe hit the button and stabbed a victory hand into the air. There were grins all around.

"What?" Christen asked, bewildered.

"That's a mighty fine piece of evidence right there," Gator said.

"Ah." Christen didn't understand all of the ramifications, but it did indeed seem that Karl had just dug his grave.

"Go on, what else is he saying?" Johnna leaned forward in her excitement.

Nutsbe tapped the key.

"Had Blaze and Gator not been out on the terrace--"

"Who's talking to Karl?"

Nutsbe played a snippet from the original. "That's Gregor." He tapped an arrow, and they were listening to the translation again.

"All would have gone as planned. Have you asked yourself through all of this why the men, who happened to have fighting skills and close protection certification, happened to be on the terrace at that exact moment? I have. There's a rat in our pantry."

"Well, put out rat poison and kill it."

"This is not going as planned, but there is some good. Your sister is dead first. With her out of reach at the Army Base in Iraq, we couldn't figure out a way to remove her first. But now it's done. Congratulations."

"Yes, I'd rather not have had to ride through the storm to give myself an alibi, but at least I can tick that off my list. It'll make a hell of a news conference when I break down in front of the camera. Everyone will think warmly of me and my brotherly affection. It might even make up a little bit for my not getting that publicity for concern over my father. Not as much. Not the same. But something that makes me look good."

"Your father can be enticed back to Tanzania, and we will get him the second time. Or…"

"Or?"

"Your father is in frail health. Perhaps hearing of your sister's sudden death, he will experience a rapid and unsurvivable decline. On the island, without the quick action of medical intervention. This could mean a second devastation for your family."

Christen swallowed hard. She tried to let that conversation sink in. Karl was so blasé over her death. She knew he didn't like her, but this sounded like he was ordering a sandwich. And her dad. Her dad was sick? Dying? What the heck!

"Okay, great, let's put a pin in that for a second," Lynx said. "It seems that Karl put a target on his father's back and that he knew Momo Bourhan. Momo was involved in the Bowman's kidnapping and was in charge of the Ngorongoro attack. Right now, I want to layer this conversation with one Christen, and Red picked up in the limo on the way to the airport, Nutsbe, if you would." Lynx turned her head in his direction.

Nutsbe played the tape.

"My father was jumped by four men and saved by his security team," Karl said.

"Do you know the names of the men he was meeting with?" Nadir asked.

"He's still trying to find the right players, the right pressure points," Karl responded.

"Momo Burhan was not at that meeting, I can assure you."

"How exactly do you know that?" Karl asked.

"He is dead."

"Momo's dead?" Karl asked. "How? When? Wait, how do you know that?" There was panic in his voice that Christen hadn't picked up at the time.

Nadir answered, "Sources. In terms of your ongoing negotiations, now that the eco-pawn is off the chessboard, we can get some work accomplished."

"The problem with the Bowmans," Karl said, "followed by the attack in Ngorongoro Crater means that this region will be considered a hot spot. The men who come to work for us will want hazard pay. The cost of business will go up."

"Experts, yes," Nadir said. "Of course, these incidences will also affect the local economy as tourism falls away, that means the locals will be desperate for new jobs, and their wages will fall. It might end up that this works in your economic favor."

"Even if this is so, the businesses will have to be extremely lucrative to follow through. Our continual cooperation is the only way to make this happen. I'm glad you were able to join our little adventure. Thank you for coming."

"Now," Lynx said. "We believe it was Karl who called the meeting together. Because of this exchange that Karl had with Lula." She nodded at Nutsbe, and he played another recording.

"Well, no. I had brought these businessmen together, we, Father and I had planned a business gathering, and so we had just invited the men."

"But why was Christen endangered? What would the purpose be? She wasn't targeted for kidnapping but murder," Johnna said.

"Nutsbe was able to hack into William Davidson's cloud as he approached his island in international waters."

Christen thought Lynx was being very specific to make sure that everyone knew they hadn't broken any laws in procuring the information.

"FYI," Nutsbe cut in. There was a break in the cloud cover, and I just downloaded the recordings from Gator and Christen's devices. I'm scrolling to the end to see the last things you both saw before you went overboard. With my first glimpses, we'll need computer enhancement for this. I'm putting them into the parameters of those we know are on the boat. We should have our suspects in just a moment, hopefully."

Christen felt like she'd been doused with a bucket of ice water. Pain started at the top of her head and flooded down.

Lynx looked at her and nodded, then cleared her throat. "Here's another interesting conversation Christen picked up."

"Christen, for someone not in the industry, you're batting a thousand," Red said.

Lynx turned to the board and pointed to a written conversation she'd posted there in her tight neat handwriting. "Gregor Zoric asked, 'Do you know someone who has a team to get the job done?' he's talking about getting a replacement team for Momo Bourhan. Nadir then asks the sheik, 'Properly?' He continues, 'Momo's activities failed three times in a row. He was not the professional he led us to believe he was.'" Lynx turned and let her gaze sweep over everyone, then rest on the camera, looking at the group huddled in Singapore. "Again, three possible activities that we might assign to that conversation: one, he might have sent the extremists to train in Paraguay where the Zoric's held Suz and her students; two, the Bowmans were kidnapped but rescued; three the attack on Ngorongoro and the kidnapped scientists including Meg Finley and Honey Honig. 'I do. I'll handle it,' the Saudi replied."

"So who do you think tried to kill me?" Christen asked. Surreal. These last few days were the poster child for the word surreal.

"Here, we go," Nutsbe said as he put up a grainy video. "This is what Gator saw. Two seconds." He tapped at his computer, up came the images, side by side, incontrovertible. She knew it was coming. But still, it was a body blow. "Daniel and Karl," she whispered. "Karl," she said again.

Johnna came over and wrapped her arms around Christen, but all Christen wanted was to bury her head against Gator's shoulder. He got up, went to the kitchen, and brought her a glass of water.

"Thanks," She said. *For nothing.* What the hell was wrong with Gator?

"The Slovakian Zoric family is helping Middle Eastern terrorists because the terrorists have illegal channels of distribution – art and drugs, some sex trafficking. Those are the three big money makers for the Zorics." She began, walking to the board and picking up a magic marker. "The Zorics, especially Gregor, are about money and power. Terrorism helps them develop political power, and the Zorics, in return, help the terrorists to manipulate the political dynamic. As far as I can tell, religion or other ideology plays no role. These attachments are strictly business dealings. It's a game of three-dimensional chess."

"You were taking a look into helium," Johnna said.

"We have some interesting folks when it comes to helium, for sure. Right now, those who want a helium crisis to bolster helium prices need Qatar to shut down their delivery of goods." As she discussed a point on her board, she'd check it off. She wasn't going in sequence, but she was painting a pretty clear picture. "Qatar created a problem by aligning with terror groups. Why would they want that? It seems counterintuitive. But having that connection meant someone else could use it as a reason to shut down their port. In steps Saudi Arabia. The dynamic means that industries are reliant on the U.S., which is far away, with helium reserves that are depleting quickly. The price of helium will go up."

"If the price of helium goes up, then the Russians and the Qatari's will make more money when they distribute their gas," Nutsbe said.

"The Tanzanians, where the new gas discoveries have occurred, doesn't have the ability to develop their own helium fields. The government doesn't want to enter into contracts with the Russians even through Slovakia, but they will consider contracts with Americans. Enter Gregor Zoric and his manipulation of William Davidson." Lynx circled that point, then drew an arrow to her father's name. "Davidson wanted the contracts – the Tanzanian government doesn't want that. They were hoping for contracts with Hesston Oil, which would mean sustainable energy and a boost to their eco-tourism trade."

"Which would put more helium in the market, by a group who was not-for-profit," Red was massaging her thumb along her jawline as she considered the data in front of them. "That wasn't going to wash with Russia, the US, or Qatar. The helium industry needed to get Bowman out of the way."

"It would make sense then for someone to arrange for Bowman with Hesston Oil to be kidnapped. Hesston steps away from the poker table once Bowman retires. Now that the field is open, there are few other companies that could compete with Davidson for the contracts. All they need is to get everything signed. A few crises in the area will scare scientists off working for environmental stability and also drive away the competition. It's not going exactly as planned but close enough."

Everyone was frowning as the enormity of the collusion was laid out.

39

CHRISTEN

Monday, Safe House, Singapore

THERE WAS a knock at the door, and another man showed up in the room.

"Special Agent Steve Finley, FBI Terror. Lynx asked me to stop by."

"Perfect timing," Lynx said.

Christen saw Johnna shifting in her seat. She wondered if Johnna thought the FBI might be treading in her territory."

Lynx turned to the camera. "Steve is a Zoric expert." She looked back at Steve,

"We already made Zoric connections to the Paraguay kidnapping. And now it looks like Momo Bourhan was a Zoric tool for the other two attacks. All that happened under a black Islamic extremist flag, but currently, it's looking more like a political play. A lot of time, money, and manpower is being invested. This must be something big," Steve said.

"Agreed," Lynx said. "Ever since your sister Meg was talking about helium, I've been playing with that idea. The market is worth billions, and it is held in just a few hands. If there were a crisis that 'B' in billions could quickly become a 'T' in trillions." She turned to face the FBI guy. "One of my questions is about the Paraguayan kidnapping. The two young boys were taken to press the grandfather to make sure a vote moved through his subcommittee. Can you tell us what the vote was about?"

Steve Finley hesitated.

"Let me tell you what I think it was," If it was classified, Lynx could probably get a yes or no out of Steve before she could get all of the information. Now, Christen absolutely understood the power and high esteem that this woman enjoyed from those around her. "Last month, at the time of the children's kidnapping, we were focused on upcoming legislation that was supposed to go through the senate arms committee, thinking that was the impetus. However, he's also a high-ranking member of the Senate Energy and Natural Resources Committee. When I looked at the tasks they had taken up, there was legislation that concerned fracking and natural gas. The industry wanted to expand its operations. And this didn't pass out of the subcommittee to a vote by the Senate. Natural gas operations are also helium operations. Is that the vote, the push, the influence that the kidnappers wanted to be exercised? Because that legislation had received a ton of public backlash and looked like it was dead in the water."

"Yes," Finley said. "That's it."

"And at the same time, the Bowmans were dragged off their yacht in the Red Sea," Lynx said.

"Well, isn't this interesting?" Johnna scooted to the edge of the sofa.

"Please," Christen stared into the little lens on top of the TV that she assumed was sending their images back to the meeting room. "My father is ill? What do you know about that?"

Johnna turned to her and put her hand on Christen's shoulder. "Your dad was diagnosed with a brain tumor. They did a biopsy. The doctors' first thought was that it looked like it might be a glioblastoma, which is an aggressive form of brain cancer. There are a few things they could try, but if he were kidnapped and didn't get the interventions, it would be a death sentence. Besides the baby-making with London, getting the lab reports back was one of the reasons your dad stayed in Singapore."

"Benign," Nutsbe said. "Lula sent that information yesterday morning. He needs an operation to remove the pressure and stop his headaches, but other than that, he's good." The computer dinged. "'Karl and Gregor have left the building. Check the video," he read.

"Check the video for what?" Johnna asked. "Is Blaze following them?"

"No, ma'am," Striker said. "He has a concussion and has been ordered to stand down." He turned to Nutsbe. "Can you put the video up on the screen?"

"Satellite's still intermittent. I'll let you know when it comes through."

"D-day," Lynx said. "Christen," she said gently. "What a terrible experience you've been through. And here, we're handing you a lot of very upsetting information. You'll need to let us know if you need a break."

"Where's my dad?"

"He's on Davidson Realm. He went with Lula and his security team on the helicopter. The weather didn't show up as a concern until after they left, and they arrived before there were any issues. The helicopter came back and took London north of the city to see a friend. She's expected back by this evening," Lynx said.

"Without outside comms, they may not know how bad the weather got on the north end of Sumatra. They are probably just now expecting the yacht to pull into the harbor," Gator said.

"And now I have a question for you, D-day. Why is it best for Karl if you died before your dad?"

Christen blinked.

"I imagine it has something to do with wills. If he died before you did, you would receive your inheritance. Then if you died, it would go to whomever you indicated in your will."

"In my will, I leave everything to The Fisher House – my trust fund and what have you."

"If your dad died first, you would have inherited from him," Lynx nodded, trying to direct her down a thought path.

Christen thought it through. "Well, there are four of us kids, and we'd divide things up equally. That would be one less. Unless London was successful in getting knocked up, but then that would be par for the…"

"There," Lynx said, "That thought. What was it."

"I'm in charge of the twins' shares until they turn thirty. That's eleven years away. I have seventy-five percent of the vote."

"Why would your dad do that?"

"I think he thought I'd be more conservative and hold Karl back until the twins were wise enough to help make decisions. I never gave it much thought. I never thought he'd die before everyone was the right age, and then, like I said, I'd arrange for someone else to manage my shares and give the money to Fisher House as they take care of wounded veteran's families. I have zero interest in the business or the money."

"With you out of the picture, your father would have to

change his will, or your older brother would have a hundred percent control?"

"Exactly."

"Here we go," Nutsbe said. He touched a key, and the lights went out.

The two men, Karl and Gregor, stood in the hallway. Blaze was watching from behind the crack of a door.

"I need to call my father and let him know all the guests and security is fine, but that Christen went overboard."

"He'll ask if there is a search," Gregor said, this time they were speaking in English.

"It was a typhoon. He won't be so idiotic. I didn't make it out with a phone. May I use yours?"

Gregor pulled it from his pocket and handed it over. "You won't be able to get through. Your father was worried about the Fivey allies intercepting what was happening on his island this weekend, so his security team put up scramblers. No signal could go in or out. It won't stop satellite images from being taken. They could see us if we were on the grounds, but that won't give them anything interesting. Have you checked in on the others?"

"The security force is fine except the new guys. Gator went overboard trying to save Christen. Blaze got conked over the head and has a concussion."

"By debris?"

"Impossible to tell," Karl smiled widely and gave every indication that it had been done on purpose.

"Mark that," Lynx said.

"Roger." Nutsbe tapped the keyboard.

"The other guests are being looked at by the doctors – we all got pretty banged up. Dehydration and nerves. Taro had to be sedated. We'll have to try this again when everyone is steady." Karl handed the phone back to Gregor. "You're right. Nothing went through. I'm going to take security with me and head out to the island."

"How?"

"Boat. London has the helicopter. I talked with the airport."

They leaned in and spoke inaudibly, then the two men shook hands.

"Hey," Lynx called out. "It looked like Gregor was palming something. Can you get in on the handshake? His lips were moving, I didn't hear that last part, but given Karl's reaction, it was important." Christen saw nothing like what Lynx described. Not a reaction, not something being passed between the two...

Nutsbe's fingers moved over the keyboard. "Here we go – you caught it, Lynx. He's palming a white screw top bottle that looks like it might be eye drops. Christen saw it now, too, as Lynx pointed at the screen to help them all focus on the right spot. The computer is working to isolate that conversation and scrub the ambient noise. Two seconds, please."

Nutsbe put the video back at the beginning again. He tapped the arrow to make it play, and they heard Gregor say, "You have yourself in a difficult spot, my friend. With your sister dead, your father will write a new will. We do not know what that will could say, to whom your father will pass power. I believe that you are the one rightful heir. You have been his right hand all these many years. You know the business. You have the contacts that have made all of this work. If it weren't for you, the whole global helium crisis would not exist. It has taken you years of plotting. Years of developing. Years of perseverance. You deserve to steer the ship as you take your place at the global table of prestige."

"Thank you. I can't say I don't disagree." Karl frowned. "I'm afraid I'll have to take matters into my own hands." He reached out to shake Gregor's hand. Surprise and curiosity filled Karl's gaze. He jerked his head back and to the left. Their hands held as Gregor leaned in.

Nope. No one could understand what was whispered. Nutsbe rewound to that point, fussed with his controls, and let it play again.

"This in his cocktail, and by morning you will find your father succumbed to a heart attack while he slept. An autopsy, if one is required, will show only natural cause."

Karl smiled slyly, sliding his hand into his pocket. "Thank you."

"What is that? What was that?" Christen was on her feet.

"The Zorics are known to use poisons to kill their enemies. It works best on those who are already in delicate health," Lynx said. "They've discovered one, that is now classified information, that would do this."

Christen took two steps toward the image of Lynx on the screen. "A Russian poison like plutonium 210 that killed that FSB guy?"

"More like the sea wasp box jellyfish, Taro was talking about," Lynx said.

"If this tape was made a while ago. It just uploaded to the satellite. Karl is heading there now. I've got to get to him. I've got to protect my dad." She was heading out the door when Johnna grabbed her.

"Don't be rash." Johnna grabbed her arm. "You don't go without a plan. And proper clothing. Christen, you're not even dressed. How are you going to convince someone to take you to the island looking like that? You need to stop and be tactical."

Christen turned and glared around the room. "Alright. Let's make a plan. But it spools up now."

40

GATOR

Monday, A helicopter over international waters west of Sumatra

THERE WERE some major problems with this mission. No one had any authority on a private island in international waters. No rules at all. Every decision would be based on a moral compass rather than a fear of repercussions. Though, repercussions meant more than just putting oneself in legal jeopardy.

Of course, he had a contract through Iniquus to protect Davidson and his family, which included D-day, in his role as part of the Davidson security team. He also had some cover in that the CIA had contracted with Iniquus and his duties there included Red and White's protection as well as the protection of their asset, Christen Davidson.

An asset, he reminded himself.

Not his heart and soul.

He could never think of her that way, for her safety.

Though suppressing, his feelings for Christen was beyond his strength. At the very least, he could try to reframe his thoughts.

She was D-day, not Christen.

He had to get her through this and get her safely away from him. Never to see her again. Those thoughts wrapped him in a dense cloak of despair. *I'll willingly wear this*, he projected his thoughts out, *just keep her safe.*

Keeping her safe on a lawless island when her brother thought he had committed sororicide and was on his way to commit patricide felt too unstable. If he were really doing his duty, he would have hog-tied D-day and kept her on Singapore soil.

Instead, he was sitting next to her in the Davidson helicopter that she flew with ease.

Fortunately, or not, the host at the CIA safe house had known they were coming in. Both he and D-day were all fitted out in tactical wear that would pass for sportswear. They even had the right sized boots. And they were armed.

Johnna White, AKA Lula LaRoe, was the reason Red offered the CIA Station Chief for flying out to Davidson Realm. With permission to rescue Lula from the island, they'd set off. Getting Lula off the island was imperative. If they could get Davidson off the island too? That would be the sauce, not the substance as far as the CIA was concerned.

D-day flew the helicopter under the grey canopy of clouds.

One step, then another.

Get Lula and Davidson, get D-day back to her unit safe and sound, then he'd deal with what came next. He spent the flight time building a wall, as high and dense as he could make it, working to keep his emotions at bay. Emotions clouded judgment, slowed reaction time. He needed to get this mission wrapped up, D-day back to her FOB, and him on to his next mission. He beat that drum: step one, step two, step three. He'd have a lifetime to mourn his loss, to patch his broken heart. Right now, those thoughts were cowardly and selfish as far as he was concerned.

D-day came first. *Her* safety. *Her* happiness.

On this mission, Red could protect herself, and she could protect White and D-day. She couldn't arrest Karl. Someone would, eventually. As soon as Karl stepped foot on US soil, he and that asswipe Daniel would be cuffed and thrown in prison. Between the video taken with D-day's contact lens and that taken by his own. The computer was able to fill in and brighten up the images until, very clearly, they saw both men's faces as they scooped D-day up and threw her over the rail. It was important, though, that those two didn't know they'd been caught on tape. If Karl and Daniel thought they'd gotten off scot-free, they wouldn't know the perils of returning to the States.

If Karl and D-day got into a spitting match, she might throw that information in the men's faces. The CIA absolutely didn't want anyone in the helium club to know their plan had been discovered. It gave the government time to think and plot their course of action, to counter the unfolding world crisis without riling up the already tenuous international balance.

The plan was to try to make it to Davidson Realm in advance of Karl. Swoop in, gather up William Davidson and Lula LaRoe and head on out so that when Karl got there, there was no one for Karl to poison.

Things didn't work out that way, though.

His satellite phone buzzed. "Gator here."

"Nutsbe here. Dude, our last satellite image shows the boat's at the harbor. You're too late for Plan A."

"Roger that, we'll have to move on to Plan B then."

"What does that look like?" Nutsbe asked.

"I'll have to get back to you."

The island was ahead. They were still a fleck of black in the sky to anyone on the ground. The harbor was on the opposite side of the island. Gator spotted the boat through his binoculars, gliding slowly toward the dock.

D-day lowered the bird to mere feet off the choppy water. They were well below the hilly topography. No one would know they were flying in.

"I'm going to set down on the putting green instead of on the helipad. We'll have a thick tree line to shield us. It could be that if they're not paying attention, we'll be missed entirely."

D-day didn't have clue one about the security precautions on this place. After conferring, they decided to wing it. They'd try to sneak in and find Lula and get a read from her on the ground situation. Until that happened, they just didn't know what they'd be facing. And now, even their satellite phone didn't function. They were on the island alone with no hope of any kind of help.

41

CHRISTEN
Monday, Davidson Realm

THE GOOD THING, she told the others, was that they weren't the enemy in her dad's eyes.

The bad thing was she didn't know if security was on her dad's side or if the security, like Daniel, was on the bad guy's side.

Bad guy meant her half-brother Karl.

She knew that comms didn't work on the island, so there would have been no heads up from Karl to those on the island about where things stood in his coup attempt. If, somehow, they did get a message through, according to Karl, she was dead.

They had landed just beside the tree line. The blades slowly circle,d losing power with each rotation. They popped off their seat harnesses and checked their weapons.

As Christen pushed open the door, she glanced at the clock. Karl and whoever came with him would be getting off the boat now. They'd be in the little golf karts that they would use to drive up to the house. They'd be getting out and taking the stairs to the front door, she thought as they lowered their bodies and ran squat-ran forward.

Clear of the blades, they sprinted. Well, that wasn't quite what she was doing. Her body was still angry and pained from her fight for life. She moved forward. She didn't give up. Okay, that much she could agree with. The other thing she agreed with herself about was that she had to get the mission wrapped. Now.

As the break in the trees showed through the foliage, she slowed to a walk. She slowed her breath. She calmed her heart rate. She was about to confront her brother over his attempt at killing both her and their dad. No amount of fly-time and crazy missions anesthetized her system against this level of adrenaline and anger. But at least not pelting out of the tree line like a bat out of hell would mean fewer guns trained her way.

"Smile," she said as they moved through the trees. A guard had his rifle at the ready. She raised her hand. "Hey there!"

He approached.

"I'm Christen Davidson, William's daughter. We had some trouble with the weather and the yacht," she walked progressively forward. "Whew, am I glad to finally get my feet solidly on the ground. We had to fly over in the heli. Is Dad in the house?" she asked, reaching out to point.

The guard turned his head in the direction of her finger, and in the blink of an eye, she had not only gotten control of the rifle, but the guy lay on the ground at her feet looking up the barrel.

Gator trained his Glock on the guard's center mass. He was in warrior mode. Remote. Hard. Stoic.

Christen blinked at him; his behavior was... confusing. They were going to have to have a serious conversation before this was said and done. But now? Eyes on the gauges, steady hand on the stick.

While Christen covered, Gator flipped the guy over and dragged him into the tree line, where he used the cuffs on the guard's belt to secure him to a tree. Christen could hear the guard hollering. But the wind was whipping over the island. If someone didn't know what that sound was, it would be lost on them.

She wasn't concerned.

About that, anyway.

Christen still wanted to get to her dad before anyone else did.

"I think we need to take the direct approach, head right into the house. Maybe we can get hold of a few more rifles along the way, in case we need them." They were all geared with tactical knives and small arms, but for precision at a distance, a rifle was what she wanted.

Christen knew Gator was itching to have the rifle in his own hands, but he said nothing to her about it as they moved forward at an angle that would make seeing them from a window all but impossible.

They followed Christen on silent feet as she made her way to the second floor, where they began a room to room search. The third room found Lula lying on her back, feet on the wall, reading a book. "Get up," Christen hissed into the room, then sent a glance up and down the hall, moved over, and glanced over the railing.

All was quiet.

"Get dressed," Johnna said, and Christen could hear Lula shuffling around the room.

"Christen's locked and loaded." There was a question mark in Lula's tone.

"Amen to that," Gator said.

"Where's my dad?" Christen asked as Lula rounded the door into the hallway.

"I have no idea. I was waiting for word that the boat had come in. My god, you guys look awful."

"I take it you didn't get a typhoon here?"

"What? No. Some rain," her voice trailed off.

There was a bang of the door and yelling.

"They all speak Slovak...I think," Lula said. "I don't understand a word."

Gator was at the opposite window. "They found our boy in the trees. One is in the woods, getting him loose the other is running. Not the best tactics, but hey."

"How many security guards are there?" Johnna asked.

"I've counted eight," Lula said, "including the ones that came in with us. There's a chef, a sous chef, a couple of maids, and a groundskeeper. Fourteen total staff that I've actually seen."

"And how are the guards armed?" Christen asked.

"Sidearms on the interior, rifles on the exterior. Unlike the Daniel guy that was playing Davidson's shadow, these guys are all military trained."

"No killing," Christen said. "Seriously, these guys are here doing a job. All we need to do is grab my dad and get him in the copter and get out of Dodge."

"They're here," William Davison called, his voice echoing up the cathedral ceiling and carrying throughout the house. "The boat has arrived."

Christen flew down the stairs and grabbed his hand. "Move it, Dad, run."

Her father didn't move. He planted himself. "What are you doing? How did you get here? Why is that boat not my yacht?"

Christen looked up the stairs as Gator hustled toward them.

"Throw him over your shoulder and run. I'll cover you," she ordered.

As Gator hot-footed it down the stairs, she could see him calculating, working on a different strategy, but when there was a rattle at the door behind them, he scooped her dad over his shoulder and started down the hall. She stayed on his heels, sighting right then left as they moved. Her dad was yelling, asking for an explanation. Christen wondered if being upside down like that would make things worse on his tumor. She was sorry. But she also knew her dad could be a mule. And he looked like he was in that kind of mood.

A guard popped around the corner, and Christen brought the butt of her rifle squarely up under his chin, making him fly backward. She aimed her rifle at him while Lula ran in, cuffed him, and took his sidearm.

Christen lifted her chin to Lula. "Take point," she whispered, and Lula complied.

"What in Sam Hill are you doing?" William Davidson yelled.

"Saving your life," Christen hissed back. "Shut up for once, Dad." She couldn't believe she'd just said that, but then again, maybe it would be such a shock that she spoke to him that way that he might just comply.

"Let me the hell down from here. I can run on my own two feet."

Gator looked at Christen for affirmation before he set her father down. Then Gator grabbed the back of his shirt in his fist, exactly like she'd seen Nitro maneuver John Grey. Gator propelled her dad forward faster than she'd ever seen her dad move before.

A bullet whizzed by her dad's ear, and she watched her dad try to swat it away like he would a mosquito. Gator bent in two and ran toward the tree line, hauling his precious cargo along.

Lula still had point. Johnna sprinted after. Christen turned to see where the shot had come from. The crack had been close. Three more bullets followed.

There he was. Karl. Rifle in handed, sighting on the group as they moved into the safety of the trees, he racked the gun and fired. Missed.

Then he turned the scope on her. Christen took off running, tripped, rolled, watched the ground lift in a puff beside her hand as the bullet dug its way into the soil.

The night she was drugged and wrapped in her sheet Karl had come and untied her from the bed. Had pulled off her life vest.

She remembered that now.

Flipping to her back, Christen sighted between her knees.

How did the life vest get back on? Was she hallucinating?

Bang, another bullet flew toward her, another miss.

Christen was so confused.

This was all so surreal.

She was so exhausted.

For all she knew, she was dreaming.

Get off the X. Get into the trees.

Gator was there by her side, hefting her to her feet. With his hand jammed under her arm, she stood, frozen, staring at Karl.

Karl waved his arms, screaming at the guards to "Get them! Don't let them leave."

"Don't let them leave," those were the words that worked their way into the cotton folds of her brain, and without any thought at all to the outcome, Christen dragged the rifle to her shoulder and pulled the trigger. She saw a spray of blood. There was a momentary howl that cut off in the middle, leaving only the wind's whistle in its wake.

"Christen!" her name echoed out past the wind. It was Gator.

He'd never said her name before. It was magic. It gave her wing. With his hand on her arm, she flew to the safety of the trees, where the others huddled and waited for her.

"I shot someone," Christen moaned, her hands on her knees, unable to breathe.

"That was Karl," Johnna said. "You shot him in the leg."

Christen realized how disappointing that was. The leg. He'd probably survive that.

"You *shot* Karl in the leg?" her father's voice boomed out, angry, volatile.

Gator had a grip on his shirt. "She saved your life. Karl came to kill you."

"The hell you say. My son? Kill me? Never."

Johnna stepped in. "When we get you back to Singapore, we'll show you the tape of his collusion. For now, we need to go." She pointed in the direction of the heli.

"Hell no. Not without Karl. He needs to get to the hospital asap. My *daughter* lost her cotton-pickin' mind and shot him for Christ's sake. You," he pointed at Gator. "Get back there and get my son. He needs medical attention. I'm not taking step one until he's here with me."

"Yes, sir," Gator said, reaching down and dragging the man over his shoulder and taking off at a jog.

The women followed.

Christen's father was apoplectic as they took him to Singapore. The CIA provided a doctor to medicate him. Singapore's hospital wasn't safe. Nowhere would be safe until her dad changed his will and made that fact publicly known. For now, Christen had seen him boarded and woozy on the private CIA jet headed for the US. What would happen to the others?

Good question.

Part of need to know.

Christen didn't need to know. She was curious, but that didn't count. She was used to that being in the military. The CIA was an intelligence-gathering entity, not an enforcement branch. Johnna and Lula didn't *need* to know and probably never would know the outcome. But someone was following through. Someone was shutting this helium crap down. Maybe. Hopefully.

As far as she was concerned, it was over. She was heading home to her cot behind the striped sheet at the FOB in Iraq. Back to Smitty, and Prominator, and Nick of Time. She'd get to hear their story. And she'd be in her element. In control. Hands on the stick, eyes on the gauges.

First, though, she needed a heart to heart with one Jean-Marie Rochambeau.

CHRISTEN EMERGED from the hot shower in her Singapore hotel room, feeling about a thousand times more human.

The mission was over.

Lula and Johnna wanted Christen gone before Karl had a chance to find her. She'd "done well." She could be "proud of her service to the country."

Christen thought the whole darn thing was a great big nightmare. The only bright side was she and Gator had met. Now, she could get on with her life. She hadn't realized that she'd been in a holding pattern waiting for him to emerge from her imagination into her reality. This was the guy she'd been waiting for.

She'd never thought about sharing her life with someone else. She thought she might be too much of a control freak to allow room for marriage—a family.

That thought put a little smile on her lips. A bunch of little

Aids creating havoc, the apples not falling too far from the trees. Lula had laid an outfit for her across the bed. She must have bought it in the hotel dress shop. When a knock sounded, Christen went to the door, thinking it was Lula coming back with some shoes.

She wrapped a towel around herself and peeked through the security lens.

There stood Gator.

When she opened the door to him, his gaze traveled down to her feet then back up to her eyes. And they brightened like he was feverish. He stepped in and shut the door softly behind him.

"I just wanted to tell you good-bye. I have a taxi waiting to take me to the hospital to pick up Blaze, then we're headed back stateside." He swallowed. He looked miserable. "I wanted to wish you the very best of luck back at your FOB and safe return home." He kept his hands at his side, fingers curled in. His body was rigid. There was nothing warm or merry about him as there had been before they'd trekked back to the headhunter's village. Again, Christen thought something significant had happened, and she'd missed it.

He looked like a man who had been beaten down.

She wanted him to look at her, really look at her. To connect. "Good-bye? Not…" Tears pressed against her eyelids.

His good-bye felt permanent.

They would never see each other again.

She knew it. She knew it in her bones.

"You're telling me good-bye?" she stammered, still not quite able to adjust to the reality of this moment.

"Yes, ma'am." His voice was husky with emotion.

Why is he doing this?

"It was an honor to work with you."

That wasn't Gator. That was… a Marine. Christen had no

354 | FIONA QUINN

power in her body. She crumpled into the chair. She was too stunned to have a coherent thought other than – *I thought we were in love. I thought this was the love of my lifetime. He's saying good-bye.*

"Why are you doing this, Gator?" She shook herself to get her mind in lockstep. She felt her system swell with anger. "You're lying to me."

"Ma'am?"

"Stop with the god damned ma'ams. The assignment is over. Tell me what the hell it is you think you're doing right now."

Anger felt better. More powerful. Right.

He opened his mouth and tried a word and shut his mouth again.

"Please," Christen shifted tone. Softened her gaze. Tried to be welcoming of what he would tell her. *I don't know him*, she reminded herself. There could be someone else in his life. My feelings might not be his. But still, she'd say what she thought and what she thought was, "This is a lie what's happening now. Just tell me the truth."

And he did.

He moved forward into the room and knelt on one knee. He reached for her hand and played with her fingers. He told her a story of desperation in Tanzania, of recognition in Singapore, of the vision quest in Sumatra, and all along how Lynx had affirmed his experiences. She'd seen the same things. Had gone through it, too. Lynx had always fought by his side, and this life-time was no different. There had always been the two women: his dearly held friend, Lynx, and the love of his life, Christen.

He lifted her hands to his lips and kissed them softly.

"I've loved you through the millennia just like I love you now. And every time we've loved, you've died in my arms. I need to go. I need to get distance between us." He held tight to her hands as he swallowed. It took a long minute until he could say, "I won't see you harmed." He pulled his gaze up to hers, and she read the anguish there.

Christen believed all of it. She'd experienced from the outside what Gator was saying. She could line up what she'd seen and heard, and it all made better sense to her, now.

"Do you think that that was literal, Gator? What you saw in the dream quest? Do you believe in many lives?"

"My beliefs don't really matter. If we live again and again or we don't. I'm not willing to chance your life on my weakness."

"You haven't a weak cell in your body." she scoffed.

"Christen, *please*, don't fight me on this. I do, for sure, have a weak spot." He cleared his throat and nodded. "I sure enough do. I'm sorry, I'm hurting you."

"Stop," Christen couldn't handle the pain in his voice. "You said there was a phrase."

His eyes snapped up. Caution. The intensity was shocking.

"I swear I won't say it." The electricity that she'd sparked now calmed. She let this all tumble around. It really all seemed tied to the phrase. "What if I were to promise you to never say, 'I will love you and the F-bomb.' Isn't that the spell? Didn't you say it was the thing you heard each time? Would you change your mind about saying goodbye if I swore never to use those words?"

Gator sat on the carpeting, so they were eye to eye. Torment in his gaze. She could tell that he was fighting his emotions and his conviction. He wanted to do the noble thing. The right thing. But he also wanted her in his life. She hoped that was what she was reading.

"Gator, Jean-Marie, please, listen to me." She turned her hands, so she could lace their fingers together. "We live dangerous lives, you and I. There is no tomorrow in our world.

There's *today*. Can't I love you for today? Wouldn't you please love me today?"

Gator's eyes flashed, and she thought she saw a spark of hope in them.

"Just today?"

"Yes, today," Christen said. "We'll decide tomorrow if we'll love tomorrow. We can wake up and decide each day. 'I will love you for today.' Or not. I may not love you tomorrow. I can't promise who I'll be or what I'll feel tomorrow. But I can tell you for sure how I feel today. In this moment. I love you today."

Their gazes held. His eyes were turbulent.

"There are no guarantees, Jean-Marie." She reached out with her free hand and slid the pads of her fingers lightly over the worry lines that ranged across his handsome face. "There are no charms or spells. There's no safety. Why not love each other and be happy – even if it's just for this moment?"

She held her breath. She watched as Gator processed the thought. Broke down his walls. Let go of his fierce protection of her. Unraveled from his coil.

Finally, he pulled her from her chair, and she tumbled onto his lap and into his arms. Right where she belonged. He kissed her, soft and sweet. Then deeper. "Christen, would you do me the honor of loving me for the whole day?" He held her hand to his lips. As he spoke, the words whispered over her skin.

"I will make that vow to you. I will, for today, have and hold you."

"For better, for worse?"

"Absolutely."

"For richer for poorer?"

"Why yes, Jean-Marie Rochambeau, I would do that."

"In sickness or in health?"

"I will, indeed, love and honor you for the whole of today.

And what's more? Just so you know, I plan on making that vow to you every single day for the rest of my life."

Peace settled in the room. Gator cradled her head against his heart. He sighed, releasing the last of his stress, and kissed her hair.

He tipped her face up to kiss her nose.

He kissed her lips.

He lifted her and moved to the bed where they crushed her new dress under their weight. Her towel slipped to the floor. And for the first time in this lifetime, Gator and Christen found the bliss of being one, once again.

The end

THE NEXT STORY in the World of Iniquus is Yours.

FOLLOW UP

I hope you had fun getting to know Christen and Gator.
They have more to their story in upcoming novels. I hope you'll
follow along.

Keep reading for a look inside THORN,

Readers, I hope you enjoyed getting to know Christen and Gator. If you had fun reading IntsiGATOR, I'd appreciate it if you'd help others enjoy it too.

Recommend it: Just a few words to your friends, your book groups, and your social networks would be wonderful.

Review it: Please tell your fellow readers what you liked about my book by reviewing IntsiGATOR on your favorite retailer. If you do write a review, please send me a note at hello@fion-aquinnbooks.com. I'd like to thank you with a personal e-mail. Or stop by my website, FionaQuinnBooks.com, to keep up with my news and chat through my contact form.

Turn the page for chapter one from THORN(Uncommon Enemies Book 4)*!*

THORN

Her past is a complete mystery…especially to her…

Juliette DuBois has no idea what happened before her traumatic brain injury. She doesn't understand why armed men just grabbed her off the streets of Toulouse, either. All she knows for sure is that she better figure out what's going on before her past gets her killed…

Retired Navy SEAL turned Iniquus operative Thorn Iverson knows that Juliette's kidnappers will stop at nothing to get what they want. But then again, neither will he. And what Thorn wants more than anything is Juliette. His gut (and heart) is telling him that she belongs with him—forever. He'll just have to keep her alive long enough to convince *her* of that…

With enemies closing in, can Thorn and Juliette overcome all that stands between them and their happily ever after? Or will their shot at love fade like a distant memory?

Thorn is an intense, action-adventure military romance suspense thriller filled with spies, conspiracies, and international terror.

1

Toulouse, France

Saturday, 7:30 a.m.

IT WAS EXACTLY LIKE THE PICTURES IN HER HEAD, BUT SHE didn't *remember* any of it.

Juliette stepped forward and laid her hand on the intricate carvings on the ancient wooden doors. They had been here since the late eighteenth century – wide enough and tall enough to admit a carriage into the cobble-stoned courtyard that was protected behind the barrier.

There was a cut out of a smaller door. If she had a key, Juliette could simply step over the threshold, walk in, and stand in the shadowed interior.

The *bijoutier* pressed his shoulder into the door frame of his tiny shop just to the right, watching the comings and goings of the pedestrians. Displays of gold necklaces and colorful earrings filled his plate glass window. To the left, there was a shop that sold leather gloves.

Her gaze traveled across the street to the corner where the bakery bustled with patrons. Juliette breathed in the warm, yeasty scent of baking bread. Every morning, while her mother heated milk on the stove to make their bowls of hot chocolate, Juliette would run down the stairs, across the street, and buy baguettes fresh from the oven for their breakfast. She had a picture in her head of doing just that. Same awning. Same baskets of *boule* and *fougasse,* same glass displays of petit fours, and the jewel-toned, glossy fruit tarts.

Picture after picture flashed in her mind like turning pages in a photo album that belonged to someone else. Juliette didn't have a single memory of actually being there in those pictures. Actually doing the running, and jumping, and climbing the stairs that she knew were just through this door on the right-hand side – wide enough for two ladies in days-gone-by to brush their hoop skirts past each other, the carved stone railing protected them from slips and falls.

It was all so recognizable. And all so eerie.

The doors swung wide, and a car drove out of the complex.

Juliette smiled and nodded at the man in his navy-blue Fiat as she slipped inside. She knew that the style of her clothes, the form-fitting jeans, and high-heeled boots, the quality of her cashmere turtleneck, the Hermes scarf wrapping her neck, would work for her. She didn't look disreputable. There was no need for concern.

She took the stairs, nestled against the inner wall, that matched the picture in her head and walked up the three flights to stand on the landing with its stone mosaic of flowers. There were three identical doors, left, center, and right. The people who had lived in the center and left had not been friends of the DuBois family. When she was six, and she was supposed to be asleep, Juliette had become frightened and went to the neighbor's for safety. Her mother had gotten in trouble with the police for leaving her child alone to go drink wine with a friend. The neighbors had been angry ever since. At least, that was the story her father told.

Turning toward the door on the right, Juliette tried to recall going in at noon for the lunch recess. Two hours of respite in the middle of the school day. An hour and a half, subtracting the amount of time it took her to walk from school to home, then reversing the pattern. One day, her father said, she had been groggy when she woke up. When she'd come home to meet the family for lunch, he had looked down at her feet and asked if the children had teased her that morning. "No, Papa, why would they tease me?" He'd pointed at her shoes; one was a sneaker and the other her patent leather dress shoe. He'd laughed when he told her that story. How did she walk all the way to school and home again without realizing that there was a difference in her gait or the thickness of the sole?

Someone opened the apartment door, *her* old apartment door. The sudden sound was such a shock to Juliette that she jumped and clutched at her chest.

"May I help you?" Juliette had to watch the woman's lips in order to comprehend all of her words.

"I used to live here as a child." Juliette smiled. "I was just taking a sentimental walk while I was in town."

"Here?" the woman asked, turning to look into her apartment. "You lived here?" She turned back to Juliette with a shake of her head.

"Not recently." Juliette thrust her fingers into the tight front pockets of her jeans. "When I was a child. A long time ago. Twenty years."

The woman shook her head again. "Madame Gigot," she called down the stairs. Her words echoed around Juliette and rang like a gong in her head. She tried not to flinch.

A woman hustled up the stairs. Her gray hair was brushed straight back and pulled into a short ponytail at the nape of her neck. She wore a faded-blue, formless dress and black tennis shoes with bare legs.

"Madame Gigot, do you recognize this woman?" the lady asked, then reached behind her and pulled her door closed.

Madame Gigot came up beside Juliette, but Juliette didn't recognize her. This woman's picture wasn't in her head at all. "I would have been a child," she explained. "I lived here before the fire. My parents' names are Marie and David DuBois."

Madam Gigot canted her head. "What fire is this? David DuBois did live here, but he didn't have a wife or child. He *did* have a boyfriend."

"You know my father?" Juliette pulled a phone from the purse hanging from her shoulder and scrolled to his photograph. Surely, Madame Gigot was just confused. It had been a long time since the family had moved.

"I know David DuBois." She took the phone from Juliette's hand and squinted down. "Yes, that's him. That's DuBois. Scientist. He moved back to the United States if I remember right."

"Yes. That's where he lives now," Juliette said. Madame Gigot obviously remembered him. Why would she think her dad liked men? Why had she forgotten her mother or their child? Yes, Juliette concluded, this woman was simply not remembering clearly.

"And we've never had a fire here, not in over two hundred years, that is." Madame Gigot handed the phone back. "I've been the concierge here since I was a teenager. I would know if there had been a fire. No fire." She waggled her finger back and forth.

Confusion pulled Juliette's brows together. "But…But there are no pictures of my mother or my childhood because they burned. Here." She gestured toward the apartment. "We lost everything. My mother saved me from the flames." And Juliette had the scars to prove it.

The two women scowled at her.

"I lived here," Juliette insisted. Her attention turned to the polished mahogany door. "You don't need a key to get in. You just bump your hip into the door, and it pops open. When I came home from school, I was supposed to pretend to use a key, so no one would know." I moved over toward the door and looked at the woman who had come from the apartment. "May I?"

She lifted her hand to give her permission.

Juliette grasped the door handle and bumped her hip into it. The door popped open, just as she had been told it would. The only way Juliette knew that piece of information was she had been *told*. Juliette had no childhood memories of her own. But, still, she felt victorious and looked up with a laugh. See? She was right. Juliette *had* lived here.

The women started speaking back and forth in very quick French, and Juliette couldn't follow along with their words mashing into each other like that. The range of their agitated voices was too high a pitch, and their mouths moved too fast from pursed lips for Juliette to read them.

Madame Gigot turned and shooed Juliette away. Literally took her two hands and shooed her away. Then Madame Gigot lowered her tone enough that Juliette caught the next sentence. "I don't know what you're up to, but you need to go now before I call the police."

Juliette saw that the woman who had come out of the apartment stood with her hands on either side of the doorframe as if to bodily block Juliette from entering. Juliette hadn't planned on going in, even if invited. She had no pictures of what the inside of the apartment had looked like. And it would be all different anyway, Juliette thought as she scuttled down the stairs. After the fire and all.

The concierge said there hadn't been any fires...

The concierge should know such things. Would she lie? Maybe that hadn't been disclosed when the new owner had bought the apartment.

What if there really hadn't been a fire. What if her father had fabricated that story? Then, what happened to the photos, the souvenirs, the things one accumulated over time? A precious doll. A beloved book. A diary, maybe. Something that would spark a true memory for her?

Juliette felt robbed as she burst through the massive front door, back out on the street. She felt lost. She rubbed her fingers through her hair, feeling the scar that ran along the side of her scalp from the surgery that had saved her life but had stolen her past.

All she had beside her physical scars was a series of flat images that she remembered, like photographs from an album.

Juliette turned left, walking toward *Place Capitole,* begging her brain to remember something.

Anything.

———

Follow along as Panther Force comes full throttle to the rescue by reading, Thorn: Book Four of Uncommon Enemies.

Turn the page to find the Iniquus World Novels in chronological order.

THE WORLD of INIQUUS

Chronological Order

Ubicumque, Quoties. Quidquid

Weakest Lynx (Lynx Series)

Missing Lynx (Lynx Series)

Chain Lynx (Lynx Series)

Cuff Lynx (Lynx Series)

WASP (Uncommon Enemies)

In Too DEEP (Strike Force)

Relic (Uncommon Enemies)

Mine (Kate Hamilton Mystery)

Jack Be Quick (Strike Force

Deadlock (Uncommon Enemies)

Instigator (Strike Force)

Yours (Kate Hamilton Mystery)

Gulf Lynx (Lynx Series)

Open Secret (FBI Joint Task Force)

Thorn (Uncommon Enemies)
Ours (Kate Hamilton Mysteries
Cold Red (FBI Joint Task Force)
Even Odds (FBI Joint Task Force)
Survival Instinct - Cerberus Tactical K9
Protective Instinct - Cerberus Tactical K9
Defender's Instinct - Cerberus Tactical K9
Danger Signs - Delta Force Echo
Hyper Lynx - Lynx Series
Danger Zone - Delta Force Echo
Danger Close - Delta Force Echo
Cerberus Tactical K9 Team Bravo
Marriage Lynx - Lynx Series

FOR MORE INFORMATION VISIT
WWW.FIONAQUINNBOOKS.COM

ACKNOWLEDGMENTS

My great appreciation ~

To my editor, Kathleen Payne

To my publicist, Margaret Daly

To my cover artist, Melody Simmons

To my Beta Force, who are always honest and kind at the same time, especially M. Carlon and E. Hordon.

To my Street Force, who support me and my writing with such enthusiasm. If you're interested in joining this group, please send me an email. **Hello@FionaQuinnBooks.com**

Thank you to the real-world military and CIA who serve to protect us.

To all the wonderful professionals whom I called on to get the details right. Please note: This is a work of fiction, and while I always try my best to get all the details correct, there are times when it serves the story to go slightly to the left or right of perfection. Please understand that any mistakes or discrepancies are my authorial decision making alone and sit squarely on my shoulders.

Thank you to my family.

I send my love to my husband, and my great appreciation. T, you are my happily ever after. You are my encouragement and my adventure. Thank you.

And of course, thank *YOU* for reading my stories. I'm smiling joyfully as I type this. I so appreciate you!

ABOUT THE AUTHOR

Fiona Quinn is a six-time USA Today bestselling author, a Kindle Scout winner, and an Amazon All-Star.

Quinn writes action-adventure in her Iniquus World of books, including Lynx, Strike Force, Uncommon Enemies, Kate Hamilton Mysteries, FBI Joint Task Force, Cerberus Tactical K9, and Delta Force Echo series.

She writes urban fantasy as Fiona Angelica Quinn for her Elemental Witches Series.

And, just for fun, she writes the Badge Bunny Booze Mystery Collection with her dear friend, Tina Glasneck.

Quinn is rooted in the Old Dominion, where she lives with her husband. There, she pops chocolates, devours books, and taps continuously on her laptop.

Visit www.FionaQuinnBooks.com

COPYRIGHT